Barbara Wallace can't remember when she wasn't dreaming up love stories in her head, so writing romances for Mills & Boon is a dream come true. Happily married to her own Prince Charming, she lives in New England, with a house full of empty-nest animals. Occasionally her son comes home as well!

Stay up to date on Barbara's news and releases sign up for her newsletter at barbarawallace.com

Carrie Nichols grew up in New England but moved south and traded snow for air conditioning. She loves to travel, is addicted to British crime dramas and knows a *Seinfeld* quote appropriate for every occasion.

A 2016 RWA Golden Heart® Award winner and two-time Maggie Award for Excellence winner, she has one tolerant husband, two grown sons and two critical cats. To her dismay, Carrie's characters—like her family—often ignore the wisdom and guidance she offers.

D0608443

Also by Barbara Wallace

Saved by the CEO
Christmas with Her Millionaire Boss
Their Christmas Miracle
One Night in Provence

In Love with the Boss
A Millionaire for Cinderella
Beauty & Her Billionaire Boss

Royal House of Corinthia
Christmas Baby for the Princess
Winter Wedding for the Prince

Also by Carrie Nichols

The Marine's Secret Daughter
The Sergeant's Unexpected Family

Discover more at millsandboon.co.uk

HER CONVENIENT CHRISTMAS DATE

BARBARA WALLACE

THE SCROOGE OF LOON LAKE

CARRIE NICHOLS

MILLS & BOON

All rights reserved including the right of reproduction in whole or in part in any form. This edition is published by arrangement with Harlequin Books S.A. This is a work of fiction. Names, characters, places and incidents are either the product of the author's imagination or are used fictitiously and any resemblance to actual persons, living or dead, business establishments, events or locales is entirely coincidental.

This book is sold subject to the condition that it shall not, by way of trade or otherwise, be lent, resold, hired out or otherwise circulated without the prior consent of the publisher in any form of binding or cover other than that in which it is published and without a similar condition including this condition being imposed on the subsequent purchaser.

® and TM are trademarks owned and used by the trademark owner and/or its licensee. Trademarks marked with ® are registered with the United Kingdom Patent Office and/or the Office for Harmonisation in the Internal Market and in other countries.

First Published in Great Britain 2019
by Mills & Boon, an imprint of HarperCollinsPublishers,
1 London Bridge Street, London, SE1 9GF

Her Convenient Christmas Date © 2019 Barbara Wallace
The Scrooge of Loon Lake © 2019 Carol Opalinski

ISBN: 978-0-263-27269-7

1119

MIX
Paper from
responsible sources
FSC www.fsc.org **FSC™ C007454**

This book is produced from independently certified FSC™
paper to ensure responsible forest management.

For more information visit: www.harpercollins.co.uk/green

Printed and bound in Spain
by CPI, Barcelona

HER CONVENIENT CHRISTMAS DATE

BARBARA WALLACE

To all the square pegs in the world.
May we love our edges.

CHAPTER ONE

THE BAR WAS one of those pop-up, themed locations that were trendy at the moment. Holiday Cheer was the name and its existence had temporarily transformed the mezzanine of the Regis Hotel into a garish, yet strangely enticing Christmas wonderland. The walls were made entirely of poinsettia blossoms, while strings of holiday lights crisscrossed the air like tiny multicolored stars.

In the middle of the cheer, at a bar framed by Christmas trees, Susan Collier was having a deep, meaningful conversation with her cocktail glass.

"So what if I don't have a date? It's not like I have the plague. Plenty of women go to weddings without a plus-one."

Her cocktail, the sympathetic ear that it was, didn't disagree.

Too bad Ginger and Courtney weren't as sympathetic. The two catty little trolls from marketing enjoyed a good laugh about her while powdering their noses. So good, in fact, they didn't realize Susan was in the stall listening to every word.

"Is it any wonder?" one of them had said. "She's got a perpetual stick up her bum. I don't know why Maria invited her to the wedding in the first place."

"I should fire them both for insubordination," Susan muttered. The cocktail offered itself up in mute solidarity. Lifting the glass, she polished off the contents in one swallow.

"You're drinking those pretty quickly. Sure you don't want to slow down?" the bartender asked when she signaled for another.

"Didn't realize there was a speed limit." She tapped the rim of her empty glass with her index finger. "Keep 'em coming. And, if you're worried about me toddling off and driving, don't. I used a car service." Because that was what women without dates did. They car serviced.

"Aren't you afraid they'll miss you upstairs?"

Susan snorted. Did he mean the wedding to which she'd received an obligatory invitation just because her office was next to the bride's? The one for which she had stuffed herself into shapeware and a vintage dress with the hopes it would make her Kardashianesque rear end look its best? Doubtful.

"Just make the drink," she told him.

"All right. But don't say I didn't warn you," the man replied.

Warning taken. Whatever the warning was.

She didn't know why she'd bothered attending this wedding in the first place. If Maria Borromeo hadn't been one of the few people who was moderately friendly toward her, Susan would have canceled when her brother Linus backed out of being her date. No one would have cared then any more than they would care if she spent the entire reception sucking back gin cocktails in the bar.

She knew her reputation. *Shrewsan*, they called her

when they didn't think she was listening. It was no secret she was the least popular Collier at Collier's Soap. Her brothers—half brothers, that is—inherited all the positive Collier traits. Things like the Collier charm and lanky athletic good looks. She, on the other hand, didn't get the Collier anything. Nor did she get any of the good Quinn characteristics either, as her mother used to love pointing out. Except perhaps a passing resemblance to a great-aunt Ruth, the dumpy one.

The bartender returned with another red cocktail with an extra cherry this time. Susan forgave him for his earlier question. He was a good guy, Mr. Bartender. She liked how his red flannel shirt and neat white beard matched the Christmas decor.

"What do you call this thing anyway?" she asked him when he set the drink down. The cocktail list had been full of cute holiday-themed names that she hadn't bothered to read, zeroing in on the first one that listed gin instead.

"A Christmas Wish," he replied. "Guaranteed to make your wishes come true."

Susan barked out a laugh. "You mean if I drink enough of these I'll meet Prince Charming?"

"Is that what you want?"

"Hardly." Clearly he wasn't as good a listener as her cocktail friend. Cinderella Complexes were for the Gingers and Courtneys of the world. She was rich and successful in her own right, and her half brothers weren't wicked. "I'm not waiting for some man to rush in and rescue me from my miserable existence."

Although every once in a while…

She stared deep into the contents of the glass where tiny bubbles rose from the bottom. Every once in a while she wished there was someone who really understood her. Her brothers…they loved her, but great as they were, they didn't really "get" her. They didn't understand what it was like to be the perpetual square peg in a round hole, always pretending she fit.

How lovely it would be to share her life with someone who saw the truth. With whom she could fit without having to pretend. Who thought her beautiful and special, warts and all.

She was getting maudlin. And the room was spinning. Maybe the bartender was right and she'd had enough. Why else would she be wishing for things that weren't ever going to happen?

"Hey, mate, do me a favor and get me a glass of soda water, will you?"

A tall, perfectly carved physical specimen of a man approached the bar, his face dripping wet. From the red stain on his shirt collar, Susan guessed he'd been the recipient of a Christmas Wish square in the face.

"Word of advice," he said to the bartender, his words coated in a Yorkshire accent. "Before you agree to be in a wedding, make sure you haven't hooked up with anyone on the guest list."

"Ran into a bitter ex-girlfriend, did you?"

"Two. And they compared notes." He grabbed a stack of cocktail napkins and began wiping the liquid from his face.

"Must have been *some* notes," she muttered.

He looked in her direction for the first time. "You're not going to lob your drink at me too, are you?"

"Why would I do that?"

"I dunno. Female solidarity or something. You're

here for Hank and Maria's wedding, right? For all I know, they're your friends too."

"That would require me to have friends." Had she said that out loud?

He arched his brow in a mixture of half surprise, half curiosity. Oh, well, too late to take the comment back now. Besides, it was the truth. She didn't have friends. She had family, she had colleagues and she had acquaintances, but friends? That would involve allowing people closer than arm's length, an impossible task when you were a square peg. It was hard enough trying to pretend your edges didn't matter.

"Sounds like I'm not the only one who got burned tonight. Weddings aren't the fun people make them out to be, are they? Unless you're the bride and groom, that is, and even then... Thanks, mate."

The bartender had returned with the soda water along with a white cloth napkin. "No problem. I don't suppose I can get an autograph when you finish? I'm a huge fan. That stop you made against Germany a few years ago? I've never seen anything like it."

"Thanks. Definitely a finer moment than this one."

Ah. Susan recognized him now. This was the infamous Lewis Matolo. Maria mentioned her fiancé knew the former footballer. She'd been in a downright tizzy over his attendance at the wedding. Matolo, or "Champagne Lewis" as the tabloids called him, came with a reputation. Then again, if your nickname involved alcohol, that was probably a given. He'd gotten the moniker after they snapped his picture leaving a London nightclub, shirtless, with a woman under each arm and an open bottle of Cristal in each hand. From what Susan had read, it wasn't an unusual occurrence.

She watched as he dipped a corner into the glass and began dabbing at a red spot on the front of his shirt. Sadly, he didn't succeed in doing anything more than turning the spot into a damp pink stain.

"You're going to need detergent," Susan told him. "Otherwise, all you're doing is making it worse."

He looked up through his long lashes. "Are you sure?"

"I own a soap company. Trust me." Scented soaps and moisturizers hardly made her an expert. More like she tended to dribble food down her front. But being a soap mogul sounded better.

"You own a… Oh, you're Maria's boss. Hank mentioned you."

Oh, good. That made two of them whose reputations preceded them. "Susan Collier, at your service," she said, saluting him with her glass.

He nodded, apparently assuming it wasn't necessary to offer a name in return. "So what's got you holed up avoiding the good times in the ballroom, Susan Collier? Shouldn't you be upstairs dancing with your date?"

"I didn't come with a date."

"Sorry."

Not him too. Why was everyone suddenly sorry for her dating status all of a sudden? "For your information, I could get a date if I wanted one. I chose not to. A woman is not defined by her dating record."

She tried to punctuate her statement with a wave of her arm only to come dangerously close to needing her own damp cloth. To make amends for her clumsiness, she took a healthy sip. These drinks were delicious.

"Again, okay. I only meant sorry for presuming.

Didn't mean to touch a nerve." Hands up in appease-
ment, he backed a few inches away.

From his place a few feet down the bar, the bartender chuckled. "Maybe you should quit while you're
ahead, mate."

"No kidding. Tonight's definitely not my night," he
said as he strained to look down at his shirt. "You're
right. Made it worse, didn't I?"

"Told you," Susan replied. "It's the grenadine. Stuff's
impossible to get out. Tastes good though."

"I'll take your word for it. Damn. Now I'm going to
smell like a fruit bowl for the rest of the night."

"I hate to ask, but what did you do to earn a cocktail
to the face in the first place?"

A better question would have been what didn't he do?
Lewis tossed the napkin on the bar. He'd been drowning
in the karma from a decade of bad decisions for the past
nine months. "Nothing," he lied. "One minute we were
talking, the next I had a maraschino cherry in my hair."

"Just like that?"

"Yeah, just like that."

She knew he was lying. It was evident from the look
she shot him over the rim of her glass.

"You're leaving something out," she said. "I can tell
by the way you're not saying anything."

"What?"

"You heard me." She was swaying on her bar stool,
the way someone did when the room was starting to
spin. Hopefully the bartender was paying attention.
"People don't toss perfectly good drinks for no reason,"
she said. "*Especially* good drinks. So what did you do?"

It was none of her business, Lewis wanted to say,

except the glint in her eye made him bite his tongue. Even drunk, she had an astuteness about her.

What the heck. She'd hear anyway. "I might have asked them for their names."

"You forgot who they were? Both of them? After you slept with them?"

He didn't say he was proud of it. In fact, he was horrified. "They were from my playing days," he replied.

"Oh, why didn't you say so? They were from his playing days," she announced to the bartender. "That totally makes it all right."

"I didn't say it was right. Just that's why I forgot them." He was lucky he remembered his playing days at all.

"I completely understand. It must have been hard keeping all those groupies straight."

Yes, it was, because there had been a lot of groupies and a lot of alcohol and they were all a giant blur of bad behavior. Lewis kept his mouth shut, however, because it was no excuse. Besides, the woman was drunk and he knew from experience that alcohol and arguing didn't mix. "Are you always this sarcastic to people you just met?" he asked.

"Meh. Depends on how easy a target."

"You're saying I'm easy."

She eyed him through her lashes. "You tell me, Champagne."

How he hated that name. If he never heard the nickname again, it wouldn't be soon enough. The irony of the situation—if that was the right word—was that he didn't remember the picture being taken.

"I'm beginning to see why you don't have friends."

His companion's lower lip started to tremble.

Terrific. On top of everything, he'd gone and hurt her feelings. Why not stomp on a puppy for an encore? "You're not going to cry, are you?"

She responded with a sniff. "Don't be silly. I don't cry."

She was doing a darn good impression of tearing up. Lewis handed her one of the cocktail napkins from his pile. "Here, dry your eyes."

"I told you. I'm not going to cry."

"Then wipe your nontears with it before they make your mascara run," he said. "And, I'm sorry. The comment was uncalled for."

"Yes, it was. It's also true."

"I'm sure it's…"

"I'm in a bar getting drunk by myself and no one from upstairs has noticed I'm missing."

"I'm sure someone has noticed," Lewis replied. Granted, she wasn't the kind of girl he'd look for, but she was hardly forgettable. Her black dress was sexy in a naughty-secretary way—prim but tight enough to show she had curves. She had black curly hair that she'd pulled into a high ponytail—to match the dress he presumed. It worked together to give her a no-nonsense vibe. If there was such a thing as a no-nonsense sex kitten, she was it.

"If it helps, no one's looking for me either," he said.

"Of course they aren't," she said, dabbing her eyes. "You insulted two women."

"And here I'd gone five whole minutes without thinking of my stupidity." Good to know her tears didn't dull the bite of her tongue.

"Now you know why no one's looking for me, except my friend here." She waved her half-empty martini glass, the red liquid sloshing against the sides. "Unless you want your reputation to get worse, you might want to slide down a few stools."

"Trust me, my reputation can't get much worse, luv." A drink in the face was nothing when everyone in the UK thought you were washed up. Maybe not everyone, he corrected, but the people who counted. Like the people at BBC Sport who thought Pete "White Noise" Brockton made a good commentator.

"More likely, you're going to mess up your reputation sitting with me," he told her.

"Whatever. Here's to our rotten reputations. Oh, no!" The liquid had splashed over the rim when she'd waved her drink. Running down the stem, it dripped onto the napkin he'd tossed down earlier. "And she'd been such a good friend."

Her lip was wobbling again. Reaching into her space, he took the glass from her hand before she could take another sip.

"Hey! What are you doing?"

"I think you've had enough." Personified drinks were never a good sign. From out of the corner of his eye, he saw the bartender hold up four fingers.

"Why does everyone keep saying that?" She went to grab the drink only to pitch forward. Fortunately, her hand grabbed the bar rail, keeping her from falling completely.

Without missing a beat, she continued. "It's Christmastime. A girl should get as many wishes as she wants."

"Christmas Wishes," the bartender supplied when Lewis frowned. "It's the name of the drink."

"Well, you're going to wish you didn't have this last

wish tomorrow morning. Why don't we switch to water for a little while? Get you hydrated."

"I don't need water. I'm fine."

"Trust me." Lewis set the drink on the bar as far down as he could reach. If she wanted it, she was going to have to stand up and walk around him. "You're an expert on soap? I'm an expert on getting drunk. You need water."

"Fine. I'll have the water." The way she huffed and rolled her eyes like a teenager proved his point. Lewis had a feeling she wouldn't be caught dead making such an expression sober.

"Thank you. Bartender?"

Giving a nod, the bearded man poured two large glasses, minus ice. "Room temperature will go down a little easier," he said.

Good man. Lewis took the fuller of the two glasses and handed it to Susan. "Here, drink up. Then I'll call a car to take us home. You'll have to pick up your car in the morning."

"Don't have one," she said in between swallows. "Took a car service."

"Even better."

"Wait a second. You're taking me home?" She looked up at him through her lashes.

Wow. Her eyes were really pretty. He wasn't sure if it was the sheen from the tears or the bar lighting but the hazel color had a copper center that looked lit from within. They were almost hypnotic.

"I'm making sure you get home safely," he told her. While he imagined she could handle herself, Lewis didn't like the idea of sending her home alone—car service or not. "We'll share a ride and I'll have the driver drop you off first."

"Oh." Her gaze dropped to her glass. "That's very nice of you."

There was no missing the disappointment in her voice. He didn't stop to think, but after going on about no one liking her, his dropping her off was probably a kick in the teeth. When she sobered up, she'd be really embarrassed.

"Bad form to leave a woman alone when she's been drinking," he said. "Or, to take advantage of her." Not that he would have taken her home, but he might as well take the sting out of his rejection.

It worked. A tiny blush bloomed in her cheeks. "You're a very decent person," she said. "Even if you did forget those women's names."

Lewis couldn't remember the last time he was called decent. "Thank you. If you get a chance, spread the word. I'm in need of an image makeover." A big one. Otherwise, he'd be stuck as "Champagne Lewis" for the rest of his life. Or worse, he'd fade into obscurity.

"You and me both," she replied.

"Amen to that, sister." Helping himself to the other water, he clinked the bottom of his glass against hers. "Amen to that."

CHAPTER TWO

IF THERE WERE two things Susan detested, they were headaches and people bothering her when she wanted to be left alone. Saturday morning brought both: a blinding headache and a phone ringing loudly right next to her ear.

Lifting her head from the sofa—where she'd collapsed facedown after stumbling from the bathroom—she glared at the caller ID, planning on killing the person.

Just her luck, it was her brother Thomas. One of two people in the UK she couldn't kill. He was also the only person whose call she had to take. As CEO of Collier's, he was technically her boss.

That didn't mean she had to be pleasant though. "Do you know what time it is?" she growled.

"Happy Saturday to you, as well. It's ten o'clock in the morning."

Really? She pulled the phone from her ear to check. When she'd lain down, it was just before seven that day. "Sorry. Thought it was earlier."

It suddenly dawned on her why Thomas could be calling. "Rosalind didn't have the baby, did she?" She pushed herself upright, ignoring how the blood rush made the room—and her stomach—sway.

"Not yet. The doctor thinks she'll go right on her due date, same as she did with Maddie. And you sound like dirt."

She felt like dirt. No longer having to worry about being alert, she slid down into the cushions. "Maria's wedding was last night. I overdosed on sloe gin."

"Sounds like a good time."

"Not as good as you'd think." And ending with her nearly falling on her face when she tripped going up her front steps—right after she'd insisted she was perfectly able to navigate the walk on her own. She could just imagine the look that had crossed Lewis Matolo's face when he caught her by the waist. A combination of smugness and disgust, no doubt. At least he was gentleman enough not to say anything out loud.

"Is there a reason you're calling?" she asked. "Because otherwise, I would like to go back to dying."

"Actually, there are two reasons, if you can stave off your demise for ten minutes."

"I'll try, but I'm not making any promises. What do you need?"

"The first thing isn't a need, it's an invitation. Rosalind and I were talking last night. About how fantastical the last eighteen months have been. Between her accident and last Christmas…"

Fantastical was a good word for it. Eighteen months earlier, Rosalind had disappeared after her car plunged off a bridge in Scotland. She had reappeared last Christmas hundreds of miles away with amnesia of all things. Rediscovering their relationship had been a challenge. Susan liked to think she helped the cause by sharing some hard truths Thomas hadn't been willing to tell his returning bride.

Of course she was the only one who thought so at the time, but the three of them had put the issue behind them.

"We thought, with the baby arriving soon, it would be the perfect time to reestablish ourselves as a family," Thomas continued.

"What do you mean?"

"We've decided to renew our vows on Christmas Eve. Nothing huge. Just family and a few close friends."

"That sounds…lovely." Susan hated the tiny knot of jealousy that twisted in her midsection. Her brother had fought hard for his life and family; a proper sister wouldn't envy his happiness.

Especially when his voice hummed with a bashful excitement. "Maddie's going to be the maid of honor," he said. "She'll be heartbroken if her favorite aunt isn't there."

"I'd be heartbroken if I missed seeing her," Susan replied, the knot easing slightly. The prospect of seeing her young niece dressed like a princess was too charming to resist.

"So you'll be there?"

"Of course." It wasn't like she had Christmas Eve plans.

"Great. I'll let Rosalind know. The other reason I called…" On the other end of the line, Susan heard the clink of a teacup. "I'm going to need you and Linus to host the Collier party again this year. I promised Rosalind I would take time off when the baby was born so we could bond as a family."

Susan groaned. Not again. Collier's had been holding

a company Christmas party for its employees ever since the days of Queen Victoria. What was once a show of largesse toward the workers had morphed into a fancy cocktail party hosted by the CEO. Last year, Thomas had begged off because of Rosalind's amnesia, leaving her and Linus to play the benevolent owners.

"Can't Linus host by himself?" Everyone loved Linus.

"I'd prefer both of you to be there. Especially since Linus has been…"

"Unreliable?" She thought of how he'd left her in the lurch last night.

"Distracted," Thomas replied. There was a pause, during which she imagined him studying his cup of tea while he thought of the right words. "Look, I know the party's not your favorite event…"

"Try least favorite," Susan corrected. The whole affair was an exercise in awkwardness for everyone involved. Smiling and making small talk with people like Ginger and Courtney. It'd be like the wedding times ten. "I was actually thinking of staying home this year…"

"You can't. You're a Collier. It wouldn't look right."

"I doubt people will care—they're more interested in the free booze."

"Susan…"

"Fine." She noticed he hadn't corrected her. "I'll host the party."

"Thank you."

"Is there anything else or can I go back to dying now?" Her head was demanding coffee and aspirin before it could handle any more conversation.

"Die away," her brother replied.

They said their goodbyes, and Susan tossed her

phone on the cushion next to her. Five minutes, she thought as her eyes fluttered closed and her body fell sideways. Five minutes and she'd head to the kitchen for caffeine.

The phone rang again, the shrillness next to her ear making her wince. She fumbled for it without opening her eyes. "What did you forget?"

"Nothing that I know of," said an unfamiliar voice. Deep and with a strong northern twang, it caused tingles to trip up her spine. "I was calling to see how your head felt this morning."

How did this stranger know she had a killer hangover? "Who is this?" Susan pushed herself into a seated position—again.

"Lewis Matolo. The bloke who brought you home, remember?"

Remember? She was hoping to forget. Nearly bursting into tears, tripping over her own two feet. She'd worked hard her entire adult life to project an image of togetherness and control to the outside world...and Lewis Matolo had seen none of that.

She also remembered him being incredibly attractive. If you were into the cocky, athletic sort.

"How did you get my number?"

"I texted Hank and Maria and asked them."

"You bothered them on their honeymoon." Her heart actually fluttered at the idea. Why on earth would he go to that much trouble to track her down? Surely, not simply to check on her well-being.

"Don't worry. They were killing time at Heathrow waiting for their boarding call. I'm glad to see you made it to your apartment safely. No tripping up the stairs?"

Thankfully, he couldn't see how warm her face was.

"I told you, the sidewalk was slippery from the cold weather," she said.

"Uh-huh." It was clear from the amusement in his voice that he hadn't bought the excuse then and he still wasn't buying it now. Susan blushed a little deeper.

"Since you didn't fall and break your neck," he continued, "how would you feel about lunch?"

"Lunch? With you?" A dumb question, she knew, but he'd caught her off guard. She needed a reality check before her heart fluttered again. Why would someone like him be asking her out?

"No, with Prince William. I have a…business proposition to run by you."

How stupid of her. Of course he would be calling about business. Doing her best to hold back a sigh, she said, "New business ideas are my brother Thomas's bailiwick. You're better off calling him directly. I don't get involved in that end."

"You misunderstand. This isn't about Collier's. It's about… Let me just say I think I have an idea that might benefit us both."

Beneficial to her but didn't involve Collier's? He had her attention. "Go on?"

"I don't suppose you've read Lorianne's blog today?"

Lorianne Around London was the UK's most popular gossip website. A treasure trove of royal, political and celebrity gossip, the blog was influential and widely read, even by those who claimed they didn't. "The only thing I've seen today is the inside of my eyelids. Why?"

"You might want to check it out on your way to the restaurant," Lewis replied. "There's a "Blind Item" you might find interesting. Now, are we on for lunch?"

Susan ran a hand through her curls. Her hair was

a stiff mess from being retro-styled and she still had a splitting headache. Without checking a mirror, she knew she looked like a plump, raccoon-eyed nightmare. Hardly suitable for public viewing.

On the other hand, Lewis's offer intrigued her foggy brain. A business venture that benefitted her, didn't involve Collier's and was somehow connected to a "Blind Item" in *Lorianne Around London*? How could she resist?

"Where and when?" she asked.

The Christmas tree next to the fountain was decorated with pairs of miniature shoes. At night, it was lit with hundreds of rainbow-colored lights, but at midday all you could see were mini sneakers and stilettos. It was supposed to be making an artistic and social commentary, but damn if Lewis could figure it out. Walk a mile in another's shoes, maybe? Guess he wasn't sophisticated enough because he preferred the lights.

Still frowning, he turned his attention back to the restaurant. It was ten minutes past their agreed-upon time. Susan didn't strike him as the kind of person who ran late. He'd done a little digging on her when he'd texted Hank and Maria. If anything, Susan was the kind of person who arrived early and grew annoyed when you didn't too. She hadn't been joking last night when she said she wasn't very well liked at her company. In fact, Maria had used a very specific word to describe her, and for a second Lewis wondered if his plan was a good idea.

He caught the eye of a waiter who immediately approached the table. "Can I get another sparkling water?" he asked.

The young man nodded. "Of course. Right away."

As the man walked away, Lewis noticed a handful of diners looking in his direction. The Mayfair restaurant was too posh a location for autograph seekers. The people who dined here were supposed to be nonchalant about dining with celebrities. That didn't mean they weren't above sneaking a peek when one was in their midst, however.

When he was a kid, places like this were a foreign country. They were for people who lived on the other side of the city, who drove nice cars and whose kids always had new clothes. They definitely weren't for nobodies who bounced from foster home to foster home. Sometimes he pinched himself that he was really able to walk into a restaurant like this one and order whatever he wanted. Sometimes he masked his anxiety with extreme cockiness.

Sometimes—most times, in the past—he'd drunk to keep from feeling exposed.

It's all right; you belong here.

For how long though? Celebrity was a fleeting thing. Washed-up athletes were a dime a dozen. If he couldn't get a broadcast job, what would he do? Football was the only world he knew. The sport defined him. Made him matter. Made him *somebody.*

It's your reputation, Lewis. That's how his agent had put it after telling him he'd lost the BBC commentator job. *People are afraid you're going to pull one of your antics again. No one wants to risk waking up to see their studio analyst double-fisting bottles of Cristal on the front page.*

In other words, he needed to prove to the world he had shed his Champagne Lewis persona for good. He'd been trying to deliver that message for the past nine months, but karma kept tripping him up. Like last night. He was surprised that the drink-tossing incident hadn't made it onto Lorianne's blog. The woman had spies everywhere.

Reading today's item, however, made him realize a few things. First, that he was damn lucky, and second, that if he wanted the world to know he was a changed man, he needed to do more than simply give up drinking and stay home. He needed to give the public proof, something splashy, that would convey the message for him.

The idea as to how had hit him like a jolt this morning. It was crazy, but it was worth a shot.

Now he needed his proposed partner in crime to appear.

He was about to turn his awareness back to the window when a flash of blue caught his attention. Finally. Susan Collier cut through the dining room, her peacock blue jacket popping amid the room's gold-and-green garlands. She wore a pair of oversize sunglasses covering her face and moved like a person who didn't have a moment to spare. Quite a different appearance from the soft, hazy woman who'd tripped her way up her front stairs the night before.

"Sorry I'm late. We got stuck in traffic."

Lewis saw it for the excuse it was. He also always seemed to have problems with the traffic on days he was hungover. "No problem. I've been sitting hear enjoying the view. It's beginning to look a lot like Christmas."

"It should. They started decorating the day after Halloween."

She looked down at the bench he sat on. Although

the alcove table could accommodate up to six people, it had been set for intimacy. This meant the only seating was the velvet bench that curved along the wall. She had no choice but to slide to the middle so they could sit side by side. "Interesting choice of table," she remarked.

"I like sitting by the window." He moved over to make room. Not too much room though. He wanted to sit next to her. That was the point.

"Don't suppose you read Lorianne's site," he said when she'd settled in—her sunglasses remaining in place.

"You mean 'Blind Item' number five? How could I resist? You had me intrigued." Reaching into her shoulder bag, she pulled out a neatly folded piece of paper. It was a printout of Lorianne's blog.

This A-plus bad-boy former athlete with the fancy name was seen playing the gentleman for a member of one of London's most established families last night. He walked the lady to the door and didn't stay the night. Fluke? Or has he washed his hands of his wild ways?

She folded the paper in half again. "Those are some of the lamest clues I've ever seen. 'Fancy name' for Champagne Lewis? 'Washed his hands' for Collier's Soap? Was this your doing?"

"I wish. Our driver must have given her the tip. Lorianne's known for her network. He must have texted her after he dropped us off and Lorianne shoved it in her column." That was the beauty of the internet. In the old days, the public would have had to wait another twenty-four hours for the news item to go public.

"Interesting, don't you think?" he asked.

"How so?" Susan replied.

"Good afternoon. Glad you could join us." It was their waiter, returning with Lewis's sparkling water. "Can I get you anything? A cocktail perhaps?"

"The lady will have a Bloody Mary." Lewis ignored the way Susan's head spun around to stare at him.

"A glass of water will be fine," she told the waiter, in a no-nonsense tone.

"And the Bloody Mary."

The poor young man looked from Lewis to Susan and back, clearly unsure who he should listen to. "She'll have water and a Bloody Mary," Lewis told him. He leaned in so he could lower his voice. "Hair of the dog, Trust me."

"And if I don't?"

"You'll be nursing that headache of yours all day." A drink wouldn't ease the pain of her throbbing head necessarily, but in his experience, it helped more often than not. "I'm the expert, remember?"

"Fine." She told the waiter to bring her both. "If alcohol is such a cure-all, why aren't you having any?" she asked once the waiter had gone.

"Simple. I'm not hungover. Plus, I don't drink. Anymore," he added when she opened her mouth.

"You don't? Since when?"

Since he'd woken up with one too many hangovers and realized what a mess he'd made of his career, that's when. "Been nearly nine months now."

"Oh. I didn't realize."

"Few people do." And those who did, didn't believe it would stick. "I decided last spring it was time to get my act together. Turn over a new leaf, as it were."

"How's the new leaf working out for you?"

"There's been a few bumps." Like last night. "Turns out being sober is only half the battle. Dealing with the mess you left behind…"

"I'm guessing last night was a bump."

"For both of us, wouldn't you say?" He took a sip of water. "Are you going to wear those glasses throughout lunch?" It was impossible to gauge her expression when it was hidden by those big black lenses. "Feel like I'm having lunch with a Russian spy." Or a woman embarrassed to be with him.

Although her lips pulled into a smirk, she removed the glasses. "Satisfied?" she asked.

Her excess from the night before revealed itself in a pair of dark circles that washed the color from her face. Her eyes' warm copper center was still visible though. Lewis had wondered if he'd imagined the unusual color. He hadn't. He hadn't imagined the intelligence in her eyes either.

"So…" She dropped her gaze, blocking his view once more. "You said you had a business proposition for me."

"Yes." Apparently they were going to get right down to business. Lewis could deal with that. "Now that I've retired, I'm hoping to get into broadcasting but no one wants to give me so much as a meeting. They're all afraid to take a risk."

"No offense, but can you blame them?"

"Maybe once upon a time, but I'm not the same guy I was nine months ago. I've grown up, and if they gave me a shot, they would see that I know my stuff. I'd be damned good."

He shifted in his seat so he could look her straight on. "It's maddening. They won't even meet with me. It's as though the world has slotted me into a role and now I'm stuck in it for life. Whether it fits or not."

"Everyone thinks they know you," she said in soft voice. She was folding and unfolding her glasses with great thoughtfulness.

"Precisely." The rush of someone understanding made Lewis want to grab her hands and squeeze them. "Telling them isn't enough. They need tangible evidence that I am not the same person. That's where you come in." Taking a chance, he reached over and laid his hand on her forearm.

In a flash, her hands stilled. Lewis felt the muscles in her arm tense. Slowly—very slowly—her gaze rose to meet his. "How so?"

Before he could answer, their waiter returned. As the man placed her drinks on the table, his eyes flickered to Susan's arm, which she quickly pulled away. Lewis tried not to smile. "Are you ready to order?" the waiter asked.

So eager had he been to discuss business, neither of them had had a chance to look at the menu. "Not—"

"I'll have the egg-and-avocado sandwich," Susan announced. "Is that all right? Or do you need to change my order?"

Man, but she had a bite to her. And here he'd thought last night's sharpness was from the alcohol. "Sounds perfect. In fact, I'll have the same. You're very decisive, for a woman who didn't have time to study the menu," he said once the waiter had moved on."

"I read the item at the top of the page and decided it sounded good. I'm not much for hemming and hawing when there's a decision to be made."

"You don't like to waste your time."

"Not if I can help it." She swished her celery-stalk garnish around in the glass and took a crisp bite off its end. "Bringing me back to my question. What are you looking for from me?"

Lewis placed his hands on the table. He thought about covering her arm again, but that might look too forward. This was where actions and word choice mattered. "You might think I'm crazy, but I got the idea from Lorianne's site. Until now, I've been staying out of the public eye, hoping people would realize I'd given up the party life, but it hasn't been working. People only believe what they see."

"Or think they see," she added.

She caught on quick. "Precisely. This morning, I read Lorianne's 'Blind Item,' and I realized I had things backward. Instead of being out of the public eye, I need to do the opposite. I need to be seen as much as possible, only, in the way I *want* to be seen."

"In other words, you want to create a new tabloid persona. Makes sense. Although I'm not sure where I come in."

"Well…" This was where the proposition got tricky. "I was hoping you'd be my partner in crime," he said. "Nothing says *changed man* like a relationship with someone completely against type. A woman who is the total opposite of all the other women I've ever dated. You."

Susan stared at him, drink hovering just below her lower lip. "Are you trying to get another drink tossed in your face?"

"Wait." She'd set her drink down and was gathering her things. "Hear me out."

"I already heard you. You spent your sporting career

dating beautiful women. Now, to prove you've changed, you want to date someone who isn't beautiful and that someone is me."

"That's not what I meant at all."

"Really?" She cocked her head. "What did I miss?"

"Yes, I dated a lot of beautiful women, but…" He threw up his hands in case the noise she'd made was the precursor to a drink toss. "They were just good-time girls."

"The kind of girls whose name you forget."

"Right. I mean, no. You should never, ever forget a lover's name." He could almost hear the thin ice cracking beneath him with each sentence. So much for making sure his words mattered.

"You're smart," he rushed on. "You own a respected business. Doesn't Collier's Soap have the queen's blessing?"

"We have a Royal Warrant, yes."

"See? You're someone society takes seriously. No one would expect to see you involved with a party boy like me. So if you *were* involved…"

"They would assume you must not be the empty-headed wild man anymore."

Forgetting about overstepping, he clasped her hand in his. "That's it exactly."

Her fingers were cold and damp from her glass. Lewis pressed his hands tight to warm them. "And it's not as though you're unattractive," he added.

She didn't smile. So much for humor. He was mucking this up big-time. "Look, you're smart. You're cute." Cute wasn't the right word, he realized. She radiated too much class and intelligence to be labeled merely cute. Sophisticated? Maybe. Different?

Yeah, different. Unique.

"Bottom line is, I need your help, if I'm to have any chance of getting a network job," he said. "Lorianne has already marked us as a potential couple. It would take a while to find another woman as qualified." Not to mention one whose company he enjoyed as much as he did Susan's, surprisingly.

"Why is being a broadcaster so important?" she asked. "Surely there are other jobs out there?"

"Because I think I'd be good at it. No, I know I'd be good at it," he told her. There was more though. "Besides, football is the only thing I've ever known. I'm not ready to leave it behind."

The field and the fans had been the only real home he'd ever had. Without them, all he'd have would be a handful of hazy memories of the glory days. He wasn't ready to be kicked to the curb, unwanted, again. To go back to being nobody.

He blinked. Susan was frowning at him from over her drink.

"Were you even listening?" she asked.

"Sorry. I drifted off for a moment."

"Obviously." She took a long sip of her drink, which, Lewis noticed, was about a third gone. "You said on the phone this proposition would be mutually beneficial. You explained what you would get out of this 'arrangement,' but what's in it for me?"

"Simple," he replied. "You get seen with me."

Thank goodness she'd swallowed before he spoke or she would have spit tomato juice all over the table. "You're joking. That's your idea of mutually beneficial?"

He leaned back against the bench, his arms stretched out along the back. "You disagree?"

Talk about ego. Like he was such a prize.

She took in his chiseled features—far more prominent in the light of day—and the way his cashmere sweater pulled across his equally chiseled torso.

Okay, he *was* a prize.

Still, did he think her so desperate she needed a fake boyfriend?

Aren't you? She ignored her own question.

"I think you have an extremely high opinion of your appeal." She paused to sip her drink. Much as she hated to admit it, the combination of tomato juice and vodka was easing her hangover. The tension in her shoulders and neck were lessening with each sip. "Why would I care whether I was seen in public with you?"

"To quote… 'my own brother didn't want to be my date.'"

"When did I say that?" It was true, but she couldn't see herself sharing the information.

"While we were waiting for the car."

Susan thought back. Much of the trip home was fuzzy. She vaguely remembered growing angry when they passed the ladies' room and going on a tirade about being single which may have morphed into a drunken pity party.

Oh, man, now she remembered. Stupid Christmas Wishes. "I was drunk. People say and do a lot of foolish things when they are under the influence, as I'm sure you would agree."

"In vino veritas."

He flashed a smirk as he reached for his water. "As

for the value of my appeal…? There are a lot of women in the UK who would tell you I've got plenty."

"Then why don't you ask one of them to be your fake girlfriend? Oh, wait, let me guess. Oh, right, they're all supermodels and party girls."

"You're not going to let that go, are you? I was trying to lighten the mood."

"Doesn't change the fact that you clearly need me more than I need you." Or the way it stung.

"You're right," he replied. "I do need you more than you need me."

Points for honesty. Sitting back, she waited to hear his expanded sales pitch.

"Believe it or not, you would get something tangible out of the relationship," he told her.

Beyond being able to rub the fake arrangement in Ginger's and Courtney's faces—which she had to admit, a part of her found appealing. "How so?"

"If my plan works, the two of us will be in the tabloids and gossip columns, a lot. Both our profiles will be raised."

"Why would I care about a higher profile?"

"You tell me, Ms. Collier."

He was appealing to her ego again. It wouldn't be only the Courtneys and Gingers of the world she'd be showing, it would be the world. The equivalent of a giant ad announcing her desirability. As if she were that lonely.

"What makes you think the tabloids, or anyone for that matter, would believe we were a real couple?" she asked. Simply out of curiosity.

"Are you kidding? Celebrities arrange public relationships all the time in order to sell an image. Remember that pop star who was dating the guy from the Brazilian team? Totally to keep people from knowing he was shagging his equipment manager."

"No way."

"It's the truth. I know the equipment manager."

Susan remembered seeing the singer on the cover of several magazines at the hair salon talking about finally finding love. She'd been a nobody newcomer before the relationship.

A thought suddenly occurred to her. "You're not…?"

"No."

Not that it mattered. She still wasn't going to say yes to this silly idea.

"Granted you and I wouldn't become an international sensation, but, if we do this right, we will get mentioned in the papers. We only need to be together a few months. Long enough for people to believe we are the real deal."

"Even though we aren't."

"Right. But the only people who will know are you and me. Everyone else will think you won me over with your brilliant mind and razor-sharp wit."

"And, if I say yes—not that I am—how long would we need to play act?"

"Just over a month. At least through the holidays."

Meaning he would be her "boyfriend" at the Collier's Christmas Party. Wouldn't that be interesting? To be part of a couple for once instead of standing around watching everyone else? Even if it was only pretend.

Despite his offered upsides, the idea struck her wrong. Did she really want to spend weeks with a disinterested man just so she could stick it to a few petty witches? Seemed like she should be better than that.

Then there was the obvious.

"Wouldn't it be easier to simply date a different category of women instead of subterfuge?"

He looked at her for a second, as though weighing his words, his sensual lips drawn in a frown. "If I were looking to get into a long-term relationship, maybe, but…"

"You don't have to go on. I get your point." He was looking to repair an image, not actually change his tastes.

"I'm not asking you to decide this very moment," he said. "Let's have some lunch, and you think the idea over. Let me know later on."

"Thank you." She doubted food would change her mind, but she'd rather not ruin the mood until after she'd eaten.

In the meantime, she was curious if she still looked like death now that her headache had eased. When the waiter arrived with their food, she excused herself and went to the ladies' room.

Whoever decorated the restaurant had the foresight to install ambient lighting as opposed to fluorescent in the sitting room so women checking the mirror would feel good about their appearance. Unfortunately, all the ambient lighting in the world couldn't brighten her washed-out complexion. She'd tried to hide the damage with powder and concealer, but the dark circles stubbornly remained. Searching into her bag, she pulled out a compact and touched up her blush. No sense bothering with lipstick since it would only wear off again when she ate. Then she combed her hands through her curls and stepped back.

Her shoulders slumped. She looked like she felt.

Tired, and hungover. The jacket was too boxy for her short frame, making her look like a squashed blueberry. People probably thought she was Lewis's agent or business manager. Certainly not a potential girlfriend. Correction, fake girlfriend.

What made Lewis think the idea would work? No way, people wouldn't believe they were an item.

Behind her, the door opened and two university-age girls slipped in. Susan immediately envied their long hair which they wore in messy topknots. Envied their cropped sweaters and leggings too. No one would mistake them for a sports agent.

All her life, she had wondered what it would be like to *fit*. To feel accepted by someone. Anyone. She had a lot to offer, if people would only look.

Don't be so dramatic, her mother would say. *People don't look if there's nothing to look at.*

Belinda was full of those little bon mots.

Lewis Matolo was offering people something to look at.

Would it be so horrible if the world saw her as someone different? Just for a little while?

Rummaging through her bag, she located a hair tie and forced her curls into a messy bun. Then, she shed her jacket. The black turtleneck wasn't stylish, but at least the world could see she had a waist.

The world. Susan chewed her lower lip. Was she really that crazy?

Lewis was biting into his egg sandwich when she returned. She tossed her bag on the bench and slid in next to him. "You've got a deal."

CHAPTER THREE

"ARE YOU SURE?"

"Positive," Susan replied. "You don't have to keep asking."

But Lewis felt like he did. They were on their second cup of tea. An entire meal had gone by and he was having trouble processing the fact that she'd agreed to play his girlfriend. "I'm surprised, is all," he said. Flummoxed was a better word. "You didn't look very enthusiastic when I pitched the idea." Which was why, when she'd come back from the washroom and announced she was all in, he'd been floored.

"I'll admit, the plan sounds insane, but it's only for a short time, right? Not like you're proposing marriage or anything."

"Dating only, I promise." Marriage was one of those concepts that made his insides squeeze, along with commitment and emotions. As it was, this arrangement would be the longest relationship he'd ever had. Then again, so would anything longer than a three-day weekend.

Her smile seemed to tighten for a second. "Right," she said, setting her teacup down. "How does this work?

Do we draw up contracts? Write out conditions? What does one do in a fake relationship?"

Fortunately, Lewis had given the matter some thought on the off chance she'd agree. "Obviously, the goal is to be seen together in as many different settings as possible. Like a real couple."

"And we do this until the tabloids notice?" she asked while pouring the last of her tea. "I know you're considered a tabloid magnet, but that doesn't seem terribly efficient."

"You're right, it's not. That's why I'm going to have my agent leak a few discreet comments. We're also going to have to attend one or two social events where there's press. Actually, I've drawn up a few notes laying out how I think this plan should proceed."

He reached into his back pocket and pulled out a folded piece of paper. Moving his teacup aside, he smoothed it flat. "We want everyone to see us, but at the same time we want to look subtle—like this is the real deal—so I've come up with a progression of steps."

Susan's arm pressed against his as she leaned in to get a better view. "Date at a public venue. Attend a society event. Be seen doing coupley Christmas things?" She turned to look at him. "Coupley Christmas things?"

"You know, Christmas shopping or walking in Kew Gardens. Whatever it is women drag their boyfriends to do during the holidays."

"I see. Clearly, you've given this a lot of thought."

"Did you think I would invite you to lunch without some kind of plan in mind?" Lewis replied. He wasn't stupid. If Susan had said yes, he knew a woman like her would expect details. "You're going to have to start giving me a little more credit."

Then again, could he blame her? The whole point behind this charade was to prove he had more to offer than being a drunken party boy.

"Considering I didn't know fake girlfriends really existed until ninety minutes ago, you'll have to cut me some slack. I do have one question," she said, tapping her cup. "How can we be sure people—the tabloids—will believe us?"

It was a reasonable question. The honest answer was they couldn't. Not entirely. "I get the impression that as long as the story gets attention, they—the papers—won't dig too deep," he told her. "However, you bring up a point I hadn't thought about. Lorianne has spies everywhere—it's how she gets her scoops—so we'll need to make sure we act like a couple whenever we're together, even when we think no one's paying attention."

"Is that why we're having lunch in a cozy corner booth? Again, I'm impressed."

Lewis was flattered. It wasn't often that the woman he was with complimented his intelligence. Other skills usually took priority. "Thank you," he said. "Oh, and another thing…we need to keep this arrangement between us. No one but you, me and my agent, Michael, will know. Will that be a problem?"

She shook her head. "I'd already assumed the arrangement would be need-to-know. If it were a problem, I wouldn't have agreed in the first place."

Good. They were on the same page.

"What are you doing?"

She'd taken a pen out of her bag and was making notes on the paper. Lewis watched her write the words *Christmas Party* with a date. "My brother Thomas has informed me that I'm cohosting the corporate Christmas party again this year. I think it's only fair that my 'boyfriend' attend with me."

"Corporate Christmas party, huh?"

"For employees and other people we do business with. The ad agency, banks, etc."

He had to admit he'd wondered if she'd insist on some type of work-related couple appearance after her speech last night. "This wouldn't be to show up those ladies from the bathroom, would it?"

Her shrug was enough of an answer.

Whatever. It was fine with him if she wanted to put a few people in their place. "I'll mark my calendar. While we're scheduling, do you need me to play arm candy for any other events? New Year's Eve? Christmas Day?"

"As it so happens…" She suddenly stopped and shook her head. "Never mind. The Christmas party will be enough."

"Are you sure?" She was holding back.

"Yes, I'm sure. Now please stop asking that question." Clicking her pen, she wrote the word *Agreed* at the top of the page along with her name and the date. When finished, she held out the pen. "Since you didn't answer my question about a contract, I hope this will do."

"Seeing as how I would have settled for a handshake…?" He added his signature below hers. It was official: one image makeover in a half dozen assorted steps. Whether it would work was anyone's guess.

"I now pronounce us a couple," he announced.

For better or for worse.

What had she gotten herself into? "When you said we were going to watch a basketball game, I thought you meant at a pub," Susan said. Some quaint place with brick walls and a fireplace. "Not surrounded by twenty thousand spectators at London's O2 arena."

She was decidedly overdressed in a pencil skirt and heels. For some insane reason she'd decided to dress daringly. Her way of showing the world she was worthy of Lewis's attention. Now she felt stupid.

"I didn't know London even had a basketball team," she said as they walked up the ramp.

"There's an entire league," Lewis answered, "but they don't play here. This is a special event. Two American teams."

That explained the crowds. It didn't explain why he'd chosen a basketball game for their first date though, so she asked.

"Why else? To send a message. I wanted people to see that I'm more than a footballer. I appreciate all sports."

"Thus broadening your appeal as a broadcaster. Clever."

"Thank you."

They stepped out of the ramp into the brightly lit arena filled with people. Susan had been to the O2 before, for concerts, but this was the first time she'd seen it prepped for a sports event. Below them, American basketball players were warming up on the shiny parquet floor. "Our seats are down there," Lewis said in her ear as he pointed toward the court. His hand molded to the small of her back as he guided her down the steep steps.

They were really doing this. Pretending they were a couple. Her legs began to shake and from more than just navigating the steep stairs in stilettos. She gripped the railing.

"What's wrong?"

She didn't realize she'd stopped moving until Lewis spoke. He looked at her, his brown eyes narrowed in concern. "Sorry. I— It just dawned on me that we're on a date."

"You're only figuring that out now?"

"You know what I mean."

"Not really," he replied.

Until this moment, their arrangement had been conceptual. She hadn't thought about the fact that in order to be taken for a real couple, they would have to behave like a real couple. Which made this evening a date complete with all the touching and other date-like behavior. Lewis was going to have to pretend he was attracted to her. Did he really think they could pull this off?

They were blocking the stairs. That was one way to attract attention. "Never mind," she said. "It doesn't matter."

"If you say so."

Their seats were in the middle of the row, close to the front, but high enough they could see the entire court. They also had a clear view of the giant electronic screen that hung over center court. It was like having a one-hundred-inch television in your living room.

She looked around at the people milling about. "I doubt anyone will notice us in this crowd," she commented.

"Oh, they'll notice us," Lewis replied. He leaned closer, his nose practically nuzzling the outer shell of her ear. "My agent has arranged for us to be outed after the third quarter."

Outed? This time she had to lean into him. "What do you mean?"

"You'll see," he replied with a grin. "Just keep your eye on the scoreboard."

She stared at the screen, which at the moment was playing an advertisement for a Christmas concert. "I don't like surprises," she told him.

"You're going to have to get used to them if you're planning to hang around with me."

Why? Was he that spontaneous?

Check that. They were talking about a man who had once jumped naked off a boat into the Thames.

Susan looked at the man folded into the seat beside her. His eyes were shining as he watched the action below. He looked back and forth, taking in everything that was going on. "You're not going to do something outrageous are you?" she asked.

"Yeah. I've got the words *I love Susan Collier* painted on my chest. I'm planning to tear off me shirt so everyone can read them."

She rolled her eyes. "Very funny."

"You're the one who asked the silly question." Before she could respond, he reached over and patted her knee, his large hand warm and firm in its touch. "Relax. This is about changing my image, remember? Plus, I'm sober," he added. "I'm far less outrageous without the alcohol."

Ironic, then, that they should meet because of her drunkenness.

"What made you stop drinking?"

It was a question she had wanted to ask. He looked so at peace with the decision, she was curious. She wasn't surprised when he shrugged as though the decision was no big deal. "Forgot one too many names. Jumped into one too many fountains."

"I would think one fountain would be too many." She gasped when he held up three fingers. "You're kidding."

"We can go for four if you're feeling adventurous. Seriously though," he said, the smile leaving his eyes, "when my career ended, so did the party. When you're on top of the world, being a wild man makes you cool. When you're out of the spotlight, you're just a washed-up drunk. I decided I'd rather try to climb back to the top and maybe remember it this time."

As offhand as he tried to sound, there was no mistaking the regret in his voice. Susan took a good look at the man to whom she'd bound herself for the upcoming weeks. If you looked past the chiseled features, you could see the signs of a life lived hard. She spied tiny scars on his chin and cheekbones and the bump of a broken nose.

"Do you miss playing?" she asked.

"Only every bloomin' day." He pointed to the court where the American players were shooting basketballs at the basket. "See that player there? Number twenty-three? He's the best basketball player in the world."

"Okay." He looked like all the other players to Susan.

"Everyone in this building is here to see him," Lewis told her. "Sure, they care about the other players too, but him…he's the reason they came."

"Because he's the best."

"Exactly. I can't begin to describe what it's like. Being on the pitch, knowing everyone is pinning their game hopes on you and your ability. Feeling the love of thousands. There's no high like it. And when you're in the middle of playing, it's like there's nothing else in the world. There's you, and the ball and the match."

His faraway gaze was so beautiful, it made Susan's throat catch.

"You were really good, weren't you?" she said, embarrassed that she didn't know.

"I was the best. When I was at the top of my game, no one could beat me." She believed him. The arrogance had too much certainty behind it to be false.

"How did you start playing?" She turned in her seat so she could look at him while he spoke. The expressions on his profile were far more interesting than anything going on below.

"Just started," he said with a shrug. "Neighborhood kids played in the street—I asked if I could play. No one else wanted to tend goal, so they let me."

"Let me guess. Soon as they saw you play they made you permanent."

A grin slid across his face. "Pretty much. After that, I played for whatever team I could until I was signed by Manchester for their academy team."

"Your parents must have been proud." Remembering the way her father used to beam every time Thomas or Linus achieved one of their many achievements, she could only imagine how his family had felt when their son joined the Premier League Under 16 program.

"Doubt they knew. I lived with foster families until I was old enough to live in digs at the academy. Never met my dad, and Mum couldn't get off the drugs. The smack pulled her back every time."

Dear Lord.

"I'm sorry."

"Don't be. I don't even remember the woman at this point. She's more of a blur than anything. What about your parents?"

"My dad died a few years ago and my mother..." Her mother wasn't a topic the family liked to talk about. "My mom is an actress. Belinda Quinn."

"That name sounds familiar."

"She played the sexy neighbor on *The Confidents.*"

"Was that the show where some poor guy inherited a ton of money from somebody and they moved to a swanky neighborhood?" His bare-bones description was about as deep as the show. "I used to watch old episodes when I was a kid. Your mom was a looker."

"She was *something,*" Susan replied. "Except into being a mother. My dad's fault she got saddled with an albatross of a daughter."

"She didn't actually say that, did she?"

Susan put on a haughty voice. "Damn near ruined her figure, I did, and her career. Not to mention the whole messy business of kids demanding attention all the time. After all, what about *her* needs?" She picked at the lint on her sweater. "My mother has what they call histrionic, narcissistic personality disorder. A fancy way of saying she's a self-centered lunatic," she said when he frowned. "Psychology's a bit of a hobby for me. I've done a lot of reading." A desperate attempt to understand why her mother didn't want her. "Anyway, when she and my father divorced, she relinquished custody. We've shared maybe a dozen words since."

"How old were you when she left?" Lewis asked.

"Eight. I came home from school and she'd gone. Last words she said to me were 'Not now, Susan, I've got a headache.'"

"So both our mothers took a flyer. Lucky us, we have something in common." Their eyes met and a beat of understanding passed between them.

Lewis cleared his throat. "Enough childhood talk. We're here to enjoy a basketball game, right?" With that, he began explaining the action on the court.

The evening passed quickly. Watching the game, with its fast pace and athleticism, was a lot more fun than Susan expected. For someone who claimed to know only a little about the game, Lewis had a very keen grip on the strategy. She imagined he would sound marvelous explaining football too. No wonder he wanted to be a commentator.

By the third quarter, they were both on their feet cheering for three-point shots.

"Exciting, isn't it?" Lewis remarked after two players came crashing together under the basketball net. "Gets the blood pumping." He popped a piece of her popcorn into his mouth with a grin. "Clock ticking. Everyone rushing at the same fast pace in organized chaos. It's fantastic."

Susan took in the glow on his face. The first two times they met, he'd been clean-shaven. Tonight, a five-o'clock shadow covered his cheeks, turning his classic-looking features dark and dangerous. Add the adrenaline shining in his eyes and the result was breathtaking. He was clearly in his element.

"You'd be amazing on television," she told him.

Her slip earned her a blush, enhancing what was already camera perfect. "Thanks," he said. "Nice to know someone thinks so. If only the networks were as enthusiastic."

If there was anything "*Shrewsan*" understood, it was being publicly judged without cause. Everyone was so certain they knew how she ticked. Without giving it a second thought, she squeezed his fingers. "We'll just have to do our best to make sure you get a shot."

On the floor, a buzzer rang announcing the end of the third quarter. While the players gathered around their respective benches, she and Lewis settled back into their seats. "I thought you said something was supposed to happen during the last quarter," she said. "Your agent didn't forget, did he?"

"Michael? No way. He's got a publicist on staff who knows her stuff. Bailed me out of public embarrassment more than once, she has."

"If something's going to happen, it's going to have to happen soon. According to the clock, there's only twelve minutes left in the game." She pointed to the center screen which was playing a highlight from a few minutes earlier.

When the highlight ended, an electronic Santa Claus came bouncing across the screen. He stopped, pointed upward and the words Mistletoe Camera scrolled by. The image fizzled away and suddenly, there was a view of the crowd. People cheered and waved as the camera zoomed in tighter and tighter until it focused on an unsuspecting couple. The pair laughed and shared a kiss.

"Mistletoe Camera?" She'd never heard of such an idea.

"An American thing," Lewis told her. "Big hit over there from what I hear. The promoters thought the gimmick might be fun to do here, as well. Crowd seems to be enjoying it."

The camera moved on, this time to a pair of middle-aged men who were clearly not together. Oblivious, they faced away from one another until the cheering crowd forced them to look up. As soon as they realized, they too broke out in laughter. The camera remained on them until they shared a bro hug.

"So it appears," she remarked. "Nothing says romance like thousands of people watching you kiss. Wait a second…?" How did Lewis know what the promoters had planned?

Her question was cut off by the crowd suddenly roaring louder than ever. She looked up at the screen to see why and her stomach dropped.

The Mistletoe Cam was pointed at *them*.

CHAPTER FOUR

"YOU…" THERE WAS a smile on her face, but Lewis could see the muscles twitching in her jaw. She was gritting her teeth.

"Wasn't me, luv. It was my agent." He murmured the words in her ear so that on camera it looked like they were sharing a secret.

While he was speaking, he slipped an arm around her shoulder. He knew as soon as Michael mentioned the promotion that Susan would hate the idea, which was why he'd kept the plans a secret. He didn't want to risk her looking annoyed for three periods. Or worse, walking out on him.

"You said yourself, nothing says you're in a relationship like kissing in front of ten thousand people."

"I was being sarcastic. I didn't mean we should follow suit."

"Why not? You've got to admit, it's a great idea. At least the crowd thinks so." The egging on had gotten louder when he put his arm around her. Lewis leaned in closer. They had a limited window before the camera moved to another couple. "They're getting restless. Better give them what they want."

Her eyes widened. "You…you don't mind?"

Why would he mind? It was just a kiss. And she was an attractive woman. He'd been watching her smile and laugh all night long. When she relaxed, her softness came out. There was real vulnerability beneath the armor. The kind that made you want to treat her special. She really was adorable and begging to be cuddled.

"I'm game if you are," he replied. "What do you say? Ready to tell the world we're together?"

"Um…" She licked her lips, making them shiny and enticing. "Okay."

Good answer since he planned on kissing her anyway. Cupping her cheek with his free hand, he bent in for what he meant to be a gentle kiss. The crowd responded with applause. Emboldened by their enthusiasm, he let the kiss linger. Susan tasted delicious. Salt, artificial butter and something indefinable that had him tempted to lick his way past her lips.

When he finally did end the kiss, she looked up at him with what he swore was wonder in her darkened eyes. The look caused something primal to click deep inside him, and for a crazy second he thought about finding some dark corner where he could demonstrate how he really kissed a woman.

If they were in a real relationship, he would. In a heartbeat.

But they weren't. The kiss was simply a hook to sell a story, and what he thought was wonder in her eyes was probably nothing more than the arena lights reflecting in their greenness.

"What do you think?" he asked, leaning back in his seat. He'd keep his arm around her shoulders for now. "Believable?"

* * *

For the rest of the game, Susan tried her best not to look as stunned as she felt. If that was Lewis's idea of a casual first kiss, what did he do when he gave his full effort? It was all she could do not to crawl into his lap and beg for more.

She *should* be angry that he kept the plan a secret. If she had known his plan involved the two of them putting on a public display, she would have...

What? Refused? Then she would have missed out on the most amazing kiss of her life. God bless the Mistletoe Cam, she decided. Were kisses like this what she could expect over the next few weeks? Well then, Merry Christmas to her.

Over her lifetime, Susan had grown accustomed to walking in on whispered conversations. It started at age five when her mother would end telephone conversations abruptly upon Susan entering the room. At the office, she could count on finding at least one or two employees with their heads together, usually complaining or gossiping. Whenever they saw her, they would break up and pretend they had been talking about work.

Today there seemed to be more heads together than usual, starting with a small group by the reception desk. Every single one of them had turned to look at her when she stepped through the front door. That could only mean one thing: There was a mention of last night in the paper.

Last night. She fought a smile as she walked toward her office. Fake or not, she had had a terrific time.

When she concentrated, she could still feel Lewis's kiss. Of course, later that night he'd dropped her off at her apartment with nothing but a friendly hug, but she wouldn't dwell on that.

Upon reaching her office, she found Linus sitting on the edge of her desk. It was an annoying habit he had, that of refusing to use a chair. When he saw her, he pointed at her with a rolled-up newspaper. "If it isn't my sister, the cover girl."

"What are you getting on about? And get off my desk. You're messing up my piles." She hung her wool coat on the back of her door before shooing him off her work with a wave of her hand.

"I gather you haven't seen this morning's edition of the *Looking Glass*." He unfurled the newspaper. "I lied about the cover. Turns out you're more page-five material."

Grabbing the tabloid from Linus, she quickly flipped to the page. There, under the headline Merry Kiss-Mas was a photo of her and Lewis.

Wildman Champagne Lewis Matolo Looks Tamed As He Cozies With A Mystery Lady, read the subhead.

The corners of her mouth twitched upward. The photographer had caught the moment just before they kissed. Her face was lifted to his, and they were looking at one another as if each were the only person in the room. There was a second photo too, which, from their excited expressions, looked like it was taken in the fourth quarter when they were cheering for a last-minute rally.

This explained all the odd looks. She gave in and let her smile bloom. Lewis had to be thrilled.

"You little minx. Why didn't you tell us you were seeing someone?"

She cast her brother a look over the top of the paper. "Minx? Seriously?"

"First word that came to mind, and you didn't answer my question. When did you start dating Lewis Matolo?"

"We…" Linus's question reminded her they hadn't worked out a proper backstory. Since she was alone, she was going to have to go with the obvious and fill Lewis in later. "We met at Maria's wedding. He went to school with her new husband. We shared a couple drinks in the bar and hit it off."

"A couple? Thomas said you were hung over when he spoke to you the next morning."

"Thomas has a big mouth, and what business is it of yours anyway?" Tucking the paper under her arm, she cast him another look as she made her way to her chair.

Much to her consternation, Linus followed, and perched himself on the edge of the desk again. "Is this where I say none?"

"Unless you'd like me to say it for you." Folding her arms, she sat back and waited for him to get to the point. Because there was a point; Linus always had a point. She just wished he'd hurry up because she wanted to call Lewis.

"Here's the thing," he said finally. "Normally, I'd agree with you, but in this case…"

"What do you mean, in this case?"

"Do you know who Lewis Matolo is? I mean really know?"

Of course she knew, and she knew exactly what Linus was driving at, as well. "Get to your point." Might as well hear him say it out loud.

Her brother tapped a knuckle against his lip, a habit he had when thinking. "How do I put this…"

"He's a drunken arse." Thomas Collier's pronounce-
ment entered the office two seconds before he did. The
chairman of Collier's Soap strode into her office wearing his standard severe black suit. Dark and handsome,
he was night to Linus's day.

Add Lewis to the mix and you would have one heck
of a gorgeous trio, thought Susan. With her as the plump
wrong note.

"Why don't you say it a little louder, Thomas? There
might be a few people at the reception desk who didn't
hear you," she snapped. "And he's not a drunken anything. Anymore. He stopped drinking."

"You just said you shared a couple drinks at the wedding," Linus said.

Oh, brother. She didn't realize they were going to
analyze every single word. "*I* drank. *He* had water,"
she replied. "Not that what I do is any of your concern.
In case you didn't notice, I'm a grown woman. I'm not
required to explain my actions to you."

"Unless your actions blow back and bite Collier's,"
Thomas replied. "Do you have any idea the kinds of
stunts this guy has pulled? Bar fights, drunken howl-
ers."

"Stop it. I've read the headlines, same as you."

"Then you know he's a degenerate. Even his teammates got tired of his antics. He bounced around to
every team in the league because the other players hated
dealing with him."

"Again, he *was* a degenerate. All of that happened
when he was drinking." The ferocity of her defense surprised her, but she didn't like Thomas's tone. Her brothers didn't know Lewis. They didn't see the vulnerability
in his eyes when he talked about his childhood. "There's

a lot more to him than the headlines would lead you to believe." Her eyes glanced down at the newspaper and their photograph. "A lot more.

"Besides," she added, "I would think you'd be glad for the potential publicity. It is the Christmas season after all."

"Oh, sure," Thomas replied, "I'm thrilled to death. Nothing says Merry Christmas like having the company name tied to scandal."

"Oh, for crying out loud. There isn't going to be a scandal." Her big brother could be such a stubborn jerk. Once he got a notion in his head, he wouldn't shake it. "I would think you of all people would be open to the idea that people change."

That shut him up. They wouldn't be having a Christmas Eve vow renewal if Thomas and his wife hadn't learned to change. "Or do you think you and Rosalind have the monopoly on personal growth?"

"Don't be ridiculous. Of course, we don't," Thomas replied. "But…"

She finished the sentence for him. "Are you saying your relationship problems wouldn't have made headlines?"

"No, they would not have because neither of us was headline fodder." Implying that her "boyfriend" was and therefore their relationship would be in the press. It was all she could do not to tell him that was the point. In fact, if things went according to plan, the two of them would be all over the paper.

Her brother looked at her with the cool intensity he usually reserved for business meetings. "Two years," he said. "Two years, it took for me to get this company stable again after Dad ran it into the ground. Doing so very nearly cost me my marriage. The last thing I want is for it to be dragged down now by a scandal."

"For the last time, there won't be a scandal." The only way that could happen was if news of their fake relationship leaked out, and she and Lewis weren't planning to talk.

"We just want you to keep your wits about you." As he so often did, Linus moved in as the voice of reason and distraction. "Guys like Lewis Matolo know how to play women to get what they want."

"You don't know anything," she told him. "You've never even met Lewis." And, so what if he was using her? Lewis had never been anything but honest regarding his intentions.

"I don't have to. Trust me, I know. We're cut from a similar cloth."

No, they weren't. The defense sprang to her lips despite her having zero evidence beyond a couple conversations, one of which centered around him using her to get what he wanted.

Linus leaned forward so his face was level with hers. "Look," he said. "We're not trying to be jerks here. We're simply looking out for our baby sister. We just don't want to see you get involved with something that might come back to haunt you."

Because God forbid her relationship have some kind of future.

That, she realized, was what really hurt. Not Thomas's worries about gossip, but their automatic assumption that her relationship was doomed. Was it so unbelievable to them that a man like Lewis could be attracted to her?

Granted it was a business arrangement but her brothers didn't know that. You'd think they would have a higher opinion of her choices.

But then why should they venture off script, right?

"I don't really care what you want," she snapped. Or what they thought of her either. "It's my life and who I date is my business. Now, if you don't mind, it's the end of the month. I have a whole bunch of work to do and you're sitting on my reports." Plus she needed to call Lewis so they could discuss their next step.

"Do what you want," Thomas said as Linus rose to his feet. "But you better be right about his being a different person. First negative article I see with the name Collier attached and I'll have your boyfriend's head on a platter." The toughness would have worked better if Linus hadn't snorted.

"He means his legal team will," her middle brother said. "Still, be careful, okay? Players are called players for a reason."

"Are we done with the lecture?" Susan asked. She really wanted to talk with Lewis now. Hoping they'd take the hint, she reached for her desk phone. It worked. They shut the door and left her in peace. Although Thomas did manage one last stern look through the glass wall.

Susan immediately picked up the paper to study the pictures again. Just who did they think they were, poking their noses in her love life? And Thomas calling Lewis a degenerate. Wait until the Collier's Christmas Party. She and Lewis would show everyone exactly how wrong their opinion was.

Even if they had to pretend to do so.

Has Champagne Lewis given up his wild ways? The former goaltender was seen canoodling with a brunette mystery woman at the O2 arena last night.

Sources say this isn't the first time the couple has been seen together. The two were spotted at Esprit last weekend enjoying a romantic Sunday brunch.

Lewis slapped the tabloid on the table with a grin. "Not bad," he said. "Not bad at all." There were two things the press loved: a good celebrity romance and a good redemption story. He should have thought of this plan months ago.

His eyes dropped to the photograph of him and Susan. Thankfully she wasn't too annoyed about the "Mistletoe Cam" incident. Yes, keeping it a surprise was a dirty trick, but it also kept her reactions natural. The way her eyes widened in surprise, the way her lips parted. You couldn't fake those kinds of things.

She wasn't the only one caught by surprise though. The original plan was to share a quick peck on the cheek. Lewis hadn't counted on her mouth looking so alluring, nor had he anticipated how good her kiss would taste. Licking his lips, he swore he could still taste her sweetness.

Kisses didn't usually linger with him. In his mind, women were more or less interchangeable. Warm bodies that kept him from noticing he was alone. He wondered if the fact that this was his first sober kiss in a long time was the reason he found it so memorable. He'd been tempted to test the theory by kissing her again at the end of the night. But then, when they reached her doorstep and Susan looked up at him with those marvelous green-and-brown eyes…he'd backed away. Susan wasn't interchangeable. She deserved more respect than to be kissed simply for the sake of kissing.

But damn, he'd wanted to kiss her again. Wanted to so badly.

On the kitchen counter, his phone began buzzing an SOS signal, the vibration pattern he'd assigned Susan. He answered and hit Speaker while at the same time opening his refrigerator. "What can I do for you, Miss Collier?" he asked as he scanned the contents.

"Did your teammates really dislike you?"

"That's an odd way of starting a conversation," he replied. It appeared his housekeeper had done some grocery shopping for him. There was a fresh gallon of orange juice next to the milk.

"Did they?"

"I never spent enough time with them to know one way or another. Hung to myself mostly. Unless there was a party." He paused to take a swig of juice. "What's this about?"

"I'm sorry. Something my brother mentioned. He said you bounced from team to team because no one liked you."

"More like management disliked paying my heavy contract fees." Although he wasn't surprised to hear his bad-boy reputation had fueled different stories. Once again, his partying ways left their mark. "I take it your brother saw the paper."

"He did. He called you a degenerate."

"I've heard worse."

The pause on the other end of the line made him uneasy. "He's worried about scandal," Susan said. "I hadn't considered how this might affect the company.

Collier's has only recently gotten back on solid footing. If people discover…"

"They won't. I promise. I'm going to be on my best behavior." He had too much to lose.

"I know you will," she replied.

Her faith surprised him. She was the first person he'd met who really believed he'd changed. "I don't want to put you in a bad spot. If you want to back out, I'll understand."

"I don't want to back out—I gave my word and I intend to keep it. Besides… I had a good time last night."

Lewis smiled at the shyness in her voice. "We're famous you know," he said.

"Everyone in my office is whispering and giving me looks. They probably don't think I've been kissed before."

"You have been, right?"

"Yes. Although never quite so publicly."

"You're not still sore about my keeping the Mistletoe Camera thing a secret, are you?"

The soft sigh on the other end of the line sounded playfully exasperated. "I've recovered. But I want a promise that next time I'll get a little advance warning."

The memory of her glazed eyes popped into his head. "No worries there. I doubt there'll be a Mistletoe Cam at our next outing." Meaning he wouldn't have an excuse—that is, a reason—to kiss her.

"I suppose there wouldn't be, unless we were attending another basketball game. That's…good."

Was the clipped tone in her voice disappointment or relief? "I think so," he said. "I mean, it being a good thing. Can't go heavy on the PDA if I'm supposed to be changing my ways, right?"

"Right. Absolutely." He still couldn't tell. There was noise in the background. Maybe she was guarding her end of the conversation.

His ego took a little kick. A *little* disappointment would have been nice. It'd been a pretty decent kiss in his book. Heck, women were known to pull off their tops just to get his *attention*.

Those were women who wanted him though. Susan was with him as quid pro quo. She didn't really want him…

"Lewis?"

He shook his head. How long had he been staring into the neck of the orange juice bottle? "Did you say something?"

"I asked about the next step. Now that people know we're…that is, you know…"

"A couple," Lewis supplied. The word felt oddly normal.

"Exactly. What do we do now?"

Good question. According to his list, step two was to be seen at a few more formal events. Fundraisers with the proper people to establish his new social circle.

And he knew exactly the event. "How do you feel about the Kew Gardens?"

"In general? They're lovely. What does that have to do with us?"

"We're going to make our first official appearance there," Lewis told her. "This Saturday night. I hope you have a formal cocktail dress in your closet."

"I think I can rustle one up," she replied.

He had no doubt. "In the meantime, I'll talk to Michael about keeping up the momentum."

There was a pause on Susan's end of the line. He

imagined her pretty pink lips drawing into a frown. "What does that mean?"

"Keeping us in the public eye, luv, of course," he said. "If all goes right, it'll be a fun week."

The next few days were unlike anything Susan had ever experienced. It was like she'd changed identities overnight.

"What's he like?" became a common question.

Along with "Is he as wild as they say?"

The photo from the basketball game—with help from Lewis's agent, no doubt—had set off a domino trail of publicity. A couple of local radio personalities had seen the story and it had become fodder for one of the morning talk show segments. That, of course, had led to more articles.

One, rehashing Lewis's past romantic rendezvous, she found uncomfortable to read. Another focused on her, with the article playing up the fact that she had ties not only to Collier's Soap, but to former sex kitten Belinda Quinn.

Thankfully, as she told Lewis, her mother was filming some island reality show in the middle of nowhere and was unreachable, saving them from having to deal with *that* particular crazy.

Susan felt like a rock star.

The best part? Courtney and Ginger were practically apoplectic with jealousy. Was it petty and childish of her to take pleasure in their envy? Yes, but she was enjoying it regardless.

The two women spent the first couple of days after the "Kiss-mas" article appeared whispering behind her back. Mostly disbelief that Susan was the woman Lewis had chosen to date.

Like he would have dated either one of you, Susan longed to say.

All right, given they were both gorgeous, Lewis probably would have dated them, but she bet he wouldn't have remembered their names. Lewis would always remember hers.

And Lewis had kissed her. It might have only been for the cameras, but it was still a kiss—something Courtney and Ginger couldn't claim.

It wasn't until Day Three that their whispers became more pointed. And louder.

"A friend of mine used to tend bar at Narcissus and he said his credit card was always getting turned down for lack of funds."

Susan was walking back to her office when she heard the comment. Glancing at the cubicle of her admin, Freema, she spied Ginger and Courtney hovering by the doorway. There was no doubt about whose credit card they meant.

"Ginger," she called over to them. The blonde's spine straightened the second she heard her name. "Shouldn't you be working on our upcoming media buys? You, too, Courtney?"

Two wide-eyed, gaping expressions greeted her. At least they had the good sense to be embarrassed over getting caught. "We, um…were just chatting," Courtney finally managed to spit out.

"Well, I suggest you save your chatting for your lunch hour and let Freema do her job. And…" Because she could, she took a couple steps closer for dramatic effect. "I'll remind you—once—that my personal life is none of your concern. Do I make myself clear?"

Ginger's red cheeks said it all. "Yes."

"Good. Because I don't want to have this talk again." Folding her arms, she stood and maintained steady eye contact until the two women moved away. As she was leaving, she swore she heard the word *Shrewsan* muttered under one of their breaths. Lunchtime would be quite the gossip session, she imagined.

Let them complain. She was a rock star.

A giant illuminated tunnel greeted the car as they pulled through the main gate at Kew Gardens a few nights later. As they passed beneath, Lewis heard Susan gasp. "Oh, my! This is amazing." Leaning forward in her seat, she looked upward. "It looks like something out of that sci-fi TV show where they enter the wormhole."

"It does at that," Lewis agreed. Hundreds of overhead lights twinkled all around them like stars. "You know what this means, don't you?"

She looked across the seat at him, the lights reflecting in her eyes. "What?"

"If the car starts shaking uncontrollably, abandon ship."

"Not in this dress I'm not."

If it were another woman, he would have started pretending to hit turbulence and saying *she's breaking up* in his best Scottish accent. She would have laughed and thought him rakishly charming, even if she were too young to get the reference.

Tonight however, he had a difficult enough time making any lame jokes. He was wound tighter than a drum. For Susan, this was just another event, but for him, it would be the first time he'd attended a black-tie event with the intention of staying and mingling. No signing autographs and blowing off early with a boot-legged bottle of whatever he could grab.

Susan's diamond earrings sparkled as she angled her head to look upward again. "I think they strung Christmas lights over the entire driveway," she said. "It looks absolutely magical."

It certainly did. Lewis had never been to Kew Gardens—nature walks weren't really his thing—but the Christmas lights were famous. "The flyer that came with the tickets did say we would be treated to a fantastical holiday light show. Guess they weren't kidding."

"What charity are we supporting anyway? I never thought to ask. Be embarrassing if I couldn't remember the names of my boyfriend's causes."

Lewis tensed. No one had ever referred to him by that word before. It unsettled him. More nerves, he decided. Susan was only joking.

"You shouldn't have too much trouble remembering," he told her. "It's for the Sports Trust for Children."

"Isn't that one of the prince's charities? You don't believe in doing things small scale do you?"

"Wish I could tell you this was part of some grand strategy, but the truth is, I've been donating to the Sports Trust for years. Usually I give the tickets to this event away though."

"Why?"

"I'm not much for brie and crackers," he replied.

"No, I mean why the Sports Trust? In case someone asks," she said.

"Do people ask those sorts of questions?" Seeing

how everyone in the room was a supporter, he would assume they didn't care.

"Never hurts to be prepared. What if I run into a reporter or some person on the board of directors? They might wonder why you all of a sudden decided to start attending boring cocktail parties. If we're smart, we'll have our stories straight. I don't want to scramble the way I had to with Thomas and Linus."

"You handled that situation well enough." Admirably actually. "But I see your point. In this case, you can tell people the truth. Football kept me off the streets. In fact, if it weren't for sports, God knows where I'd be." He wouldn't be attending charity cocktail parties, that's for sure. More likely he'd be working some dead-end job and trying to stay out of trouble. "Sports gives kids a way to escape and be kids, if only for a few hours. If my money can help a kid out of trouble then that's a good thing, right?"

"A very good thing," she replied.

He wasn't sure why, but her smile made him feel like he'd aced a test. It mattered that she knew he was capable of sincerity.

In keeping with the season, the Victorian greenhouse hosting the event was illuminated with soft pink-and-blue spotlights, giving the building a purple glow. Lewis directed their driver to pull into the valet line to let them out.

"I haven't been here since my grandfather took us as children," Susan said as they stepped onto the sidewalk.

"Puts you one up on me," Lewis replied. "I've never been."

He looked around at the rolling lawns. They looked lush and manicured, despite it being winter. The building itself was an astounding stretch of glass and metal, its doorway guarded by a set of robed statues. "Lot fancier than I expected," he said.

"I always assumed my memory of this place was distorted by childhood, but maybe not. If I remember correctly, this particular building was filled with all sorts of rare plants."

They followed the other guests up the granite steps to the entrance where they were welcomed by a pair of giant poinsettia towers and a whoosh of warm, moist air. It was like stepping into a giant tropical forest. Plants of every shape and size surrounded them.

"Smells like spring," Susan said.

Indeed. There was definitely a hint of fresh dirt to the air. A sharp contrast to the cold night air.

The coat check was in the corner, marked by a pair of ferns decorated with tiny Christmas ornaments. If he hadn't been looking for it, he might never have found it. He turned to Susan intending to help her with her coat only to find she'd already slipped the garment from her shoulders. His breath caught at the sight of her. She'd been waiting on her steps when he picked her up, so this was the first time he'd had a chance to see what she was wearing and the sight took his breath away. At the wedding, she'd gone for a retro look: black, white and tight. Tonight she had a more graceful look. Her pale pink dress had a gathered bodice and long flowy skirt. While the dress didn't hug her curves the way the dress at the wedding had, the outfit fit tightly enough to let people know she had a shape while the V-neck showed off her ample cleavage. He liked that her breasts were soft and natural looking too. He'd seen enough enhancements in his life to actually find them boring.

In fact, he liked how everything about her looked soft and natural, right down to her hair which she let curl around her shoulders.

"You look great," he said.

Her skin turned the color of her dress. "Thanks. I don't go to a lot of formal events so I wasn't sure if this would work. I was afraid this might be too..." She paused as a woman in a sequined minidress and with mile-long legs sauntered by. "Dowdy."

"Nonsense. It suits you." Shoot. That sounded like he was saying dowdy suited her. "I mean, not everyone is the sequined-mini type."

"I'm certainly not, that's for sure," she said before adding in a lower voice, "Think I'd catch a cold baring that much skin."

"Skin is overrated. Seriously." She was giving him a look of disbelief. "I'm not saying I don't appreciate a miniskirt as much as the next guy, but there's something to be said about maintaining a little mystery, know what I mean?" He handed over their coats and waited for his claim ticket.

"Really? I always got the impression men wanted to get down to business as quickly as possible."

"Obviously, you've been hanging around the wrong type of man."

She blushed again. This time the color went past the V and the effect hit him square in the gut. He meant what he said. It was much more fun wondering how much of her very white skin was capable of blushing than seeing it from the start.

He reached out and twirled one of her curls around his index finger. "Trust me, luv. You look as good as anyone here. More so, even, because you've got class."

"And you are a very smooth talker, Mr. Matolo," she replied with a smile. "If things don't work out in the broadcast world, you can always get a job selling used cars. Come on, we've got mingling to do."

Lewis watched as she started along the leafy walkway. She didn't believe him, but it was true. She projected a level of class that came from years of breeding. Even when drunk at the wedding, she'd held herself with refinement. Lewis could barely muster it when he was sober. Sure, he had looks and charm, but at his core he was the little street kid being kicked from home to home. The one whom, if he hadn't been able to block a ball, wouldn't have been looked at twice by the people in Susan's world. The one who didn't belong...

"Are you coming?" Susan asked.

"One minute. Thought I'd enjoy the view a moment, first."

Score blush number three, although she tried to cover it with an exasperated eye roll. "Now you're just trying to get a rise out of me. If you really want a view, come check this out."

It was a Christmas jungle. In addition to the tropical plants, strategically placed Christmas trees dotted the walkway intersections. Each was decorated with a different color of the rainbow. Red. Orange. Yellow. Green. Blue. Violet. Only they weren't covered with traditional ornaments. Instead, silk butterflies and flowers mixed with the lights.

It wasn't the Christmas display that captured his attention, however. It was the dozens of men and women clustered around the display. All dripping with money and status. A couple close to them turned in his direction, their gaze subtly looking them up and down. Judging. Whispering.

Suddenly he was that little boy again, waiting to be told he didn't belong.

"I need a drink," he said. He headed to the bar.

CHAPTER FIVE

DID HE SAY he was getting a drink? Susan hurried after him, wishing her legs were longer so she could keep up. Amazing how the man could cut through a crowd like butter.

She finally caught up with him—nearly collided with him, actually—when he stopped cold about a foot from the bar. "What are you doing?"

"I—I…" He washed a hand across his lips. "Something stupid."

Exactly what she'd feared. The question was why? After all his talk about reforming his image, why would he risk sabotaging himself right as his plan was taking off?

There were too many people around to have this conversation. Lewis's arrival had most of the room starstruck. She could see people all around them sneaking glances.

Grabbing his hand, she moved past the bar and down the back pathway where she spied a water display in the far corner. The splashing water from the falls discouraged most people from standing too close. They would have privacy there.

There was only one other couple lingering by the water's edge. The pair shot them a look upon arrival, with the woman, not surprisingly, looking a bit incredulously at Susan. Ignoring them, Susan pulled Lewis off the walkway and into the foliage. There was only a small spot of bare ground, but if they stood close together, they wouldn't trample anything. "What are you doing, Lewis?" she hissed, just loud enough to be heard over the water. "I thought you were a 'changed man.' Pretty sure making a beeline for the bar isn't one of the sobriety rules. And don't try to tell me you meant to grab a glass of water, because I saw the look on your face." It was like a mask had dropped over his features. The muscles by his jaw began to twitch.

He wore a different expression now. Eyes lowered, his brow drawn together. "I know. It was stupid. I wasn't thinking."

Something had flipped his switch. "People don't just fall off the wagon without some kind of trigger. What happened?"

He shook his head. "It doesn't matter."

"Yes, it does matter," she told him. "I didn't agree to this little charade only to have you muck it up and embarrass us both."

Plus, not that she'd say so out loud, his sudden change in demeanor worried her. He was supposed to be this sexy, confident "reformed" playboy. The man she saw a moment ago had looked vulnerable and dare she say, insecure. Insecurity was *her* albatross. Men with perfect faces and perfect lips didn't experience self-doubt.

"You don't have to worry," Lewis told her. "It was a momentary blip. Nothing more."

"I believe you." After all, he'd stopped himself before

even getting to the bar. "Still, I'd feel better if I knew what set the blip off."

"Silly really," he said, looking downward. "I've faced down some of the world's toughest players with thousands of people watching without flinching, but put me in a room full of tuxedo-wearing strangers and I'm a bundle of nerves." Susan's breath caught as he moved his hand toward her shoulder, only to fiddle with a frond hanging behind her. "I'm sure that sounds ludicrous to someone like you."

"What do you mean *someone like me*?" The branch he was playing with was brushing against her curls, causing little ripples of awareness.

"This is your world. Sophisticated. Highbrow. You belong in it."

Hardly, but this wasn't the time to argue. At least about that. "Excuse me, Mr. Celebrity Millionaire. This is your world too."

"You know," he said, "I tell myself that very thing all the time. That I belong."

"But?" She could hear the doubt in his voice.

"But then I look at these people and I can hear them thinking *What is he doing here?* It's like they know where I came from."

"So what if they do?" she asked. "You have nothing to be ashamed of. Heck, half of this room is probably wondering how they can wrangle an introduction. More than half, likely."

"For now."

Susan frowned. "I don't understand."

"You said it yourself. I'm a celebrity. The more distance between me and my playing days, however, the less it'll matter. Until eventually I'll be just some bloke who was once a somebody and they'll wonder…" He shook his head. "Never mind."

"Tell me. Please." If whatever was on his mind was distressing enough that he would consider drinking, she wanted to help.

He answered so softly, she almost didn't hear. "And they'll wonder why they ever wanted me around in the first place. Silly, huh?"

A piece of her heart broke for him. "No," she told him. Illogical perhaps, but far from silly. He wasn't talking about reality; he was talking about a feeling that dwelled deep down inside a person. A feeling logic couldn't always touch.

"The Collier men are all very tall," she told him. "Very tall, very handsome and very charismatic, like my father. My mother is very beautiful. Like stop-traffic beautiful."

He was looking at her with dark, fathomless eyes. "I'm not following."

"When I was seven or eight—right before my mother took off—my parents threw a party. I wore this fancy party dress and my father told me how pretty I looked. I asked if I was as pretty as Mommy. And when he replied, *Absolutely*, my mother replied, *Don't lie to the girl, Preston*. That was the moment I knew that I wasn't like the rest of them. No matter how hard I tried, I would always be the odd one out."

Now it was she who felt judged as Lewis's gaze bore down on her. She'd meant the example as a sign of solidarity. Instead, she'd revealed that she was the Ugly Duckling of her family. He must think her daft. Why did she share anything?

His deep brown eyes moved closer. "Thank you.

Knowing you understand means a lot." He ran the back of his hand down her cheek. "More than you could know."

A shiver worked its way through Susan's body. Odd, since she'd suddenly grown very warm. Between the greenhouse temperature and the warmth emanating from Lewis's body, the air around her had grown thick. It was making her light-headed.

"Everything all right?" Lewis asked.

"Can we sit down somewhere?"

"Of course. Come with me." He tucked a curl behind her ear.

Since the other couple had departed—escaping the awkwardness of standing near a couple whispering in the bushes no doubt—Susan assumed they would head back to the walkway. Instead, Lewis took her hand and together they picked their way toward the waterfall.

"You were looking a little pink," he said, as he guided her to a seat on a nearby rock. The air was noticeably cooler by the water.

"We're going to get in trouble for being off the walkway."

"We won't stay long. Besides, the gardeners or whatever walk through here, don't they? That's why there are paths."

Susan shook her head. "You're funny. One minute you're telling me you worry about fitting in and the next you're flouting the rules. One would think you're self-sabotaging."

"Psychoanalyzing again, are we?"

"I told you, psychology's my thing." Fat lot of good it ever did her though. Being able to psychoanalyze everyone but herself.

"Bit of an odd hobby, isn't it?" Lewis asked.

"What can I say? I'm rubbish at arts and crafts. I got into it when I was a teenager. My attempt to understand my mother better."

He touched her knee, his hand bringing a steadying warmth. "Did you? Understand her better?"

"I learned a bunch of terms, all of which boiled down to her being a selfish piece of work who didn't want to share the spotlight with a child. They want so much attention, you know."

She tossed aside the last part with an overdramatic voice, but the sting never really left. When she was younger she blamed her looks, thinking if she was taller or thinner or elegant like the Collier boys, then her mother might have wanted her around. As she grew older, however, she realized her mother wouldn't have wanted the competition. The sad truth was her mother just plain didn't want her.

"At least you knew how she felt," Lewis said. "My mum cried holy hell when they took me away, but not so much that she couldn't get her act together."

"Just like Belinda," she said. "Guess that makes us two odd peas in a pod."

"Guess so," Lewis replied with a smile.

She slipped her hand over his, and their fingers entwined. With the connection came a strange, full kind of feeling. Kinship, Susan realized. For the first time she felt understood. It was a heady, seductive feeling.

Ironic that she would set out to comfort him and end up being the one comforted.

"I'm not the only one who's an enigma," he continued.

"What do you mean?"

"Well, for one thing, I keep looking for this unlikable shrew part of you, and I can't see it. I mean, you've got sharp edges, but who hasn't, right?"

He couldn't have said a nicer thing if he tried. "Thank you."

"Just calling it like I see it. And what I see looks pretty nice. Very nice, in fact." His smile sobered as his gaze dropped to her lips. Susan's pulse quickened, remembering the last time he'd looked at her mouth.

Instead of leaning in like she thought he would, however, Lewis suddenly released her hand and rose to his feet.

"We should get back on the path before we get in trouble," he said. "Won't do either of our reputations any good if we get tossed out on our ears. I can see the headline now. Stay Off the Grass, Lewis!"

"I'm sure they'd come up with something punnier than that." Although an example escaped her. She was too busy hiding her disappointment behind smoothing her dress. Her embarrassment too, for thinking he'd been about to kiss her. Talk about foolish. There were no cameras, no giant screen. Why would he want to kiss her if there was nothing to gain?

They snuck out of the plants the way they'd come, emerging to the backs of several other partygoers who were standing on the path.

"And here we thought we were being so sneaky. I bet half the party saw us." She looked over at Lewis who was smoothing the front of his jacket. He looked as crisp and elegant as before.

"If they did, no one would say anything," he said. "My guess? They didn't care."

"Or they were too polite to make a scene with photographers about." She and Lewis might have joked about negative headlines, but in reality, the sponsors of the event wouldn't want the bad press.

"Either way, we lucked out then, didn't we? Come on, I'll buy you a glass of champagne before we mingle. I don't suppose you know anyone here?"

Other than one or two faces she recognized from Collier's functions, not really. Since attending solo wasn't much fun, she only went to charity events when Linus needed an emergency date, which wasn't often. She didn't want to tell him that though, because it would reveal how pathetic her social life was. This faux romance was the most social activity she'd had in who knows how long.

"Excuse me, Mr. Matolo?"

They'd managed to go no more than a handful of steps before they were stopped by a pair of official-looking gentlemen. The younger of the two reminded Susan of a thinner, nerdier version of the Duke of Sussex with red hair and a neatly trimmed goatee. The other resembled an owl. Rotund with tortoiseshell glasses and an extremely receding hairline.

It was the younger one who addressed them. "I'm Christopher Redmayne, from the Sports Trust for Children and this is Graham Montclark."

She felt Lewis's body stiffen from six inches away. "As in Montclark Communications?" he asked. Montclark was Britain's largest private media corporation. "I believe I've read your name atop a scoreboard or two."

The balding man didn't return Lewis's smile. "I'm sure you have. The company sponsors several sporting venues."

"The two of us have been waiting for you to step away from the water display," Redmayne said.

So much for escaping comment. "I'm sorry about that," she said. "I—"

"Susan was feeling a bit light-headed. I thought the air might be cooler by the water." Lewis clasped her hand and squeezed. "Didn't want her keeling over or anything. I hope that wasn't a problem?"

"No, of course not," Redmayne replied. If it was a problem, Lewis's explanation coupled with the fear of a guest fainting kept him from saying so. "Are you feeling better, Ms…?"

"Collier, and yes. Thank you. Lewis knew exactly what I needed. In fact, he was just about to get me something cold to drink."

"Good. Good," Redmayne replied. "A cold drink is always a good idea."

Interestingly though, the two men didn't make a move to step aside or leave. They remained planted in the middle of the path, apparently intent on having a conversation.

"Collier," Montclark said. "Any relation to Thomas?"

"My brother."

The businessman nodded. "Good man. Miraculous story, that business with his wife."

"Yes. The whole family was shocked when she returned. In a good way of course. We like to think of it as a true Christmas miracle."

"Graham is one of our advisors. I was telling him how generous you've been to our organization," Redmayne said. "Your support is very appreciated. It's always a surprise, to see who is willing to step up and help."

"You do good work," Lewis replied. "Why wouldn't I support you?"

"That's nice to hear." At that moment, a server walked by carrying a tray of champagne. Holding up a hand, Redmayne stopped the man from passing. "Could you get a glass of water for Ms. Collier?" he asked.

"Actually… Champagne will be fine." This conversation defined the term awkward. If it was going to continue, she would need more than water.

"I'll take the water, if you don't mind," Lewis said. You could tell both of the other men were struggling not to look surprised. "I'm a teetotaler these days."

Susan smiled at him with pride. The admission couldn't have been easy for him. Not in this environment where he already felt judged.

Redmayne recovered first, with the grace one expected from an experienced networker. "I should take a page from your book. Every holiday I swear I'm going to cut back on excesses and every year I'm filled with regret because my pants are too snug." The four of them shared an uncomfortable chuckle.

"Anyway," Redmayne continued, "I hate to talk business when the two of you are here to enjoy yourselves, but we're hosting a Christmas event for our young ambassadors on December eleventh. Heath Chilton was supposed to lead a sports clinic but we found out this morning that he's having a second knee surgery and won't be able to attend so…"

"You're wondering if Lewis would be able to step in!" In a voice suiting a loyal girlfriend, Susan finished the sentence for him. Actually she suspected Redmayne wanted to ask if Lewis could use his contacts to get a current player—hence the awkwardness—and she jumped in to get Lewis's name on the table first. From the look Redmayne shared with Montclark, it was a good thing she had. "I think that's a terrific idea. Lewis was just saying how he wanted to get more involved with the program. Weren't you?"

He picked up her train of thought immediately. "Yes, I was, and I'd be honored to step in."

Redmayne was scrambling for a polite way to escape the hole he was in. "That's very generous of you, but, um…" He looked at Montclark, who opened his mouth to finish.

Lewis cut them off. "In fact," he said, "I know what Heath charges for public appearances. If it would help the organization's bottom line, I would be glad to donate my time free of charge."

Well done. Susan smiled into her champagne. A light gleamed in Montclark's eyes. The idea of saving a sizable amount of money clearly appealed to him. "We're looking to inspire these kids. Can we count on you to show up, ready to perform?"

"Mr. Montclark, I always show up ready to play," Lewis told him. "You have my word."

The reassurance didn't seem to impress the businessman, but the organization had its back against the wall. That they'd approached Lewis for any kind of assistance this close to the event said they were desperate. Susan knew what the two men were thinking. A free-of-charge, former player was better than no player at all.

The waiter returned with Lewis's water. "Here's your water, Mr. Matolo," he said. Servers probably didn't usually address the guests by name but the young man's starstuck expression as well as the excited tremor in his voice explained the break in protocol.

"Thanks, mate. Appreciate it."

Tucking the tray under his arm, the young man prepared to leave only to pause. "I've watched every game you ever played in."

"Wow," Lewis replied. "What'd you do? Start watching when you were in diapers?"

Susan watched Montclark taking in the exchange, particularly the waiter's starstuck face. After a few minutes more of conversation—and a request for a selfie—the young man moved on and Montclark cleared his throat. "Very well," he said, "since you are willing to make a firm commitment and waive your appearance fee…"

"Anything to help the organization," Lewis replied.

"We appreciate you stepping up on such short notice. Redmayne will send your agent all the information." The three men shook on the arrangement.

"Remind me to tip that server extra," Susan said once Redmayne and Montclark had moved on to the buffet table. "His timing couldn't have been more perfect if we paid him." There was no doubt his enthusiasm was what had finally convinced Montclark.

"Should I tip you too?" Lewis asked.

"Beg your pardon?"

"For backing them into the corner in the first place. We both know they wanted to use my connections, not hire me. If you hadn't jumped in with the idea, it never would have come up."

"You wanted to rehab your image. What better way than to dazzle them with your newfound dedication to charity?"

"Not to mention impressing Graham Montclark."

"Oh, do his stations carry the matches? I hadn't realized." Putting a hand to her chest, she blinked with false innocence.

Lewis chuckled, his accompanying smile devilishly crooked. "Well played, Ms. Collier. I knew I picked the right woman."

His words had the smoothness of raw honey dripping from a spoon. They ran through her, leaving a slow warmth.

He means the right woman for the arrangement.

She needed a dose of reality to counteract the sweetness. None of this was real. She'd be wise to keep that in mind before she did something incredibly stupid.

Like fall for the man.

CHAPTER SIX

LEWIS HAD DATED a lot of women in his adult life. Too many really. None of them, though, were like Susan. Granted, that was the point, but never had he thought that different would be so interesting.

They were on their way home, still in character, as it were. He had his arm slung across the back seat while Susan sat close to his side. Not overly close, and certainly not draped across his lap like a lot of his dates. Susan was far too classy for that kind of behavior.

Susan was a lot of things. She was smart and sophisticated, not to mention perceptive. When he had freaked out, she'd known exactly what to say.

An odd experience, it was, being understood. When she touched his hand, the warmth shot straight through him, the sensation simultaneously comforting and terrifying.

He wasn't used to sharing pieces of himself. Better to maintain distance, he always said. It made leaving easier. With Susan, however—and maybe it was because they were so alike—with Susan, sharing felt normal.

The car turned a corner. In spite of the late hour, there were plenty of lights on. Some of the windows already had candles and in one or two, he spied Christmas trees. "Early birds," he murmured.

"Who are early birds?" Susan asked. When she turned to look at him, he caught a whiff of vanilla shampoo. Reminded him of cookies.

"The trees," he replied. "Some people already have theirs up. They're early birds."

"Probably the same people who start playing Christmas music the day after Halloween and have their shopping done a month early."

"I'm going to go out on a limb and guess that you aren't one of those people."

"Definitely not." Even in the dark he could see her eyes widen in horror. Whether she realized it or not, her little protest had shifted her closer to him. Her shoulder brushed against the edge of his coat. "No shopping until December first. That's my rule."

Lewis looked at his watch. "Good news then. You can start officially start shopping. It's after midnight."

"Huzzah! I'll fire up my computer as soon as I get home."

"That's the Christmas spirit." Unable to help himself, he wrapped his arm around her shoulder and squeezed, pulling her body into the crook of his arm as he did so. He liked that she was huggable. When you pulled her close, her body was warm and comfortable. The kind of body built for cuddling.

He'd never been one for cuddling before.

"I don't know what I would have done without you tonight," he said. "You were brilliant."

Despite the shadows, he could feel she was blushing. "I told you before, you played as big a part in convincing Montclark as I did. If you really want to thank someone, thank the waiter."

"Man's timing *was* impeccable." It was Susan, though, who made him feel confident. "I don't think I would have made it through the entire party if you hadn't been there to talk me off the ledge."

"Don't be silly. You righted yourself all on your own," she said.

Perhaps, but her gentle reassurance was what had kept him righted from that moment on. "The stories you shared…"

Her gaze fell away. "Who knew sharing my childhood angst would be so powerful?"

"Don't sell yourself short." They both knew the real meaning behind her story. She'd peeled back a layer of herself to let him know he wasn't alone. That she, in her own way, understood how it felt to be on the outside looking in.

For as long as he could remember, he'd been left of center. Separate and alone, even when surrounded by people. Oh, he put on a good face, but in the end that's all it was, a face. Even when he was part of a team, he never truly felt a sense of solidarity. Why bother when you were only going to move on?

But tonight, he didn't feel alone. He and Susan were a team. The idea was headier than anything he ever felt. It took his breath away, and at the same time, scared him. He didn't do close. He did self-preservation.

Regardless, she deserved to know just how much her honesty meant to him. "All that stuff I told you tonight…" He chose his words carefully in case the driver was listening. "I've never told anyone before."

Her breath caught, and a second later her head came to rest on his shoulder. "Me neither," she said.

"Your apartment is right ahead, miss," the driver said.

His announcement was a switch, ending the moment. Almost immediately, the two of them straightened, with Susan shifting one way and Lewis the other. The gap that formed was imperceptible, but Lewis's side grew cooler nevertheless.

He busied himself with watching the traffic while Susan fiddled with her bag and the driver parallel parked.

"Tonight was fun."

At the sound of Susan's voice, he turned his head. "I'm glad you enjoyed yourself."

"I did. Between this and the basketball game, you've set the bar pretty high. Makes me wonder what you'll come up with next."

"You'll have to wait and see."

The driver opened the door, and they stepped onto the sidewalk.

"Should I wait?" the driver asked.

"I… No. I'll be right back," he replied. "I have an early morning tomorrow."

Ignoring what looked like a flash of disappointment flaring in Susan's eyes, Lewis guided her up the walkway to the red door marking the entrance to her apartment building. "If you give me your keys, I'll open the door for you."

"I think I can handle a key," she replied before reaching into her bag and pulling out a large key ring. "It's hardly complicated."

"Yes, but the driver is watching. Since we don't know

if he'll try to sell us out, I should make a point of unlocking and walking you in the door."

"Absolutely. We've got to keep up appearances, don't we? However, the front door has a keypad. The lock is for my apartment door."

There it was again, that distance, and he couldn't figure out why. Nothing he had said seemed inappropriate. "All right then, why don't you give me the key code."

"Fine," she said with a sigh.

As he punched in the numbers, Lewis fought the urge to turn around and check on the driver who might or might not be paying attention.

No sooner had he opened the door, than Susan started over the threshold.

"Wait." He grabbed her wrist to keep her from disappearing. "I need to kiss you goodnight. The driver might be watching. We want to give him something he can peddle to Lorianne or another columnist."

"Right," she replied. "We want to give the right impression."

Lewis couldn't tell if the sarcasm in her voice was meant to be humorous or not. With the shadows obscuring her expression, it was impossible to tell. It didn't matter though. Appearances needed to be maintained. Slipping his arm around her waist, he closed the space between them and kissed her. Just as he had at the game, he only intended a brief, chaste peck. The moment his lips touched hers, however, any thought of chaste flew out the window.

Her mouth was made for kissing. Their lips slanted together like links in a chain, Susan's mouth yielding without urging. Her head fell back and her body arched against him. Lewis's body, still humming with awareness from earlier, reacted immediately. Pulling her close, he pressed his hips to hers, delivering a deep, soulful kiss while his free hand tangled in her curls.

Susan's eyes were glazed when they finally broke apart, or so he told himself. Again, he couldn't see her expression, but since *he* was dazed, he hoped she was, as well. From one kiss. His body was on full alert now, wanting nothing more than to take her upstairs and continue.

Fortunately common sense had maintained a tenuous grip, and he was able to step back. "Continuing" wasn't part of their deal.

Taking a breath, he stepped backward again, down to the step below. "Well, that should give the driver some gossip to peddle," he said.

Hopefully his grin didn't look as shaky as it felt.

"I think it's time we slept together."

Susan tripped over a crack in the sidewalk and nearly dropped her coffee. It was three weeks into their "relationship," and they were spending the weekend afternoon Christmas shopping. Until now, they'd stuck to highly visible social events where their status as a couple was documented by official photographers and social reporters. Lewis felt the timing was such that they should embark on Step Three of his plan, or what he called "doing coupley things." His agent said he would tip off the tabloids that the two of them would be spending the day on Regent Street on the off chance they wanted to snag a photo of the budding romance.

At the moment, the only thing they'd snag would be a shot of her staring at him bug-eyed.

"Not literally, obviously," Lewis said catching her elbow.

No, of course not. Susan focused on adjusting her jacket so he wouldn't see her disappointment. Sleeping together didn't involve an audience, and Lewis didn't initiate any displays of affection unless someone was watching.

How could he turn his emotions on and off like that? All gentle touches and intimate glances in public only to back away the moment they were alone. They'd even taken to stepping inside the doorway of her building to say goodbye so he wouldn't have to kiss her goodnight.

Clearly she'd been a little too enthusiastic in her response the other night. Honestly, what did he expect though after essentially telling her she was special on the drive home?

Then again, maybe the admission had been for show too. They hadn't been alone.

Recovering herself, she made a show of taking a sip of coffee. "What would be the point of pretending we're sleeping together?" she asked. Besides frustrating her.

"Because people expect to see a real relationship move forward. It's the twenty-first century. People in serious relationships sleep together."

"I know that." She may not have had a serious love affair in her lifetime, but she had dated people for more than a few months. "I mean, what would be the overall goal? We'd get a blind item saying you spent the night or a pic in the *Looking Glass* of us heading out to breakfast?"

"You got a better idea?"

"Not really, but…"

She'd been thinking about this a lot the past few

days. There was a hole in Lewis's plan. "Blind items aren't read by everyone. There's no guarantee your message is going to reach the people you need to influence. Same with attending a few social events." The more she thought, the more she wondered if their plan was a waste of time.

Or maybe it was that the phoniness of it all was beginning to chafe. Tipping off photographers, pretending for witnesses. Every gimmick was a reminder that she wasn't good enough to be a real girlfriend.

It wouldn't be so bad if he weren't so damn amazing when they were together. Like today when he'd shown up on her doorstep bearing coffee for their shopping adventure. He even tucked in her scarf under the guise of keeping her warm while they walked. All for the benefit of anyone who might be watching.

Why wasn't she worthy of such treatment in private? Susan sighed. When she agreed to play along, it was so people like Courtney and Ginger would stop calling her pathetic. Now she wondered if she was merely proving them right.

"Earth to Susan..." A leather glove waved in her face. "You there?"

"Sorry," she replied. "You were saying?"

"I was saying you're right. We need to make a bigger splash. I'll talk to Michael about scoring a profile article in one of the weekly mags. How do you feel about becoming a cover model?"

Awkward. "Who on earth would want to read an article about me?"

"I would. You're a fascinating woman." His smile made her stomach tumble. There he went again, making her feel special. "But I'm thinking about a profile about both of us. One of those 'How Love Saved Me' articles. What do you think?"

Terrific. So not only did he want to take their fake romance to the next fake level, he wanted to give an interview about how much he fake loved her. The idea gave her heartburn. "I think I need to check your coffee," she said.

"Nothing but Italian roast, I swear. Here, do you want to test it?" He held out the cup.

Susan pushed it back. "I'll take your word for it."

"The more I think about it," Lewis continued, "the more I can't believe I didn't think of the idea sooner. A feature article would convince people a lot faster and it would give Collier's some good publicity, as well."

"I didn't realize you were in a rush," she said.

"I'm not looking to dawdle—the season will be starting soon enough."

"You're going to have to hustle if you want to be featured before the holidays," she said. "Even weekly magazines have a lead time. Too close to the holidays, and you'll have to keep up the ruse through January. We only mapped out an agreement through the holidays, so unless you want to extend things..."

"I'll call Michael first thing on Monday morning," he said. "I don't want to tie you up longer than necessary."

What he really meant was tie him up. The sooner he established himself as a reliable potential commentator, the sooner he could go about finding a woman who was more his type. She swallowed the bad taste that suddenly filled her mouth.

No sense dwelling on the inevitable. They had nearly a month to go before they parted company. Today was about "being coupley."

"Is there a game plan for this shopping expedition or are we just going to parade up and down the street letting people stare at us?" she asked.

"Up to you. I'm more of an online shopper myself."

"How personal."

"How convenient," Lewis replied. "One click and you're done."

Susan wondered if she was part of his "one click." They'd decided they weren't spending Christmas together. Did fake couples bother to exchange gifts if they weren't being watched?

Stop whining. You knew what you were getting into.

"As much as I enjoy people staring, I think we should do something. Do you feel up to tackling a toy store? My niece Maddie wants Bugnoculars."

"Bug-what?"

The way he scrunched up his face in confusion was adorable. "Binoculars that let you look at bugs close up," she explained. Her niece had become a budding entomologist. "Actually, she wants two pairs. One for her and one for her stuffed pet, Bigsby. Oh, and a kitten too, but I was informed she's already put in an order for the animal with Santa."

"Hope for her sake, he comes through."

"Last year she asked for a visit from her dead mother, and got her wish. A 'gray tiger kitten with a red bow' shouldn't be too difficult, considering."

Naturally her sister-in-law's reappearance at Christmastime was merely coincidence, but Maddie believed it was all Santa. Susan saw no sense bursting her bubble. In a few years the little girl would learn the truth about Santa and that part of her innocence would die forever. "How old were you when you stopped believing in Santa?" she asked.

"Six," Lewis replied. "I told one of the other kids at the foster home that Santa was bringing me a race car set, and he let me know the score."

Six years old. It saddened her, thinking of how disappointed he must have been.

"Wouldn't you know, *his* mom got her act together for the holidays and showed up with the exact set I wanted. I got to watch him and his brother play with the thing all day."

She didn't dare ask about Lewis's mother, suspecting she knew the answer. "Didn't they let you join them?"

"Nah. Wasn't part of the family," he said, eyes looking off in the distance. In that moment, his profile looked so forlornly beautiful it made her throat clutch. She squeezed her coffee cup to keep from pulling him into a hug. Lewis shook his head. "I was too young." Maybe she was projecting, but his offhand comment came out flat. "What about you," he asked. "When did you figure it out?"

"Fourth grade." She remembered well. "My classmates told me. Turned out I was the only one who was still a believer. The whole class got quite a laugh." The memory of her embarrassment swirled in her stomach. "Oh, well," she said. "Whatever. It was a long time ago. I've recovered."

"My resilient little pea?"

His what? Right, they were two odd peas in a pod. Was it strange that whenever they shared sad childhood tales, she ended up feeling warm from the inside out?

She decided to change the subject before things became too maudlin. "Hamleys is only a block away. Ready to tackle the crowds?"

Breaching the gap between them, Lewis took her arm and tucked it in the crook of his own. "Crowds are what we want, luv. Remember?"

Good thing too because it was the opening weekend of Santa's grotto. As a result, the toy store was filled with children dressed in their Christmas finery waiting to go upstairs for their chance to speak with the man himself while their parents snapped a photo for the annual Christmas card. If ever there would be a place where they'd be noticed, this was it. Most of the kids would be too young to recognize Lewis, but their parents weren't. Susan saw a number of heads turn in their direction as they walked in.

"I think the science toys are on the second floor," Susan told him.

She made it halfway to the staircase before she realized Lewis wasn't following. Figuring someone must have stopped him for an autograph or photo, she turned and scanned the crowd. It wasn't difficult to find his tall form in the crowd and she soon spied him by the animatronic display. The store was famous for its fantastical panoramas. This year, the wall was a winter resort with animals of all sorts enjoying the great outdoors. Teddy bears rode a ski lift. A pair of rabbits were ice skating on a pond. There was even a cutout of a lodge where a sloth lay stretched in a hammock by a roaring fire.

Lewis was mesmerized. His eyes were wide and shining and he had an almost slack-jawed look of wonder about him. Maddie wore a similar look when Susan had brought her last year. Lewis's expression caused warmth to spread through her chest. He looked beautiful when his guard slipped. She wanted to wrap her arms around him and soak him up.

Suddenly it hit her. He was viewing the display with a child's eye for good reason. "You've never been in here at Christmastime, have you?" she asked.

"Never been in here period," he replied. "No reason to."

And probably too far away when he was a child. How much childhood had he lost moving from home to home? While she was the odd person out in her family, she at least had one. Her heart ached picturing the little boy watching his foster siblings play with the toy he wished for. It wasn't just the toy that caused the pain; it was being shut out.

Without giving it a second thought, she wrapped her arms around his biceps and rested a head on his shoulder. Her way of saying he wasn't frozen out anymore. The shifting of muscles beneath her cheek told her Lewis had looked down in surprise, but he didn't say a word.

"Pretty amazing, isn't it?" she remarked. "It must take them months to plan everything out. All the little details."

Lewis chuckled. "There's a red squirrel dancing in one of the trees. I had a teammate who danced like that. Hector Menendez. Called it his booty dance. I should send him a video to show him how awkward he looked." He took out his phone.

Susan was watching another set of rabbits, this pair chasing one another around a tree trunk. "My grandfather used to bring us here when we were little."

"Same one who took you to the Kew Gardens?"

Susan nodded. "He took us a lot of places. The company museum was his favorite—always a good time."

"Didn't like learning about soap?"

"Thomas and Linus liked it. I was four years old. I just wanted ice cream. Come to think of it, there are days when I'd still rather eat ice cream than be at Collier's. For that matter, I'd take ice cream over anything."

"Anything?" Lewis asked. Actually he purred, making her insides flip. "I can think of a few things I might like better."

There must be someone nearby watching because he had his nose dangerously close to her temple. Very well. She'd play along. "Is that so? Like what?"

"Sugar cookies, for starters."

Susan nearly snorted. That was so not what she expected. But then, this was a show, not a seduction. Why shouldn't he give a nonsensical answer? "Cookies over ice cream? Close call, but I don't think so."

"That's your opinion. Lately I've been finding the aroma very tempting. Has anyone ever told you that you have gorgeous hair?"

The non sequitur threw her, along with a brush across the top of her head that felt a lot like a kiss.

For the crowd.

"I've gotten a few compliments," she replied.

In reality, her hair was a source of vanity for her. She had the Collier black hair, one of the few family traits—maybe the only family trait—from that side of the family that had been passed down to her.

"Good. Glad to hear it didn't go unnoticed."

Like the rest of her, she almost said. Instead, she whispered, "Thank you," and, closing her eyes, rested her cheek a little more firmly against his woolen coat.

"Did you know your hair smells like sugar cookies?" Lewis whispered back.

Susan's eyes flew open. Pulling back, she looked at him expecting a grin. He was dead serious though. If anything, his eyes were slightly hooded. "Your shampoo," he said. "Reminds me of sugar cookies."

He just said he preferred sugar cookies. Was he trying to say…

The sound of her phone interrupted her thoughts before they could become coherent. Pulling her phone from her bag, she saw her brother Linus's face on the caller ID.

"Might want to head to the hospital," he said when she answered. "Baby number two has arrived."

CHAPTER SEVEN

"THE BABY'S HERE! The baby's here!" Susan's niece nearly lifted off the ground, propelling herself into her aunt's arms. A wispy little live wire she was, bouncing up and down on her toes even as she hugged Susan's midsection. "I'm a big sister," she announced in a loud, proud voice.

"And everyone in the hospital knows," Susan replied. "You need to keep your voice down though, so you won't wake the babies in the nursery."

Lewis watched the moment unfold from a few feet away. They stood outside one of the birthing suites in the maternity ward having hurried over as soon as Linus had called. He noticed Susan wore a giant smile as she admonished the girl, a clear indication she didn't really mind the boisterous greeting. She pressed one hand to her niece's back, while the other gently smoothed her bobbed brown hair. Even if she hadn't told him how much she adored Maddie, he'd have known from the tender expression on her face.

She knelt down so she was eye level with the girl. "Do you have a brother or a sister?"

"Brother. His name is No-Well."

"That would be Noel." A man joined them. Judging from his lanky frame, Lewis assumed it was one of Susan's brothers. Linus, the middle one, most likely. He looked too laid-back to be a new father. "She read the name card on the bassinet and thinks he's named after the Christmas song," he said. "Noel Christopher Collier."

"Got a bit of a Christmas theme going there, don't they?" The remark was out of his mouth before he could catch it.

Susan didn't seem to mind. In fact, she laughed. "My brother and his wife have a thing about Christmas. They think some kind of Christmas magic brought them back together."

Whatever floats their boat. Someone needed to believe in Christmas miracles.

He listened while Susan peppered her brother with questions about the baby's weight and other pertinent details.

"When did she go into labor?" she asked.

"Middle of the night, from what Thomas said. I'm not too clear on the details. Maddie was with the housekeeper when I picked her up."

"You weren't home," Maddie said. "We called you."

"I'm sorry, sweetheart. I didn't hear the phone. I was out Christmas shopping."

"With a friend," Linus noted. He'd finally acknowledged Lewis's presence. A pair of extremely intelligent blue eyes looked him up and down. "Hello."

There was definitely scrutiny in the greeting. As well as a good dose of protectiveness. Lewis's eyes darted to Susan who blushed and looked away. Lewis couldn't blame the man. If he had a sister and thought she was dating someone like him, he'd scrutinize the guy too.

"Lewis Matolo," he said, extending his hand. "Pleased to meet you."

"Linus Collier. Likewise." If he was insincere, the man's smile didn't show it. "Sorry to interrupt your shopping date."

"No problem. We can shop anytime. It's not every day someone has a baby."

"I'm Maddie." The little girl had her hand out, mimicking her uncle. When Lewis accepted, she yanked his arm up and down with enthusiasm. Had she been an adult, he would have popped an elbow.

"Hello, Maddie," he said. "Congratulations on your baby brother."

"I'm getting a kitten too. Santa's bringing him," she replied before tilting her head and switching gears in the way only children could. "Are you Aunt Susan's boyfriend? Uncle Linus says you are."

Lewis's cheeks grew warm. He wasn't expecting the third degree from a six-year-old. "I...um..." From his place behind his niece, Susan's brother was waiting for his response.

Susan stepped in before he could answer. "Lewis is a very good friend," she said. "He was helping me pick out your Christmas present."

"Really?" Maddie's eyes widened. "What did you get?"

"We can't tell you that," Lewis replied. "It would spoil the surprise."

"Aunt Susan says surprises are overrated."

"Yes, I know. She told me how she felt about them when we went to a basketball game recently." Susan ducked her head to hide her pinking cheeks. Lewis waited until she glanced at him through her lashes and then he grinned.

The exchange didn't escape her brother who scrutinized them both. "I'm sure Aunt Susan meant unpleasant surprises," Linus said. "Not good surprises like presents."

"Absolutely," Susan answered. "Some surprises are definitely worth waiting for. Like Christmas presents. So you're just going to have to wait, little munchkin."

"Okay." Maddie's disappointed expression didn't look very permanent. In fact, the frown disappeared about a second after it appeared, in correlation with the suite's door opening up.

"Daddy!" the little girl bounced away from Susan and toward the dark-haired man who'd stepped into the corridor. He immediately scooped her up in his arms.

Thomas Collier, Lewis presumed. His shirt and slacks were wrinkled, and he had the shadowed cheeks of a man who'd been up for hours. "You made it!" He flashed a grin in Susan's direction. "Linus said he was having trouble finding you."

"I didn't hear the phone," Susan said. "I was out shopping."

"With a friend," Linus added.

"So I see." Thomas turned his attention to Lewis. "Hello."

"Congratulations," Lewis replied. There was no welcoming handshake as the man had his hands full with his daughter, but part of Lewis wondered if there would have been one anyway. Clearly, Thomas was the more serious of the two. His gaze, laser-like in its focus, had a hint of wariness.

"Thank you," he replied. "Kid was an impatient little

guy—Rosie barely got settled before he decided to appear. Fifteen minutes later and he might have popped out in the lift." The second half was directed at Linus and Susan.

"Sounds like a Collier," Linus said. "Susan was born in the back seat."

"Only because Belinda thought a back seat delivery would make for better drama," Susan replied. Her face was beet red, the poor thing.

Not knowing what else to do, Lewis wrapped an arm around her waist. "If you're going to make an entrance, might as well make it memorable, right, luv?" He pecked her on the cheek.

Out of the corner of his eye, he saw both Collier brothers raised their eyebrows.

"Daddy, can I see Mummy now?" Maddie asked.

"Sure, sweetheart. Everyone can."

One by one, the family stepped inside the pastel-colored room where a beautiful and tired-looking brunette lay in bed. A few feet away, in a clear plastic bassinet, a tiny bundle lay swaddled in a soft yellow blanket.

"Noel Christopher Collier." Pride filled Thomas's whisper.

"He looks like Dad," Linus said. "Only with a little more hair."

"You're a jerk," Susan said. "He's beautiful. Really, really beautiful."

"All Rosalind's doing. She's the one who did the work." The adoration in Thomas's voice was palpable.

Lewis stood by the door and watched the scene evolve. So much love and pride in one small room. Susan had told him on the way over that the Collier legacy meant everything to her older brother. It was evident. You could feel the sense of family in the air. How could Susan not see it? That she was part of the circle.

He wasn't. He was the outsider. The unexpected, unwanted guest being politely tolerated.

His eyes sought Susan. She was frowning at him from across the bassinet. "Why are you standing by the door?" she asked.

"Coffee. Thought I'd pop down and get us some." It was the first excuse that came to mind. He needed space to clear his head. A cafeteria run fit the bill.

Coward that he was, he slipped out the door without waiting for her reply.

"Hold on! I'll go with you." Linus's voice called out.

Great. Instead of an escape, he was going to get an escort. The sandy-haired man caught up with him just as the elevator door opened.

"I figured you might need some help carrying everything," he said with a grin. "Both Maddie and Rosalind put in an order for milk and cookies. We might as well buy a half dozen. Susan never met a cookie she didn't like either."

Something about the joke grated on his nerves. "So what? Lots of people like cookies."

"True, but Susan's love of cookies is legendary. We've been teasing her about it since we were kids."

"I'm sure she loved that," Lewis muttered. Already self-conscious because she didn't look like her mother or brothers, her being teased about her eating habits must have stung. Now he understood why she thought she didn't fit in.

"Did you say something?" Linus asked.

"Talking to myself," Lewis replied. Wasn't his place to pick a fight with Susan's brother.

Linus however, wasn't ready to let it go. He moved so he was in front of Lewis, his back to the elevator buttons. Arms folded across his chest, he gave Lewis another long, studious look. "You're annoyed, aren't you?"

"No," Lewis lied. "Just don't think you should be singling her out when everyone has a sweet tooth."

"Huh," Linus said.

"What's that supposed to mean?"

"Nothing," the man replied. "It's nice to know you're protective of Susan's feelings."

Lewis felt his shoulders tightening. "Shouldn't I be? Seems to me, a lot of people should care about Susan's feelings."

"Perhaps, but not all of them are known to go through women like water."

"No. Some of them are related."

Linus's eyebrows shot up and for a second, Lewis worried he'd pushed his luck too far. Then he saw what looked like a gleam of respect.

"Are we going to see you at the gathering at Christmas?" her brother asked, changing the topic.

"Your company party? Absolutely. I promised Susan I'd be there with bells on."

"No, I meant the wedding on Christmas Eve. Well, vow renewal, second wedding. Whatever you want to call it."

Lewis thought back to the day they'd signed their agreement and the way Susan had hedged when he mentioned the holidays. She clearly didn't want him at a family event.

"The holidays haven't really come up yet," he replied. "We're taking things one day at a time."

"Oh," Linus said. Awkwardness filled the small space. "Well, perhaps we'll see you there," he replied.

"Maybe." Probably not. Weddings were for family, not fake boyfriends.

Why the thought made his stomach hurt, he didn't know.

"Your friend Lewis seems much more low-key than I expected," Thomas remarked shortly after Linus and Lewis left the room. Susan had hoped new fatherhood would distract him, but no such luck.

"What did you expect?" she asked. "That he'd show up…" She was about to say shirtless and carrying a bottle of Cristal, but a quick look at Maddie reminded her that wasn't appropriate. "…ready to go crazy? I told you, he's not that person anymore."

"Relax. I wasn't trying to criticize the guy."

No, only lobbing a passive-aggressive comment in his direction. "Lewis is a lot…more…than people give him credit for," she told him. "He's smart, he's gentle, he's considerate…"

"Handsome."

Her sister-in-law lay in bed, her eyes half-closed, with Maddie curled up by her side. Exhausted from the excitement, the little girl was nearly asleep but Rosalind had clearly been listening.

Rosalind stroked her daughter's hair. "He's very handsome," she repeated. "The tabloids don't do him justice."

"No, they don't," Susan agreed. There were times when she would look at him quickly and the sheer perfection of his profile made her breath catch.

"I still can't believe my sister is going out with Champagne Lewis," Thomas said.

"Why?" Because she wasn't a supermodel? Because she was a pathetic shrew? "Is it really such a big stretch?"

"You've got to admit, you two are different."

"Not as much as you'd think," she replied. Maybe on the outside, but on this inside they were two odd peas in a pod. The thought made her smile. "Anyway, it doesn't matter. We're not..."

Her brother, who'd been staring at his newborn son, turned his head. "Not what?"

"Running off and getting married anytime soon."

She almost said they weren't really dating. But it was a secret and if she told Thomas the truth, he'd use it to justify thinking Lewis was still some kind of "bad boy." Which he wasn't. He was everything she said and more.

And she was going to hold on to the illusion for as long as she could.

"For goodness' sake, stop interrogating the woman," Rosalind said in a sleepy voice. "Her love life is none of our business. We don't need to butt in."

"If you remember, she had no problem butting into ours," Thomas said.

Susan winced. She *knew* he still held a grudge over her interference last winter.

"That was different," Rosalind said. "We had our collective heads in the clouds. We wouldn't have had Noel if she hadn't said anything. Now be quiet so I can get some sleep."

"Thank you," Susan replied. Her brother looked down at his feet.

"You're welcome," Rosalind said. "Besides, we already know he's special or you wouldn't have brought him to the hospital."

We already know he's special or you wouldn't have brought him to the hospital.

Her sister-in-law's words stuck in Susan's head the entire way home.

When Lewis and Linus had returned from the cafeteria, she noticed a distinct change in her faux boyfriend's manner. He seemed distant.

"Thank you for coming to the hospital with me," she said. "I know it wasn't quite the fun day you had planned."

"You're welcome. I just hope I wasn't in the way."

"Hardly. I was more worried my brothers would pin you down and interrogate you. They didn't, did they?"

"No."

"Linus didn't say anything stupid when the two of you went to get coffee?"

"No."

The distance was driving her insane. Reaching across the seat, she brushed her fingers across the back of his hand. "What's wrong?"

"Nothing. Seriously," he added as though sensing she was about to press. "It... I'm not used to being included in family events is all."

And he felt out of place. The pieces suddenly came together. "I'm glad you were there," she told him.

"Were you?"

"Yes. Very much. I'm glad my brothers got to see firsthand how good a man you are."

"Now you're reaching." He gave a soft laugh.

"All right, maybe a little. But I think Linus will come around. Thomas…he might be a harder sell. He has a highly overdeveloped sense of responsibility. I used to tell him he had *monomania*, which is a fancy way of saying he's hyperfocused on the business. Comes from listening to our grandfather drone on about the family legacy during his formative years."

"You're playing armchair psychologist again."

"Force of habit." Understanding what made people tick made dealing with them easier. If she could link a reason to an action, then it took away some of the sting. Sometimes, anyway. "Plus, I've spent a lot of time observing my brothers."

"Are you sure you studied the whole picture?" he asked.

"After more than two and a half decades, I'd better have. What makes you ask?"

He shrugged. "No reason. Just that I didn't get the impression either man was acting out of responsibility. Doesn't really matter, though, does it? What they think? After all…"

After all, it wasn't as though he would be a long-term part of her life.

"I'm curious," Lewis said suddenly. Turning sideways, he rested an elbow against the back of the seat. Grateful to have him in her orbit, Susan shifted as well so that they sat face-to-face, their knees touching. "What would your psychology books say about me?"

"You want me to psychoanalyze you?"

"Haven't you already?"

"Maybe." She looked at her lap. "I might have kicked around a few concepts." They only served to depress her.

"Like what?" he asked.

"Why do you care?"

"Color me curious. You sound so certain about your brothers. Makes me curious what you think of me."

Was it really curiosity or was he trying to send her a message? Reminding her not to get too attached.

"What if I don't want to share?"

"Then I'll presume the worst." Lewis's grin was overly wide. "And I'll pester you until you give up the info."

"Fine." He *would* pester her too. "Keep in mind this is completely nonscientific, but if I had to make a hypothesis, I would say children who grew up in foster homes are prone to anxiety, commitment issues, low self-esteem and often have a resulting fear of abandonment."

Lewis didn't answer and the shadows made it impossible to read his expression completely. Susan's stomach sank. "It's only a theory," she said, turning to face the front once more.

"Low self-esteem? Seriously?" she heard him say. "Do I seem like I have low self-esteem to you?"

"I wouldn't say low," Susan replied. Although, he *had* been worried about being accepted at the fundraiser.

"No offense, luv, but I think you might want to rethink your theory. Excepting for the other night—which was an extraordinary circumstance—my self-esteem and anxiety are just fine."

"And fear of commitment? Am I wrong about that one?" She probably shouldn't ask with the driver present, but she couldn't help herself.

"Depends. Is fear the same as disinterest?"

"No." Fear was better. Fear implied there might be a chance.

"Good to know," he said, nodding.

So much for an answer. On the other hand, did she really need one? The warning was clear. There was a warning hidden in his question—*don't get too attached or think long-term.*

Fine. Then she would take what she could for as long as she could get it.

They moved on to other topics. Thanks to Noel's arrival, they never finished their Christmas shopping and now Susan had to buy a baby gift in addition to the other items on her list.

"Why don't we go tomorrow?" Lewis said, for the driver's benefit, Susan suspected. "I know a great restaurant in Soho. We can grab brunch and then hit Regent Street again. What do you think?"

"Sure." She noticed he was pulling out his wallet to pay. Did that mean he intended to stay? Her heart skipped a beat.

"So, what's the plan?" she asked once they'd stepped outside. The car's taillights disappeared into the traffic.

"Tonight? We grab some takeout, watch a movie and I sleep on your sofa."

A right proper sleepover. All aboveboard and completely phony. But she was tired of phony. She was a woman, dammit. She wanted to be held and kissed like a woman.

The moonless night left his face bathed in shadows, making it impossible to read his expression. His eyes appeared dark and hooded. The warmth from his body floated around her, enveloping her with his scent. One she couldn't label and that was uniquely him.

Take what you can, a voice whispered in her ear.

"You…you don't have to sleep on the sofa."

Lewis stepped back. "I'm not sure that's a good idea."

"Oh." Rejection cut through her. Hugging her mid-section, she struggled to keep the disappointment from her voice.

"It's not that I wouldn't want to sleep with you," he said. "In fact…"

"Don't," Susan said. She so didn't want to have this conversation. "The last thing I need to hear is a lot of phony flattery and excuses. You made it very clear that you weren't interested in me in that way. It was stupid of me to think you might change your mind."

Beyond stupid. She wanted to go inside, pull the covers over her head and pretend the last five minutes had never happened.

"Susan…"

"It's been a really long day, Lewis," she said, cutting him off again. "Why don't we say good-night. We can wake up superearly and pretend we spent the night together, okay?"

"Susan…"

"Good night, Lewis. I'm sorry you have to…"

He kissed her.

He closed the distance between them and he kissed her. Like an animal springing on its prey, his mouth covered Susan's before she could make a sound. Her eyes fluttered shut as she melted into him. Wow, could this man kiss. This wasn't gentle or sweet like the other kisses though. This kiss was primal. The kind of kiss that claimed a person. Clutching his shoulders, Susan met him need for need until neither of them could breathe. They broke apart, their breaths loud and ragged in the night air.

"Still think I don't want to sleep with you?" Lewis asked between gasps.

If he didn't, he was a damn good liar. Her body, from head to toe, believed him. "Then why?" Why did she feel like he was still about to reject her?

Lewis's hands were tangled in her curls, combing them away from her face over and over. "A woman like you is made for serious relationships," he said. "The kind a man dates when he's thinking about things like homes and kids. If I…" He smiled. "If I were the kind of guy who thought of such things, I'd tether you to my side for eternity."

"But…?" Susan asked. There was definitely a but coming whether she wanted to hear it or not.

Lewis's hand slid from her hair to cup her cheek momentarily. "But I'm not that kind of guy."

"I know." He'd made his views on commitment quite clear in the taxi.

Take what you can, the voice reminded.

"What if I said I didn't care?" she asked. "What if I'm okay with here and now?"

She reached down and entwined her fingers with his. "Houses and kids are nice dreams, but sometimes a woman just wants to feel wanted."

Her heart was in her throat when she finished. Talk about laying it all on the table. It was up to Lewis now. If he rejected her, so be it. At least she'd know.

Lewis's hand was cupping her cheek again. The whites of his eyes were brilliant in the dark as he searched her face. "Are you sure?"

Could he not see the certainty on her face? Releasing his hand, Susan slid her palms upward along the padded front of his jacket until she reached the point where the zipper stopped. He was layers of darkness. Navy jacket, black sweater. With a deep breath to steel her nerves, she slipped her gloved hand under his jacket. "What do you think?" she asked.

What felt like the longest beat of her life passed. Susan kept her eyes locked with his; the knot of nerves in her chest twisted.

There was the rustle of nylon and suddenly, Lewis's hands were at the front of her wool coat. One by one, he undid the buttons, his eyes never leaving hers, until her coat hung open.

"I think," he said, playing with the hem of her sweater, "that we should go inside."

"This is new," Lewis said later, wrapped together with her in a cocoon of blankets, in Susan's king-size bed. Her cheek was resting over his heart and the taste of her kisses was still on his lips.

"What's new?"

"Staying awake." He buried his nose in her curls, inhaling the vanilla scent of her shampoo. "Usually I fall asleep." Or start planning his escape. Pulling a woman close to savor in the afterglow wasn't his style.

And yet, here he was, with Susan curled against his body, drawing lazy circles on his torso.

"You romantic devil."

"Never said I wasn't a player, luv."

For some reason he was determined to hammer that shameful point home tonight. He immediately regretted the statement when Susan's hand stilled. There was no reason to be harsh. She knew this was a temporary arrangement.

"Did you know that you're the first woman I've slept with stone-cold sober?"

"Seriously?" She lifted her head. Even in the dark, he could see her surprise. "You mean you haven't…?"

"Nope. Been too busy keeping my head down, proving I'm a good boy."

"Oh, you were good…"

"I know," he replied. Her laugh vibrated through him, and he pulled her close. Could you feel someone rolling their eyes? "You weren't so bad yourself, you know."

"Glad I didn't disappoint."

"Definitely not." Being with her was…well, it was amazing. He'd mapped every inch of her soft curves with his hands, and then went back and did the same with his mouth. Something else he'd never felt the need to do: savor the experience.

All this newness made him uneasy. Different was turning out to be unnerving.

"You didn't tell me your brother and his wife were renewing their wedding vows."

Her hand stilled again.

"Linus told me. He seemed surprised I wasn't attending."

"I didn't think you'd want to go," she replied. "You can, of course. If you want."

Gee, with that kind of enthusiasm… "Don't worry about it. I only mentioned it so you wouldn't be caught off guard if Linus mentions we talked about it."

Honestly, he didn't know why he'd brought it up.

Maybe he was looking for further affirmation that she wasn't looking for more.

Or was he hoping for the opposite?

Listen to him. One night with the woman and he was psychoanalyzing too. It was a short-term arrangement. No need to turn the affair into anything deeper. Once they holidays ended, he and Susan would go their separate ways.

And he was fine with that.

Really.

Truly.

Wasn't he?

CHAPTER EIGHT

"I WANT TO TELL you a story. Once upon a time there was a boy who really, really loved sports. Every chance he got, he practiced. Good weather. Bad weather. He worked at becoming the best he could be. And you know what? It paid off. He became a superstar.

"But then you know what happened? He stopped working so hard. He started taking his skills for granted. He developed bad habits. He told himself, 'I'm a superstar. I don't need to practice that much.' For a while, he got away with it. Eventually though, his athletic skill started to slip. Suddenly, he wasn't the superstar anymore. He was just a guy with a lot of bad habits who'd forgotten what was really important."

Susan sat in a far row of the indoor facility listening to Lewis tell the youth ambassadors his story. He'd told her last night that he wanted to use the opportunity to teach the kids what happened when they lost sight of what mattered. It was impressive, how honest Lewis was being about his own failings. Heartbreaking too, when you realized how much his partying had cost him. Thank goodness he'd seen the light before the lifestyle killed him.

Otherwise, the world would be a bleaker place. Not

to mention her bed. She smiled recalling the last few nights. Since the night Noel was born, the two of them had been engaged in a full-fledged affair, and it was better than she could have imagined. The way Lewis touched her when they made love made her feel like the most beautiful woman in the world. It was going to be awfully hard going back to life without him after their fake love affair was over.

Something inside her cracked a little at the thought. They'd attend a few more events, the company party and then say goodbye. Unless, that is, they needed to continue the arrangement a little while longer.

How sad was that? Hoping Lewis's image didn't improve enough so she could keep him in her life a few weeks longer.

"He's doing a marvelous job. Goes to show people love a good redemption story. Even kids."

A man she didn't recognize sat down in the seat next to her.

"Michael Ryder," he said.

So this was the infamous Michael, Lewis's agent. He looked like a talent agent. His pinstriped suit was very expensive and his hair very styled. He also obviously had a penchant for cigars. The scent clung to his clothes. Trying not to wrinkle her nose, Susan shifted herself a little farther away.

"I have to admit," he said after they'd shaken hands, "that when Lewis first came up with this crazy scheme, I had my doubts. But it looks like it might have some value after all. He never would have scored an event like this without you."

On the field, the kids broke out in laughter over something Lewis had said. "He doesn't need me to help him secure speaking engagements," Susan replied. "He's perfectly capable of charming people on his own."

Ryder smirked. "Spoken like a true loyal girlfriend."

"Don't have to be a girlfriend to recognize his abilities."

"Wow. You're good. I can see why Lewis was so keen on partnering up with you."

"Is there something I can do for you, Mr. Ryder?" Susan decided she didn't like the man. He was too keen on reminding her she wasn't Lewis's real girlfriend.

"I came by to tell you that *Personal Magazine* is interested in doing a story about the two of you. A reporter's going to sit down with you both next week."

"Great. Lewis will be thrilled."

"Yeah. They loved the whole love as the redeemer angle. They're bringing a photographer to get some shots of you both at Lewis's apartment. Readers love that homey behind-the-scenes stuff. You *have* been to his apartment, haven't you?" he asked in a low voice.

"Yes." Just the past night, as a matter of fact. Although his tone was so annoying she wouldn't have admitted if the answer was no.

"Good. Make sure you know where all the glassware and stuff is. We want to ensure you look at home. Know what I mean?"

"Why don't I leave some intimates on the bathroom floor to really hammer home the message?"

"Funny. Stick to leaving an extra toothbrush."

"Fine. I'll make sure to buy one tonight." She seriously did not like this man. "Unless there's something else you need to discuss, I'd like to continue watching Lewis."

Unfortunately though, it looked like she'd missed

the end of his talk. The kids were breaking into groups for some kind of skills training. While the volunteers played shepherd, Lewis walked to a nearby bench and stripped off his sweatshirt. Susan's eyes automatically sought out the strip of skin on his back that came exposed when his shirt pulled up. He had the most beautiful back. She loved watching the muscles play across his shoulders when he moved his arms. She loved running her hands over those shoulders too.

"Oh, man, you've got it bad."

Hadn't the agent moved on? Susan slid her gaze sideways. "I beg your pardon?" she asked.

"The look on your face. You look like you're worshipping the guy." Susan rolled her eyes. "Don't get me wrong," Ryder said. "If you look at him like that during the interview, there won't be a person alive who won't believe you're not madly in love. Problem will be getting him to look at you the same way. The Lewis I know has trouble remembering girls' names."

So did the Lewis she knew. "That was when he was drinking," Susan said. "He's not the same person now."

"Only, I'm not sure sobriety translates into acting skills. If he were really a one-woman man we wouldn't be doing this crap."

The man made a very good, albeit harsh, point. One that settled hard in the pit of her stomach.

"You needn't worry. Lewis knows how to put on a show when he has to."

"Good." The agent started to stand, only to sit back down. "Hey, do yourself a favor, will you? Don't get too sucked in by our boy."

"Don't worry," Susan replied. "I'm not stupid. I know exactly where I stand with Lewis."

Besides, his warning was too little, too late. She was already irreparably sucked in.

When Lewis was a kid and played his first game in net, he had been on top of the world. Sure, it was only a street game, but he remembered how it had felt like he'd won the World Cup. He'd succeeded and the neighborhood kids liked him. Over the years, he'd had many moments of victory, but as amazing as they were, none had the pureness of that first game.

Until today.

He lay prone on the turf, the smell of rubber backing tickling his nose. "That's it," he said. "I'm done."

Thirty-six kids faced off with him. Thirty-six kids beat him and scored. Lewis had to work harder than he'd ever worked to make sure each ball just missed his outstretched hands. By the tenth or eleventh goal, the kids knew he was letting them win, but they didn't care. If the laughter was any indication, they were having too much fun. So was Lewis.

Pushing himself to his knees, he blew the whistle around his neck. "All right. Fun as it's been, we've got to pack it up." A loud moan filled the facility, pumping him even higher. "What's with the booing? You're going to a Christmas party! With cake."

That got them moving to the sidelines quickly.

A girl, who looked to be around nine years old, approached him. "Mr. Matolo? Can I take a selfie with you?"

"Sure. Give it over and we'll take a proper one," he said. How much things had changed. When he was nine, he barely knew what a cell phone was let alone had one stashed in his equipment bag. And when he was playing, he'd been too arrogant to give fans the proper time.

He stayed on his knees so the two of them would be the same height. Of course, as soon as the others saw what was happening, more came running over with their phones to do the same. Not all though. Several of the kids looked over and went back to their bags. Lewis noticed a couple pulling out scraps of paper including one who tore off part of his lunch bag. Some things hadn't changed after all. There were still kids going without.

An idea came to him. Cupping his hands into a megaphone, he called into the stands. "Hey, Susie! Come here for a moment, and bring your phone." He smiled as she got up and started toward the stairs. Susan didn't know it, but she'd been his good luck charm. Knowing she was in the stands, believing in him, gave him the courage to tell his story. He loved the way she believed in him. Every time he looked in her direction, an empowering warmth spread through his insides. Different from the heat of attraction, it made him want to prove her trust wasn't misplaced.

"Mr. Matolo? Can I have your autograph?" It was the kid with the torn lunch bag bringing him back to the moment at hand.

"Hold on for one minute," Lewis told him. "I need to make a quick announcement."

He cupped his hands once again. "If anyone wants to take a picture, but doesn't have a camera, come get in line. My friend will take the pictures and have Mr. Redmayne send you a copy." Surely the director wouldn't mind doing a little extra to make sure the kids were happy.

While waiting for Susan, he signed paper scraps and

several of the kids' T-shirts. He was in the middle of writing on one kid's shoulder when he noticed a shadow fall across the crowd.

"I owe you an apology," Graham Montclark said. "I came by because Chris was a nervous wreck over hiring you. You never mentioned you were a motivational speaker when you made your offer the other night."

"I'm not," Lewis replied. "I simply told these kids the truth. If it stops one of them from making the same mistakes I made, all the better."

The other man digested his words. Lewis hoped they'd come out as sincerely as intended. A word from Graham Montclark would be the in he needed.

"Do you have any idea how many stairs there are between the stands and this playing field?" A slightly out-of-breath Susan came walking toward them. From her adorably flushed cheeks, he guessed she'd run the entire way. "Not to mention security guards. I almost had to cheat on you in order to gain access. Hello, Mr. Montclark. Nice to see you again."

"It's good to see you as well, Ms. Collier. I was just telling Lewis here that he should consider a career as a motivational speaker."

"He was inspiring, wasn't he?" The way she beamed in his direction made Lewis's insides turn end over end.

"While I appreciate the compliments, all I did was give the kids some straight talk and attention. Nothing special about that."

"Don't sell yourself short," Susan replied. "Perhaps you should consider doing events on the side."

"On the side of what?" Montclark asked. "You're retired aren't you?"

Bless her. Once again, she'd opened the door for him.

When they got home, he was going to kiss every ivory inch of her. "My agent has been talking with a few outlets about my being involved with the media side of the sport. In fact, I think one of the stations might be yours."

"Is that so?" Montclark replied. "I hope they're treating you right."

They weren't treating him at all. "They're being fair." To his surprise, he found he meant it. "After all, as you know, I come with some past baggage."

"I don't usually get involved in day-to-day operations myself, but if anyone gives you trouble, let me know. You've more than impressed me today."

"Thank you. I appreciate the vote of confidence." His eyes caught Susan's. Unbelievable. Was it possible this whole crazy plan was actually going to work? Was he actually going to rebuild his reputation and return to the spotlight? If so, it was all because of the woman he'd picked for a partner. She really was his good luck charm.

His stomach immediately sank. What was he going to do when their arrangement ended?

Nothing. He didn't know why he kept asking himself the question.

"Mr. Matolo, will you take our pictures now?" one of the children asked.

"Absolutely! We've wasted enough time." He turned his attention back to the task at hand. "Miss Susan, snap away. We've got a Christmas party to attend."

He could dwell on end dates another time.

Susan had to hand it to her brother. He didn't do things halfway. Thus it was no surprise when she walked into the annual Collier's holiday party to discover Christmas had arrived early. The ballroom was a winter wonderland of crystal and white like the ice castle in Maddie's favorite animated film. In fact, there was an ice castle. A giant sculpture in the middle of the room, around which were tables laden with hors d'oeuvres. Behind her, outside the ballroom, there was a staircase decked with white poinsettias. She hadn't gone upstairs yet, but she'd been told it led to a rooftop bar where people could sit around a fire pit and sip hot chocolate.

It was magnificent, and she was standing in the doorway alone.

Only for a moment. "Who takes home the castle?" Linus asked, joining her. Susan breathed a sigh of relief. As substitute host and hostess, she and Linus were expected to arrive early in order to greet all the guests. After his flakeout over Maria's wedding, she'd been worried he'd leave her to the wolves again. She looked him up and down. "You made it," she said.

"Thomas would have killed me if I hadn't, same as you," he replied. "I wasn't in the mood to court death this holiday."

"Good call." If Thomas hadn't killed him, she would have. "Let's hope next year he doesn't decide to have another baby so we can hand the job back to him."

"Sounds good to me." He looked around the room, then back to her. "Where's your boyfriend?"

"He had some business to take care of." That was exactly how Lewis put it too. Business to take care of. "He'll be here soon," she replied.

Her answer came out more defensively than she meant. Of course he would be there. He'd promised.

She adjusted the neckline of her dress again. The red-and-silver brocade was flashier than her usual style. Knee-length and classically draped in the front, it had a plunging back. The minute she saw it, visions of Lewis kissing her exposed back danced in her head. She couldn't wait for him to see her in it.

At the current moment, she'd settle for just seeing him come through the door. "Where's your date?" she asked Linus. "Or are you going solo again this year?"

Her brother shoved his hands in his pockets. "What do you think?" he asked.

Single then. If Lewis didn't show, then she'd at least have a dance partner.

Honestly, why was she worrying about Lewis? He'd promised. Maybe it was because the holidays were drawing closer. After this, Lewis had no obligations to her. She thought after Graham Montclark's comment the other day that he might discuss their future, and whether he thought they should continue their faux romance past New Year's. Instead, he'd said nothing. When they were together, it was easy to pretend they didn't have an arrangement; other times Susan felt like she was in a holding pattern. One ruled by nights of incredible wonder.

"You're making that face again," Linus said.

Susan frowned. "What face?"

"The one you've been making all week. Where your eyes glaze over and you get this dreamy smile. Somebody's in love." He nudged her with his shoulder.

"Stop being an ass," Susan replied as her cheeks warmed. "I'm not in love."

"Could have fooled me. Little Miss Dreamy Eyes."

Oh, brother. Please don't tell her she was going to be stuck listening to his stupid nicknames. Linus loved his stupid nicknames. "Lewis and I are enjoying each other's company, that is all," she told him.

"Uh-huh."

"We are. I'm not in love with Lewis Matolo."

Aren't you? After days of being ignored, the question slammed into her brain. How long was she going to pretend the man hadn't gotten under skin?

Easy, she answered back. For as long as it took. Fake it till you make it, as the saying went.

Since she was having the conversation in her head, however, Linus felt comfortable continuing. "He certainly seems to care about you. Nearly took my head off in the hospital elevator the day Noel was born."

"What? What did you do?" Besides mentioning the wedding. She *knew* something had happened that afternoon.

"Why are you assuming I did anything?"

"Because I've known you since birth," Susan told him. "You always do something."

Linus was insistent. "I swear I did nothing. At least not on purpose. All I said was that we needed to buy extra cookies because you love them so much. He suggested I stop picking on you."

Warmth seeped through her veins. She couldn't remember the last time someone had defended her honor.

"I'm not surprised. Lewis likes to look out for the underdog," she told her brother.

Linus gave her a look. "You're an underdog?"

"He was defending me against a comment you made. What do you think?"

"Either way, he's not what I expected," Linus said.

"I told you but you and Thomas refused to believe me. Thomas still doesn't believe me."

"Meh." Linus waved off her complaint. "You know

Thomas. Anything that could remotely impact the company gets him uptight."

Susan looked away. He would really hate if he knew the truth then.

"If it will make you feel better, I'll talk to him," Linus said. "Let him know Lewis passes my sniff test."

"Thank you. I'd appreciate that. And for the record... I hate when you make jokes about my sweet tooth."

Linus leaned back in surprise. "We've been making those jokes since we were kids."

"I know. Thanks to my mother." Belinda used to love to point out how calories weren't Susan's friend and never missed an opportunity to remind her with a subtle jab. "Might as well just say you think I'm fat."

"We don't think that." Linus continued to look shocked. "We just know you like cookies."

"Well, it feels like you think so. Especially since that's how Belinda meant it."

"Belinda was a piece of work. None of us should take anything she said seriously."

Easy for him to say; Linus and Thomas weren't her children. "Still, I would appreciate if you stopped making the joke. Especially around my... Lewis."

"No need to worry there," Linus said. "He didn't find the comment funny either. In fact, he pretty much said the same thing as you did. About you feeling like we were calling you fat."

Because Lewis understood her. Susan couldn't help her smile or the fullness in her heart. She'd always wondered what it would be like, having someone in her life who knew what she was thinking or feeling without her having to say a word. To be able to look across a crowd and know she wasn't alone.

"You're getting that dreamy look again," Linus said. "You really like this guy, don't you?"

"Yeah, I do." More than liked, to be honest.

"I can tell. How come you didn't invite him to Thomas's vow renewal then?"

The question caught her by surprise. "Because it's a family thing."

"Doesn't mean you can't include your boyfriend. You brought him to the hospital."

"That was different. He was with me when you called. The ceremony on Christmas Eve is going to be intimate."

"And gathered 'round Rosalind's hospital bed eating cookies and letting Maddie climb on him wasn't?" He frowned. "You're afraid we're going to give him a hard time, aren't you?"

"Wouldn't you?"

"Absolutely, but in the best-natured way possible. That's what big brothers do. Tell you what," he said. "If you're worried, the five of us can go out beforehand and bond with him properly."

Oh, yeah, she could see Lewis jumping at the opportunity to have a "bonding" dinner with the Collier clan. She could picture the scene now. The three of them eating curry and peppering Lewis with questions. Her temporary relationship was going to be short enough; she didn't need their curiosity ending the arrangement prematurely.

"That isn't necessary," she told him.

"Sure it is. You said yourself, we weren't being fair to him. This will be our way of letting him know we approve of his dating our sister and we welcome him to the family."

"Really, you don't have to," Susan said.

"Why are you fighting the idea. You just asked me to be nice. If the guy's going to be around for a while…"

"He's not."

Her brother's eyes narrowed. "What are you talking about? Don't tell me you two are on the outs already? Is that why he's not here tonight?"

"No, no. I told you, Lewis will be here."

"Then what gives? Why so certain you two will be done? You've got to have a little more faith than that, Susie."

"Maybe I would if I didn't have an exit date."

"I beg your pardon."

Susan sighed. If she'd known they were going to start suggesting family get-togethers, she would have told them the truth from the start. But since when did her brothers bond with anyone? Let alone someone connected with her? "We aren't really dating." Briefly she explained their arrangement.

"You're kidding," Linus said when she was finished. Susan was stunned by his stunned expression. Maybe she and Lewis had done a better job pretending than she thought. "Why would you do something like that?"

"I told you, Lewis needs…"

"I mean you. Champagne Lewis I get, but why would you get involved in something like this?"

She shrugged. "Maybe I wanted an image make-over too."

"Unbelievable. Thomas is going to have a cow, you know."

A big mad cow too, which was why she kept silent in the first place. But only if Thomas found out. Which didn't have to happen. "Then don't tell him," she said.

"The whole affair will be over before Thomas gets back from paternity leave. There's no reason for him to get involved."

"Except for the whole Collier's thing. You know how he is about the company reputation."

"All the more reason to not spoil his time with the new baby. There's no need to trigger him unnecessarily."

"True." Her brother let out a long, frustrated breath, a sign he was seriously considering the suggestion. "We'll have to talk about this later," he said. "People are starting to arrive."

And the last thing they needed was someone to overhear. "I'm going to go check my hair," she said. "The bun feels loose."

"I'm going to go make sure everything is in order, or whatever it is Thomas expects us to do." He headed toward the back of the room where the event coordinators were congregated.

"Oh, hey," he said, stopping and speaking over his shoulder. "About that other thing we were talking about. You know, the cookies?"

"Yeah?" The abrupt change of topic would throw her except it was Linus, and Linus was known for it.

"You're nowhere near being fat."

"I know," Susan replied. She was normal. And even if she wasn't, Lewis loved her body. Every porcelain inch, he said. That was all that mattered.

Smiling to herself, she turned and headed to the powder room. On the way, a flash of black caught her eye. It was Courtney minus her partner in crime. Ever since Susan had told them off at work, she and Ginger had limited their interaction to only the most necessary business. Tonight, the woman smirked like a cat as Susan passed her.

Susan was surprised to discover she didn't care.

Imagine that. All this fuss about paying them back tonight, and it no longer seemed to matter.

CHAPTER NINE

FOR THE NEXT forty-five minutes, Susan smiled and said hello to every person who stepped off the elevator. Most responded politely and kept going, way more interested in the free drinks and food than in talking with her. Thankfully. It wasn't until Maria and Hank arrived that she had to make any kind of real conversation.

"Welcome home," she greeted the newlyweds with a smile. "How was America?"

"Big. We had a marvelous time. Especially in Hawaii," Maria answered. "I hated to come back. Don't worry, though, I'll be in the office on Monday. I know you're eager to discuss a few things."

"Maria, honey, it's a Christmas party," Hank said, his voice gently admonishing. "There'll be plenty of time to talk work next week."

His bride blushed. They were still in the phase where bickering in public required restraint. "I know, but this is Susan. I'm sure she wants to bring me up to speed."

Did she do that? Did she spend time at parties working? Susan thought back to different functions. Damn. "Not tonight," she quickly replied. "It's Christmas. I don't know about you, but I have more important things to talk about."

"So we read." Maria's remark had all three of them turning a subtle pink.

"Where is Lewis?" Hank asked. "I was hoping to catch up with him. We didn't get to talk very long at the wedding."

Indeed, where was Lewis? Nearly an hour into the party and he still hadn't arrived.

"He…um…got tied up with business and is running late," she repeated for the umpteenth time. "I'm sure he'll be here any minute."

"See? I'm not the only one distracted by business," Maria said.

"Apparently not." But as Hank answered, he flashed a sympathetic look in Susan's direction. It was the look of someone who knew Lewis's past habits. He's not the same man, Susan wanted to holler. A hard sell seeing how it was at their wedding that Lewis had a pair of drinks tossed in his face.

Just then the elevator dinged. The doors slid open and there was Lewis looking like he'd stepped off a runway in a black velvet blazer. Susan's heart leaped to her throat at the sight of him.

So much for faking not being in love. It'd be easier pretending Lewis wasn't gorgeous or Collier's sold auto parts.

She broadened her smile. Her feelings—or rather, their repercussions—were an issue for another time.

"I am so sorry I'm late, luv. My meeting went far longer than I thought." The apology tumbled from Lewis's mouth as he slipped an arm around her waist. "You look delicious," he added, kissing her cheek. "Maybe it was a good thing I wasn't there when you were getting ready or we'd both be late."

"If you're trying to flatter me into forgiving your lateness, it's working," Susan told him.

"Good. I'll flatter you some more later. Welcome back from the honeymoon, you two," he said, turning to Hank and Maria with a smile.

This was one of those times when the relationship felt real. Although they were sleeping together so it was also real in that sense. Deeper was the better word. This was one of those times when the relationship felt deeper. There was a sparkle in his eyes that was easy to mistake as adoration. She needed to remember though, he was just playing a part. Tonight he was honoring his half of the agreement by playing the doting boyfriend.

"I can't believe you two met at our wedding," Maria was saying.

"I told her when you RSVP'd as single, that you wouldn't be going home that way," Hank remarked.

"Which I admit, had me worried. Especially after that thing with Diane and Trish."

Lewis looked up at the ceiling lights. "Diane and Trish! Those were their names! I am really sorry about that little scene. I met those girls during a dark time in my life."

"Well, I'd be more annoyed if I didn't know they're total gold diggers. Hey, I love them," she said to Susan's stunned expression, "but that doesn't mean I don't know what they're like. It's why I agreed to give Lewis your phone number. I figured if he was chasing after you, he wasn't the promiscuous man Hank had made him out to be. Although you should apologize to them," she added, turning to Lewis with a reproachful look.

"I agree," Susan said.

"So do I," Lewis replied. "Which is why I sent them

both apology letters explaining everything after the wedding."

"You did?" She smiled at him with pride. "Wait a second," she said. "I thought you just remembered their... You jerk."

Laughing, Lewis pretended to rub the shoulder she'd playfully slapped. "Hey, can't a guy joke around about his bad-boy past? I can't believe you didn't think I would apologize."

"You're right." She was properly chastised. "I should have realized you're too good a man not to own your mistakes."

"Well, I did lead you on, so I can't be too annoyed, can I?" He leaned over and kissed her temple, causing Hank to offer a mock groan.

"Oh, man," his friend said. "You are smitten with a capital *S*. Never thought I'd see the day. Must be a Christmas miracle. Say, the four of us need to go out after the holidays."

Susan tensed. "You mean, in January?" What was it with people suddenly inviting them places?

"Sure. Lewis can help me lie about my glory days before I left academy league."

"Left?" Lewis said. "You were dismissed because your foot couldn't find the ball. You sure you want to ruin whatever lies you told your bride?"

While the three of them laughed, Susan drifted away into thought. January was only a few weeks away. She and Lewis would be done. This marvelous fun-filled night out they were planning would never happen.

"Tuesday?"

Giving a blink, she realized Maria was talking to her. "I know you usually choose to eat at your desk but the wedding proofs will be in so I thought maybe you'd like to join us for once." Maria and several other women went out for lunch every Tuesday.

"Um…maybe," Susan replied.

Maria looked pleased. "Great."

"Hey, babe, I want to grab a drink before the lines at the bar are too long," Hank said. "We'll catch up with the two of you later."

She waited until the couple disappeared into the ballroom before turning to Lewis. "Did I agree to go to lunch and look at wedding photos?"

"Yes, why?"

"No reason. Other than I'm surprised she asked." In the past, when Maria made the offer to join the group for lunch, Susan assumed it was because she'd happened across them as they were headed out.

"Perhaps she's seeing you in a new light," Lewis replied. "Congratulations. Means both of us are getting the makeover we wanted."

"Maybe." Changing the subject, she asked, "How did your business meeting go?"

"I'll tell you all about it later. When we have a chance to talk," he replied.

"We can't talk here?"

"Nah," he said, shaking his head. "This is your night. I'm going to help you make the entire company jealous."

"That was never my goal," Susan said. "Not all of it anyway."

"What was your goal then? Because I seem to remember a woman telling me she wanted to show the whole lot of them."

"I did. I…do. At least that's part of it."

"What do you mean?" The way he looked at her, his

expression direct and focused, it felt like he was trying to read her mind. He played with a tendril of hair by her ear. "Is there another reason?"

How did she explain? "I'm not sure I can put it into words," she told him.

"Try."

"All right, but not here." Looking around for a quiet area, she saw that the staircase was empty. It was too early for anyone to venture to the roof. Most of the partygoers were still busy milling about near the bar. "Come with me."

"This is cozy," he said when they stepped outside. "I like the way you think."

"I didn't want anyone listening," she told him. She'd been right about the crowd. The rooftop was empty except for the bartender who was tucked away behind the Plexiglas wall of the bar, out of the cold.

The flames in the gas firepit flickered brightly. Susan led Lewis to one of the sofas making up the surrounding circle.

No sooner had they sat down than the bartender emerged from his shelter, carrying a plaid blanket.

"Welcome to the rooftop," he greeted as he handed the blanket over to Lewis who promptly draped the material around them.

"Wouldn't want you to get cold," he murmured, his breath warm against her temple.

The shiver that followed was anything but cold.

"Can I get you something to drink?" the bartender asked. "The special tonight is peppermint hot chocolate. Guaranteed to warm you from the inside out."

"Depends," Susan mused. "Does it have a holiday name?"

The man looked confused. "Peppermint hot chocolate," he said.

"Then I think we're good," Lewis replied. "We'll create our own warmth." He scooped Susan's legs up over his lap. She gasped as the cold from his hand touched her leg, but then snuggled against his chest. Being in his arms was like being nestled in a wonderfully safe cocoon.

"Now," he said. "Tell me this reason you can't put into words."

For a second, Susan had forgotten what they'd been talking about. "I hate this party," she said, laying her head on his shoulder. "All parties really, but this one most of all. Usually I make up an excuse and stay home, but this year Thomas didn't give me a choice."

"Why do you avoid it?"

"Isn't it obvious?" She was always alone, in a room where she felt like everyone was dreading having to talk with her. "Think of the wedding times ten."

A frown formed on Lewis's face. "It makes you feel like a pathetic loser?"

"Bingo. All these groups of people who know each other chatting away and there I am, with a stupid smile on my face, wondering if any of them will invite me to join them."

"And you were too afraid to join them yourself."

"Not scared." Scared was the wrong word. "More like I could feel the barrier between me and them, if that makes sense. Like I could go over to them, but I would still be the outsider without anything to say. You saw Maria. The only thing she could talk to me about was work." At least it was, before they had Lewis to talk about. "And she's one of the friendliest."

It was embarrassing, listening to herself complain like this. She didn't like revealing this side of herself. For some reason, however, it seemed to happen around Lewis. Whether because the way he looked at her when she spoke loosened her tongue or because she felt he understood, she didn't know.

Losing herself in the blue of the fire, she continued. "Normally, I don't care what they think. We're talking about coworkers and employees. I don't need to be their friend. Every once in a while though…well, that's why I stay home. Being in my apartment is a lot more comfortable than being a wallflower."

"You could simply hang with your family," he said.

"I try, but Thomas believes in mingling and Linus is friends with the entire company. I look like the sad baby sister tagging along." Just like when they were kids.

"So along with getting a little revenge on those bathroom chicks, you wanted me to be here to keep you from feeling alone. Is that what you're telling me?"

"Sort of." The words still weren't completely right. "Have you ever wanted to be that person who everyone noticed? I mean, noticed in a good way? The person the whole room wants to be? Never mind. Forget I asked that." Of course he knew.

"You want to be one of the cool kids," Lewis replied.

"When you put it like that, it sounds so childish." Maybe it was. High school was a long time ago.

She felt Lewis's thumb stroking her dress, right above her hip bone. A slow, steady massage. She focused on the tempo, back and forth, back and forth until the feelings jumbled inside her formed a coherent sentence. "Not cool. Special," she said finally. Lewis went to speak, but she stopped him with a shake of her head.

"My brothers, my mother, even my father when he was alive. People pay attention to them. Notice them. People care about what they think because their opinions matter. *They* matter. I want to matter too," she said in a soft voice.

Lewis stared at the woman curled into his side. How could she think she wasn't special? "Oh, luv," he whispered, brushing a wispy tendril from her face.

He knew what she meant. That feeling of being less than the rest of the room. Of waiting to be called out as a fraud and asked to leave. And while Susan was the last person who should feel that way, he knew all the reminding her in the world wouldn't make her believe him. The feeling came from deep inside where words couldn't reach. Only thoughts.

Still, it didn't hurt to tell her. "You don't need me on your arm to matter."

"Don't I though?" She shifted her position, her legs leaving his lap. It added space between them, and he didn't like it. "Do you know how many people have wanted to talk with me at work since we started dating? They look at me differently now. And Courtney and Ginger? They've practically twisted themselves into knots trying to get on my good side. Call me immature," she said, "but I like the attention. That's the reason I wanted you as my date for the party. This might be the one time I get to be the popular girl."

"I'd never call you immature," he told her. She began to pick at the plaid material of the blanket. "If wanting to be popular is a crime, then half the world would be guilty." Including him. Heck, his glass house was probably ten times the size of hers.

"You're wrong though," he told her. "You don't need the spotlight to matter."

Like he expected she would, she scoffed softly. "You can have all the adulation and popularity you want, but all you really need are a few people who care. One person even."

"Easy for you to say."

Was it? There was a lesson for him in those words, but now wasn't the time to pick them apart.

"You sell yourself too short. You matter to your family. I know you don't believe it, but you matter to your brothers. And Maddie…"

She smiled at the mention of her niece. "Maddie's my little angel."

Noel would be one soon enough as well, he suspected. She wasn't the horrible, unlikable shrew she painted herself out to be.

She was amazing really.

If someone had told him a few weeks ago, when they hashed out this arrangement, how much he would enjoy their time together, he wouldn't have believed them. Today wouldn't have happened. He wouldn't have achieved half the success if she hadn't been by his side.

An inexplicable fullness gripped him. Looking at her now, white lights twinkling about her, he'd never seen anything as lovely.

"You matter to me too," he said. The reverence in his voice didn't come close to capturing how he felt. "A lot. You matter to me a lot."

The look in her eye said she didn't believe him.

Very well. He would just have to show her the best way he knew possible. Pulling her close, he kissed her.

And kissed her again.

"Let's get out of here," he murmured against her mouth. There was more he wanted to tell her. Plus he hadn't been kidding about how delicious she looked. Between her chocolate-tinged kisses and her creamy bare back, she had him starving.

"I can't. I promised Thomas." Her argument would have been more persuasive if she weren't kissing him back in between sentences. Eventually, she pulled away, out of his mouth's reach. "Besides, at the very least I deserve a dance downstairs."

Lewis took a good look at her mussed hair and swollen lips. There was no hiding what they'd been up to, that was for sure.

Well, she'd wanted people to notice.

Linus was stepping onto the dais to speak when they entered the ballroom. As soon as he saw them, he motioned impatiently for Susan to join him. Lewis stepped back into the shadows and watched as she hurried to the front of the ballroom. At least a half-dozen heads turned in her direction.

And she thought no one noticed her.

When she reached the stage area, Linus whispered something in her ear. Judging from the way she turned crimson, he could guess the commentary.

"I promise I won't stand up here long," Linus said, "because I know you'd much rather eat and drink free food than listen to anyone named Collier drone on. But my sister Susan and I wanted to take a few minutes and say thank you. This has been a true comeback year for Collier's. Thanks to your efforts, the Collier name is poised to continue succeeding, not only for the upcoming year, but with luck, for another four hundred!"

When the polite laughter subsided, he raised his

glass. "Seriously, Collier's would be nothing without our employees. So on behalf of Thomas, Susan and myself—along with all our executive staff—thank you, happy holidays and a very happy New Year. Now get out there on the dance floor and have a good time!"

The crowd applauded, and the deejay struck up a party song. Lewis waited until Susan stepped off the stage before sauntering toward her.

"Now can we go home?" He already knew the answer, but he wanted to see her skin blush again when he made the suggestion.

At the same time, Linus walked by. "Nice of you to join us," he said, giving them both a look. "We'll talk later, Susan."

Lewis looked back at her with a frown. "Are you in trouble?"

"Nothing dire. Although you could have told me my bun was falling."

"Is it? I hadn't noticed." His hands settled on her hips, fingers splaying outward. "Everything seems in place to me." He paused. "Oh. Now that you say something, it does look a little disheveled." Dipping his head, he whispered. "As if you were snogging on the rooftop."

Score another blush. If he thought she'd agree, he'd drag her back to the rooftop for a repeat performance. Seeing as how they couldn't, they'd have to find another way to fill the time. "Since we're going to stay," he said, "would you rather eat or dance?"

As if to help his argument along, the deejay began to play a Christmas love song. Susan's arms looped around his neck. "Dance," she said.

Good. Food was overrated.

They did eat eventually and mingle, as well. He

wished Susan could have seen herself from his vantage point. She was charming and funny as she moved from group to group. Not a shred of shrewishness or unlikability in sight. "For a wallflower, you are amazingly charismatic," he told her later, while they were dancing. It was the end of the night, and the deejay was playing the last slow dance of the evening, or rather the fifth last slow dance as Lewis had slipped him a few bills to keep the songs coming.

"If I was, it's because I had a star on my shoulder," Susan replied. She had her cheek against his lapel and her arms wrapped around his waist. They probably looked more like they were hugging than dancing. "You make me feel charismatic."

Nonsense. She was her own star. She didn't need him to be anything. Someday she'd realize that.

"People are leaving. I don't suppose Linus will release you from duty."

"Afraid not," she replied. "Even if I weren't in the doghouse, I'm stuck here until the last employee leaves. Turns out that's the tradition. Something Linus said I'd know if I hadn't skipped out all the time."

"Any way we can convince all the employees to leave now? Pull a fire alarm or something?" He was dying to get her home so he could peel off that dress and share his good news. In that order.

"I wish." Letting out a long sigh, Susan burrowed closer. "Why don't you just tell me your news now? You know you're dying to, and I'm dying to hear it."

"Won't be as fun though." Still, she was right about him being eager to tell her. "Let's sit down though." It was the kind of news best told face-to-face.

"Do you remember when Graham Montclark said he

would vouch for my character if necessary?" he asked once they'd settled in at a nearby cocktail table. Susan nodded. "Turns out, he went ahead and vouched anyway."

"I don't understand."

"I got a call this morning from his network asking me to come in for a meeting. They've decided to add a new face to their game-coverage team and they think I'm the right face."

Slowly, Susan's eyes widened as the meaning of his news settled over her. "Are you saying…?"

"It worked." Man, but it felt amazing to finally say the words out loud. "Our crazy plan worked!"

CHAPTER TEN

Susan let his news sink in. Lewis was going back to football. He would feel like he had a home again. "That's…" It was a good thing. It was what he wanted. Rising from her chair, she threw her arms around his neck. "I'm so happy for you," she whispered. Lewis was getting his dream.

Meaning hers was over. With his mission accomplished, there was no more reason for their arrangement. Stupid her, telling him the affair could end with their agreement. Had she really thought she could sleep with Lewis and escape unscathed?

"I couldn't have done it without you," he said. "You believed in me."

"No, it was all you. You're the one who did the work and actually changed. All I did was help get the word out."

And now he didn't need her. She blinked away the lump in her throat.

"Look at me. I'm so happy, I'm getting teary," she said wiping her eye. "We need to celebrate."

"That's kind of the reason I wanted to go home."

Her heart twisted at the words. Wouldn't be too many more times she'd hear him say them. Not now that he no longer needed her. "How about we settle for a toast in the meantime? Champagne for me, water for you. I'll go get it."

Immediately he reached for her arm. "You don't have to do that."

"I want to." She needed the moment to shake the thoughts from her head. "This is your celebration. You sit and let me wait on you."

Pushing her lips into a smile, she scurried to the bar, choosing the one outside the ballroom so she could duck into the powder room and wipe her nose. Someday she'd get through an event without having to hide in the bathroom at some point, but not tonight.

And, because the world really wanted to mock her, Ginger and Courtney were seated along with a few of the PAs at the table nearest the door to the restroom. Both of them shot a trademark smirk in her direction as she approached.

Whatever. She didn't have time for them.

That is, until she was almost through the door. That's when she heard Courtney.

"Fake," she said.

Susan stopped in her tracks. Stepping behind the door, she leaned her ear close to the crack to listen, the nerves in her stomach doing a tap dance.

It was probably nothing.

"…heard her clear as day," Courtney said. "She told Linus that the whole romance was a scam to get him some publicity."

"You mean they aren't an item?" someone asked. "What about those pictures of them kissing?"

"Totally for the camera," Courtney said.

Susan's stomach felt like it had been punched. No

wonder Courtney had smirked at her. She'd overheard everything. The witch had probably spent the whole party spreading the story to anyone who would listen.

What was she going to do? Lewis was going to kill her.

She found a different entrance and rushed back to the table. Lewis frowned upon seeing her. "Where's your champagne? Did they cut you off?"

The ballroom wasn't the proper place for this discussion. There were too many people still gathered at the tables nearby. If they hadn't heard the story, she didn't want them to overhear anything now.

"You know what?" she said. "Screw Linus. Let's go home and celebrate properly."

Under any other circumstance, the way Lewis's brown eyes lit up would have made her knees weak. "Are you sure?" he asked.

"Definitely." They'd talk when they got to her place.

As it turned out, Lewis gave the driver directions for his place. That was fine. They could talk there, as well. She chewed the inside of her mouth while he pressed the combination on his apartment lock. It would be fine, she realized. Courtney could spread the rumor all over the company if she wanted. She and Lewis could always debunk it. Who would they believe—a known company gossip or the two of them? And even if they didn't believe her and Lewis, it was only Collier's. Wasn't like anybody who worked there was going to alert the press.

Yeah, she would tell Lewis and it would be fine.

The first time she saw Lewis's apartment, she'd joked that it looked like a set for a bachelor-life reality show. Lots of chrome and retro-style furniture and a hot tub with a view to rival the London Eye. She thought that again as she dropped her wrap on the glass dining room table.

Lewis stepped up behind her, his large hands curling around her shoulders. "Finally," he murmured. "I've been waiting all night to get you back here."

Preoccupied or not, Susan's eyes still rolled back at the growl in his throat. "Lewis, there's something I need to…"

His lips found the curve of her neck and those were the last words she said on the subject. It could wait until morning, she thought as her head fell back against his shoulder. There was still plenty of time to nip the gossip in the bud.

It was snowing when Lewis woke up. Big slow-falling flakes like the kind in TV movies. They blanketed the trees and parked cars with white. He pulled a nylon jacket over his running shirt and grabbed a knit cap. Running in the snow had always been a favorite pastime, even as a kid. While his teammates complained and moaned about working out in unseasonable weather, he embraced it. There was something strangely invigorating about cutting through the snowflakes. Besides, he could always count on the snow to clear his muddled head.

This morning, his head was clear as a bell, but he had too much energy to sit still. Susan was still asleep, wrapped up in the covers. He smiled and for a second he considered waking her up instead of running. But there would be plenty of time later. It was going to take a lot more than a run to burn off his high.

Other than the Youth Ambassador Event, Lewis couldn't remember the last time he'd felt this good about life. All the pieces of his goals were coming together. He was back in sports where he belonged, back on a team. And maybe now that he was back on top, he could convince Susan to continue their arrangement a little while longer.

Being with her was as close to belonging as a man could get.

After a few laps around the park, he made a quick stop for scones and a copy of the *Looking Glass*. The vendor sold *Personal Magazine* as well so he grabbed a copy of that too since Susan and he were scheduled to do that interview with the magazine later in the week. He was half tempted to cancel since the article wasn't needed. On the other hand, he liked the idea of Susan gracing the pages of a national magazine. Letting the whole country see more of her uniqueness.

That reminded him, he'd have to find a place for a Christmas tree. When he was done "waking up" Susan, he would ask her what she wanted to do for decorations.

The bed was empty when he unlocked the door. Susan was in the bathroom. It was that last loop. He knew he should have cut it short. Oh, well. He'd give her a few moments of privacy, and then join her. The shower wasn't built for two for nothing.

As he kicked off his running shoes, he idly flipped through the paper where he'd dropped it on the kitchen island. It was the usual headlines. The prime minister was fighting with Parliament. One of the royal duchesses had made an appearance in an expensive designer coat. He turned to page six and froze when he saw the headline.

Scam-pagne Lewis? Fans Duped by Publicity Stunt.

What the…? This was not good. Not good at all. This was…

He ran a hand over his mouth. This was a disaster.

Quickly, he scanned the article. It detailed how he and Susan had conspired to improve his image and get publicity for Collier's at the same time, even implying that he was paying Susan and that he was the same drunken playboy he'd always been. Half of it wasn't true at all, and that mattered. Once a narrative was cast, it was near impossible to sway public opinion.

This was going to ruin everything. Goodbye new career, new reputation. Men like Montclark would want nothing to do with him now.

Snatching the paper in his fist, he stormed into the bedroom and thrust open the bathroom door. Susan was just stepping out of the shower. Upon his bursting in, she grabbed a towel.

"What the heck, Lewis," she snapped.

"We've got a problem." He held up the paper so she could see the headline.

A curse escaped her lips. Taking the paper, she continued reading as she padded past him into the bedroom. Lewis followed, reaching the bed in time to hear her swear again.

She'd turned pale. "I didn't think it would make the papers," she said in a low voice.

"What are you talking about? Did you know something like this might happen?"

"Not this." She ran a hand through her curls, sending droplets of water across the comforter. "This is my fault," she said. "I told Linus last night and Courtney overheard. I didn't know she was there but at the end of the night I heard her and Ginger telling others. I'm not sure how it got in the paper though. One of the servers or bartenders must have heard her."

"Dammit. Didn't we agree that we couldn't tell *any-body* for this exact reason?"

"I'm sorry."

Sorry wasn't going to change the fact his reputation was ruined. Again. "Why would you tell Linus in the first place?"

"I didn't set out to," she replied. "He was going on about some family-bonding trip and it came out. I didn't know Courtney was there."

"Well, she was," he snapped. "And now all of London knows."

"I'm sorry." Her eyes were wet with tears.

Blowing out a breath, Lewis got up and retrieved a bathrobe from his closet. He couldn't have this conversation with her wrapped in a towel. She looked too vulnerable. The rational part of him knew it was an accident. That she hadn't intentionally set out to ruin their plan, but he wasn't ready to listen yet. Not when everything he wanted was tumbling out of reach. "I need to go for a run," he said.

"But you already went."

He looked down at his damp running clothes. "Another one. I need to clear my head."

"Don't." Her hand landed on his arm. Lewis turned around. His robe was oversize, the sleeves hanging several inches below her fingers. It was worse than seeing her in the towel.

"It's only one article," she said.

"Right now. You saw how the first one spread." By tomorrow they would be dissecting it on the morning talk shows.

The shrill sound of a phone ringing cut through the tension. "Yours," he said.

She rummaged through her bag. "It's Thomas."

He'd heard about the article, no doubt. "You better take it."

"He can wait until we're done talking."

"What more do we have to talk about? The damage is done."

"Not necessarily. We just need to get out ahead of things. We'll tell people it was a vindictive ex-girlfriend or someone with a grudge. If we do it right, we can spin this in our favor."

"How, when it's the truth? We aren't a real couple."

Her lower lip started to quiver. Lewis had to look away.

"We both said it that night in front of your apartment. A casual hookup that doesn't mean anything. We aren't some grand romance."

Why would she want to be with him now anyway? His chance at redemption was done. If he was untouchable before, because of his reputation, surely, he was doubly so now that the papers branded him a fraud.

He couldn't see bouncing back. Not this time. Might as well walk away from Susan too, and end everything in one cut.

"You should go talk to your brother," he said walking away. "Fix what you can."

"What were you thinking?" Thomas asked. With the baby sleeping in the bassinet a few feet away, he kept his voice a whisper. That didn't hide his frustration however. "A phony romance?"

He paced back and forth in front of the ornate giant tree the decorators had installed in his living room as Susan watched his progress from the couch. "I knew something was odd from the start, but Linus convinced me that you were the real thing. I couldn't believe when he told me last night. And now this?"

He pointed to the paper that lay on the cushion next to her.

"That," Susan replied, "is not my fault. Gossip columnists have spies everywhere. All it takes for things to spiral out of control is for someone to overhear a single conversation."

"If I find out one of my employees leaked the information, they're going to be out the door."

Susan kept quiet. As satisfying as it would be to toss Courtney and Ginger under the bus, she wouldn't. If they were guilty, Thomas would find out easily enough and deal with the problem. Susan didn't need to add fuel to the fire without proof.

"What did you and Lewis think you were going to gain by doing this?" The question came from Rosalind who, until she spoke, had been sitting quietly next to the bassinet watching.

"A new reputation," Susan replied. Still pacing, Thomas let out a loud scoff. "He really is a different person," she said. "About as far from Champagne Lewis as you can get. Only no one would believe him. Everyone was waiting for him to slip up."

"So to prove he was reliable, he decided to lie to the press. Fabulous." Her brother rolled his eyes.

"It's called a contractual relationship and it's done all the time by actors and athletes. Especially if they need a socially acceptable partner or have a project to promote. I wouldn't be surprised if my mother's had one."

"Oh, by all means, let's copy your mother's bad example."

"Thomas," Rosalind admonished.

"It's all right," Susan told her. Belinda certainly wasn't the best role model. "My point is, this wasn't some nutty scheme Lewis dreamed up. There's precedence."

"Let us get this straight," said Rosalind calmly. "You're saying that Lewis needed to be seen with someone like you to look respectable?"

"Precisely. I'm the complete opposite of the women people picture him dating. The idea was that being seen with me would prove he was no longer the same man. And he's not." Didn't matter if he'd broken her heart a half hour ago. She would defend Lewis's character until the end.

"He needed an image makeover and this seemed like the best and most subtle way to do it," she said. "It almost worked too. Graham Montclark vouched for him to the network. They were talking about giving him a broadcast job."

Until this morning. Susan couldn't imagine Lewis's despair. To be so close to what you wanted only to have it taken away.

Actually she could imagine. She wanted to curl up and cry her broken heart out for a week. Only thing stopping her was maintaining a front for Thomas's inquisition.

Thing was, she couldn't blame her brother for being angry.

"All right." He sat down in a chair across from her. "I get what Lewis was trying to do. Why would you agree though? What could you possibly be getting? And don't say publicity for the company, because we both know that couldn't have been your main driver."

She shrugged. "Maybe I needed an image make-over too."

"What?" Thomas and Rosalind spoke together.

"Come on, there's no need to act all shocked," she said. "We all know I'm the unloved elf of the Collier family."

"The what?" Thomas asked.

"The one who doesn't fit in and who everyone would rather just went away."

"No one wants you to go away," Thomas said. "You're our sister."

"Half sister," she reminded him. "And please, I know I drive everyone crazy. People at the company only tolerate me *because* I'm your sister."

"I don't believe that," Thomas said. "Linus told me last night that you were the belle of the ball."

"Because I had Lewis with me. When I'm with Lewis I feel different. Likable." Wanted.

"Is that why you agreed to the idea?" Rosalind asked.

She nodded. "Yes. Kind of." Close enough anyway. "I wanted people to see me as more than I am. I thought if people think someone like Lewis could fall for me, they would see there's something likable about me after all and I wouldn't..."

"Wouldn't what?" Thomas asked. For the first time since the conversation began, his voice was gentle. The kindness threatened to dislodge her withheld tears.

"Be the loser outsider anymore."

"What are you talking about? You're not an outsider." Thomas said. "You're my sister."

"Half sister," she corrected again.

"Whatever," he replied. "It's not your fault who your mother is."

"A woman who took off and stuck you with me," Susan added.

He waved off the comment. "Linus and I always figured you dodged a bullet when that happened. You call yourself a loser outsider now. Imagine the damage if she'd stuck around and raised you. Imagine the kinds of issues you might have had to face."

Susan didn't know how to respond. He was right; she would have been worse off. The three of them sat quietly for a few minutes, listening to the baby's gentle sleeping noises.

Eventually, Thomas leaned forward, resting his forearms on his knees. "Linus told me last night he didn't believe you. About the relationship being fake. He said you two looked pretty into each other and he thinks you only said it because you wanted to get him off your back."

He'd whispered something similar to her when they were on the dais. *You don't look like you're faking to me.*

"That was wishful thinking on his part." On her part too. "We had to put on a show in order to make people think the relationship was the real deal."

"By loving it up on the roof?" Susan looked up from her lap. "He told me on the phone."

"I've got to say, that doesn't sound too fake to me," Rosalind said.

"It was nothing serious. We figured since we were going to spend the month together and were attracted to each other, we might as well enjoy ourselves. We weren't some great romance," she added, quoting Lewis.

"And how'd that arrangement work out for you?" Thomas asked.

Susan didn't answer. Couldn't answer really, without her voice cracking. She studied the wrinkles in last night's dress.

"I'm sorry," her brother said.

"Me too." But hey, for a few glorious weeks, she'd felt special. "I've got no one to blame but myself. The whole point was to go against type, so I knew going in he wasn't going to stick around. Caveat emptor or something like that."

A tear escaped. The first of the day. Swiping it away, she looked over at Thomas. "I never meant for Collier's to get stuck in the middle of this. I'll step away from the company."

"What? Why would you do that?" he asked. "No one is suggesting you step down from anything."

"But the bad publicity. You're going to need to do something."

"It won't be firing my sister. You're a Collier. The company is as much a part of your legacy as it is mine and Linus's. Was I the only one who listened to Grandfather when he brought us to the company museum?"

He crossed the room to sit next to her. "Bottom line is that family is what makes Collier's. We've survived four hundred years. We'll survive a few weeks of tabloid coverage. Might even help. We're getting a lot of free advertising."

Susan gave up trying to rein in the tears. Letting them escape, she hugged her brother tight. "Thank you." It was the first time she'd ever truly felt like a Collier.

"You're welcome. And you're not an unloved elf. Just an annoying one."

Annoying, she'd take.

"Now," Thomas stood up and smoothed the front of his sweater. "I'm going to call the office and see what kind of statement they're putting out before Rosalind and I go Christmas shopping."

As she watched her brother head upstairs to his office, Susan felt moderately better. At least things were okay with her family.

Family. She repeated the word to herself with a sense of shame. Lewis had tried to tell her that she mattered to her brothers, but she hadn't believed him. Turned out Lewis was right. Someday she'd have to thank him. If she ever saw him again.

Baby Noel was starting to fuss in his bassinet. Must be nearly feeding time.

"I'm sorry. I disrupted your morning," she said to Rosalind, rising to leave. "I'll get out of your way."

"Hold it right there, unloved elf." Wearing a very deliberate expression, her sister-in-law rose from her chair. "It's high time you got a dose of the truth."

CHAPTER ELEVEN

"Do you remember last Christmas when you read me the riot act?" Rosalind asked. "You told me I was as much to blame for my problems as Thomas?"

"Of course, I remember."

"You said things no one else was willing to say. Things that were uncomfortable for me to hear."

"Someone had to."

"You're right. Someone did," Rosalind said. "And if you hadn't, we might never have had our little Christmas miracle here." She paused to scoop up the baby and cradle him. "That is why I'm going to return the favor."

Susan's skin was starting to twitch again. "How so?"

"I'm going to tell you some truths," Rosalind said. "Starting with the fact that for someone who's so obsessed with psychology, you suck at self-awareness."

Susan felt as though she had been slapped. "Excuse me?"

"You heard me," Rosalind said. "Do you honestly believe you're some ugly little lump that no one likes? Give me a break. If that's the case then why were you invited to a half-dozen weddings this year?"

"I don't know. Maybe because I'm the boss?"

"Correction. My husband is the boss and Thomas wasn't invited to half as many."

He wasn't? Susan always assumed he didn't attend because he'd scaled back his business commitments since their reconciliation. "Probably because they know he's been preoccupied, and figured they'd invite the one most likely to attend."

"What about Linus? Did they figure he was too busy, as well?"

"I…" She couldn't answer that. Everyone loved Linus. "He's been distracted lately too."

"So these people knew Thomas and Linus wouldn't attend their weddings, but figured you would and that was why you got an invitation?" Rosalind folded her arms. "Do you hear yourself?"

"If you're going to put it like that, of course it's going to sound ludicrous," Susan said.

"How would you put it then?"

Susan opened her mouth only to shut it again. She wasn't sure. "Company social invitations don't mean anything. There could be any number of reasons why I drew the short straw."

"And what about last night? Linus said you mingled with the best of them."

She'd already told them the reason. Lewis had been by her side. "Mingling is easy when you're dating a celebrity. I've been a rock star all month. Everyone wanted to chat."

"Or maybe," Rosalind said, "it was that for once, you were willing to chat back."

Susan frowned. What did that mean?

"I've seen you at Collier's functions," her sister-in-law went on. "You tuck yourself in the corner and act all aloof. When someone comes up to talk to you, you're fine, but otherwise you pull yourself away. You're the one being antisocial, not them."

"That's not true."

Rosalind arched her brow. "Really?"

All right, maybe she did stand off to the side, but it was only as a matter of self-preservation. Pretend you're not hurting, and you won't.

"You would too if your coworkers thought you were a shrew."

"What?"

At the sight of her sister-in-law's shocked expression, Susan felt a twinge of satisfaction. "*Shrewsan*. That's my nickname at work."

"Who calls you that?"

"Everyone."

"Seriously."

"Well, almost everyone," Susan said, feeling defensive now. "Courtney and Ginger…" She paused. Come to think of it, they were the only two people she'd heard use the term. She only assumed the rest of the company did, as well.

Was it possible she was allowing the nasty opinion of two trolls to color her opinion?

No, because her problems had been going on far longer than that. School. University. She'd been separated from the world her entire life.

She offered her final argument, daring Rosalind to come up with a counterpoint. "If I'm so damn likable, then why isn't my phone ringing with invitations? Why am I stuck spending weekends alone?"

"Probably because people think you'll say no if asked." Rosalind adjusted the baby on her shoulder.

"I've heard you back out of plans with Linus. I'm sure you back out of others."

Like invitations to lunch.

"Look, I get it," her sister-in-law continued. "Thomas told me what your mother is like. But did you ever think that the reason people don't socialize with you is because you don't socialize with them?"

"Why should I?" Susan said. "They're only going to…"

"What?"

"Leave." She didn't need to listen to this. Not today. "I've got a headache," she said, starting for the door.

"How do you know?" Rosalind asked. "How do you know people will leave if you don't give them a chance to stay?"

Was that what she did? Susan sat on the edge of the sofa and thought hard about Rosalind's words. All this time she was protecting herself, was it possible she was being her own worst enemy?

"Lewis left," she whispered.

"He's just upset." Rosalind's voice softened, the way Thomas's had earlier. And like before, Susan felt the tears threatening.

"You're worth a lot more than a fake boyfriend or a casual hookup. You're pretty and you're smart, and if Lewis Matolo didn't appreciate that for anything beyond what you could do for him, then he's the one missing out."

Susan would listen to a lot of things, but disparaging remarks about Lewis weren't on the list. "Lewis is amazing. He's the most amazing man I've ever met. I don't think he even knows how amazing he is. I'm just not in his league."

Rosalind sat next to her. "Yes, you are. You're a Collier. You have four hundred years of legacy behind you. You can be in any league you want."

She didn't know what to say. For the third time in twenty-four hours, she was being told she mattered to the family.

All you really need are a few people who care. That was what Lewis had said. Looked like she had those people.

If only she could make Lewis care for her too. "I think I'm in love with him," she told Rosalind.

Her sister-in-law snaked her free arm around Susan's shoulders. "Then let's hope he smartens up and realizes what he had."

Susan didn't know if that was possible.

Rosalind's lecture stuck with her the rest of the day and into the evening. How appropriate that it would be her sister-in-law who delivered the tough love. Last year at this time, it'd been Susan reminding Rosalind of something similar. As she nursed her glass of wine, she found herself circling a familiar cliché: the pot calling the kettle black.

Looking across the street, she saw most of her neighbors had their Christmas trees lit. One apartment was throwing a party. Seeing the people laughing in the window, she wondered if it was true and her insecurities were her own worst enemy. She'd certainly been wrong about her family. All those years of feeling like a square peg, unwanted and unlike the rest, and it turned out her brothers didn't care what shape she came in.

Of course, that didn't change things with Lewis. All the tough love in the world wouldn't make him want her. She'd laid herself bare and he'd rejected her.

Did he? Or did you hold him at arm's length too?

From the very start, she'd been waiting for their affair to end. Pretending for both their sakes that their lovemaking didn't mean anything.

But it did. She loved him. What they shared had been real on her part. She'd never told him though. In fact, she'd pretended she didn't care. She hadn't even invited him to Christmas Eve for crying out loud. How was he supposed to know she cared unless she let him in?

Downing the rest of her wine in one swallow, she grabbed her phone. Lewis's number was on speed dial. Number one. She pressed the button before her courage ran out.

His voice mail answered.

"Hey, Lewis, it's me." She rushed the words as fast as she could. "I know I'm the last person you want to talk with right now, but I wanted to let you know I'm sorry for..."

No, that wasn't what she wanted to say.

"I wanted to let you know that you were the best fake boyfriend around and that I love...loved every minute we spent together. As far as I'm concerned, the relationship was real—very real—and I'm sorry that I ever said anything to Linus. If I could take it back, I would because you deserve nothing but the best. Oh, and Lewis..."

She stopped herself from disconnecting.

"If there's any chance you feel the same or *could* feel the same...please come to Thomas and Roseanne's vow renewal on Christmas Eve. Not because I need a date, but because I want to see you again and there's nothing I'd like better than to spend the holidays with you. You...you matter to me."

There, she thought with a sniff. No one could say she hadn't made the effort. The rest was up to Lewis.

There was only one thing to do when the going got tough, and that was turn off his phone and belly up to the bar. And, because he was a glutton for punishment, he picked the place where the whole debacle had started. The bar was as empty as it had been a month ago. Emptier. Because a particular brunette wasn't perched on a stool nearby.

"Hey, welcome back."

Just his luck. It was the same bartender.

"Are you here alone or is your girlfriend with you?"

"Haven't you read the papers?" Lewis replied. "She wasn't my girlfriend."

"Could have fooled me. You two looked crazy about each other."

"Goes to show, you can't always believe what you see. Lady was way out of my league."

"Huh."

"What?" Lewis asked. He couldn't believe he was discussing his love life with a bartender. On the other hand, he was in a bar so who else was going to talk with him? It beat staying home and wondering what he was going to do with his life. "If you have an opinion, you might as well go ahead and say it."

The bartender shrugged. "You didn't strike me as someone who hesitates about going after what you want, no matter how out of reach it seems."

"Once upon a time maybe." When reaching meant getting out of a lesser situation. "Unfortunately, just because you want something doesn't mean it'll last." Especially if you didn't belong in the same world. People walk away.

Unless you send them away. Like he had Susan. Why wouldn't he though? He was washed up. His chance at redemption had blown up in his face. Why would Susan want to stick around when she could do so much better?

"Here." The bartender set a bright red drink in front of him. "You look like you could use this."

"What is it?"

"A virgin Christmas Wish. On the house."

Lewis had to laugh. There was a joke in there.

He stared at the bubbles rising in the red depths. Susan. The bubbles reminded him of Susan. Oh, how he wished he could fix what he'd messed up.

If wishes were horses, beggars would ride. He remembered someone telling him that as a kid. His first foster mum maybe. The one who was like Susan. Because of course.

"Excuse me. Are you Lewis Matolo?"

Looking up from the glass, Lewis saw a man in a bellman's uniform. "I saw you walk in," the man said.

He was middle-aged, with salt-and-pepper hair and weathered brown skin. "My name is Darcus Alajua," he said. "You met my grandson David at the Youth Ambassador Event."

The man pulled a phone from his jacket pocket to show its wallpaper—a picture of Lewis and a young boy of around eight.

"I remember him," he said. "Speedy little thing. Good footwork."

"I wanted to thank you. Meeting you is all he's talked about for the past week."

"Wow, with Christmas right around the corner, that's a pretty big feat," the bartender remarked.

Lewis was surprised. He remembered praising David's skills a few times, but he hadn't given the boy any additional attention or singled him out in any way that would merit the boy being that impressed.

"I'm glad he enjoyed himself" he said.

"It's more than enjoyed," Darcus said. His eyes dropped to the screen for a moment and grew misty. "David came to live with me a year ago because his mother...my daughter...has some demons. He's been discouraged, feeling sorry for himself. Sports has been the one thing he's enjoyed."

"I know the feeling." He'd been in David's shoes once.

"I know and when you talked about how football saved you, how it helped pull you out of tough times, it lit a fire in him. He's excited about something again."

"I'm glad. You tell him not to give up, and to keep playing. Sports isn't about being a superstar. It's about belonging and being a part of a team and learning to work at what you love."

The older man smiled, the lines on his cheeks fading and his face turning youthful. "I can see why he enjoyed your talk."

"I enjoyed giving it. Being with the kids reminded me of why I fell in love with football to begin with. When you grow up like I did, you need that escape."

"Yes, you do," Darcus said. "That's why it means a lot to the kids when someone like you comes back home."

Comes back home. Was that what he'd done? "Can I see that photo again?" he asked Darcus.

This time he studied David's face. The kid was looking at him like he had hung the moon.

Who else had looked at him like that? Susan.

Lewis handed the phone back with a smile. All his life he'd needed—wanted—a place where he belonged.

He thought that place was football. But it wasn't. Athletic stardom had never come close to how he felt when working with those kids. The only thing that made him happier had been when he was holding Susan.

You don't need the spotlight. All you really need are a few people who care.

Susan's smile had felt more like home than any stadium or spotlight ever could. She'd believed in him. Understood him. He hadn't needed the spotlight to win her support.

And he'd sent her away. Since when did he not go after what he wanted? He was Champagne Lewis Matolo, for crying out loud!

He pulled out his wallet. "Do me a favor, will you?" he asked Darcus. He handed the man a hundred-dollar bill. "You take this and buy David the best football cleats and shin guards money can buy. Tell him his friend Lewis owes him for making him see something very important."

If the company Christmas party had taken place in a winter wonderland, then Thomas and Rosalind's vow renewal was being held in its more glamorous cousin. Her brother had spared no expense in making the Christmas Eve ceremony special, right down to the grand piano he'd had installed in the living room for the occasion.

"I may have gone a little crazy," Thomas admitted as he took Susan's coat along with the bags of Christmas gifts she'd brought for the next morning.

"Rosalind would have been happy renewing our vows in the middle of a field, but Maddie wanted to have a sparkly wedding."

Susan took in the myriad of lights and candles,

enough to rival the Kew Gardens display. The regular lighting had been turned off because the decorations provided more than enough illumination.

"Good thing you don't overindulge your daughter," she said.

"Hey, it's Christmas Eve. If you can't go crazy with decorations at the holidays, when can you?" He kissed her cheek. "Merry Christmas. You look lovely."

"Thanks." She'd splurged on an evening gown for the occasion. Silver with sequins. No more hiding herself in the corner. If she was to be a square peg, she was going to own her edges. "I'm afraid I don't feel very lovely though."

"No word from Lewis?"

"Afraid not. We had an interview with *Personal Magazine* scheduled for yesterday, but I got a call from his agent saying the interview was canceled."

No surprise there. For a short while she'd hoped they might go through with the interview to contradict the negative publicity, but apparently not. Like Lewis had pointed out, how did you contradict the truth?

The answer was, you don't. She had this pipe dream that Lewis would use the article to make their casual encounters into something more. But he hadn't.

The fallout from Scam-pagne Gate, as it was lovingly called in the press, was swift and loud. Radio stations all over the UK commented on the story all weekend, which in turn, led to the morning shows holding round-table discussions about celebrity ethics and England's search for gossip. Lewis was once again a bad boy while her reputation vacillated between coconspirator to besotted victim.

As for Collier's? The company was experiencing their best holiday season in years so either people didn't care that she was involved with Lewis or her being involved with Lewis had helped the company project a saucy, youthful edge. Either way, at least something good had come out of the scheme.

Thomas eyed her with concern. "Are you going to be okay?"

"I feel like a right idiot," she said. She'd fallen for a man when she'd known from the start he wasn't interested in a long-term relationship. "But, I'm not the first person to have had their heart broken. I'll survive." It killed her when she thought of how good she and Lewis could have been together, but she couldn't make him love her. As magical as the past few weeks had been, she deserved more. First and foremost, a man who loved her back.

"Yes, you will," Thomas replied. "Just remember, you're not alone. Your family will always stand by you."

She smiled. "I know." Now.

Perhaps more than one good thing had come out of the debacle.

Rosalind's dose of reality had been hard to hear, but it also gave her a lot to think about. It made Susan take a good look at her behavior over the years. She'd become such an expert at pretending she didn't care about being an outsider, that she failed to see all the times she'd been offered a place inside. She had brothers who cared about her. Sure they were all completely different, and she would never mesh completely with them in a million years. But as Thomas showed the day she and Lewis were outed, when the chips were down, they had her back.

"By the way," Thomas continued, "we found out how the paper got the story. Turns out one of the bartenders at the hotel has a cousin who writes for the *Looking Glass*. She overheard Courtney and Ginger talking at the bar and convinced them to tell her the entire story. She then turned the info over to her cousin."

"Lewis warned me there were spies everywhere. What are you going to do about Ginger and Courtney?"

"Since I don't handle personnel issues anymore, I told senior management that while I wasn't happy with their behavior, I would leave the final decision to them. And you."

"Me?"

"Last time I looked, you were the one who handled human resources," he said. "Plus, you were the victim. If anyone should weigh in with an opinion, it's you."

In other words, Courtney's and Ginger's fates lay in her hands. How circumstances had changed.

Over the week, she'd thought quite a bit about the gossipy twosome. She finally realized that their need to put her down said more about them than it did her. What their reason was for disliking her, Susan didn't know, but that didn't mean their opinion was correct either. In fact, a long talk over coffee with Maria proved their opinion was in the minority. Susan was simply so busy wrapping herself in protective distance that she hadn't noticed.

The question now was how bad a punishment did they deserve? "They didn't purposely leak the story," she said. "More like they were being petty and foolish." On the other hand, their pettiness had caused her and Lewis a lot of pain. Mostly Lewis. When it came to Susan, the story had only hastened the inevitable.

"Still, they did do damage. It's only by sheer luck Collier's didn't suffer some kind of backlash."

"You can say that again. Personally, I think we should fire them," Thomas said.

"Not me." Susan couldn't believe what she was about to suggest. "I'd rather suspend them for two weeks and give them a stern warning."

Her brother lifted his brows. "Seriously?"

"And I want them to know that I was the one who saved their catty little butts." She wasn't so magnanimous that she didn't want them to owe her.

"Excuse me, you two." Linus stepped into the entryway. "Do you plan to spend the entire evening talking in the entryway or do you plan to attend the party?"

"Merry Christmas to you too." She kissed him on the cheek.

He looked past her shoulder. "Are you here alone?"

"What do you think?"

"Just checking. I need a drinking companion. Come with me to the bar." He tucked her arm into his. "By the way," he said over his shoulder, "your wife wanted me to tell you the maid of honor is getting antsy. She's worried you'll take too long and prevent Santa Claus from coming."

"You know," Susan said as they stepped into the main living room, "Thomas insists that Maddie will be running Collier's someday. I'm beginning to think he's right."

When Thomas said only a few friends and family would be invited, he hadn't been joking. Only a handful of people, a dozen at most, were in the room. Most were gathered by the piano listening to the Christmas carols. Four stockings, fire-engine red, hung from the mantel, the newest one a miniature version of the other three. The magic of it all was like salt poured into her heart, but she forced a smile for her brother's sake. It was just a broken heart. She would survive.

Linus led her to the opposite side of the room where a portable bar had been staged. Susan's eyes nearly popped out of her head.

"You again!" she said. "Are you the only bartender in London this holiday season?" The bartender let out a hearty laugh. "I'm beginning to think so. I was drafted into service by my uncle Chris. He's over there by the guests." He pointed to a portly man with a white beard and red reindeer sweater.

"Well it's good to see you…?" She realized she'd never gotten his name.

"Nick," he replied. "Is your boyfriend with you?"

A little more salt burned her heart. "I'm afraid we aren't together anymore."

"That's too bad. You two made an adorable couple."

She'd thought so too. "Some things don't always work out," she said sadly.

"Or maybe they just take time," he replied. Evidently they taught positive thinking at bartending school. "Can I get you a house special?"

"What's it called this time? Nick likes to name his drinks," she told Linus.

"Yep, and in honor of tonight's special event, we're serving True Love cocktails."

"Fabulous," Linus replied, sounding slightly more enthusiastic than she felt.

"Trust me," Nick told them. "You won't regret the choice."

Their cocktails were barely in hand when the pianist played a loud fanfare. "If you could take your seats," he announced. "Our ceremony is about to begin."

Maddie appeared at the top of the spiral staircase, and as the pianist played a soft classical piece, she began picking her way down the stairs. When she reached the bottom, she scurried to the front of the room to hug her father. She looked adorable. Susan smiled, then looked at the empty seat beside her.

How she wished Lewis were here.

Rosalind was next, looking resplendent in a simple white silk dress. She positively beamed with happiness. No wonder Nick named the drink True Love.

Feeling a little nauseous, Susan took a large sip and watched the ceremony. The look of utter adoration in her brother's eyes made her heart ache. How wonderful must it be to be loved the way Thomas loved Rosalind.

Some day, she told herself. Some day she would have that. At the moment, her heart still wished it were Lewis, but after a week, it was time for her to accept that that wasn't going to happen. Instead, she'd be grateful for the time they'd had.

As she blinked away the dampness from her eyes, she felt someone settle into the empty seat beside her.

"I hope those are tears of joy."

Susan stopped breathing. She was almost afraid to turn her head. Was that really Lewis sitting beside her? "You… I…"

He put his fingers to his lips. "Shh. There's a wedding going on." A second later, his hand captured hers.

The rest of the ceremony passed in a fog as the only thing Susan could focus on was the man beside her. Did his being there mean he returned her feelings or was he simply fulfilling one last obligation? A tear slipped down her cheek.

"Hey, now," Lewis said as the rest of the group burst

into applause. "What's this?" He reached across and
fanned her cheek with his thumb, his fingers lingering
on her jaw when he finished.

What was he doing, smiling at her like she was the
most important person in the world? People were still
applauding and congratulating the happy couple, but
she needed to know. The moment was too surreal to
believe. Or rather, too perfect to believe.

"Come with me," she said. Slipping past the crowd,
she led him to the vestibule where they could talk in
private. There, partially hidden by a poinsettia tower,
she turned to him and finally asked what she'd been
dying to ask the entire ceremony. "Why are you here?"

"I got your invitation."

A week ago. She'd left her message a week ago.

She tossed her drink in his face.

"What was that for?" Lewis wiped the True Love
from his face.

"Why do you think?" It was an instant reaction and
probably over the top, but dammit! "You left me hanging for an entire week!"

"Is everything okay?" she heard Thomas ask.

All five members of her family appeared in the doorway, prepared to stand by her. Even distracted by Lewis,
the show of solidarity squeezed her heart.

"Thanks, but I've got this," she told them. "Lewis
was just about to explain what the hell he was thinking
showing up here after being MIA for a week."

"I was trying for a romantic gesture."

"You call leaving me hanging romantic?"

"Don't be daft. I wanted to call you back as soon as
I got the message."

Out of nowhere Nick joined the group, brandishing a cloth napkin. Lewis took the cloth and wiped the last of the liquid from his cheeks. "Okay, I *should* have called you back as soon as I got the message, but I was out of town on business. I decided it would be better if I waited until I saw you in person so I could say I love you properly. Clearly I made a mistake."

"Clearly you did... Wait." Did she hear him right? "What did you say?"

"I said I made a mistake."

"No, before that."

Lewis smiled. "I said I love you, Susan Collier."

Before she could say another word, he drew her into a kiss. He tasted like peppermint and True Love.

God bless silly cocktail names.

"I'm the biggest idiot on the planet," he whispered when they parted. He rested his forehead against hers, his eyes shut tight. "I was so afraid of... I spent my entire life certain the only reason anyone would want me was because of what I could do on the field. That if I weren't a star...if I weren't in the spotlight, that people wouldn't care. I wouldn't be good enough for anybody." Pulling back, he opened his eyes to reveal unshed tears. "Especially not for you."

"You are an idiot." Her lips were trembling so much, the words barely made it out. "I don't care what you do. I never did." The irony of his confession hit her and she started to laugh. "I thought *I* wasn't good enough for *you.*"

"Oh, sweetheart, you are so far out of my league. I consider myself lucky that you would ever give me the time of day."

"We're both idiots," she said. Letting their insecurities keep them from happiness. "I love you, Lewis Matolo."

He brushed her cheek. "I love you too, Susan Collier."

They were the three most beautiful words she'd ever heard.

"My last grand gesture didn't go right, but maybe this one will," he said. "I know we both have a lot of issues to work out, and I can't promise what the future is going to hold for us. But I'd like to find out."

There was a gasp from the room as he dropped to one knee. "Therefore, in front of your friends and family, I'm asking if you'll...date me. For real."

"Yes," she replied, wiping the tears from her cheeks. "I would be honored to be your real girlfriend."

"Daddy, are we having another wedding?" Maddie called out.

"Maybe someday," Susan replied, her heart giving a leap at the smile her answer brought to Lewis's face. "Right now, I think I'll focus on having a very merry Christmas."

Lewis Matolo: How a Fake Relationship Brought Me Love

It doesn't take a genius to see that Champagne Lewis is happy with life. Once the king of London nightlife, he's content these days enjoying a cup of tea and babysitting his girlfriend's niece and nephew.

"I love kids," Matolo says. "They remind you of what's important."

It's that love of children that led the star of *Football Tonight* to establish the Matolo Chil-

dren's Foundation, which aims to help underprivi-
leged and foster children develop leadership skills
through sports. His partner in the venture is his
girlfriend, Susan Collier.

"To think," he says, "it all started with a fake
relationship..."

Susan stopped reading and tucked her copy of *Personal Magazine* under her arm. "It's brilliant. I told you we could spin this into something positive."

"Yes, you did, and it only took twelve months," Lewis replied. He laughed when she gave him a playful smack.

Hard to believe a year had passed since that horrible night they'd met, which in retrospect had turned out to be the best night of her life. It'd given birth to the best twelve months she'd ever had. Both she and Lewis were making an effort to work through their insecurities. Taking Rosalind's advice, she'd begun trying to be less standoffish and to be open to people. As a result, they were heading to the Regis to help their friends Maria and Hank celebrate their wedding anniversary.

Meanwhile it turned out Lewis hadn't blown his shot after all. The network loved Lewis's new notoriety. The executives thought he brought an extra edge to the broadcast.

"It's too bad the article's going to be out of date soon," Lewis said. "I've already given the network my notice." He'd decided the joy he felt working with kids was far more rewarding than broadcasting.

"I'm sure the world will forgive you," Susan said. "It's not like you left to chase wine and women. You didn't, right?"

"No way, luv. I'm a one-woman man these days."

Susan smiled. The best part of the year had been making their journeys together. Lately they'd even started talking about merging those journeys into one shared life, and if the little square box she'd accidently found in Lewis's drawer was any indication, that merger was right around the corner. Two odd peas no longer unwanted and alone.

Just as they reached the hotel, the first snowflakes of the season began to fall. "Looks like the Christmas season has officially started," Susan remarked. "They'll be playing carols on the radio next."

"A little early Christmas isn't so bad," Lewis replied. "Means the pop-up bars will be setting up shop."

"That's true." Hard to hate those when it was a pop-up bar that brought them together. "Do you think the same bar is here this year? We could stop in and say hello to Nick."

"We could see."

They walked up the stairs to the mezzanine, expecting to find the temporary structure. Unfortunately, when they reached the top step, the space was empty. There was nothing but a pair of high-back chairs and a table with a small Christmas tree.

"Sorry, luv," said Lewis. "Looks like we're out of luck."

No, she wasn't. Her luck was only beginning.

"That's all right," she told him. "I've already got my Christmas wish."

* * * * *

THE SCROOGE OF
LOON LAKE

CARRIE NICHOLS

This is dedicated to the two Jills.
My agent, Jill Marsal, who believed in my writing voice before I knew how to plot or write conflict, and my walking partner, Jill Ralph, who not only pulls me away from my desk twice a day but is the perfect sounding board for story problems.

Chapter One

Desmond "Des" Gallagher heaved a frustrated sigh as he stared at the scattered pieces of colorful glass laid out on his workbench. This was the third day in a row he'd come to the former business office in the spacious barn he now used as his workshop and done nothing but sit and stare. The scarred and chipped wood that made up the table's surface attested to the fact that work did indeed get done here. Just not today. Or yesterday. He rubbed a hand over the stubble on his face. And not even the day before that. Normally, seeing the glass laid out before him was enough to spark an idea, even if he had no concrete design in mind.

Today's project was an unfinished stained glass window that could be installed in place of an existing window frame or framed and hung like a painting. While those remained popular, his new love was shattered glass sculptures. Shattering the glass himself, he enjoyed taking those broken pieces and creating something new and better from them. Although he'd experimented with small, blown glass items, he'd shunned the much larger ones because crafting those required more than one person.

Having to think about a project stifled his creativity. His best work came when his brain sent signals directly to his fingers and he assembled pieces without conscious thought. Crazy, but who was he to argue with something that had served him well enough to earn a living? He wasn't getting rich from it but his art supplemented his military disability.

Stretching his neck, he scowled. *Christmas.* That was the problem. He couldn't escape the dreaded holiday nor the painful memories the season triggered. He did his best to avoid going into town from Thanksgiving until well into January because Loon Lake loved its Christmas celebrations. Main Street, with its quaint, brick-front shops huddled around the town green, would soon be decked out in lights, garlands and, God help him, holiday cheer. If he couldn't get an item at the gas station mini-mart on the edge of town or by ordering online, he went without until after the holidays.

And what was his excuse for avoiding the town the other ten months? He reached for his stainless-steel insulated mug and took a sip of his favorite Sumatran coffee from beans he'd ground that morning. Yeah, he took his coffee seriously. Maybe if he pretended he *had* an idea one would come. Pfft, talk about clutching at straws. Shaking his head, he set the mug down and reached for the grozier pliers.

"Yoo-hoo? Lieutenant Gallagher?"

His head snapped up at the interruption. A petite blonde woman, dressed in a bright red parka, stood in the doorway. One hand held a red and green tin; the other clutched the hand of a towheaded boy who looked to be about four or five. What the…? He discouraged visitors and studiously shunned community activities to avoid becoming embroiled in the residents' lives—and thereby ensuring they, in turn, stayed out of his.

How did she even find her way out here? He lived in the back of beyond; his fifty-acre former horse farm could be considered isolated, even in a sparsely populated state like Vermont. His nearest neighbor, Brody Wilson, was five miles away and that was as the crow flew. And unlike Brody, Des had no interest in keeping horses, so the numerous paddocks surrounding the barn remained as empty as the day he'd bought the place. Summers working on a dude ranch had cured him of the romance of horse ownership.

The woman, who appeared to be in her mid- to late-twenties, stepped closer. Close enough for a subtle lavender scent to reach him.

"Hi. I was hoping I could have a minute of your time." Her broad smile revealed a crooked bottom tooth.

He had no business noticing that tooth, even less thinking it was…what? Not sexy, but appealing in some wholesome, girl-next-door way. He scowled at his thoughts. "Why? Are my minutes better than yours?"

"Sir?" She shook her head, her long, corn-silk hair

brushing against, and contrasting with, the cherry-red of her jacket. "No. I—I meant—"

"Unless you know something I don't, you taking one of my minutes won't increase yours." He was acting like a first-class jerk, but she'd set off warning bells. And what was the deal with that *sir*? It grated on his nerves. Here he was checking her out and she was addressing him as *sir*. At thirty-four, he couldn't be more than eight or ten years her senior. He sighed. It wasn't her language that had him spooked. No, it was his reaction to her that had him acting like a complete ass.

A small furrow appeared in the middle of her forehead. Damn, but she even frowned cute. That clinched it because he wasn't into *cute*. And certainly not ones who addressed him as *sir*. *Let it go, Gallagher*. His type might be blondes but they were also tall and blatantly sexy with a mouthful of perfect teeth. That disqualified the five-foot-nothing woman with the crooked tooth. Considering how many women he'd been with in the past three years, though, his type would appear to be fictional women.

Her full bottom lip now hid the tooth and he looked away. He rose from the stool he'd been perched on, careful not to put too much weight on his left leg after sitting for so long. Staggering or collapsing in front of her was not the look he was going for. Ha! She'd probably rush to help and his ego had taken enough beating with the *sir*. *That's letting it go?*

Bottom line, he needed to get rid of her before she regrouped, started using that killer smile on him again. He hitched his chin at the tin she carried. "If you're here from the town's welcoming committee, you're three years too late."

She shook her head, causing her hair to sway. "That's not why I'm here. I—I saw your work at the General Store and—"

"Then you should've bought it there. I don't sell pieces out of my workshop. Didn't Tavie explain that?" His location wasn't a secret, but the tourists and residents of Loon Lake bought his stuff in town and left him alone, and that was the way he liked it. "How did you even find me?"

"It wasn't easy, believe me." She gave him a tentative smile.

He grunted. "And yet, here you are."

"I can be quite resourceful and frankly—" she glanced around the cavernous barn, empty and scrupulously clean except for his cluttered work area "—it's not exactly some Bond villain's supersecret lair."

Her smile seemed to be an invitation to join in, but he deepened his scowl. It was either that or start grinning foolishly. She was charming, and he remembered he didn't do charming. And, by God, he wouldn't allow himself to *be* charmed.

She licked her lips and swallowed. "Tavie gave me directions."

"That figures," he muttered.

Octavia "Tavie" Whatley might be proprietress of Loon Lake General Store, but general busybody was her true occupation. Not much went on in town without her knowing about it, but she'd sold more of his pieces than anyone, so he grit his teeth and put up with her.

Even with his frugal lifestyle, the military disability only went so far.

"Dear me, where are my manners. I'm Natalie Pierce." She let go of the boy's hand and placed her palm over the top of his head in a tender gesture. "And this is my son, Sam."

The kid grinned up at him, his eyes the same clear August-sky blue as hers. Des nodded to the boy. He had nothing against children. *Just women with bright sunny smiles? And let's not forget that oddly appealing crooked tooth.* Damn. He didn't want or need these distractions. *Yeah, because you're so busy being creative.* He told his nothing-but-trouble inner voice to shut up.

"I hate to interrupt—" she began.

"But you're doing it, anyway." And the jerk behavior continued. Her presence was flustering him so he was repaying the favor. See if he could fluster her a bit. His reaction wasn't her fault, but he was in survival mode because that weaponized smile of hers had scrambled his thought process. He'd gone too long without female company. That was it; blame this on self-imposed celibacy.

"Lieutenant Gallagher, I—"

"Call me Des. My navy days are behind me." His days of being catapulted at one hundred and sixty-five miles an hour from the deck of a carrier in a metal casket worth seventy million dollars were over. He grit his teeth and rubbed his knotted thigh muscles. Why did he want her to call him Des? Saying his given name shouldn't matter because he was trying to get her and that way too appealing smile out of his barn. Wasn't he?

"Des," she said, drawing it out.

"Yeah, but it's generally one short syllable." But her version worked. Worked a bit too well, as a matter of fact.

"Sorry." She inhaled as if she was about to launch into a prepared speech.

He opened his mouth to—

"I'm here to talk to you about handcrafting some items for an auction we're having. Christmas ornaments would be a real hit this time of year. And it's for a great cause. There's this fantastic hippotherapy program that needs—"

"Stop right there." He held up his hand like a cop halting traffic. "Doesn't matter the cause. I don't do Christmas. Period."

"What? No Christmas? But…but… Why?" She blinked owlishly. "What's not to love about Christmas?"

How about being a child and spending it with a suicidal mother? Always worried she would disappear. He would've been left alone because his biological father wanted nothing to do with Des. In his dad's mind, Des was proof of an indiscretion while attending an out-of-town conference. "I have my reasons."

She opened her mouth, but Sam tugged on her sleeve. She looked down, and the boy up, his eyes large and his stare intense, both standing still like they were having a telepathic conversation. One that excluded everyone else, even him. She glanced at her watch, sighed and nodded her head.

"To be honest, it took me much longer than I expected to find this place," she said, gnawing on her bottom lip, calling his attention to it again.

"Maybe that's the way I like it," he said, even though

he wasn't sure if she'd been talking to him, her son or herself. He'd been too distracted by that bottom lip.

She set the tin on the workbench next to his tools. "I have to leave, but I warn you, I don't give up easily, even if you do cloak yourself in that grumpiness like it's a virtue."

The boy tugged on her sleeve in another silent plea and she nodded. There was that nonverbal communication again, reminding Des he wasn't a part of their world. Not that he wanted to be. Nope. Not one little bit.

She took the boy's hand in hers. "I'll be in touch," she said as if it was a threat and headed for the door.

"Wait," he called and she turned her head to look over her shoulder. He pointed at the tin. "What's this?"

"Don't worry, it's not a bomb," she said and smiled briefly. "It's homemade Christmas bark. Even a grinch like you can't say no to that."

"What the heck is...?" He glanced up, but she was gone.

Shaking his head, he opened the tin to reveal irregularly shaped bars of white chocolate covered with red and green M&Ms and crushed candy canes. Grabbing one and taking a large bite, he sank back on the stool and thought about the mystery that was Natalie Pierce. What the heck had just happened? Her soft, lilting voice, coupled with that appealing smile, had taunted him and he wanted to know more about her. Her speech was devoid of the flatter, more nasal vowel tones he'd grown accustomed to since moving here. But neither could he peg her as having a Southern drawl. And the kid hadn't spoken at all, but he'd smiled and made eye contact. Maybe the boy—Sam—was shy. Des shook his head. None of this was his problem, so why was he wasting time on it?

He glanced at the pieces of colorful glass sitting idle on the bench and his fingers itched to create something. He popped the half-eaten piece of candy into his mouth, brushed his palms together and picked up the pliers.

The next morning Des stood and thrust his shoulders back to work out the kinks from sitting hunched over the workbench. He couldn't remember the last time he'd pulled an all-nighter, but he wasn't about to leave and have his muse desert him again. He scratched the scruff on his jaw with his fingertips and glanced at the now-empty tin. Huh. As he'd worked last night, he'd munched on her delicious candy. This stained glass window was of the lake during winter when many of the trees were bare. Up close, the lake and trees were individual pieces, but when standing back, those pieces became shades and ripples of the lake water.

A car door slammed and he scowled as his heart kicked up at the thought that the visitor might be Natalie. Uh-oh. Was she back? Who else could it be? Natalie Pierce had been his only visitor in recent memory. He didn't know whether to be glad or annoyed. He started to rise but his leg and his inner voice protested. *Down, Gallagher. You're not an addict waiting for your dealer.*

It was indeed Natalie Pierce and she was holding her son's hand again. In the other, she carried a plate wrapped in aluminum foil. What did she bring today?

"I told you I'd be back." She smiled, the crooked tooth peeking out.

He quirked an eyebrow. "So I should take your threats seriously?"

"Maybe you should." She laughed.

Heat coursed through his veins at the sound. "Are you in the habit of threatening all the men in your life?"

"Is this your way of asking if I'm married?" she asked with a significant lift of her eyebrows.

Yeah, he was about as subtle as a sidewinder missile. He grunted instead of replying.

"I assure you that Sam is the only man in my life." She showed him her crooked smile. "One thing you need to know about me, Lieutenant. I follow through on my promises."

"Des." He'd enjoyed hearing his name yesterday in that musical voice. Liked it a little too much but he'd worry about that later.

"Des," she repeated and set the plate on a clean corner at the end of the workbench. "I hope you like gingerbread men. They're quintessential Christmas, don't you think?"

He grunted, trying not to give her any encouragement, but his stomach rumbled, reminding him he hadn't had any breakfast yet.

"I used my grandmother's recipe and her forged tin cookie cutter." She let go of the boy's hand and began removing the foil. "They're fresh, but I'll let you in on a little secret. Even after a few days, you can warm them in the microwave and they will have that fresh-from-the-oven taste. Sam likes them best that way. Don't you, Sam?"

She glanced down at the empty space next to her. "Sam?" Her voice rose. "Sam?"

She uttered something under her breath and raced out of the barn. He'd been so fascinated by her mouth as she spoke, he hadn't noticed the boy's disappearing act. But then the kid couldn't have gotten far, and there wasn't anything nearby that could hurt him. Des grabbed a cookie and followed her as quickly as his bum leg allowed.

Natalie's heart hammered as she rushed from the barn. She'd never forgive herself if— She choked back a sob. She was overreacting but couldn't prevent it.

She had no idea Sam was capable of disappearing so fast or so stealthily. He'd overcome many of his balance issues since starting equine-assisted therapy. Another reason she needed to save the program. And as soon as she found him, she'd celebrate his acting like an adventurous five-year-old boy.

She was gasping for air by the time she located him standing next to a sleek, top-of-the-line, black-and-red snowmobile parked on the side of the barn. He must've spotted it on their way in. She'd been so consumed with the prospect of seeing Des again and what she was going to say that she hadn't paid attention to her surroundings. Shame on her.

She didn't know a lot about snowmobiles, but she guessed this one was expensive. "Sam, honey, don't touch."

Not that she could blame Sam for being curious. Weren't all little boys fascinated by that sort of stuff? A lump in her throat threatened to cut off her oxygen. For all of his challenges, and Lord knew there were many, Sam was still like all boys his age. After suffering life-threatening injuries, he'd had to learn to walk again but still had occasional balance issues. She'd been warned that his ability to speak might never return. "Be careful. You could hurt yourself."

"There's not much chance of that."

Natalie turned. The lieutenant bit the head off the gingerbread man in his hand. Was his cavalier attitude toward Sam's safety bugging her, or was it the fact that looking at him had her insides clamoring for…for what? For something she hadn't wanted in such a long time, she had no name for it. But the strange yearning she couldn't name made her want to snarl at him in a primal reaction similar to fight or flight. *Remember you want his help with the auction.* Neither fight nor flight would get her what she wanted for Sam.

"Easy for you to say. He's not your son," she pointed out and grit her teeth, not understanding her reaction to Des Gallagher. Grumpiness aside, he wasn't menacing, despite his disheveled appearance, and yet, he threatened her on some visceral level.

"Even if he was," he said, brushing cookie crumbs off his shirt as if he didn't have a care in the world, "it doesn't change facts."

She narrowed her eyes at Des as if he represented some sort of threat. *He does*, a voice screamed at her. But the danger wasn't physical…well, unless you counted her body's reaction to him. He wasn't her type, she argued with herself. For one thing, he was too tall, at least two or three inches over six feet to her mere five foot two. Okay, okay, five feet and one and a half inches. He couldn't be called charming or even pleasant.

His face was covered in stubble, his eyes a little

bloodshot. He appeared to be wearing the same clothes as yesterday, a red-and-black buffalo-plaid flannel shirt over a cream-colored, waffle-knit shirt and faded jeans. Had he been up all night? Working or drinking?

She was going with *working* because she hadn't smelled any alcohol or even breath mints on him. Besides, Tavie hadn't said anything about a drinking problem, and she would know. Natalie was convinced the owner of Loon Lake General Store knew everything about everyone.

Des muttered something under his breath and limped toward Sam. How come she hadn't noticed that limp before? *Maybe because he'd been sitting down.* As her neighbor's little brother might say, "Duh, Natalie." Being around this man had her on her toes. Too bad being around him also drained IQ points.

"Have you ever been on a snowmobile?" Des hunkered down next to Sam with an exhaled grunt.

What was the matter with his left leg? Was that why he was no longer in the navy? She took back every nasty or unkind thought she'd ever had about Des Gallagher. *Except the thoughts you were thinking last night weren't unkind.* Some might call them *nasty* but with a totally different connotation of that particular word.

Tavie Whatley had talked about Des but hadn't said anything about permanent or debilitating injuries. Was it simple politeness or was Tavie caught under his spell, too?

What's this too *business? I haven't fallen under his spell.*

"This will be our first winter here," she said, hoping to steer her thoughts to more wholesome topics. "We didn't get much snow where we lived before. We're looking forward to real snow, aren't we, Sam?"

His blue eyes wide, Sam nodded enthusiastically.

"Real snow? What other kind is there?" Des snorted and threw her a questioning glance. "Where the heck did you live before?"

"Nashville. We'd get some snow accumulation, but it didn't last much past noon on sunny days. Sam and I are looking forward to building our first snowman, going sledding and having snowball fights."

"Be careful what you wish for," he said. "Along with all those snowmen come shoveling, scraping your car, crappy driving conditions, salt and sand all winter long. To name a few of the exciting perks."

"And yet, here you are." She parroted his words from yesterday and made sure the challenge was evident in her tone.

He made a noise, blowing air through his lips. "Maybe I'm a glutton for punishment."

She laughed. He was enjoying this too much to be as fractious as he wanted her to believe. "I'll bet you enjoy every minute of the snow. The more miserable, the better."

He rolled his eyes. "Remind me not to play poker with you."

She frowned at his comment. Wait, was he groaning? "Why? I don't understand your meaning."

"You see too much." He shook his head. "I predict if we have a bad winter, you'll be crying uncle long before mud season."

"Mud season?"

"It's Vermont's fifth season and comes between winter and spring." He glanced at her sneakers. "You might want to invest in a decent pair of rubber boots before then, not to mention snow boots for the snow you're wanting."

"We're here to stay. It would take more than snow or mud to chase us away." She squared her shoulders and forced strength into her voice. "And that's a promise, not a threat. In case you were wondering."

"Thanks for clearing that up." The side of his mouth lifted a fraction, the only indication he might be amused.

She moved closer and rested her hand on the padded seat of the snowmobile. "I must say, you have an impressive piece of equipment."

"Gee, thanks, it's been a while since anyone has complimented me on my...equipment," he said in a deadpan tone.

She turned toward him. What did she—*Oh!* So much for wholesome. She closed her eyes, wishing the ground would swallow her up because now her imagination was going there. The last time she'd flirted could be measured in years, definitely before her marriage to Ryan. Her face burning up, she opened her eyes and met his gaze. His face was impassive except for an ever-so-slight lift of his eyebrows.

Her mouth opened and closed. Great, she couldn't manage anything except an imitation of a goldfish. His expression didn't change, but she had the distinct feeling he was relishing her discomfort. When she narrowed her eyes at him, he rubbed a hand over his mouth, his fingers making a scratching sound on the stubble. How would those dark whiskers feel against her skin? *Stay away from there, Natalie. You're way out of your depth.*

Okay, so the man had a sense of humor hidden under that ill-mannered exterior. What would he be like if—No, she wanted him to make some ornaments for her auction. That was all. Nothing more. But there was no harm in noticing how his chest filled out that flannel shirt, was there?

"...on a snowmobile before?" Des had been talking to Sam while she'd been daydreaming about things she shouldn't.

Sam, who seemed to be hanging on every word Des said, shook his head. Natalie's chest tightened. Last year her dad had suffered one of those widow-maker heart attacks, and Sam had lost the closest male role model he'd had since his dad and her late husband, Ryan, passed away. Sure, he had plenty of doting women in his life, but she knew they couldn't fill the void the same way a man could. Her father had been a crusty career army drill sergeant but had had a soft spot for Sam she could have hit blindfolded.

She listened as Des explained how the snowmobile worked and she made a mental note to look for a toy one Sam could add to his beloved collection of die-cast miniature cars. It would make a nice stocking stuffer. There wasn't an abundance of extra money for Christmas presents, so she was making sure each gift from Santa was well thought out.

Des rose and stepped back until he stood shoulder to shoulder with her. "He doesn't say much."

She knew she could agree with him and that would be the end of the matter. That was what she'd learned to do with people who passed anonymously through their lives. She'd even perfected her smile when people said things like "I wish mine was that quiet."

"That's because he can't. Three years ago, when Sam was two, a car jumped the curb into a crowd of people leaving a minor league baseball game in Nashville, where we were living. That crowd included my husband and my son. Ryan was killed and Sam suffered a TBI." She cleared her throat. "Sorry, a TBI is—"

"Traumatic brain injury," Des interrupted. "I'm familiar with the term."

She glanced at Sam, who was still enamored with the snowmobile. "I'll spare you all the fancy medical jargon and say he understands words, but his brain can't plan and sequence the movements to say them. *Apraxia of speech* is the official term."

Des nodded. "And this hippotherapy you mentioned helps?"

"Not with speech but it helps with muscle memory and balance," she said. "Plus, he enjoys it. Being with the horses is more of a reward than just another therapy session like with the speech-language pathologists or physical therapy."

"Is that why you left in such a hurry yesterday?"

"Yeah, that's one appointment he doesn't like to miss. Sam, don't climb up there. It's—"

"It's fine. He won't hurt anything," Des interrupted and motioned to Sam. "You can sit on the seat if you want, bud."

Natalie tamped down the automatic protest that sprang up and pressed her lips together. It wasn't easy, but she needed to allow Sam room to explore. Smothering him only helped her, not him.

Des shifted his stance, bringing her attention back to him. She longed to ask what had happened to him, but politeness made her hold her tongue. Telling him she'd noticed his limp seemed a bit too forward, despite his mentioning Sam's lack of verbal skills. Her Southern mother had drilled proper manners into her with the zeal of Natalie's drill sergeant father. Plus, she was enjoying the sunshine on this final day in November. Not to mention being in the company of a male over the age of five. She didn't want to spoil either with awkward questions.

"Is he in school?"

She shook her head. "I held him back an extra year. You can do that with kindergarten. He still had a lot of weekly therapy sessions and he's made great strides in almost everything this year, which was why I felt comfortable enough to pick up and move here."

"So will he ever be able to…" Des trailed off and winced.

"Every individual's recovery is different." Even to herself, her answer sounded rote and unconvincing. "We're working with an AAC device. Sorry, that's his augmentative and alternative communication device. Ha, my dad was career army so I grew up with all those military acronyms, but I must say medical experts love them just as much."

"Ah, an army brat. That explains it." He weighed her with a critical squint.

She shifted under his scrutiny. "Explains what?"

"You have a slight accent, but I haven't been able to place it."

"Yeah, I guess my speech patterns are a mixture

of everywhere. My mom is from Georgia, so I have a bit of her accent but did my best to fit in wherever we were living at the time." Her stomach did a little fluttery thing. He'd tried to pick out her accent? That meant he'd thought about her. A little thing like that shouldn't please her as much as it did. *Why not?* her inner voice demanded, because she'd given him enough thought since yesterday. Des Gallagher had occupied a lot of headspace for such a brief meeting.

His face was impassive, but his gaze roamed over her. "Georgia? Huh, maybe that explains it."

"My accent?"

He shook his head. "Nope."

"Sorry? You've lost me." Her knees wobbled under his examination. What the heck was he on about?

"How old are you?"

"Twenty-six. Why?" She stood straighter. Despite a few silver strands threaded in his thick, lustrously black hair, he seemed no older than his midthirties. They were contemporaries.

He grunted. "There's eight years separating us. Hardly calls for you to *sir* me."

"When did I call you *sir*?" She couldn't recall a faux pas like that.

He rubbed the back of his scalp. "Yesterday. When you first walked in."

"You must have flustered me." *Should I be admitting that?* "Between my drill sergeant father and Southern mother, *sir* and *ma'am* comes naturally. I—I sometimes fall back on that if I feel like I've been put on the spot."

He swiped a hand across his mouth, his dark eyes amused. "In that case, I apologize for flustering you."

"Bless your heart, you can't help it," she said in a perfect imitation of her mother, not that he would know that.

His eyes narrowed in suspicion. "Am I detecting an insult in there somewhere?"

"If you are, then that's on you." Natalie shook her head, doing her best to look innocent. "Are you from Loon Lake?"

"Colorado. I settled here after leaving the navy three years ago."

Her gaze went to his white American foursquare home with its hip roof, black shutters and wide brick steps leading to the front entrance. The house seemed large for one person and she wondered if he'd planned to share it with someone when he'd invested in the property. Tavie had mentioned he lived alone. Again, not her business if he had a dozen girlfriends. "So have I changed your mind about those ornaments?"

"Not a chance, Ms. Pierce." He took a step back as if needing to put distance between them. "Don't waste your time on a lost cause."

Great. She'd managed to kill the camaraderie they'd shared moments ago. She plastered a smile on her face. "I gotta warn you. I'm a champion of lost causes. A regular St. Jude." Holding out her hand, she said, "Come along, Sam, I think we've taken up enough of Lieutenant Gallagher's time for one day."

Chapter Two

Des watched them walk away and felt…what? *Relief, that's what you feel.* He shook his head and limped toward the house. He didn't need or want a woman in his life, especially one with a child. Sam was a cute kid and seemed bright and curious, despite his lack of verbal skills. No, this had nothing to do with Sam. His reluctance was all down to Natalie. She was making him feel things, think about a future he'd given up wanting a long time ago.

Natalie's gingerbread men.

Halfway toward the house, he stopped. That plate of delicious cookies was still on his workbench. Heaving a sigh, he turned back toward the barn. Those were too good to take the chance of some critter getting them. He'd caught a crow hanging around the barn and had

had small items go missing from his workbench. No proof the bird was the thief but he had his suspicions. Yeah, that wasn't crazy or anything.

He retrieved his cookies, eating one on the way back to the house. In his mind's eye he could see Natalie's striking blue eyes, pert nose and Cupid's bow lips that kept forming a smile. From the first words she'd uttered, her voice had grabbed him in the gut…and elsewhere. *Damn.* He needed to stop thinking about the beautiful Natalie Pierce. A blind man could see she was a white-picket-fence-kids-dog-soccer-practice type of woman.

He might have had a similar dream once upon a time, but it died the day he had to punch out of his aircraft. Those three seconds, the most violent experience of his life, had changed the course of his future. That was the amount of time it had taken from pulling the lever until he was under the chute. A textbook low altitude ejection. Except for the part where his parachute lines had gotten twisted and he'd lost precious time correcting them while plummeting toward the earth.

He'd hit the ground hard, shattering his left leg and fracturing his spine. After two surgeries and endless months of PT, he'd regained his ability to walk but not to fly jets. Although Ashley had stuck by him during his recovery, once she realized he'd no longer be flying jets, she began voicing concerns over their engagement. She'd said perhaps they wanted different things from marriage. Evidently being married to him wasn't her dream so much as being the wife of an aviator. Any aviator.

As a last-ditch effort to salvage their relationship, he showed her the horse farm he'd stumbled across and had admired while visiting Riley Cooper in Loon Lake. Stupidly, he had thought maybe the beautiful family home and the prospect of having room for horses would appeal to her. At one time she'd claimed to be a horse lover, but she'd taken one look and said she hadn't signed on to live in small-town Vermont. The place wasn't even on Google Maps for heaven's sake. She'd thought after a career in the navy, he'd work for a major carrier, they'd live in a metropolitan area and would take advantage of all of the travel perks. Yeah, she'd had their future all planned out, except he wasn't sure where his wishes fit in.

Going into the house he'd gone ahead and purchased after their final split, he set the plate of cookies on the counter and slipped another one off the stack. He had a crazy thought that he would never confess under the threat of torture, but he swore he could taste the love Natalie put into her baking. He suspected she put her heart into everything she did. Sam, with his big grin, was proof of that. A woman like Natalie deserved someone who had a heart.

He glanced around at his state-of-the-art kitchen with its stainless-steel appliances, granite countertops and the off-white cabinets with glass inserts on the upper doors. The kitchen had been remodeled by the previous owner. When he and Ashley had toured the house, he'd figured the updated kitchen would be another point in his favor, but like everything else it had gone bust. So for the past three years, he'd rattled around in the immaculate kitchen using the refrigerator, microwave and coffeemaker.

Too bad he had nothing more than a dream kitchen to give a women like Natalie.

* * *

Des set the pliers back down. His new piece had stalled and it had nothing to do with the fact that Natalie hadn't returned for two days. Two days and no cookies, no pleas for him to make something for her auction. He'd listened for the sound of a car but all he heard was the silence. Silence was why he'd chosen this place. He liked silence. Huh, he and Sam would get along fine. It sure beat her chattering nonsense.

And he didn't care if Natalie's blue eyes reminded him of the adrenaline rush he'd gotten—and missed—when successfully landing his jet on the rolling deck of a carrier. He would've sworn there was nothing in the world to compete with going from one hundred and fifty miles an hour to nothing in the two seconds it took for the arresting wires to do their job. But looking into those clear eyes… He shook his head to shake some sense into it. What was he doing thinking that way about this woman? Hadn't he learned his lesson? First his mother, then Ashley. How long would it take for Natalie to see the flaws in him?

His mother still lived in Colorado, in the bungalow he'd grown up in. Although he dutifully called on a regular basis to see if she needed anything, the answer was always no. But he called anyway, just as he'd contacted the man who'd fathered him and been rebuffed. So he lived half a continent away and used his acres as a buffer between him and the rest of the world.

Disgusted with his unproductive thoughts, he got up and put another log into the woodstove in the corner of his work area. They'd had some unusually warm days at the end of November, a truly long autumn, but December had come, bringing much colder temperatures.

Back at his workbench, he held up the piece he'd cut this morning when he'd first come to his workroom. The curve of the glass still wasn't to his exacting standards. He'd have to redo it. Again. Maybe he should abandon adding the loon—except he'd gotten the idea the day Natalie had barged into his barn.

I follow through on my promises. Natalie's words, in that lilting, slightly husky voice, taunted him as he worked.

Yeah, right. Forty-eight hours and she hadn't been back. He tossed the piece of incorrectly cut glass into the box that held rejects. Those could be recycled and used another time. The pile had grown since yesterday, but he could use them in a future glass sculpture. Yeah, that was putting a good spin on the situation. He barely knew this woman and her absence for two days didn't give him the right to mope.

I'm a champion of lost causes. A regular St. Jude.

Maybe he was one lost cause too many. Maybe Natalie saw the same thing in him that his mother did so that no matter what he'd accomplished, it wasn't enough. It would never be enough because he wasn't his half brother. Though he and Patrick shared the same mother, they had different fathers. He chose another piece of glass, determined to get this one right. His muse had returned and he wasn't going to let a couple of mistakes stop him. He'd—

A car door slammed in the distance. He started to rise from the stool he'd been perched on but forced himself to sit back down. *What is wrong with you, Gal-*

lagher? He ground his back teeth, but deep down he enjoyed sparring with Natalie, enjoyed being the kind of guy who could attract a wholesome single mother, even if that was temporarily. Even if it was because she wanted something from him.

"Hello? Lieutenant?"

His heart thudded at the sound of her voice and he scowled, angered by his reaction. Making a fool of himself was not on today's agenda.

She appeared around the corner, her straight, blond hair billowing out behind her as if she were a model at a photo shoot. Once again she carried a tin in one hand and had a tight grip on Sam's hand with the other. The boy's bright blue eyes danced above ruddy cheeks as he held up a fistful of colorful candy canes and grinned. Des shifted in his seat and his throat clogged up with emotions at the sight of Natalie and her winsome son.

"Boy, it's windy today. Don't you think so?" she asked but didn't wait for an answer before rushing on. "Sorry we're late but we stopped at the store and well, you know how Tavie is. Talked our ears off, didn't she, Sam? Anyway, that's why we're so late today. Have you wondered where we were?"

Only for two freaking days. "No."

She stepped farther into the barn. "Sam's pediatric neurologist wanted a colleague to exam him, so we drove to Montpelier."

"What's there to do for two days in the state capital?" Damn. He hadn't meant to ask that and he detested the thread of need evident in his voice. What was that about not making a fool of himself?

"You'd be surprised at how much there is to do."

She gave him a blinding smile. "Maybe you should check it out."

"Humph."

"Grumpy again today? Maybe these will help." She set the tin on the bench. "I made you my special home-made minty shortbread cookies dipped in chocolate and topped with sprinkles. Sam put the Christmas sprinkles on them, didn't you, Sam?"

The boy grinned and nodded his head and Des bit back the snark that threatened to roll off his tongue. It wasn't Sam's fault he was such a dumbass around the boy's mother.

"Huh, maybe I should've asked if you liked mint before I inundated you with it, but I see you ate all the bark, so I guess that answers that."

She opened the tin and the scents of peppermint and chocolate wafted out. The green cookies were partially coated with chocolate and red, white and green sprinkles on top of that. They looked delicious, but Des scowled at them, refusing to be coaxed out of his mood by her or her baked goods.

"Problem?" Her gaze flicked between him and the cookies.

He fisted his hands to keep from reaching out and caressing her cute little frown. Or better yet, running his tongue over those furrows in her forehead. He swallowed a groan. "If I keep eating what you bring, I'm going to end up as a carnival sideshow."

She broke into a wide, candid smile, transforming her from attractive to unforgettable. "Didn't you get the memo? Calories don't count in December."

He grumbled but grabbed a cookie and took a bite,

closing his eyes as butter, mint and chocolate exploded in his mouth. These were the best yet. No doubt left, he was a goner.

Natalie gave him an expectant gaze. "What do you think?"

That I've died and gone to heaven. He shrugged. "They're pretty good."

"So…" She met his gaze. "Have you given any thought to making ornaments?"

"Yeah," he said and winced at the hopeful expression on her face. "The answer's still no, but—" he held up the half-eaten cookie "—I applaud your effort."

"Ah, you have a sweet tooth." She gave him a smile that had him wishing he was the kind of man she deserved. "Good to know."

"You can bring a whole bakery and the answer would still be no," he warned and grabbed another cookie. He did not need her getting under his skin any further. The fact that he'd been looking for her for the past two days rankled. And she never quite answered why she'd been gone that long. How many appointments did Sam have? *Yo, Gallagher, none of your business.* So why was he fixating on it? She didn't owe him an explanation, just as he didn't owe her one for refusing to make Christmas-themed glass art pieces.

"But don't you enjoy the feeling you get from doing a good deed?"

Give the lady points for tenacity. He shook his head. "It might alter people's expectations of me."

Instead of being cowed or annoyed by his surly attitude she seemed buoyed, ready to take on the challenge he represented. Des admired that. Yeah, admiration was a nice safe name for what he felt for Natalie Pierce.

"I must say, you're quite the conundrum."

"Really? I've always considered myself more of an enigma." He handed a cookie to Sam and winked. Sam grinned and bit the treat in half.

"Tell you what," Des said and popped the rest of the shortbread into his mouth, but it lost its appeal when her expression turned hopeful again. He was going to disappoint her, but he should be used to disappointing the women in his life. Not that she was *in* his life. Nope. He didn't do charming. Why did he always forget that around her? "I'll make a cash donation to this auction of yours."

"Thank you. And don't think I don't appreciate it, but we would have more earning potential if you made ornaments. More people would attend if we were able to advertise that we'd have your exclusive crafts. Ones that you can't get anywhere else. I don't want to seem ungrateful, but more people would be bidding on them and that would drive up the price."

"I thought it was a silent auction." He tilted his head and raised his eyebrows in a "gotcha" gesture.

Natalie stabbed her finger at him. "Okay, you got me there, but when people see all the bids piling up for your ornaments, they'd bid higher."

"Are you sure you're not overestimating my appeal?"

She blushed. "I don't think that's even possible."

His stupid heart did not stutter. What was he, fifteen? He cleared his throat. "You know I was referring to my art."

She gave him a wide-eyed, innocent expression, but

those baby blues shone with amusement. "Of course. That's what my answer was based on. What did *you* think I meant?"

Sam tugged on her sleeve and she glanced down. "You're right. It's getting late." She glanced up and met Des's gaze. "He has another hippotherapy session today."

He might not do charming, but he admired the heck out of the strong bond she had with Sam. "I wouldn't want him to miss that."

"Especially if it means getting rid of us, *hmm*?"

He held up his hands. Hey, even his jerkiness had its limits. "Honestly, I didn't mean it that way. You said he enjoyed the sessions."

"I was teasing," she said and laid her hand on his arm.

Incapable of speech, Des couldn't think of anything except that she was touching him. The warmth of her hand penetrating the flannel of his shirt had muddled his brain.

"Contrary to the popular consensus, I believe you have a lot buried under all that grumpiness, including a sense of humor." She squeezed his arm before letting her hand drop.

As reason returned and he became capable of speech once again, he lifted a finger and wagged it. "See? That's where you'd be wrong. I'm grumpy on the outside, morose and malcontented on the inside. Unlike you, I don't do optimism."

"Oh, my, you say *optimism* like it's a communicable disease." Her eyes sparkled. "And maybe I choose to see more in you."

He snorted a laugh. Damn, too bad he didn't do cute. Except that argument died a little more each time he saw her and soon that feeble excuse would be on life support. He shook his head and tried to arrange his face in a scowl, but for once those muscles refused to cooperate. His grin snapped back like a rubber band. "Then I seriously question your choices, Ms. Pierce."

"Question them all you want, but it won't change my opinion." Sam tugged on her sleeve again and she nodded to him. "I'll be seeing you soon."

He quirked an eyebrow. "Making threats again?"

She exited the barn, leaving behind her subtle lavender scent and the echo of her laughter. What would it be like to be in her orbit? To know her so well that silent communication was possible?

Des sighed and cut the piece again. This time the curve was perfect. "Coincidence," he muttered as he put the glass in place to create a loon rising from a lake. He believed in a lot of things but coincidence wasn't one of them. Which meant he was in a whole heap of trouble.

Standing, he stretched his back and took a sip of coffee from the insulated mug as he eyed the tin of cookies. He was going to have to add time to his workout regime if he kept this up much longer. He reached for another cookie.

"Umm… Des?"

His head snapped up to find Natalie and Sam still standing in the doorway of the barn. The smile that had started at the sight of her slipped when Sam sniffled as if he'd been crying. Des jumped up and nearly tripped when his leg protested.

"What's wrong? What happened? Is Sam okay?" His

heart pounding, he ignored the pain in his leg to get to them. "Did he get hurt?"

"He's okay… I'm okay…we're both fine." She waved her hand. "I didn't mean to alarm you. It's my car. It won't start. I could call Ogle Whatley's garage, but Sam's session would be over by the time Ogle came out here and fixed it."

Des exhaled, but his heart was still pounding. "Is that why he's crying? He doesn't want to miss his session?"

"I'm sorry. We didn't mean to frighten you." She appeared as distraught as her son. "I'm sure it must seem silly to you but—"

"It's not silly when you're five, is it, Sam?" He held out his hand to the boy. "Want to help me look for the jumper cables? I have some in my truck. If it's your battery, it won't take long to get you going. C'mon, Sam, let's go take a look."

He should resent having his work interrupted now that his muse was back, but the fact was, the sight of either one of them in distress made him want to help. And when Sam slipped his hand in his, Des had the urge to start whistling some stupid, sappy tune.

Natalie hung back as Des and Sam left the barn. She'd thought Des might be put out at having to help her, but he seemed strangely happy. *Don't read too much into it*, she cautioned herself. Maybe he didn't want to upset Sam. As gruff as Des tried to project, he'd been nothing but kind to Sam.

She followed them outside to where Des was pulling jumper cables from a locker in the bed of his pickup.

Sam was standing on his toes, trying to see. "Sam, please don't get in the lieutenant's way."

"Why don't you get back in the car?" she suggested. Sam frowned and she added, "You can watch him from your seat. I'll lower your window."

"I think your mom has a good idea, bud. You might even get a better view than standing on tiptoe," Des said.

After she made sure Sam was buckled into his car seat, she got in the driver's seat and lowered her window. Like son, like mother? She shook her head, but couldn't help gawking as Des leaned over the hood of her Camry to hook the jumper cables to her dead battery. To prevent drooling, she ordered herself to think about the cost of a new battery—and at Christmastime—instead of how luscious his butt looked, caressed by all that faded denim. But it wasn't just his glutes making her mouth water. The stubble that peppered his face, the two-haircuts-past-due thick, black hair and the intense dark brown eyes all sent her pulse racing.

"Natalie?" Des asked, his tone laced with impatience.

Nothing like getting caught daydreaming about the super-hot naval officer. How many times had he called her name? "Sorry. What?"

"I'm going to start my engine and I'll let you know when to try yours again. Wait for my signal."

She nodded and he went to his truck. Once they got her car started, he came back and removed the cables, rolling them up as he walked toward his pickup. She was glad to see that his limp wasn't as pronounced today.

Grabbing the roll of paper towels she had on the passenger seat, Natalie tore off a few. He came back to her car, and she offered him the towels through her open window.

"Thanks." He wiped his hands. "Stay here while I shut the barn door."

"Why?" She checked her watch. Sam's session would be starting soon. "What are you doing?"

"I'm going to follow you and make sure you make it to the therapy place." He spoke as if his actions were a given.

His concern brought delicious warmth to her insides. Again making her yearn for something she hadn't even realized was missing from her current existence. Okay, maybe she'd realized it, but she'd been ignoring the vague discontent. *There's nothing missing. You have a full, satisfying life,* she repeated to herself. And she did. So what if she hadn't dated in the three years since Ryan's death? Sam had been her top priority during that time. Ryan's generous life insurance payout gave her financial stability and the nursery school in Nashville where she'd been employed part-time had permitted Sam to attend free of charge. Here in Loon Lake she'd met Mary Wilson through volunteering at the weekly payment-optional luncheons at the church. When the Wilsons' summer camp cook had taken ill, she'd stepped in. The Wilsons had also allowed her to bring Sam and even invited her back next summer.

Full life or not, since meeting Des she'd wondered if she had room for more. Something more. Or rather, some*one* more. And that was disconcerting.

She stuck her head out the car window. "I'm sure we'll be fine. I've already taken up too much of your time."

He shook his head, his dark hair falling across his forehead. "Unless you plan on letting the car run the entire time you're there, you might need another jump."

She fought the urge to brush his hair back, to touch it to see if it felt as soft as it looked. "That wouldn't be good for the environment, would it?"

"No, ma'am, it wouldn't."

She snickered at his use of *ma'am*. "Aha, I see what you did there."

"So it's settled. I'll follow you."

She'd love for him to come along, but she didn't want him to see her and Sam as a nuisance. Yeah, as if he didn't already, considering the way she'd barged into his life with her demands for Christmas ornaments.

He crossed his arms over his chest. "Besides, aren't you the one trying to convince me to support this enterprise?"

That did make sense. "Are you saying you might be so overcome by what you see, you'll do whatever I ask?"

Des dropped his arms and snorted a laugh. "Too late for that."

A flush of warmth spread through her and she couldn't contain her grin. Was he saying he felt an attraction, too? Was that a possibility? Des might act all gruff and surly but she suspected beneath all that he was a caring man bent on protecting himself. *Don't go spinning fairy tales*, she cautioned herself. Des might be a case of WYSIWYG—What You See is What You Get. Yeah, the problem with rainbow optimism was that you often got your heart broken.

On her wedding day, she'd assumed they'd happily grow old together, but two years later a stranger's careless actions had taken Ryan from them and changed the course of their lives in an instant. Because of it, Sam would have to grow up without his dad.

Ryan had convinced her to drop out of college when Sam was born. He'd had a decent paying job at a tech start-up in Nashville so her degree hadn't been a priority then. Now she understood how short-sighted she'd been.

As much as she needed optimism, facing reality was key to planning for the future.

She waited for Des to come back and climb into his truck before she put the car in gear and made her way to the therapy center.

Conflicting thoughts vied for space in her head during the drive to the stable. She hardly knew Des. Or what had happened to make him keep the world at arm's length. Few wounds healed without permanent scars. She'd have to be crazy to even try bringing him out of his self-imposed exile. She had enough on her plate with Sam, finishing her degree and starting a career, as opposed to the lower-paying jobs she'd had since Ryan's death.

Last year, she'd inherited her grandmother's summer home, a duplex in Loon Lake. After careful deliberation, Natalie had decided not to sell the place, but to move to the quaint town she'd remembered and loved from childhood visits.

Thanks to the inheritance she lived mortgage-free plus collected rent from the tenant on the other side of the two-family home. That monthly rent paid her utility bills and helped with upkeep. With Ryan's generous life insurance payout, she'd been able to spend time with Sam when he'd needed her during his recovery and rehabilitation. But now was the time for a concrete plan for their future. Finishing her degree so she could get a decent job was the first step. She'd set aside a portion of the life insurance for Sam's college fund and had refused to draw from it. Next year, when Sam started school, she'd have more time to devote to online studies or attend classes at the nearest university.

She pulled into the packed earth parking lot of the hippotherapy center and chose two spots together in case Des needed to jump-start her car again. She smiled. It was nice to think someone had her back. Even though she'd lived in Loon Lake for a short time, many of the residents remembered her grandmother and were friendly and helpful, treating her as if she'd lived there all her life. But it would be nice to know she had someone more permanent to share life's ups and downs with. What was she doing? She barely knew this man, so no more spinning fairy tales.

Once the auction benefitting the equine therapy center was over, maybe she could still take baked goods to Des. *And maybe he'd have to take out a restraining order on me.* She laughed at herself as she turned off her engine and got out and opened the rear door. Sam scrambled out of the car and she held out her hand. He dutifully took it, but she knew the day was coming when he'd refuse to comply. She'd gotten into the habit of insisting on holding his hand because he couldn't answer if she called to him.

He'd gotten away from her once when he darted under a rack of clothes in a department store. She'd frantically called to him, despite knowing he couldn't answer. After five agonizing minutes that felt like fifty, she'd found him, but from that day forward she'd insisted he hold her hand in public. She suspected that his seeing her anguished tears that day had scared him and he hadn't fought holding her hand since then.

Turning to Des, who'd parked and was getting out of his truck, she said, "I'm going to take Sam in to get saddled up. Over there by the fence is the perfect spot to watch his session."

He nodded and she took off toward the barn with Sam.

Des leaned against the fence and studied the dirt arena where the sessions were held. He'd used his laptop the second day Natalie had visited to look up information about how hippotherapy worked. At the time he'd justified learning more about it because he'd planned to give Natalie a cash donation for her auction. It had nothing to do with wanting to learn more about the woman who'd barged into his life with an endless supply of chatter and baked goods. But it wasn't the sweets that had invaded his dreams every night. She and her crooked-toothed smile, her big blue eyes and that sweet voice had kept him company the past few nights.

He caught movement in his peripheral vision and turned as Natalie made her way over to him. His heart kicked as it always did when he saw her, but her face lacked its usual sunny expression. The sight of her distress was like a blow to the chest with a two-by-four.

He wanted to reach out but forced himself to stand still, keeping his arms along the fence to keep from pulling her into his arms and crushing her against him. "What's wrong?"

She heaved a sigh. "I found out the program's financial situation is worse than I thought. The owner is close to being evicted from this place."

"If they lose the lease, what will happen to the horses?" he asked, her unhappiness weighing on him.

"I don't know. But without the horses, getting the lease paid up-to-date or getting the business on sound financial footing won't matter. This place relies a lot on volunteers, but there are two part-time employees, in addition to the owners, who would be affected. I'd hate for anyone to lose their job. Not to mention, the nearest therapy center is three hours away." Her bottom teeth scraped her upper lip in what appeared to be a nervous habit. "Driving that far for twice-weekly sessions would be out of the question."

He shoved aside his urge to soothe that lip with his tongue. He needed to concentrate on practical matters, like finding out what sort of business operation was Natalie getting involved in? "How did this place get into such a financial bind to begin with?"

She gave him a sharp look. Yeah, his tone had been gruffer than he'd planned, but he didn't want her getting hurt. Financial or otherwise.

"From what I understand, the owners are going through a contentious divorce," she said.

"So raising money might not even help?" His instinct was to interfere in order to safeguard Natalie and Sam. But he had no right to feel the protective feelings that rose up. They'd known one another a short time. They weren't even friends, just acquaintances.

"I had hoped raising funds would keep the horses safe and in place until something better could be figured out." She waved at Sam, who was smiling proudly as he sat on his horse.

Sam looked at ease atop a seal-brown gelding with one white rear leg. Des considered Sam a sunny, happy child, and he could see how much pleasure he got from riding the horse.

Des cleared his throat. Did he want to bring this up? It was none of his business, but he'd be damned if he stood by and let her be harmed in any way. "You haven't done anything other than organize this auction, have you?"

Her head snapped back and she narrowed her eyes. "What do you mean?"

"I'm talking about infusing this place with cash…as in, your own cash." He curled his hands into fists on top of the cross posts for the fence, waiting for her answer.

She shook her head and raised a hand. "I would never ever do anything to jeopardize Sam's future by putting money into a failing enterprise. And I don't appreciate the inference that I would."

He took her hands in his and winced at how cold they were. He rubbed them to try to warm them up. "I'm not accusing you of anything, Natalie. I wanted to understand what we're dealing with."

"Thanks. I've had a lot of support from family and friends ever since the accident, but sometimes, late at night when I'm alone, I second-guess all my decisions." She grimaced. "I didn't mean to snap, but sometimes guilt—warranted or not—makes me a bit defensive."

He squeezed her hands. "I was worried about you pouring your own cash into a dying business."

"No chance of that." She shook her head and visibly relaxed. "I've been extremely frugal with our finances. I take my obligation to Sam seriously. I want him to be happy, but not to the point where I might jeopardize his future. I'm the parent and need to make the hard decisions."

He let go of her hands. He barely knew Natalie so his relief at her answer was disproportionate to the situation. If she wanted to go bankrupt supporting a failing business that was her problem, but he admired her fierce protectiveness toward her son. As a kid, he would've given anything to have had a mother like Natalie. Heck, he would've been thankful for one who'd taken any interest at all. He cleared his throat. "What if nothing can be figured out?"

She frowned. "Are you always such a pessimist?"

"I'm a realist. I would think you'd be one, too." He regretted the words as soon as they were out of his mouth. "Look, Natalie, I—"

"No, you're probably right." She turned to face the dirt track and Sam. "But I can't think that way. I have to choose optimism. If that's rainbows and unicorns, then so be it."

When he didn't respond, she brought her gaze back to him. "No comeback about my choices?"

He gave in to his urge, running his fingers across her cheek and tucking strands of silky hair behind her ear. "No glib comebacks. Sam's one lucky guy to have you for his mother. Not all mothers practice the kind of unconditional love you have."

"I like to think I'm the lucky one." She smiled at Sam before turning her gaze back to Des. "So you believe not all mothers practice unconditional love? What makes you believe that?"

"I know they don't," he said, thinking of his own. He'd always known Patrick was the golden child but it wasn't until after his brother's death that—

She cupped her hand around his cheek. He should pull away because it wasn't just her mothering he admired. How could she be offering comfort after his callous remark? What kind of woman did that? He leaned into her touch. What would it be like to pull her into his arms, let her warmth sink into those cold places inside him?

She started to pull her hand away, but he reached up and captured it in his. "I apologize for my comment. I may be an insensitive jerk but normally I practice my antisocial tendencies when I'm alone and especially not when I'm in the company of a beautiful woman."

"Apology accepted." She blushed. "After his session, Sam and I always go to the café in town. I hope you'll join us. I want to thank you for getting my car started."

"You should go straight to the garage and have Ogle check the battery. Your old one may not even have kept the charge."

"You're right," she said and frowned. "I know I should've gone straight to Ogle's but…" She turned her head to watch Sam, a tender expression on her pretty face.

He studied her profile as Sam and his horse continued to be led around the ring. Sam grinned and waved to them each time he passed. Des waved, but his attention was on the woman beside him.

"I see how much he enjoys riding," he said.

"He's calmer since he's started spending time with

the horses." Her voice sounded resigned. "We've had our ups and downs. He gets frustrated and can be quick to anger but being around the horses soothes him."

He reached for her hand again. "And what soothes you?"

"Me?" She stared at him, surprised. "I don't think anyone has ever asked me that."

"Maybe they should." He touched her cheek with his other hand. "So tell me what you find soothing."

She looked off in the distance as if trying to decide how to answer.

"I bet I know." His hand moved from her cheek to her hair, unable to resist touching the corn-silk strands.

"Oh? What do you think it is?" she asked, sounding a little breathless.

He contemplated, stalling for time. Then something occurred to him. "Baking. I'll bet baking soothes you."

She seemed to be thinking it over, her gaze meeting his. "I believe you're right, but how did you know?"

He cleared his throat and broke eye contact, glancing at Sam on the horse. "I can taste it."

Before she could say anything, he pointed to Sam, whose horse was being led back into the building. "Looks like he's finished."

To his relief, her focus shifted back to her son. He was not about to admit his feelings about her baking.

After his session, Sam came out from the building and carefully made his way toward them. His gait was slightly stiff, but a huge grin split his face.

"You looked like a jockey up there on that horse, bud," Des told him and held out his hand, palm up. The kid slapped it and although it seemed impossible, Sam's smile got even bigger. What was it about this boy and his mother that called to Des?

"You did great, Sam, but I'm afraid I have some bad news for you. We won't be able to go to the café like I promised. I need to take the car to Ogle's garage for a new battery. We can get some snacks at Tavie's store while we wait if you're hungry."

Even though the Loon Lake General Store was next door to Ogle's garage, Des didn't think a few packaged snacks were as much fun as going to Aunt Polly's Café. And he was right; the boy's face fell. "You like Polly's pancakes, don't you?"

Sam grinned up at him and nodded his head vigorously.

Natalie's eyes widened. "How did you know that's what he always orders?"

"Because having pancakes when it's not breakfast is fun, right, Sam?"

Again, the boy grinned and nodded. Des answered with a wink.

Natalie put her hand on Sam's shoulder. "I'm not sure how long it will take for the battery to be replaced, if that's even what's wrong. The café is only open for breakfast and lunch, but we'll try."

Des cleared his throat. "I have an idea. I'll follow you to the garage and we'll go to Aunt Polly's while Ogle is checking out your car." What was he doing? Did he suggest they go to eat? As in *together*? As in a public place? Not only would he be seen in public, but also with a woman *and* her son. Gossip would be flying from one end of town to the other.

She turned to Des, her eyes wide. "Are you sure you don't mind?"

No, he wasn't sure, but he wasn't about to change his mind and disappoint Sam. But it wasn't just about Sam, was it? He wanted to spend time with Natalie, plain and simple. But could he do that without falling under her spell? And he had no doubts this woman could cast a spell. So he'd take them to lunch, make a donation to her charity and that would be the end of it. He could handle that, right? It wasn't as if he was getting involved with her or anything. She'd have her car fixed, Sam would have his pancakes and afterward Des would go back home and things would return to normal. "I don't mind. Let's go and see if your car will start."

Her car did need another jump. Good thing he'd insisted on coming with her. In a town like Loon Lake she wouldn't have been stranded for long, but he didn't like the idea of her stranded at all. Yeah, because he was a regular Dudley Do Right. His sudden altruism had nothing to do with his burgeoning feelings for Natalie... right?

Chapter Three

As soon as Des walked into the café with Natalie and Sam, he knew he'd made a grave tactical error. The other customers did a double take at the sight of the three of them together. Natalie was popular and well-liked because everyone smiled and waved or nodded to her. He could see the reputation he'd cultivated as someone unapproachable crumbling before his eyes.

A short, blond waitress pointed to a booth. "Be right with you folks."

Once they were seated, Natalie pulled a small packet of crayons out of her purse along with a pad of paper and handed them to Sam. Reaching back into the voluminous bag, she set a miniature car next to the pad. Sam began drawing a picture of the toy.

She glanced up and caught Des watching her. "What?"

"Just wondering what else you have in there." Des hitched his chin toward her humongous bag.

Wiggling her eyebrows, she grinned. "Wouldn't you like to know."

He shook his head and chuckled. "That's one challenge I'm not crazy enough to take on. I know that a woman's purse is sacrosanct. You do not touch without permission."

Amusement flickered in her eyes. "Someone taught you well."

"Any woman I've ever known has always said 'get my purse' instead of 'look in my purse.'"

She laughed. "Yeah. I guess you're right."

"Of course I am. Don't you agree, Sam?"

Sam looked at him, then his mom. When he turned back, his expression said he knew better than to get involved. Des couldn't hide his grin.

Her gaze bounced around the restaurant. "Do you have any idea why everyone is staring at us? Sam and I come here every week and that's never happened before."

He shrugged. "I can't say for sure, but I'll bet it's because you're with me."

"Oh." She swallowed. "So you're…like more famous than I thought."

He bit back his laugh and shook his head. "*Infamous* is more like it. I bet they're all wondering what the heck a nice girl like you is doing with someone like me."

"Now, why would they be thinking that?" she asked, her face suffused with color.

Des loved seeing that flush, knowing he'd put it there. If he wasn't careful, he'd be getting in deeper than he intended. But when she looked at him like that, he found it impossible to stop teasing.

He shrugged. "You said it yourself. I cloak myself in grumpiness like it's a virtue."

She blushed again. "I shouldn't have said that. I apologize."

"Why? Have you changed your mind about my behavior?"

"No, but I've changed my mind about calling you out on it." She gave him an impish smile that once again melted his resolve. "My mother would be appalled at my being so openly rude."

He quirked an eyebrow. "But it's acceptable if you hide it?"

"My mother definitely would have preceded any insult with 'bless your heart,' Lieutenant."

"And that would mean?"

"That you couldn't help your behavior." She leaned across the table. "Bless your heart. I just love how you don't care what people think."

He barked a laugh and swore that a hushed silence descended on the whole place as if everyone else was holding their breath. Damn, he was ruining his reputation.

The waitress who'd pointed them to the booth appeared with a tray containing two ruby-red pebbled plastic tumblers filled with water. She also had a white disposable cup with a cover and a straw, which she handed to Sam. "Hey, little man, welcome back. And I see you've brought a new friend with you today. I often wondered what it would take to get our resident hermit into town." She set the glasses on the table. "What did you two have to threaten him with to get him here? As far as I know, he'd never come here willingly. And smiling about it, too."

Des rolled his eyes and shook his head, but winked when Sam caught him.

"Hi, Trudi," Natalie greeted the waitress. "Most people don't know this about me, but I was a lion tamer before I had Sam."

Trudi held the empty tray across her chest and looked Des up and down. "Nah. This one is more grizzly than lion, if you ask me."

"Then maybe it's a good thing no one is asking you," Des said. Being with Natalie and Sam may have stunted his gruffness, but he couldn't let Trudi's comment pass without a response.

Trudi blew out her breath and grinned. "Is he always this entertaining?"

Natalie gave him a smile that increased his heart rate, then said, "I wouldn't be here with him if he wasn't."

If he wasn't careful he'd start grinning like a lovesick idiot. How the heck had she gotten him to do any of this? He glanced across the booth at Natalie and scowled. If he wasn't careful, he might start thinking he could still have the happy ending he'd dreamed about once upon a time.

Natalie shifted in her seat in the café across from Des, who was scowling at her. He seemed to do that every time she thought she'd drawn him out of his grumpy self. Was he angry with her for the quips with the waitress? No, he had a sharp sense of humor buried under all the surliness. Maybe that scowl was a defense mechanism like her fake smile when people commented on Sam's lack of verbal skills.

"Is Sam wanting his usual?" Trudi asked into the sudden silence. She stood poised to take their orders, pencil in one hand, pad in the other.

Sam frowned and pointed at Des, who looked to her with a helpless expression and Natalie had to clear the sudden clog in her throat.

"I think he wants you to order first." She'd grown accustomed to deciphering Sam's wants and needs, but Des seemed lost. She wanted a male role model in Sam's life, but she needed one that wouldn't simply be passing through. She needed to be careful Sam didn't get his heart broken. She made a mental note to see if Loon Lake had any sort of a Big Brother program.

"What's Sam's usual?" Des asked the waitress.

"Malted pancakes with warm maple syrup and a dollop of whipped cream on top," Trudi said.

Des turned to Sam. "You recommend that?"

Sam gave him a thumbs-up.

"Sounds perfect. I'll have that." Des handed the menu back to the waitress and nodded to Sam. "You have good taste."

Relieved by the easy exchange between Des and Sam, Natalie laughed as she handed the menus back. "What the heck, it's the holidays. Make it three."

"I have it on good authority that calories don't count in December," Des said after the waitress had scurried away.

"So my chatter isn't all background buzz for you. Good to know." She was teasing, but on some deeper level she was serious. Not that she'd ever admit it to him. Nor did she want to admit that she cared about what he thought.

He grunted. "You do tend to talk a lot." He glanced at Sam, then met her gaze. "But I guess it's understandable."

She swallowed against the sudden burn in the back of her eyes. Reaching over, she took a sip of water to collect her thoughts before speaking. "We've been practicing communicating with his iPad, haven't we, Sam?"

Sam scrunched his nose and shook his head before going back to his crayons and paper. Natalie looked out the window at the Christmas wreaths hanging from the lampposts lining Main Street. She loved how the town exuded Christmas spirit and in times like this she was glad she'd moved to Loon Lake to raise Sam. Even if living here meant driving an hour or two for appointments with specialists in pediatric neurology. But in the end, what if she'd been wrong to move away from all that Nashville had to offer Sam? Was she doing right by her child? Or simply doing what she wanted?

A warm, callused hand squeezed hers and interrupted her brooding. She lifted her head and her gaze collided with deep brown eyes.

"Recovery's not always a straight line. It doesn't mean you've done anything wrong," Des said softly.

It was as if he'd read her mind, recognized her self-doubt. Was that one of the many reasons she was drawn to him? Did it have to do with his hiding pain the way she did? She knew all about that. Natalie had meant it when she said she chose to be cheerful and optimistic, but that didn't mean that she didn't have her doubts when she was trying to fall asleep at night.

Des chose to mask his pain behind a gruff exterior. She didn't know what had happened to him but she suspected his limp had to do with the end of his naval career. Why had she never asked him? Scolding herself for being so selfish, she said, "Thank you. I—"

"And here we go, malted pancakes with whipped cream." Trudi stopped at the end of the booth with her tray. The plates were piled high with pancakes topped with mounds of whipped cream.

Des removed his hand from hers, but Natalie knew his gesture had piqued Trudi's interest. Yup, she and Des would be the next hot topic of conversation and endless speculation. She may not have been in Loon Lake long, but she knew how small-town gossip worked.

Trudi set the tray down and passed out the plates before putting a clear glass syrup dispenser in the middle of the table. "And warm maple syrup. The best part, right, Sam? If you need anything else, let me know." The waitress wiped her hands on her apron. "And if Sam here needs a refill on these pancakes, it's on the house."

"You've got a sweet deal here, Sam," Des said and gave him a thumbs-up.

Sam grinned. Natalie's stomach fluttered and she mouthed "thank you" to Des over Sam's head as he bent over his plate to dig into his pancakes. His questioning expression told her he wasn't sure why she was thanking him. But then, neither was she. Perhaps it was that she appreciated the way he treated Sam. Or could it be the way he treated *her*?

She and Des talked about the hippotherapy center and the horses while they ate. Des did his best to include Sam by asking direct questions that her son could answer with a nod or shake of the head. By the time they'd finished the pancakes, her admiration of Des Gallagher had increased twofold. And not just because of the way he treated Sam. She wasn't so naive as to think her feelings only had to do with her son.

Trudi came back to the table and asked Sam if he needed more, but he shook his head and patted his stomach.

"You folks will need to walk off all those calories. You three might want to go across the square to Libby Taylor's quilt and craft shop," Trudi said as she collected their empty plates and stacked them, piling the utensils on top with a *cling-clang*. "I hear Libby's setting up one of those miniature Christmas villages in the front window complete with a train." She juggled the dirty plates against her chest and slapped the bill facedown on the table. "I'll bet Sam will love the train."

Sam's eyes widened and he looked toward Des. Sam didn't have to say anything because the pleading look on his face said it all.

Natalie's scalp prickled at the thought of Sam looking to Des for permission after having her son to herself for three years. Of course she didn't want to limit Sam's world, but neither did she want him to get his heart broken. She couldn't protect him from all of life's hurts, but as a mother she had to at least try.

"It's up to your mom," Des said in a neutral tone.

She tried to gauge how Des felt about going to see the window display. He'd made it pretty clear how much he disliked Christmas.

"You're probably champing at the bit to get back

home. If you don't want to go, I can bring him some other time," she said, giving Des an out if he wanted one.

His brow furrowed as he seemed to be thinking it over. "What I have waiting at home will still be there tomorrow. We'll settle up here and head on over before we go to pick up your car. How's that sound to you, Sam?"

Sam looked as though he was imitating a bobble-head doll.

"Okay." She had a feeling she looked as excited as her son but for different reasons. Nope, it wasn't a ceramic village with a train that she found so appealing but a handsome six-foot-two former navy lieutenant.

She reached for the bill, but Des was faster and scooped it up. "My treat."

"But I invited you so I should pay." She held out her hand.

He gave her his usual scowl and held the bill close to his chest. "When I go to a restaurant with a woman, I like to pay."

"You're not going turn out to be some sort of misogynist, are you?"

He grinned. "Nah, just old-fashioned."

Impulsively, she reached over and brushed her hand across his arm. It wasn't skin-to-skin contact but it proved as powerful to her psyche. "In that case, Sam and I thank you, don't we, Sam?"

As Des paid, she made sure Sam's jacket was zipped up and cautioned him to put his mittens on. Her son gave a long-suffering sigh but put them on.

"They were talking about snow by the end of the week," she remarked as the three of them left the restaurant.

"Glad someone is excited for it." Des chuckled as he zipped up his distressed leather bomber jacket.

She gripped Sam's hand as they crossed the street, but let go when they reached the paved path that led through the town green. He ran a little ahead of them. She and Des strolled side by side along the walkway that meandered through the park. Birds chirped in the pine and aspen trees and squirrels darted about, gathering food as if they'd all listened to the same weather forecast predicting snow.

"Does the weather bother your leg?" she asked.

"Only when I walk."

"Oh, dear, then maybe we shouldn't—"

He bumped shoulders with her. "I was joking. Walking is good. Keeps it limber."

"Does it get stiff often?" she asked, her gaze on Sam as he walked ahead, his arm outstretched at a ninety degree angle with the toy car as if it was driving through the green.

Des made a strange sound, a cross between a laugh and a cough, but hadn't answered her question, so she turned toward him. "I was asking if— Oh."

He was rubbing his hand over his mouth, his deep brown eyes full of humor.

She choked back her hoot of embarrassed laughter, not wanting to attract Sam's attention. She gave an exasperated sniff. "You do know I was asking about your leg?"

He nodded, his lips twitching. "Of course. What else could you have meant?"

"I think that sense of humor you do your best to hide has a wide streak of juvenileness running through it."

He bumped his shoulder against hers. "I think juvenile humor attaches itself to the Y chromosome."

"I think you're right." She bumped him back. "Ryan's humor could be juvenile at times."

"Ryan's your late husband?"

Damn. Bringing him up couldn't be a good idea, but she'd started to feel comfortable with Des. "Yeah, but maybe I shouldn't have brought him up. Didn't mean to cast a pall over everything."

He shook his head. "You didn't. He was a part of your life and you shouldn't have to apologize for saying his name."

"Thanks." She sighed. "Next year he will have been gone longer than we were married. What about you? Have you ever been married?"

He stared straight ahead. "Came close once."

"Oh?" She tilted her head to look at him, wanting to know more, and yet, not.

"I dodged a bullet there." He stuck his hands in his jacket. "She seemed to think pilots were interchangeable."

Did he still care for her, mourn the end of their relationship? This mystery woman from his past might have changed *her* mind about marrying Des but that didn't necessarily follow that he had. "I'm sorry."

He gave her a curious look. "Why? You had nothing to do with it."

She chuckled. "Sor— Um, I must warn you, along with all my other shining qualities, I'm a knee-jerk apologist."

"As far as faults go, that is one I could live with," he

said. Then, as if realizing what he'd said, he cleared his throat. "So how did you come to settle in Loon Lake?"

"I inherited a duplex from my grandmother. I remembered visits to Loon Lake from my childhood and decided to come back as an adult before I decided what to do with the home."

"Obviously, you liked what you saw."

She smiled broadly. "I did. Took one look at Main Street and fell in love. After living in so many different places growing up, I felt as though I'd come home. And the people are so friendly and caring. So how did you end up here?"

He scrunched one side of his face and closed one eye. "Because the people are so friendly?"

She burst out laughing and bumped shoulders with him. "Juvenile or not, you have a wonderful sense of humor."

"Glad you think so." He chuckled, then grew serious. "Actually, I met Riley Cooper at Walter Reed and he mentioned he was coming here for R&R, so I decided to check it out."

"I know Riley's wife, Meg. I've volunteered a few times at the weekly luncheon at the church—" she motioned toward the soaring steeple at the end of the town green "—and she mentioned he'd been in the marines before they got married."

"Yeah, he came and basically never left. Got married, started a family and now he's a sheriff's deputy for Loon Lake."

"So you're friends with Riley?" Had Des wanted

with his ex-girlfriend the happy family that Riley now had with Meg?

"Not really. He mentioned Loon Lake and since I didn't have anywhere else to go…" He turned away and kicked a small stone.

Having no ties to anything was sad, but she decided not to call him out and embarrass him. She'd had a rootless childhood, so she knew the feeling of not belonging to any one place, but she'd had her parents to anchor her. They weren't a location but they represented home to her. Perhaps that was why she'd wanted to raise Sam in Loon Lake, give him some deep roots to fall back on. "You couldn't have picked a better place than Loon Lake. And I must say, you have a beautiful home."

"Yeah, I had thought that maybe Ashley would change her mind about a future with me when she saw it."

So the former fiancée had a name. Ashley. And it sounded as if maybe he did want what Riley had. Natalie had a love/hate relationship with a woman she'd never met. She hated her for hurting Des, and yet if she hadn't, he might now be a married man and not sharing this pleasant day with her. "Then it's her loss. Your house is gorgeous." She touched his arm. Sensing his withdrawal, she searched for a lighter tone. "Of course, I haven't been inside. The interior could be hideous."

Her deflection worked, because he chuckled again. "Not hideous. Perhaps a bit sparse. I spend most of my time in the workshop in the barn."

"Have you worked with stained glass for a long time?"

"I was interested in all forms of art before—" He stopped, then cleared his throat. "A long time ago, and did some projects during my recovery and continued to work on them after I left the navy. I kept on when I found out people were willing to pay money for them."

Before what? What had he been about to say? They were reaching the end of the path and Sam was getting close to the road, so she didn't pursue it. "Sam, wait for us."

Des was glad she didn't press him about what he'd been about to say. He never talked about the loss of Patrick. Maybe that was wrong. Maybe he should be more like Natalie, who talked about her late husband.

They'd caught up to Sam, who was waiting on the sidewalk that bordered the town square, and crossed the street together. Sam hadn't even tried to dart into the street, but Des understood that was Natalie's fear. What had happened to Sam must have increased her fears.

Natalie motioned with her hand. "Libby's shop is right down there. The one with the navy blue awning in the middle of the block."

Sam pocketed his toy car and hustled ahead of them toward the shop.

He tipped his head in her direction. "Don't tell me you make quilts as well as all that delicious baking?"

"I'm a woman of many talents." Her teasing smile was dazzling.

Catching his breath, he leaned closer to whisper, "Mmm…tell me more."

She turned to face him and her eyes sparkled with

mischief. "Isn't a woman supposed to preserve some mystery?"

He gave her a mock scowl. "That's the way you're going to play it?"

"I am." She nodded firmly but her lips twitched. "For now."

He shifted so his arm brushed against hers. "That sounds promising."

They reached the shop and Sam had his nose pressed to the window, watching a small train chug along a wooden track.

"He's into trains," she said. "And planes and fire trucks, police cars, race cars. You name it. He's hoping Santa Claus will bring him a big LEGO set, but he can't decide between an airport or a fire station or police station."

Sam tugged on Natalie's sleeve and pointed to Des.

An expression Des couldn't read flitted across her face before she said, "I think he wants to know which one you'd pick."

Des chuckled. "I'd pick the airport for obvious reasons, but they all sound exciting and you should ask for the one you want the most."

Sam seemed to consider this advice, then nodded and went back to watching the train run through the miniature village.

"Were you always interested in flying?" she asked.

"My older brother had the dream first. I guess it rubbed off." He left out the part about how he'd tried and failed to fill Patrick's shoes after his brother's death. Even before then, though, he hadn't measured up in his mother's eyes. And he knew how his biological father felt. Despite the man's lack of interest when he was growing up, Des had still reached out as an adult. But his father had felt responding to his own child wasn't important enough, since it might jeopardize his marriage. He pushed the past away, wanting to enjoy this day with Natalie.

"I'm glad you got to fly, even if it did come to an end." She touched his arm. "You should be proud of what you accomplished."

Huh, maybe she had a point. He'd spent a lot of time thinking about what he'd lost and not enough on what he'd done. A weight near his chest shifted and eased at her admiring tone. "Thanks." And he found he meant it.

He stood close enough so the slightest movement from either one caused them to brush against one another, close enough to breathe in her scent. And close enough to be in her orbit, if only for a short time. He pretended to watch the train chugging along a track, weaving between colorful ceramic houses and businesses, but he was concentrating on Natalie, attuned to her slightest movement.

"Oh, look, Sam," Natalie said and pointed to a poster taped to a lower corner of the plate glass window. "They're going to have a tree-lighting ceremony. Remember that big evergreen we passed in the park near the gazebo? They're going to light it up for Christmas. That sounds like fun."

Sam nodded and looked over to Des. She threw him an apologetic look over Sam's head.

"I think he wants you to come with us," she said.

68   THE SCROOGE OF LOON LAKE

He was caught off guard and hesitated.

She put her arm around Sam's shoulders. "How about we let the lieutenant think it over? It's not until the weekend."

Sam nodded but kept shooting him furtive glances as they started to walk back toward the green.

"I apologize if Sam put you on the spot by inviting you to the town tree-lighting," she said after they'd crossed the street.

"No problem. I'm flattered that he wanted me to go with you guys."

"Well, you're welcome to come but don't feel bad if you choose not to. There'll be lots of people there that I know."

Did she not want him to go with them? After all, the invitation had come from Sam. But it had come via Natalie. Could she have interpreted Sam's request to coincide with her wants? "Yeah. You've met more people in three months than I've met in three years."

"I'm not the town's hermit," she pointed out with a grin.

"Me? Really?" He'd never cared what the townspeople called him or thought of him...until now.

"Yes, you. I wasn't here before Brody Wilson got married and became a father, but I hear he was a bit of a loner. But he's become an upstanding pillar of the community, now that he and Mary have a family and run summer camps from their farm on the edge of town. So I think the moniker now belongs to you."

"Bah, humbug, he wasn't a true hermit. Before he and Mary even started their summer camps, he had an

animal sanctuary on his farm and from what I understand, he used to allow farmers to drop off unwanted
animals. Obviously, he was a soft touch." Des had made
sure no one did anything like that with him.

"Are you saying you wouldn't let that happen?"

"Exactly."

"Well, his animals are well cared for and his camps
are successful. He has programs for foster children and
at-risk youth. And now I hear he's planning one for kids
with cancer."

"The poor guy." He tsked his tongue but didn't believe it. "You wouldn't catch me opening my place to
people or animals."

She scowled at him, but the sparkle in her blue eyes
gave her away. "Every time I see him, he's got a big
smile on his face."

He chuckled. "I'll bet that smile has more to do with
Mary than camps or animals."

"So you believe in true love?"

"Ha! That's about as believable as—" He glanced at
Sam, who was still walking ahead of them, and leaned
closer. "That guy in the red suit."

She bumped his shoulder. "I hope you're not letting
one bad experience sour you on love."

"You can hope all you want, but it won't change my
mind."

"Just like with the Christmas ornaments?"

He nodded. "Exactly."

"And I'm still determined not to give up on lost
causes."

"In that case, I'll take care not to get lost."

They walked through the town green and back to his truck. He couldn't help wondering what it would be like to have Natalie believe in him. She didn't seem to mind that he couldn't fly fighter jets anymore.

Being with Natalie gave him a calm feeling because he didn't have to justify any of his choices or try to be something he wasn't. She accepted him as he was.

Chapter Four

"**W**ill you be glad to get home?" Natalie glanced in the rearview mirror and smiled when Sam nodded his head. Three days had passed since they'd gone to the café for pancakes with Des and she'd missed talking to him. Once she'd gotten home, she'd received a phone call from her mother-in-law, Bev, whose sister had had a stroke. Natalie had driven to Boston that night so Bev could see her grandchild. This morning they'd taken Bev to the airport; she was going to catch an early flight to Tampa, Florida, to care for her sibling.

Would Des wonder what had happened to them? She hadn't driven to his place to tell him she'd be going out of town. It wasn't as if they had a proper relationship. Did they even share a friendship? Or were they more like acquaintances? She and Sam had been gone three days, but it felt longer. Truth was, she'd missed Des more than she could imagine, and that could become a problem if he didn't feel the same. She still couldn't be sure he wasn't still in love with his ex, Ashley. He'd said he'd come close to getting married. Had they been engaged when she broke up with him?

She had been married before, so she had no right to her jealousy—and yet, there it was. But emotions were not always rational, were they?

Enough thinking about Des Gallagher. For all she knew, he might be celebrating her absence, wondering how he'd gotten so lucky. He'd made it clear he wouldn't become part of the community the way Brody had. But that fleeting expression she'd glimpsed on his face when Sam indicated he wanted Des to join them for the tree-lighting haunted her. She'd recognized yearning in that brief, unguarded moment. She'd recognized it because she was intimately familiar with that particular feeling.

Trying to force her mind onto another topic, she glanced in the rearview mirror at Sam. "I'm sure Shadow will be glad to see you."

They'd adopted a black-and-silver tabby two months ago when the stray had shown up at the hippotherapy center. Sam had fallen in love with the sweet, loving cat the moment he'd laid eyes on it and she hadn't been able to say no. They'd named him Shadow because the kitten followed Sam from room to room as if afraid Sam would disappear if out of sight. Obviously, the cat returned Sam's feelings.

"I'll bet Shadow missed you, but I'm sure Miss Addie and Teddy took good care of him for you."

She pulled into the driveway and parked in the three-sided carport. Sam had unbuckled his seat belt by the time she opened his door. He scrambled out of his booster seat and ran toward the entrance leading to the laundry/mud room, eager to get to his kitten. She followed him to the door and unlocked it. He ran inside to look for Shadow.

She was taking off her jacket in the kitchen when there was a knock at the back door. Natalie smiled when she saw her neighbor through the window in the door and let her in.

"Welcome back," Addie said. Addie Miller had moved into the other side of the duplex with her much younger half brother several months ago. Natalie didn't know the whole story but their mother couldn't take care of Teddy, and Addie had temporary custody. Sam and Teddy had bonded over LEGOS and the boy had accepted Sam and made allowances for his lack of verbal skills.

"Glad to be back." Natalie gave Addie a hug. "Thank you for taking care of the cat."

"Happy to help out. I wanted to let you know what's happened while you were gone." Addie leaned against the kitchen counter. "There's a rumor going around that the horses are gone from the hippotherapy center."

Natalie and Addie had become fast friends as well as neighbors. Natalie had told her all about Sam's therapy sessions and how much he enjoyed the horses.

"Gone? What happened?" Her stomach began to cramp at the news.

"I don't know." Addie shook her head. "I found out about it an hour ago when one of the parents stopped by to see if you knew anything."

"Do you know who could have taken the horses?" Had the owners or creditors auctioned them? Bile rose in her throat. Sam had made such great strides since he'd started the therapy six months ago. His balance issues had almost disappeared. She couldn't be sure if it was all due to the horses or part of the recovery process. But more importantly, he'd bonded with Augie, the dark bay gelding he considered "his" horse.

Addie shrugged. "I'm sorry. I don't. All I know is what that other mother said. Why don't you go and see for yourself? Maybe you can find out something."

Natalie took a deep breath and searched for calm. "Are you sure? I hate to—"

"I understand," Addie interrupted and patted her arm. "Let him stay. Teddy missed him."

"I can't tell you how much it means to me for Sam to have a friend like Teddy." And she meant it. It was good for Sam to interact with boys close to his age.

"I could say the same. Coming here has been an adjustment for Teddy, too. He refuses to talk to me about it, but I fear he's having some trouble fitting in at school. The other kids in his class have been together since kindergarten."

"I'm sorry to hear it. I hate that for Teddy. I hope you can figure out how to get him to open up. I have a feeling Sam will be facing challenges, too."

Addie patted Natalie's shoulder. "We'll be able to form our own support group."

"It's a deal. But for now I've got to see what's going on with the horses. As long as you don't mind keeping Sam." She hated leaving him, but she wouldn't be able to rest until she learned the fate of the whole operation. Yes, she worried about the horses, but also the employees and the children like Sam who depended on the therapy sessions.

"Sam will be fine with me." Addie made a shooing motion with her hands. "Go. Take care of your stuff and don't worry."

"Okay, you have my cell number if you need me." She was convinced and grateful for her friend. It was times like this that she knew she'd made the right choice in moving to Loon Lake.

Natalie drove first to the hippotherapy center, her stomach in her throat the entire way. She wanted to get all the information she could before having to break the news to him. Augie wasn't just Sam's therapy horse; he and the gentle horse were friends. They seemed to have a bond that didn't need words. Good thing, since Sam didn't have any. Why was parenting always one step forward and two steps back?

She inhaled deeply. Enough feeling sorry for herself. That wasn't who she was. She'd get there and find out what was going on and how she could help. Then she'd set about helping. That was what she did, and continued to do, after learning how the TBI had affected Sam.

The first thing she noticed when she pulled up to the center was a for-lease sign. Not a harbinger of good things to come. She parked her car and got out. The place looked deserted. And she couldn't hear the usual activity. Normally at this time of the day, someone would be cleaning out the stalls and feeding the horses.

"Hello?" she called as she approached. Nothing.

She anxiously picked up her phone and called Roberta, one of Sam's therapists.

"Hi, Roberta. I'm at the hippotherapy center, but it's deserted. Do you have any idea what happened?"

"I'm so sorry, Natalie. All I know is the owner called yesterday and asked me to contact my patients and cancel their appointments. You had already told me you were out of town, so I hadn't called you yet. The owner said something about losing the lease."

Her breath hitched. How naive she'd been for believing she could pull off a miracle. "I had no idea things were that bad."

"Believe me, you're not the only one."

"I'm worried about the horses. Do you know where they are?" Her heart pounding, she waited for the other woman's answer.

"I'm sorry but I have no idea."

"Okay. Thanks." She shuddered at the sour taste flooding her mouth.

"Please keep me up-to-date."

"Of course." Natalie ended the call.

Trudging back to her car, she had the overwhelming need to talk to Des. That was crazy; she barely knew him and yet she felt the urge to talk to him. Des Gallagher wasn't a demonstrative man and yet she sought the comfort of his presence. She ignored the voice that accused her of avoiding going home and telling Sam as she headed toward Des's place instead of hers.

If he asked her why she'd come, she could always explain that she might not need his help on the auction after all. She could make up excuses, think up reasons to justify going, but the simple truth was she'd missed him and wanted to see him. It had barely been three full days and she was missing him. Oh, man, she was in trouble. She'd just gotten back in town and here she was racing out to his place.

What if he didn't want to see *her*? What if he was enjoying the peace and quiet without her chatter? And it wasn't as if he could do anything himself about the horses. They were gone. As was her excuse to continue to see Des unless he wanted to see her, too. She pulled into his driveway and parked next to his truck. Leaving her purse on the passenger seat, she got out and went in search of him.

The barn seemed the best bet so she headed there first to look for him. As she approached, noises emanating from the building had her slowing her steps as she listened. It couldn't be what she thought, could it? She quickened her steps. The closer she got, the harder her heart pounded. Were those horses? The echoing whinnies and nicker sounded like it. She inhaled. The air smelled like hay. What was going on?

She entered the barn and stopped dead in her tracks. The hooks on the rough wooden barn walls now held bridles, lead ropes and halters.

Des stood in front of one of the stalls, talking to…a horse? A familiar-looking animal stuck his head over the door.

"I know this is all very confusing to you, but I'm sure Sam and his mom will be stopping by sometime soon. You looking forward to seeing your buddy Sam?" Des rubbed Augie's head. "You've got to eat or you won't have any energy when Sam gets here."

Was she dreaming? She blinked, but Des and Augie were still there. "Des?"

He turned toward her. "You're back."

She took several steps toward him and noticed the color high on his cheeks. She smiled. Looked like the gruff lieutenant was embarrassed to get caught chatting with a horse. "What's going on?"

He looked past her. "Where's Sam?"

"He's with my neighbor. I didn't want to take him with me to an empty hippotherapy center."

Several more horses stuck their heads out of different stalls at the sound of her voice. She counted and all five of the horses from the center were here. *In Des's barn.* Shocked, she rubbed her eyes, but the horses were all still here. What did this mean? Thoughts tumbled over one another in her mind, leaving her disoriented.

She tried to swallow but her mouth was too dry. "Des, what's going on?"

He crossed his arms over his chest. "First, I have a question for you. Where have you been?"

"Boston," she answered automatically. "My mother-in-law—Ryan's mother—needed to fly unexpectedly to Florida. Sam and I wanted to say goodbye since she'll be gone during Christmas. We gave her a ride to the airport." Why was she babbling? "Never mind all of that. I have to know how the horses got here."

"In a livestock trailer. That's the best way to transport—"

"Very funny." She poked him on the shoulder. "Tell me why."

"Hey, in my defense, *how* was your original question." He chuckled and grabbed her hand when she tried to poke him again. "Brody Wilson called and explained, or rather begged, for my help. Seems that Riley Cooper heard that the owner of the center had walked away and abandoned the horses. Riley mentioned it to his wife, Meg, who told Mary, who got Brody involved." He exhaled loudly. "Small-town life in action."

She blinked back tears. "And you brought them here."

He shrugged. "Brody had no room for them at his place. His stalls are all full."

He tilted his head from side to side. "Brody threatened to get Tavie Whatley involved. And I wasn't about to find out if his threats were serious. I know when I've been bested."

"Do you know how to take care of them?" While working at the Wilsons' summer camp, she saw how much care horses required.

"Yeah, I worked on a dude ranch enough summers to know what to do and if I need help or information, there's always Brody for advice."

"I can't tell you how wonderful this is! Desmond Gallagher, you're my hero."

Throwing her arms around him, she pressed her lips to his. She'd intended the kiss as a quick thanks, but when she would have pulled away, his arms went around her. He urged her closer, turning the chaste contact into something more.

He ran the tip of his tongue along the seam of her closed lips and she opened her mouth. This was the kiss she'd been thinking about, dreaming about, longing for, since her second visit. His tongue slipped in and caressed hers as she sighed and gave herself over to the exquisite things his lips and tongue were doing to her. She rejoiced as parts of her, dormant for so long, came alive again.

* * *

Des tightened his hold on her. Kissing Natalie was everything he'd imagined. Literally. But this was better because it was real. She kissed with that same curious mixture of enthusiasm and nervous shyness she'd shown since barging into his barn that first day.

A horse whinnied and she pulled back.

"Umm…uh… I guess I got a little carried away. I—I hope I didn't embarrass you." She smiled but her lips trembled, letting Des know that she wasn't unaffected by what had happened.

Oh, he was embarrassed, too, but not by her or the kiss. It was his reaction to having his lips on hers that was tying him in knots, making him feel like a hormone-pumped teenager.

"No. I think we…uh…we both got caught up in the moment." He cleared his throat. "I'm glad I could help with the horses."

"I don't care what you say, you're my hero for stepping up."

He shook his head. As much as he enjoyed hearing those words from Natalie, he didn't deserve them. His actions didn't come from a place of altruism. Quite the opposite. She thought he was someone he wasn't. That was why he shouldn't get involved with someone like Natalie. She'd always be looking for the good in him. What happened when her search turned up empty? "I'm no hero. For you or anyone."

"To these horses you are. Who knows what might have happened to them if you hadn't rescued them." Joy shone in her eyes.

As much as it pained him, he needed to set her

straight because he liked that look in her eyes, liked it too much. It started giving him ideas for a future he'd put away three years ago. "I didn't rescue them… I'm giving them a place to stay while you sort out what's going to happen with the therapy program as a whole."

"Even so, I appreciate what you did and I know the others who've benefited from the program will, too." Her smile broadened.

He shook his head. "I didn't do it for them."

"What do you mean? Why did you do it?" she asked, confusion evident in her features.

"I did it for you. I knew how concerned you'd been." He sighed and ran his hand through his hair. Maybe he should've left the situation alone. "When Brody called, he sounded desperate. And since this used to be a horse farm…" He shrugged.

At least all the running around he'd had to do to get all the supplies for the horses had kept him from stressing over her disappearance. The physical labor of getting the stalls ready and hauling in hay and straw helped him catch a few hours of sleep at night.

"If they'd been abandoned, were they okay when you brought them here?" she asked.

"Yeah, Brody's large-animal vet came and checked them out."

She swallowed and her eyes shimmered with what looked like unshed tears. *Damn.* He needed to steer this conversation away from himself or he'd be taking her in his arms again. "Have you ever thought about taking over the administrative running of the program?"

"Me? Why would you think I could do something like that?"

He shrugged. "You know a lot about it and you work miracles."

"Miracles?" Her head snapped back "What makes you think I work miracles?"

"You not only got me into town during December but also got me to eat at the café like a regular person." And she had him questioning why he'd given up all his hopes and dreams, setting them aside as if they had meant nothing.

"And the world didn't come to an end! Now, that's a miracle."

He reached over and flicked the end of her nose. "You're going to be ruining my reputation. I won't be able to growl at people and have them run in fright."

She laughed. "It's like a *Scooby-Doo* episode. I lifted the sheet and underneath all that frightening bluster was simply a grumpy man trying to scare people away."

"At least you didn't say grumpy *old* man."

"No, sir, I wouldn't do that."

"Careful or I'll…" He stared at her lips, plump from his kisses.

"You'll what?" she asked in a breathless challenge, her chin at a pert angle.

Did she want him to kiss her again as much as he wanted to? He started to lower his head, but one of the five horses kicked against the stall.

"We have an audience," he muttered, regaining his senses. Had he lost his mind? What was he doing repeating mistakes? And that first kiss had been a mistake. Hadn't it? Of course it had because it left him wanting more. More kisses, more everything.

"We do," she agreed and sighed. She checked her

watch. "I need to go, but I promise I'll be back bright and early tomorrow to care for the horses."

She put her hands on her hips. "I thought you said you wouldn't end up like Brody, taking in unwanted animals."

He scowled. "Did I?"

Her expression softened and she leaned closer. "You know you did."

Before he could give in to temptation again, he held out his hand. "Give me your cell phone."

"My phone? Why?" she asked but reached into her jacket pocket and pulled it out.

He put his hands on his hips to keep from snatching the phone from her hand. "So I can program my number in. In case you…uh, in case you need to contact me."

At first she looked confused, then her eyes widened and she nodded. "Oh, right. Of course you'll need my number because of the horses."

That would be a plausible, safe excuse, but it would be a lie. And when push came to shove, he couldn't lie to her. He shook his head. "I want it so you can let me know next time you go out of town."

"Did…did you miss me?" She handed him her phone.

"I didn't say that." He didn't look up from the screen as he programmed his number into her contacts. He hated to admit this, but if she hadn't shown up today, he'd planned to go into town and talk to Tavie—of all people—to ask where Natalie and Sam lived. He'd needed to reassure himself that they were both okay. He never would have lived it down with Tavie, but that was how desperate he'd become by day three.

She grinned. "You didn't have to."

He grunted and handed her back the phone, but when she reached for it he captured her hand and tugged her closer. Raising his head, he looked at the horse stalls. "Any objections?"

Augie snorted and whinnied, shaking his head as if he'd understood the question.

"Tough," Des muttered to the opinionated horse and cupped his hands around Natalie's face.

He gently brushed his thumbs across her cheeks as his lips touched hers again. She tasted like peppermint and new beginnings. It was then that he knew he was lost. And he didn't care. If this was lost, he never wanted to be found.

Natalie was lost in the kiss. His lips were firm and gentle and she craved what he was doing to her. She groaned and he pressed closer, letting her feel what she did to him. She reveled in that knowledge.

One of the horses whinnied and stamped its foot, breaking the spell. She sighed and pulled away. It was for the best, she told herself, but it hurt all the same. She took a step back.

"I don't want to, but I need to go," she said and licked her lips. He'd kissed all the lip gloss off them.

"Why the rush?"

She tried to decipher his expression. Did she detect hurt? Did she have that much power? "I—I can't stay. I need to get ready for tonight."

"Hot date?" he asked, his voice tight, his eyes dark.

She shook her head, meeting his gaze straight on. "I promised Sam we'd go to the town tree-lighting to-night. He was worried we'd missed it when we were in

Boston. I assured him we didn't, so I have to keep my promise to take him."

He cleared his throat. "Am I still invited?"

She reached up and cupped his cheek, his scruff scratching her palm. All her nerve endings tingled at the touch. "Of course. Sam will be thrilled. Do you want to pick a time and spot to meet up?"

He shook his head. "Give me your address and I'll pick you up."

She told him where she lived and he walked her back to her car.

He opened her door but touched her arm, preventing her from getting in. "I'm glad you're back."

"Me, too."

"Who told you the horses were here?"

"No one."

"Then why did you come out here?"

Heat crept up her face and settled in her cheeks. "When I found out the horses were gone…coming here was my first reaction. I felt an overpowering need to talk to you."

She searched his face for a clue as to how he felt about her admission.

He tucked strands of hair behind her ear. "I'm glad."

Later that day Des pulled into Natalie's working-class neighborhood of older but well-loved homes. The pleasant, well-lit street ended in a cul-de-sac, the dead end a plus for families with young children like Natalie. His GPS indicated Natalie's was coming up on the left: one of two duplexes on the street, the home had brick on the bottom and blue clapboards on the upper half. It was set back from the road and had a decent-sized front yard. A cement sidewalk led to three steps and a small covered entry with an overhead light shining down on the entrance. The black door and window shutters gleamed as if freshly painted.

He pulled into the blacktop driveway and shut off the engine. He stared at Natalie's house, thinking about the woman inside, and the last time he'd been on a date. Date? But this wasn't a date. Would she see it that way? They were taking Sam to the town tree-lighting, that was all. More of a community thing they were doing together. They were both attending anyway, so together made sense, really. *You were going, anyway?* If not for Natalie and Sam, he wouldn't have been caught dead anywhere near the town square this evening. And yet, he'd been looking forward to this outing after talking with Natalie in the barn. Talking? *More like kissing.*

He got out of his truck and went to the front door. An evergreen wreath with a giant red velvet bow hung on the inner black painted door. He could picture her placing the wreath with that appealing smile, asking Sam if he liked it. And Sam giving his thumbs-up, smile in place and his blue eyes bright. Before he could ring the bell, the inner door opened, disturbing the wreath. His breath caught in his throat at the sunny smile that lit up her face and reached her eyes.

"Hi, c'mon in." She opened the glass storm door.

He stepped inside, caught the outer door so it didn't bang, then closed the inner one. The front entrance opened into a small but cheerful living room. Shoes were lined up by the door, a stack of Harry Potter books and magazines piled on the coffee table and miniature cars and LEGOs scattered on the floor.

"Sorry we're not ready. The kitten ran away with one of Sam's mittens and we've been searching for it."

"The kitten or the mitten?"

"Both. I bet you weren't expecting to walk into a nursery rhyme, huh?" A giggle bubbled out. "You look confused. I was referring to the Mother Goose rhyme about three little kittens who lost their mittens. I used to read it to Sam."

He swallowed, thinking how cheerful Natalie's home was compared to his. His might be larger and not as cluttered, but Natalie's place was warm and inviting. His? Not so much. Could Natalie and Sam bring their warmth and cheerful chaos to his place? He scowled. Ever since she'd barged into his barn that day, Natalie had been messing with his head. She'd made him want things, made him think things were possible.

Blushing, she wrung her hands together. "It's okay to say 'Natalie, shut up' if my chatter starts to get on your nerves."

Damn. She must've interpreted his silence negatively. He reached out to stop her hand-wringing by taking one of hers in his. He stroked her palm with his thumb. "That's not what I was thinking. I apologize if I gave you the wrong impression."

He pulled her closer so their bodies were practically touching. Gazing into her eyes, he saw an emotion lurking in their blue depths. It looked like hurt and he hated that he might have put it there. "It's not what I was thinking at all."

"You had one of those mightily menacing scowls of

yours going on." She swallowed and shifted, bringing herself even closer to him. "So tell me what you were thinking."

Mightily menacing? He shook his head, disturbed that she saw him like that. "I was thinking that—"

Sam came running down the hall followed by a black-and-silver tabby jumping up, trying to grab a mitten in his hand. Sam giggled as he tried to keep the mitten away from the lunging cat.

Des threw Natalie a surprised look.

She met his gaze. "I don't hear that sound often enough. But I've heard it more since we've had the kitten and he's been in hippotherapy. As happy as he was to get spoiled by his grandmother, he missed that crazy cat while we were in Boston."

She laid her hand on Sam's shoulder. "Put your jacket on, please. You were supposed to be ready when Mr. Des got here."

Sam looked up at him, those big eyes so like Natalie's, and thrust out his lower lip. Des felt as if his insides were melting.

Des rubbed a hand over his mouth to hide his smile. "Better do as your mom says," he told him but winked and was rewarded with a giant grin.

Des reached down to pet the cat, who was busy sniffing his pants. "Hey, there, what's…?" He glanced at Natalie.

"His name's Shadow." She hunkered down and got the zipper on Sam's jacket started. "Because he was Sam's shadow from the moment we got him."

She scooped up the cat and cradled it close to her chest. The kitten huddled closer and nuzzled Natalie's neck.

"Wow, I never knew they could purr that loud," Des said. Not that he could blame the kitten. He'd be purring, too, if she was letting him snuggle her neck, her subtle lavender scent filling his nostrils.

"Yeah, he's a regular motorboat. Let me put him in the kitchen and give him some treats and a toy. It'll distract him while we leave. He's an indoor cat." She disappeared into the kitchen, cuddling the animal. "Sam, put your mittens on," she called from the other room.

She came back without the cat and picked up her giant purse and slung the straps over her shoulder. Outside, she got Sam's booster seat out of her Camry and secured it in the backseat of the truck. Sam was bouncing on the balls of his feet as he waited. He tugged on Des's sleeve.

That laugh made his chest expand and Des couldn't stop grinning. He was as proud of Sam as he would be of his own son.

Sam handed the tablet back to Natalie, who slipped it into her purse. Sam climbed into the truck, and she double-checked that the booster seat was secure. Des hurried to the front passenger side and opened her door.

"So you're an officer and a gentleman," she said.

He grunted. "The door sometimes sticks and you have to maneuver the handle just right."

She shook her head. "Why do you fight it so much?"

"What do you mean?"

"You don't want me to see you as an admirable man."

"I'm simply saving you future disappointment." Was he that transparent? He had been trying to keep some space between them.

"I can't imagine ever being disappointed in you."

"Give it time," he said and shut her door.

After leaving Natalie's place, he drove to Main Street and found a parking spot in the church's lot. They got out of the truck, crossed the parking lot and headed toward the festivities on the town square.

"Sam, it's crowded here tonight. You need to hold my hand."

After watching other boys darting around, Sam shook his head. He crossed his arms over his chest, tucking his hands into his armpits.

"Sam," Natalie said in a warning tone laced with frustration.

Des understood the boy's reluctance, but he wanted to tell Sam how lucky he was to have a mother who was so concerned about him. Except he couldn't do that without going into stuff he wasn't about to get into with anyone, even Natalie. Instead, he held out his own hand. "Would you hold mine?"

Sam's eyes widened and he uncrossed his arms, holding out his hand.

"Do you mind?" Natalie asked, sounding surprised.

Des couldn't blame her; he'd surprised himself with the offer.

"Of course not," Des said and took Sam's hand. His heart squeezed when the boy grinned shyly up at him. *Oh, man, don't look up to me, kiddo. If your mom knew how messed up I am, she'd be running away and taking you with her.*

They crossed the street and entered the crowd on the green.

"Are you guys warm enough?" Des asked as they made their way to the front of the crowd so Sam would have a better view. "I know this is your first real taste of winter."

"I will have you know, Lieutenant Gallagher, that we had winters in Nashville."

He barked a laugh. "Yeah, right."

She playfully poked him. "You laugh, but I guarantee we're here to stay."

"A promise and not a threat, right?"

She rolled her eyes at him, but she had that giant grin he enjoyed and her eyes sparkled. He not only enjoyed that smile but also rejoiced at putting it there.

Despite standing near the front, Sam was jumping up, trying to get a better view of the tree, so Natalie adjusted her purse straps on her shoulder and started to bend down to pick him up.

"Let me," Des said and put a hand on her arm to stop her. He then swung up Sam and put him on his shoulders, hanging on to his feet. "That better, bud?"

"He's nodding." Natalie patted her son's leg.

A choral group sang several Christmas carols with the high school band accompanying as a prelude to the tree-lighting.

The mayor stepped up to the podium. "We're going to light this tree in a minute but first I want to urge everyone to stay and enjoy refreshments provided by the town's restaurants. Our businesses are donating tonight's proceeds to the high school music program."

He then went over to the ceremonial switch and pulled it with an exaggerated flourish. The huge evergreen came alive with thousands of twinkling lights and the crowd cheered.

Sam clapped and bounced with excitement, causing Des to tighten his grip on the boy.

Des set Sam back on the ground and took his hand. "How about something hot to warm up? That sound good to you, Sam?"

Attracted by the smells of cinnamon and warm dough, they strolled over to a booth that served hot cider, hot chocolate and doughnuts.

As they waited in the long line, an older man tapped Natalie on the shoulder. "Natalie, hi. Glad I ran into you. Saves me a phone call."

She turned and greeted him. "Hey, Mitch. Good to see you, too. Do you know Des Gallagher? Des, this is Mitch Makowski."

Mitch stuck out his hand. "You're the fella who rescued Natalie's horses."

Des shook Mitch's hand. "Well, I—"

"They're hardly *my* horses, Mitch." Natalie shook her head.

"Whatever." Mitch waved his hand. "My neighbor's grandson has benefited from that program, so I know they do good work. You still taking donations for that auction of yours?"

"Yes, we're always on the lookout for more items now that the horses are safe. Pastor Cook has been kind enough to let us use the church storage shed until the auction. Do you have something?"

"My wife's sister sold painted wood crafts at local flea markets for years, but she's packing it in. Moving to Florida to enjoy retirement. Anyway, she's got a bunch of Christmas things she's willing to donate. Even the artificial trees she used to display them."

"That sounds great. We might even be able to auction the trees as is."

"That's what she thought. Only catch is, you'll have to pick them up. I don't suppose you have a pickup." Mitch glanced at Des before turning back to Natalie.

"Hmm, maybe I could ask Br—"

"We'll use mine," Des said. The words were out of his mouth before his brain could stop them.

"We could?" Natalie turned to him.

Mitch pulled out a business card and handed it to Natalie. "Give her a call if you want to set something up."

"Thanks, Mitch. I appreciate this." Natalie shook his hand.

"Glad to help out with a good cause." The older man grinned and wiggled his bushy, snow-white eyebrows. "And I knew your grandmother back in the day. Sorry to lose her so soon."

"Thank you." Natalie gave Mitch one of her special smiles.

They moved forward a few paces in line as Des wondered what had gotten into him. Since he'd moved to Loon Lake, he'd done his best to avoid interactions with the residents. And yet, here he was, offering to drive around and do just that.

She put the business card in her purse. "You're sure you don't mind helping?"

"I offered, didn't I?" Exactly why did he? He glanced at Natalie. Ha, that was easy. It was a chance to spend more time with her and Sam, to be a part of her world, bask in the glow of her smile.

"Yes, you did, but that didn't answer my question."

Yeah, because he didn't want to admit that he had his own selfish reasons for offering to help. Did he want to admit that to her right now? "Are you always this gracious when someone offers to help?"

She glanced sharply at him as they stepped forward. "Are you saying I'm not acting gracious?"

"You seem reluctant. Is this how you normally act?" He hadn't meant to anger her, just deflect.

"No." She sighed and grinned. "Normally, I would smile and say thank you."

"So I'm an exception?" Why was he pressing her? Did he really want to know how she felt?

She tilted her head and placed her open palm across his chest. "You are. Does that bother you?"

His heart pounded under her palm as if trying to get to her. "No, but I am curious as to why."

Her smile held a hint of sadness. "Don't you think you're an exceptional person?"

"Exceptional? Me?" He rolled his eyes and shook his head, but in that moment he longed to be that man she saw. Could he? "That's stretching things a bit."

They reached the front of the line and Des ordered three hot chocolates and a bag of mini-doughnuts. After getting their order, he carried the cardboard tray over to a spot that had been set up with long tables and chairs.

Natalie made sure Sam was settled with his drink and doughnut before sitting. "So you're okay with helping collect auction items? Boarding the horses is above and beyond."

He took the cover off his drink. "I offered so I'll do it."

She exhaled. "The truth is, I didn't want you to feel

as if you'd been put on the spot in front of Mitch. You know, saying you'd help to be nice."

"Wow." He snapped his head back in mock surprise, but couldn't hide his grin. "That's the first time I've been accused of being nice."

She gave him a thoughtful assessment. "Well, I think it's better if people are honest about their feelings. You don't have to be cruel but honesty is important."

He shook his head, the humor evaporating. "Honesty in relationships in overrated."

Her jaw dropped. "How can you even say something like that?"

It's easy when your own mother tells you things you never wanted to know. In the days following Patrick's suicide, their mother had made it clear that when her favorite son had died she'd lost the only link to the man she'd worshipped—the man who'd been Patrick's father but not his. Weeks later she'd offered a stiff apology, saying she'd voiced sentiments in the depths of grief that she shouldn't have. Although he'd accepted it, he couldn't help notice that the apology was for voicing her feelings, not for having or that they weren't true. "Because once something is out there, you can't take it back."

"But if you keep your feelings hidden, that can cause problems, too."

"Those problems are nothing compared to the ones that honesty can cause." And he should know. He grew up, knowing no matter what he did, he couldn't hold the same place in his mother's heart as Patrick. And Ashley came along and let him know he was interchangeable with whatever man could give her the future she'd envisioned.

"I guess we'll have to agree to disagree." Natalie touched his arm. "Let's not let a difference of opinion spoil this fun night."

He put his hand over hers on his arm. "So you're having a good time?"

She nodded. "Yes. Aren't you?"

More fun than he'd had in a long, long time. "I'm getting a kick out of watching you two enjoy it."

"Then I'm glad you came with us."

Sam's eyes started to droop as soon as he'd finished his doughnut and hot chocolate. Des squeezed Natalie's hand and when she met his gaze, he hitched his chin toward Sam.

"Ready to go?" she asked as she began gathering up their trash. "I think we're all tired."

Sam's eyes popped open and he shook his head.

"You need to get your rest so we can go to the lieutenant's tomorrow and take care of the horses," she told him.

Sam straightened up and looked to Des for confirmation.

"That's right." Des snapped his fingers and pointed to Sam. "I'll be needing all the help I can get taking care of those horses. Are you up to it, Sam?"

His eyes wide with excitement, Sam nodded.

"Then we all need a good night's sleep and you can come over bright and early with your mom," Des told him and stood up with the trash. He had plenty of competent potential help lined up, but Sam was so excited he didn't have the heart to tell him his wasn't necessary. "But be ready to work hard."

Sam laughed and jumped out of his seat and raced around the table toward Des. When he reached Des, Sam threw his arms around him. The cardboard tray with the trash wobbled and Natalie grabbed it. Des patted Sam's back, trying to swallow the sudden clog in his throat. He might not deserve the boy's devotion, but he decided he'd do his best to live up to it.

Chapter Five

Sam had fallen fast asleep in the backseat by the time they'd gotten back to Natalie's place.

"I'll carry him in," Des told her when he pulled into her driveway.

He opened the rear door and leaned in. He unbuckled the restraints and lifted a sleeping Sam out of the booster seat. The child wasn't heavy but his weight caused a strange new sensation in Des's chest—around the area of his heart. He'd never been around young children and wouldn't be if he remained single. He didn't have nieces or nephews to interact with. A lot of the men his age in Loon Lake had started or were adding to families, but Des only knew them in passing. A nod hello here and there but that was all. Not enough to interact.

When they'd been together, he and Ashley hadn't gotten around to discussing children. Huh, maybe that right there was a warning sign that their relationship was doomed. How could they have contemplated marriage without discussing something so important? He glanced down at Sam and clutched him a little tighter. At least he and Ashley hadn't brought an innocent child into their lives because their relationship hadn't weathered its first storm. He'd met Ashley while out in a group with fellow officers. They were all celebrating getting their various assignments. At the time, he'd considered their meeting a lucky coincidence. Now, the cynic in him wondered how much calculation had gone into that night, along with her easy acceptance of all the difficulties his training posed for a relationship.

Had he let his need for acceptance blind him to their problems?

He shifted Sam's weight in his arms and followed Natalie to the door. She unlocked it and pushed it open and stepped aside so he could go first.

"Could you bring him straight to his room?" Natalie whispered, then put her hand on his arm. "Wait a sec."

She leaned down and scooped up the black-and-silver cat. "He likes to trip people when they're carrying something and can't look down."

"I suppose it wouldn't be any fun otherwise," he whispered and was rewarded with one of her crooked-tooth smiles.

She followed him into Sam's bedroom and set the cat on the bed. The tabby walked around the bed and began kneading his claws on a royal blue fleece with orange moons and white spaceships.

"Let me get some of Sam's clothes off before you put him down."

Des nodded and she pulled off Sam's boots, hat and mittens. Des shifted and held the boy so she could unzip his jacket.

She pulled back the covers. "You can lay him down and I'll slip off the coat."

Des laid Sam on the bed. Natalie pulled off his jacket and put a ragged stuffed rabbit next to him before pulling up the blankets. He stirred and hugged the rabbit to his chest. The cat curled up next to the stuffed rabbit.

She smoothed the hair back from Sam's forehead in a tender gesture. "Bunny Rabbit kept him company when he was hospitalized."

Des watched her with her son. What would it be like to have her touch him as a lover? To have those hands explore him as they learned one another's bodies. Then afterward, for her to get that soft look in those big blue eyes as they—

Damn. What was wrong with him? He shook his head. Had he lost his mind? A warm, loving woman like Natalie deserved the same from a man and he'd already told her he didn't believe in everlasting love. Because he didn't. And he wasn't going to let Natalie change his mind. Was he?

Pushing away the things he felt watching her, he said, "I guess I should be heading out."

She gave him a puzzled look at his gruff tone. "Do you have to go already?"

Did he? "Well, I…"

She touched his arm. "Please. Have a seat in the living room."

He nodded and went into the other room, but instead of sitting he prowled restlessly around the cluttered room. He stopped in front of a framed photo of Natalie, a baby he assumed was Sam and a smiling man who must've been Natalie's husband, Sam's father. He had no business being jealous of a dead man. That was low and he should be ashamed of himself.

He took a last look at the photo, yearning for something he'd never had and never would. Or could he? For the first time since punching out of the cockpit of his F/A-18 he was starting to see a future that involved something more than what he had. A future that held more than what he'd had with Ashley. A future with a woman like Natalie, kids and—

"He's out like a light." Natalie came into the living room.

He'd turned at the sound of her voice, and once again he felt that tug around his heart. What was wrong with him? He was a man of logic, not emotions. In order to make it through those dark days following Patrick's suicide, he'd had to lock down his emotions. Soon it became habit, especially when his mother had started drinking and made it clear she'd lost the wrong son. How many times had he heard that Patrick's dad had been the love of her life? As if it had been his fault who his biological father was.

At first he'd chosen the navy because Patrick's father had been a career naval officer. But he found concentrating on a goal helped to block out his untenable situation with his mother. Then the rigid structure of the military became a haven.

"Des?"

He blinked and shoved the past aside, where it belonged. "Sorry, what did you say?"

"I asked if I could interest you in something?"

Yes, but not with anything I'm willing to voice out loud. What if he'd misinterpreted this whole situation? "Like what?"

"I have coffee, tea, hot cocoa or…" She grinned. "I have a bottle of Baileys if you want an adult version of hot chocolate."

"I'm not sure that's a good idea."

"Oh." Her disappointment was obvious in the confused look she gave him.

He put his finger to her lips. "I was thinking about the fact that I have to drive home."

She put her hands on his chest and gave him a shy smile. "Well, there's nothing that says you have to leave as soon as you drink it. I'm sure we could think of something to keep us occupied while you let the alcohol work its way out of your system."

He raised his eyebrows and stared into the depths of her eyes. "Are you sure? Because I'm not the kind of guy who—"

She silenced him by pressing her fingers to his lips. "Tonight let's pretend you're the kind of guy who sits and watches a movie with a woman on her sofa."

Okay. Not what he'd been imagining, but now he wanted nothing more than to watch a movie with her.

He gave her a quick kiss. "That sounds like fun. Did you have a movie in mind?"

She blushed and pointed to a small collection of movies sitting on a round table at the end of the couch. "I pulled out my Christmas movies the other day, but feel free to pick whatever kind you want. I have nonholiday ones on the shelf over there." She nodded at the built-in bookcases next to the television.

"Let me get the drinks started," she said.

"Do you want some help?"

"No, I'm good. Pick out a movie." She disappeared into the kitchen.

Watching a cheesy Christmas movie was the last thing he wanted, but if it meant sitting next to Natalie, he'd put up with the saccharine sentimentality.

He looked through her collection of holiday titles, pulled one out and grinned. He'd put the DVD into the player when she came and stood in the doorway between the kitchen and living room. The light from the kitchen glinted on her hair and he had the urge to run his hands through it and capture a bunch of strands in his fist while he—

"Did you find one?"

"Hmm?" He reined in his wayward thoughts and tried to concentrate on her question, but all he wanted was to kiss her senseless.

"A movie? Did you pick one out?" She squinted at him.

That was right. As much as he longed to kiss her, he also wanted to sit next to her while watching a movie. "Yup. I figured it must be one you like since it was in your stack of holiday films."

"Let me guess." She put her hands on her hips. "You didn't pick *The Holiday* or *While You Were Sleeping.*"

"Uh, would you rather one of those?" He had no desire to watch either one of those, but he'd do it if it meant sitting next to her for the next ninety or so minutes.

"No. *Die Hard* is fine," she said and laughed.

"Hey, how do you know that's what I picked?"

She lowered her chin as she studied him. "Did you?"

He couldn't hide his grin. "Yeah."

"Let me get the drinks," she said before leaving the room.

He frowned. Was she regretting inviting him to stay? Before he could say anything, she reappeared, carrying mugs topped with whipped cream, a cinnamon stick stuck in each one. He took the one she offered.

They settled on the sofa and he rested his arm along the back, his fingers brushing her soft hair. He couldn't remember the last time he'd enjoyed an evening as much as this one. She took a sip of her drink as the movie began, then set the mug back on the small coffee table in front of them and snuggled against him. Her tongue darted out and licked off the whipped cream mustache and he groaned.

She looked up. "Something wrong?"

He brushed his finger along the corner of her mouth. "You missed a spot."

"You did, too." She reached up and skimmed around his lips with a featherlight touch.

"I better make sure," he murmured and leaned down.

As his lips brushed across hers, a small bundle of fur landed in his lap. What the…? The cat began to stroke its head across his chest and purr.

He straightened but kept his arm around Natalie's shoulder, anchoring her to his side. The cat curled up on his lap and settled in. "What did you say his name was?"

"Shadow. Why?"

He grunted. "Are you sure it's not Chaperone?"

She laughed and snuggled closer as the movie started. He sighed and scowled at Shadow, who looked up and slowly blinked at him. If he didn't know better, he'd swear the cat was smirking at him.

Halfway through the movie, Des noticed Natalie's breathing had evened out. He glanced down at her asleep against his side and grinned. He let the rest of the movie play but his attention was on the woman sleeping next to him. He ran his fingertip along her cheek and tucked strands of hair behind her ear. She smiled in her sleep and burrowed closer with a sigh.

As the movie was ending, she awoke with a start and startled the cat, who dug his claws into Des's thigh before jumping down to stalk off.

"This is embarrassing." She sat up and yawned. "Sorry. I guess I wasn't much company."

Des chuckled and touched the mark on her cheek from the button on his shirt pocket. "I thought I might have to carry you to bed and tuck you in like Sam."

She blushed. "I'm sorry."

"I didn't mind." And he found that he didn't. He enjoyed being with Natalie.

The following morning, Natalie drove to Des's place, dressed for mucking out the stables or whatever else she needed to do. She'd been serious about helping with the horses and so had Sam. He'd been raring to go from the moment he got up. Jiggling in his seat as he ate his oatmeal. She wasn't sure who he was more excited to see, Des or Augie. As much as she wanted to see the horses, Des was the bigger draw for her. No question about it.

Warmth rose in her face as she recalled dozing off

while cuddled up to Des last night. Despite that embarrassment, she'd enjoyed spending the evening on the sofa with Des as much as any date in a fancy restaurant.

Des must've heard them pull up because he was waiting in the doorway to the barn when they drove up and parked.

He came over as she turned off the engine and opened her door. "Good morning."

"Good morning. Your helpers have arrived," she said and got out of the car. "I hope you haven't started having all the fun of mucking stables without us."

He laughed and opened Sam's door. "Not a chance."

"Good because we're ready to work hard. As a matter of fact, if you want to work on your art, we can handle this."

He chuckled. "I'm sure both of you are eager and willing to help, but be warned, caring for horses is no easy task."

She swallowed. Didn't he want them there? He'd seemed keen on the idea last night. "I don't think it's fair to you to have to do everything."

"Don't fret. When I agreed to help, Brody offered to share his stable hands if necessary and one of them, Kevin, has already been here this morning to get us started. And I'm sure with Sam's help we'll be done in no time if you two have plans for later."

"As a matter of fact, we're going to look for a Christmas tree. A couple people on the street already have theirs up. Of course they probably have fake trees, but Tavie said the garden center will have the freshest trees, so we'll check there first to see if they have any yet."

"Even those will have been cut down a while ago," Des said as they made their way into the barn.

She laughed. "Unless we go chop one down ourselves, I guess we'll run into that."

He handed her a pair of work gloves. "To help prevent blisters if you're not used to raking."

"Thanks." She took them.

Sam held up his hands and Des laughed. "I didn't forget you, buddy."

He pulled out a pair of child-sized gloves from his pocket. "Specially for you."

Natalie swallowed, remembering the first time they'd come to the barn. He'd been brusque with them, but she'd been right to sense something more underneath that crusty exterior. She'd been a little afraid that first day. And now? The thing that scared her was how much she was beginning to care for him.

"Were you interested in chopping down a Christmas tree?" Des asked as they started cleaning out the stalls. With advice from the therapy center employees as to which horses got along, he'd sent the them into the various fenced paddocks before Sam and Natalie arrived.

"As wonderful as that sounds, I fear we may have to settle for a garden center tree." She had even debated on getting an artificial tree, but for their first Christmas in Loon Lake she wanted to go all out. Sam was getting older and the time was coming when he'd consider himself too old for many of the traditions they enjoyed now.

"I have quite a bit of wooded property here. I'm sure we can find a suitable tree and it's best to do it today before the snow makes it more difficult to go tramping in the woods."

"For real? You'd do that for us?" Every time she thought she had Des figured out, he surprised her. "Sam and I thank you."

Sam gave an enthusiastic thumbs-up.

After they'd finished cleaning the stall that hadn't been touched yet, they took a break in the workshop then followed Des to his truck.

"We'll drive out to the edge of the trees. There's a dirt road that leads down there," he explained.

"Do you go into the woods much?"

"Why? You thinking you need to leave a trail of breadcrumbs?" He put his hands on his hips.

"Should I? You haven't built a gingerbread house in there, have you?"

He looked confused and she scolded herself for yet another children's story reference. *For crying out loud, he's a grown man with no kids, Natalie.*

Heat rose in her face. "*Hansel and Gretel* ring any bells?"

"Ah. The old witch with the oven."

"Yes. See, you remember."

He laughed and opened a rear door for Sam. "More like a good guess."

"I'm planning to make a gingerbread house for Sam and me to decorate." She climbed into the passenger seat.

"That I've got to see," Des said before he shut her door.

"We'll let you know when it's done, won't we, Sam?" She turned to look into the back.

"I'll hold you to it," he said as he slipped behind the wheel and started the engine.

The truck spewed up gravel behind it as he drove along the dirt road toward the tree line.

"So you've never cut down your own tree before?" he asked.

"No. In the past Sam and I would walk around the garden center attached to the big home improvement store, checking out trees that had been cut at least a month before."

Des brought the truck to a stop near the tree line. They piled out of the truck and Des retrieved an ax. She and Sam followed him into the woods.

"Pick out your tree, bud." He adjusted Sam's knit cap. "This one may not be perfect like the cultivated ones, but it will definitely be fresh."

"You're right." She took a deep breath and released a contented sigh. "It even smells like Christmas out here."

She turned her face up and frowned. A few wispy clouds spread across the blue sky, not the kind that foretold of snow, the one thing this holiday was missing.

"You'll get your fill of snow soon enough." Des elbowed her and chuckled.

The hair on the back of her neck stood up at the sexy sound. "I was promised snow."

"You don't want snow today. We need to get your tree first." He hitched his chin toward Sam. "He's taking this task quite seriously."

She nodded, blinking back sudden tears. Des had made this possible and she would be forever grateful. As much as he tried to make everyone believe he was a Scrooge, his generosity told a different story. And she was falling for him, even the grumpy parts. She prayed she wasn't making a mistake, but then her heart seemed to have a mind of its own when it came to Des.

"He's safe out here," he said, interrupting her thoughts.

She lifted her face up to look at him. Had he seen her tearing up? "What do you mean?"

"You don't have a death grip on his hand today." He motioned his head toward Sam, who was examining each tree, no matter how big or small. "But I see how nervous you are."

Let him think that was the cause of her tears. She wasn't ready to admit her innermost thoughts and feelings yet. "Am I that obvious?"

"I can't say I blame you." He reached out his hand. "You can hold my hand if it will make you feel better."

"Are you in danger of wandering off?" She laughed, enjoying his playful mood.

"You never know." He held up his hand.

"Then perhaps I'd better." She took his hand, her skin tingling when it made contact with his.

As they followed Sam on his quest for the perfect tree, she explained about the time she'd lost track of him in the department store. "So now I keep a death grip on his hand."

"I wasn't criticizing." He lifted her hand to his mouth and pressed his lips against her knuckles. "I can't imagine how difficult it must be."

"Thanks." She had trouble concentrating with his lips on her skin. "I'm grateful he survived the accident and how far he's come, but I still worry."

Des put his arm around her. "Are you warm enough? I imagine you Southern gals have to get used to our winters."

She shivered but not from the cold; it was his deep voice and warm breath so close to her ear. "I'm fine. I'm learning to dress in layers. I started with thermal underwear. First time I've worn it. Probably not sexy but it keeps me warm."

"Maybe that calls for a second opinion." His mesmerizing gaze lingered on her lips.

Her heart thudded under his dark-eyed gaze. "To be sure I'm wearing it correctly?"

"Call me quality control." He grinned and squeezed her against his side.

"Oh, I can think of a lot of names to call you," she teased, enjoying the lighter side of him. So much different from the side he'd shown her that first day. But still, she'd seen past that facade, because he'd stayed on her mind all day and into the evening.

"Ouch." He brought their linked hands to his chest.

"Hey, who said they were bad names?" Having fun, she batted her eyes and adopted a drawl. "Why, Lieutenant, I think you're projecting."

"Have I told you how much I love listening to you?"

"You like the accent?"

"I do indeed." He bumped her shoulder and pointed toward Sam, who was stopped in front of an evergreen that had to be ten feet tall and nearly as wide. He glanced back at them with a hopeful expression.

She smiled. "It's beautiful but it's way too big for our living room, I'm afraid. Look for something smaller."

Sam nodded and ran ahead, stopping every so often to examine a tree.

"He's enjoying this. Thanks." She leaned against Des, enjoying being in his company. He made tramping through the woods special. "You're being a good sport, considering you don't even like Christmas."

He shook his head. "Walking around my property isn't a hardship. Uh-oh, looks like he found one."

"That one?" Her dismay came through in her tone.

Des glanced at her and turned back to Sam. "Are you sure that's the one you want, bud?"

Sam nodded his head and reached over and touched the tree again.

"We can get something a bit bigger," she told him. How was she going to handle this? She sighed.

Sam shook his head, touching the tree again.

"Serves me right for reading *The Littlest Christmas Tree* to him," she whispered to Des.

He chuckled, showing no sympathy. "It'll be fine once you get lights and decorations on it."

Says the man who dislikes Christmas. "It will still be a Charlie Brown tree."

"Look how happy he is," Des whispered back and winked. He glanced in Sam's direction and leaned down and gave her a kiss. "That's important, isn't it?"

"I suppose." She shrugged and struggled for an explanation. "I wanted this Christmas to be perfect."

"Why?"

"Because it's our first year in Loon Lake." That sounded lame even to her. She couldn't put her finger on why this was so important. Was it because this was their first year in Loon Lake? Or did her reasons run deeper than she was willing to admit?

He turned and stood in front of her. "His challenges aren't your fault," he said quietly.

"What?" How could he know what she'd been thinking? "What are you saying?"

"I think you're bending over backward to make up for the hand life has dealt your son."

"I'm his mother." She shook her head. "I'm supposed to take care of him."

"You are. Look at him." Des pointed to Sam, who was walking around the tree as if he couldn't believe his luck in finding it. "He may not be able to speak, but he communicates. And he knows he's loved by you. From what I've seen, he's well adjusted."

She sighed. Des made a lot of sense, but it was still hard for her not to want to hold Sam and be able to make everything better. She knew he would be facing numerous challenges in the years to come, and the thought made her heart ache. "I confess I'm worried about what will happen when he starts school. I won't be there to protect him. I need to get a job, so homeschooling is out and I'm not sure I should. Maybe being around other kids more is what he needs."

Des put his arm around her shoulder and pulled her close. "You're giving him a solid background...a loving home to help him navigate life's ups and downs. Don't beat yourself up."

He kissed her temple.

"Thanks. I..."

"You what?" Des asked.

I think I'm falling for you. "Nothing."

The earth was shifting beneath her feet. Was she falling in love with Des? No, it was too soon. Love should take longer than this, be more gradual. This could be a crush, that's all. She swallowed the words before they could escape. He wouldn't be amenable to hearing them yet. And she wasn't ready, either. It was too soon for any big declaration.

Guilt burned in the back of her throat at the thought of falling in love again. Ryan had been dead for three years. No one could accuse her of moving on without a backward glance, and yet, loving another man was a big step. Was she ready to risk her heart again?

He gave her a quizzical look but didn't press and she was grateful. She wasn't ready to tell him something like that yet. She would have to get used to that herself. When had her feelings deepened? She'd been attracted to him from the start. Her feelings had been a mixture of lust and like for a while. And yes, some exasperation with him at times.

"So you're good?"

"Huh?" She needed to pay attention or risk having Des suspect something.

He pointed. "With the tree. I'll chop it down."

"That's right. We have to chop it down." She grimaced. The tree was, after all, a living thing.

"It's a tree, Natalie."

"I realize that." This was silly because this was the whole reason they'd come out here. She sighed. "It's up to Sam."

"Do you want to help me chop down your tree, Sam?" Des asked.

Sam did a thumbs-up and grinned.

"I see I've been overruled."

Des chuckled. "Would you have felt that way about chopping down a Hallmark-worthy tree?"

She crossed her arms. "No comment."

"We'll be giving this less than perfect tree a chance to shine. Like Cinderella." He grinned. "Looks like it's my turn to involve you in a children's story."

"You are way too clever." She elbowed him and laughed. "Okay. Okay. You've sold me, but I still need to get a stand and pull out all the ornaments from the basement before I can get it set up."

"It'll be fine once you get it decorated. You'll see," he whispered to her.

He chopped down the tree and Sam helped him carry it to the pickup. Seeing the look on Sam's face, she knew Des was right. She might have picked out a fuller tree with a better shape, but she had a feeling this tree would be a wonderful memory for Sam. And that had been part of her reason for moving to Loon Lake, to create lifelong memories for them both.

Des and Sam seemed to have bonded over the tree. Her stomach knotted. Ryan would never get the chance to do something like that with his son. That was sad, but she couldn't let regrets prevent Sam from enjoying moments like this. She did worry about Sam's growing attachment to Des, because his tender heart was at the mercy of the adults around him.

"I'll bring it to your place as soon as you're ready," Des told her as he closed the tailgate with a *thunk*.

Back at the farm, Des parked his truck next to her car and glanced into the mirror. "Come into the house. Sam looks like he could use some refreshments. How does that sound to you, Sam?"

Sam gave him a thumbs-up.

Natalie's gaze went from her son to Des. "You're offering refreshments?"

"I may not be Martha Stewart, but I have been known to do a little entertaining."

"This I've got to see," she teased.

"Are you insulting me? Because you didn't preface it with 'bless your heart.'"

She laughed and undid her seat belt. "Bless your heart, but by your own admission you've been chasing people away for the past three years."

"But that doesn't mean I don't know how to be a gracious host. I simply choose not to."

"Okay, point taken."

Des led them to the back door and into a mudroom paneled with bright white wooden panels, a brick floor and built-in benches on either side.

"Sam, honey, sit and take your boots off," Natalie said as she slipped off her own footwear. "Your mudroom is gorgeous. Puts mine to shame, that's for sure."

Des shrugged as he toed off his own boots after loosening the laces. "It was this way when I bought the house."

Boots in hand, Sam touched her arm and pointed to one of the cubbyholes under the bench across from the one she was sitting on.

"Is it okay if he puts his boots under there?" she asked and motioned toward the bench.

"Sure." Des picked up his own boots. "Here, I'll put mine next to yours, bud."

She put her hands on her hips as she faced Sam. "How come you're not this neat at home?"

Sam shrugged and giggled.

Natalie set her boots in the available space next to theirs and paused at the sight. Closing her eyes, she recalled childhood memories of placing her shoes next to her dad's giant army boots and her mom's ballet flats. But the three of them weren't a family and she needed to put the brakes on those thoughts. Sam's heart wasn't the only one in danger. She may have survived her grief when she lost Ryan, but her belief in fairy tales had been steadfast when she'd married him. Now, she understood love didn't protect people from life's tragedies.

Blinking and pushing aside the maudlin thoughts, she straightened and followed Sam and Des through the door into the kitchen.

Her gaze roamed around the beautiful but sparse kitchen. Raising an eyebrow, she asked, "Previous owner?"

Des chuckled. "Good guess."

Sam tugged on her sleeve and gave her a look.

"Bathroom?" she asked. When he nodded, she turned to Des. "Where's the bathroom?"

Des set the loaf of bread in his hands on the counter and pointed. "Through the dining room and into the front hall. First door on the left."

"Thanks. Let me show him."

She led Sam through an empty dining room and into a hall that led to the front of the house. After Sam closed the bathroom door, she glanced down the hall and drew in a sharp breath as her gaze landed on the stained glass inset in the front door. The colorful glass depicted a loon taking flight from a lake. Unable to resist, she went to the door and reached out to run her fingertips over the bird. She'd never seen such intricate stained glass work. Looking at it, she'd swear she could feel the disturbed air from its fluttering wings.

A man who created such inspiring beauty had to be capable of deep emotions, but being able wasn't the same as being willing. She herself was leery of opening herself once again to the vagaries of love. Des might be capable, but was he willing to open his heart? From what he'd told her, he might not be.

Des stepped into the doorway to the dining room and glanced down the hall. Standing at the front door, Natalie was tracing the stained glass insert he'd installed as soon as it was finished. Her fingers lingered on the depiction of the loon rising from the lake. It may have taken him numerous tries to get it perfect, but seeing her reaction made it all worthwhile. After all, she'd been his muse. She'd made him want to make what had started as a simple piece more complex, like her. And as close to perfection as he could get.

Des went through the dining room and into the hall to stand behind her. With his limp he wasn't exactly Mr. Stealth, but she hadn't turned around at his approach. Was she that engrossed in the piece?

"Like it?" Des asked from behind her.

She startled and turned to face him. "It's stunning. I'm going to assume you made it."

"Yeah." He shrugged, but pride made him puff his chest out. "Finished it recently and decided to keep it."

"Do you keep a lot of what you make?" She touched his arm as she spoke.

Her hand on his arm made the hair on the back of his neck stand up. In a good way. A very good way. "No. Very few, actually."

"But you kept this one. Why? I mean, it's beautiful,

but so are the ones Tavie sells in the General Store. That's where I first noticed them." She dropped her hand.

"I have my reasons." He wasn't about to admit that he'd feared he'd lost his muse until the day she showed up with her crooked-tooth smile and tin of candy. She'd inspired this piece and he couldn't part with it. No matter what happened between them, the piece would always hold special meaning for him.

"Are you always this mysterious?"

He lifted his chin as he contemplated her. "Wow, I've graduated from conundrum to mysterious? Is this a good thing? A step in the right direction?"

She crossed her arms. "What do you mean?"

This time he reached out to touch her. "Are women more apt to be attracted to mysterious as opposed to flat-out grumpy?"

She gave him a side eye. "Depends."

"On what?" He scowled, but was enjoying the verbal sparring. He couldn't remember the last time he'd liked being with someone as much as he did with her.

"On how well they entertain their company?"

The fact that she posed it as a question had him laughing. He couldn't help himself. She was charming and she had succeeded in charming him. No doubt about it. He was smitten.

She pointed at him. "You should do that more often."

"Entertain?" He didn't think that was what she meant, but he needed to know what she meant, hear her say it.

She shook her head. "Laugh. It makes you more… more…"

"More what?" He held his breath, waiting for her answer. Her opinion mattered to him. His gut clenched. What was he getting himself into? Did he want to leave himself open to the possibility of getting hurt? Again…

"Approachable," she said.

He laughed again. "But don't you see? I've been trying to be the opposite."

"Are you?" She looked up at him. "Because you haven't been that way with me."

He rubbed the side of his thumb across her cheek. "That's because—"

The bathroom door opened and Sam came out and headed toward them.

Des ached to pull her into his arms and drag her upstairs to the bedroom, but that would have to wait. "You two ready for some mean grilled cheese sandwiches?"

"Mean ones?" Her brow wrinkled.

He nodded. "The only kind I make. I hope you two can handle them."

"Considering I have a mean appetite, I think I can handle your wimpy grilled cheese."

"Wimpy?" He winked at Sam. "You are going to eat those words, Ms. Pierce."

"Gee, and I thought I was going to eat the sandwiches."

He gave her a look and she laughed, putting her arm through his as they went back toward the kitchen. "I love your dining room." Her head swiveled around to take in the empty, beige-painted room. "What's the style called?"

He rubbed his chin. "I think the proper term is *minimalist.*"

She laughed and hugged his arm closer to her side before letting go. Even after she released him, he felt the warmth of her body against his arm. And in the heart he'd been so convinced was stone cold.

Chapter Six

Shadow lifted his head when Natalie pushed the door to Sam's room open even wider, but the cat didn't move from his spot, curled up next to her son. Not that she could blame him; the old furnace was working overtime trying to keep the place warm. She tucked the covers around Sam and ran her hand over his hair. They'd had such a good time that afternoon, picking out a tree. Today, she'd felt as though she were part of a family again, something she'd missed since Ryan's death. She and Sam had both blossomed under Des's attention. Did Des feel the same way? Or would he run as fast as he could if he knew her thoughts?

Her cell phone vibrated and she pulled it out of the pocket of her bathrobe. *Des*. She smiled and left the room before answering. "Hey, everything okay?"

"Yeah, I wanted to say good-night."

Say good-night? Hadn't they done that when they'd left his place? "Oh. Okay."

"I hope you and Sam had fun picking out a tree."

She smiled. "I should be asking you about that. I hope your leg isn't bothering you after tramping around the woods today."

"I'm good. How's Sam?"

She glanced at Sam. "He's out like a light."

"I'm glad he had fun. How about you? I hope you enjoyed yourself, too."

She smiled even though she knew he couldn't see her face. Maybe it would show in her voice. "I did. Thank you for helping us pick out the tree and chopping it down for us."

"I should let you go. Good night and be sure to let me know when you're ready for me to bring the tree over."

"I will. Good night, Des."

She was still smiling when she hung up. She wouldn't have pegged him for late-night, sleepy-voice calls. But then, he was continuing to surprise her. All in a good way.

Natalie spread white frosting on the edges and put the last gingerbread piece in place. She held the pieces together, waiting for the icing to set. She pulled her hand away, stepping back to admire her work. Sam was going to love it. It had been two days since they'd picked out their tree and she wasn't going to be able to hold Sam off much longer. At least the evergreen was fresh enough she wouldn't have to worry about bare branches come Christmas morning.

She wanted Christmas in their new home to be perfect. She wanted to believe that moving to Loon Lake had been the right thing to do. Even if she'd sold the duplex, the proceeds wouldn't have covered buying a similarly sized home in Nashville. Plus, she knew in her heart when she'd visited Loon Lake that she'd found home. Being uprooted hadn't been easy for Sam, but he was settling in and she'd promised him Santa would find him in their new home. She hadn't been able to prevent what had happened to him or the loss of his father, but she was determined to do the things that were in her power. Like having a perfect Christmas.

With Des having the horses at his place, they'd been able to cobble together some hippotherapy sessions for established clients. Des had even been good-natured about putting up with it. Of course, *amiable* was a relative term when it came to Des Gallagher.

Stepping back, she wiped her hands on a dish towel. As she turned to hang the towel back on the oven door handle, a black-and-silver blur raced past her, heading toward the table: the table where she'd left the gingerbread house.

"No!" Natalie yelled and simultaneously lunged for the kitten.

She managed to grab Shadow before he could jump on the table, but in doing so her foot hit the table leg, knocking over the bottle of water she'd set there. It swayed then toppled over onto the completed house, smashing through the back half. Part of the back wall was gone and there was a hole in the roof.

Setting Shadow on the floor, she shooed him away. Why did he have to pick today to try mastering jumping high enough to get onto the kitchen table? Natalie swore, using phrases that would've made her drill-sergeant dad proud. Not that the swearing helped with anything, except maybe her blood pressure, for letting off steam.

Her cell rang and she checked the screen. She inhaled and answered. "Hey."

"What's wrong?"

"What?" She frowned at the phone. Was Des psychic? "What makes you think something is wrong?"

"I can hear it in your voice."

"You can?" His perception made her stomach do a funny little flip-flop.

"Yeah, your voice doesn't have that usual—" he cleared his throat "—sparkle."

She smiled despite what had happened. "You really are an enigma."

"And just yesterday I'd graduated to mysterious." He chuckled. "Quit trying to distract me. I want to know what's wrong."

He was going to think she was silly for being so upset over a house made from cookies. She sighed. "It's my house. One of my walls collapsed and—"

"What?" There was a short pause followed by some of the same words she'd used. "Are you okay? Were you hurt?"

"Hurt? No, I'm mad abou— Oh! You thought I meant my real house. No. No. It was the gingerbread house I was making. I was going to surprise Sam when he got home and now it's ruined."

He swore again. "A gingerbread house? You mean you gave me a heart attack over a cookie house?"

"See? I knew you were going to think I was silly."
Damn. Why did she tell him. He was going to think she
was nuts. And maybe she was, but the picture-perfect
house was now in ruins.

He exhaled. "I never called you silly. I was upset
thinking you could have been in a situation where you
might have gotten hurt, that's all."

"Sorry. I didn't mean to upset you. And I didn't mean
to mislead you. I was making this elaborate house and
it was almost finished. I was waiting for the cement to
harden and—"

"Hold up. By cement you mean…"

"Sorry. It's icing—you know, like frosting—but it
hadn't set yet and the cat tried to jump on the table and
well, long story short, half the house is in ruins. The
pieces broke and part of it is nothing but rubble. Looks
like some sort of earthquake or natural disaster took
out half the house."

"I'm sorry."

"Thanks, but I guess it will work out for you and
Sam since you'll be able to eat the pieces."

He snorted. "Yeah, like I need to eat more baked
goods."

"I had promised Sam I'd have it ready when he got
home. Mary Wilson took a couple of the kids to a mati-
nee." She looked at the gingerbread again and grimaced.
"Even if I try to get the pieces patched together, a chunk
of the roof will be gone and a hunk of one of the walls."

"And that's bad?"

"If you saw this mess, you wouldn't have to ask."
She sighed, but was surprised he hadn't brushed off

her concerns. Another point in Des's favor. They were adding up fast.

"It might not be a mess to a five-year-old boy."

"Yeah, right."

"Have you ever been a five-year-old boy?"

She grinned. "Okay. I see your point, but it makes it hard to decorate."

"You were going to decorate it?"

"I had planned to let Sam help me." She shooed the curious cat away from the table.

"How do you decorate a cookie house?"

"With gumdrops, candy canes, stuff like that." She glanced at the ingredients she'd laid out on the counter with high hopes.

"Where's the house now?"

"It's still on the kitchen table. Why?"

"Can you patch the bigger pieces together?"

"Yeah, but why would I want to?"

"Do it. I have an idea. I'll be right over."

"Are you some sort of gingerbread house whisperer?" she asked.

"Something like that. Patch together what you can and then leave it. Don't get rid of it. Promise?"

"I promise." She was still confused but decided to go along with it if this meant Des was coming over.

After she patched together what pieces of gingerbread she could, she raced into her bedroom to change. Rolling her eyes at herself in the mirror, Natalie brushed her hair and applied lip gloss. *Eager much?* she asked her reflection as her doorbell rang. She smoothed her festive sweater over her jeans with shaky hands. When was the last time she'd experienced these heady sensations? The breathless anticipation, the racing pulse, the grin that wouldn't quit? She'd been a college freshman getting ready for a first date with that cute senior, Ryan Pierce.

Des waited for her to answer the door, hoping his idea would work. If not, he was going to look like a fool.

The door opened and Natalie greeted him. For a moment he stood speechless. She was smiling at him, her lips shiny and begging to be kissed. He ached to lean over and kiss her until they were both breathless and—

"Des? Is something wrong?" She peered at him.

Recovering, he quirked an eyebrow. "You didn't tell me this was Ugly Sweater Day."

"What?" She glanced down at her herself. "I…"

He laughed and gave her a chaste, no-tongue kiss—unlike the messy one he'd been craving—before stepping inside. "I'm joking."

She narrowed her eyes but her smile stayed in place. "Joking? Or trying to save your hide?"

"I confess I've grown attached to my hide. It's been with me for thirty-four years now. I'd hate to lose it over a googly-eyed reindeer with a red pompom nose."

"So we're in agreement my sweater is kitschy and not ugly?"

"Yes, ma'am."

She swatted his shoulder. "What's in the bag? Did you bring replacement gingerbread?"

"Call me Mr. Fix-It." He pulled away when she tried to reach for the bag. "Show me to this disaster house."

"Disaster is right, but unless you have replacement gingerbread it's a lost cause."

He cupped her cheek in his free hand. "Let me be the judge of that."

She pressed her face against his palm. "It's in the kitchen, what's left of it. The house, not the kitchen."

He chuckled. "I guessed that much."

"I wanted to be sure to clarify. I don't want you having any more heart attacks."

"I like a woman who's concerned for my health." He couldn't resist and gave her a kiss. His lips lingered but he force himself to keep it light or he might not be able to stop.

Following her farther into the house, he licked his lips. Peppermint. He'd never again taste or smell peppermint and not think of Natalie.

In the kitchen, she pointed to the gingerbread like Vanna White revealing a vowel. He stood in front of what was left of the confectionery disaster and studied it. "I'm impressed."

She snorted a laugh. "Is that good or bad impressed?"

Straightening up, he cleared his throat. "Just impressed."

He opened the bag and pulled out the die-cast airplane that sat atop the dresser in his bedroom. He held up the jet. "Naval aviation to the rescue."

"Oh."

He frowned. "What's wrong?"

"That looks much too expensive for a five-year-old boy." She shook her head. "Granted, Sam will be disappointed by the ruined gingerbread house, but I don't think we need to bribe him. He'll get over it."

"Oh, ye of little faith." He studied the mess and then

strategically set the plane so it appeared the jet had crashed into the house.

"Oh, wow," Natalie said. Grateful as she was for Des coming to her rescue, her feelings went much deeper than gratitude. And they were turning into something more. Much, much more. Those emotions elicited as much fear as they did excitement. And had nothing to do with gingerbread houses.

Before she could say anything else, Sam burst through the side door from the carport.

A dark-haired woman appeared in the doorway and waved. "Hey, I wanted to let you know we had a great time with Sam, but Elliott's asleep in his car seat so I can't come in," she said, even as she glanced toward the driveway. "And I see you have company anyway so I'll call you later and we can catch up. Wow, clever gingerbread house. Oh, hi, Des. Sorry, but I don't want to leave Elliott alone with the car running."

"Thanks, Mary." Natalie shut the door after the woman dashed off and turned back. "That whirlwind was Brody Wilson's wife, Mary. She recognized you, so I'm assuming you've met her before. She took a group of the kids to see that new Christmas movie and included Sam."

Sam stood staring at the gingerbread house with the tail end of the plane sticking out. She smiled at Des and put her hands on Sam's shoulders. "As you can see, there was a little accident."

Sam shook his head and ran off down the hall toward his room. Des met her gaze and his gut clenched. He'd hoped to save Natalie's project but should've known he was no one's hero.

"Well, at least you tried and I appreciate it. I'm sure Sam will…" She trailed off when her son came running back into the kitchen, the cat following on his heels. He held up a miniature fire truck and set it next to the house along with a toy police car.

Natalie choked out what sounded like a mixture of a laugh and a sob. Sam pulled something out of his pocket and placed LEGO people around the scene, his tongue in the corner of his mouth as he concentrated on his work.

"That's exactly what it needed," Des said and nodded his approval when Sam looked up to him. "Great job, bud."

The look on Sam's face was priceless. Des had trouble swallowing past the frog in his throat. Who knew something so simple could mean so much? He met Natalie's gaze and fought the feelings tightening his chest. He supposed he'd accomplished a lot of things in his life to be proud of, but being responsible for that expression on Sam's face topped the list. Who would have thought a five-year-old with a gingerbread house could mean so much to him?

Sam opened and closed his mouth, stamped his foot and ran again toward his room with the cat scampering after him.

Natalie pulled out a chair and sank down. "I can't imagine what it must be like not to be able to express myself using words."

"Have you tried sign language?" Des pulled out a chair and sat next to her. He reached over and took her hand in his. It had been a long time since he'd tried to comfort anyone and he wasn't even sure if his attempts would be welcome, but he had to try.

"Yeah, we—"

Sam appeared once again in the kitchen with his tablet. He tapped a picture and a computerized voice said, "Love" and Sam pointed to the gingerbread house. He tapped again and the voice said, "Thank you."

"You're welcome, bud."

Natalie wiped her cheeks with the backs of her hands and jumped up. "Let's get your jacket off."

While Natalie was hanging it up, Des got up and went to the counter. "Are these candies what you were going to use to decorate?"

She came to stand next to him. "Yeah, but gumdrops and candy canes hardly seem appropriate now."

"I guess Sam and I hijacked your Christmas house." He rubbed his knuckles across her back.

"I might be able to get into the spirit." She opened a cupboard, rummaged around and pulled out a food coloring set and held it up.

"What can you do with that?"

"I can color the icing and use it to enhance your scene with some flames."

Sam held up his tablet again. The computer voice repeated, "Love."

She sighed. "Not what I had in mind this morning when I was making the pieces for the house, but don't let anyone say I can't go with the flow."

"That's getting into the spirit of things." Des squeezed her shoulder.

"Says the man who hates Christmas."

He leaned close and kissed her temple before straightening up and taking a step back. Was she changing his mind about Christmas by replacing bad memories with good ones?

She cleared her throat. "So what are we calling this?"

He put his hand under his chin as he studied the house. "How about we call it a simulated disaster scenario?"

"Simulated?" She raised her eyebrows.

Sam jumped up and down and tugged on her sleeve, nodding his head.

"Okay, I'm outnumbered. Simulated disaster scenario it is. Now, let's get this decorated and find someplace to put it where the cat can't reach it or the disaster won't be simulated."

She mixed up some red and orange icing and put it into pastry decorating bags. Des picked up Sam and held him over the house so he could decorate with less chance of bumping into the building. Sam took his time and piped icing flames on with a precision Des admired.

After Sam finished, Des lowered him to the floor and put up his palm. Sam gave him a high five and giggled.

"Great job, sport." Des wondered if Sam would someday find solace and satisfaction in creativity as he had. Sam might enjoy making a simple stained glass item. Maybe he'd suggest it sometime and if Sam was interested, he'd teach him what to do.

Natalie found some black coloring she'd had left over from Halloween and they used it on some of the bigger broken pieces to make them look charred from the fire. She'd been quick to switch gears from her original vision for the cookie house. What would his life have looked like if he'd a more structured family life growing up? He pushed the thought aside. He could only go forward, not back.

Natalie stood back and admired their work. "I think it needs one more touch."

Des turned to Sam but the boy shrugged and shook his head.

"To look like soot," she explained as she sprinkled cinnamon over it.

Once it was all finished, Des helped her carry the house and the cardboard square she'd built it on into Sam's bedroom. They set it on top of a tall dresser after deciding the cat hadn't mastered leaping that high. Natalie turned on the small light located on the dresser to illuminate the scene.

Sam stayed in his room so he could admire the gingerbread creation. Natalie walked down the hall with Des. "Thank you for this. I can't tell you how much this whole thing has meant to me. And I feel as though we crossed a hurdle when he went and got his tablet. In the past, I've had to give the iPad to him and ask him to use it."

Des squeezed her hand. "Maybe he wasn't ready."

She heaved a sigh. "I've been torn between letting him develop at his own pace and giving him the support and encouragement he needs."

He glanced down the hall to be sure Sam was still in his room before taking her in his arms. "I'd say continue to do what you have been."

"Thanks." She reached up, cupped his face.

"Glad I could help." He let her go when she pulled away. "I need to get back home. I want to get the horses into the barn and get the plow ready to attach to my truck. If the weather forecast is correct, I'm going to need to attach it soon."

"Finally, our first snow," she said and laughed when he rolled his eyes.

"We'll see how you feel about it this time tomorrow."

She stuck her chin out. "You know you don't scare me. Even that first day when you were so rude."

"Was I rude?"

"Yes, very," she said but her grin gave her away. "But I knew you were all bark, no bite."

"And how did you know that?" He was glad he hadn't scared her away for good. He couldn't imagine not getting to know her.

"I'm a good judge of character. Besides, you winked at Sam."

He clicked his tongue. "Was that my mistake?"

She patted his chest. "Told you I was a good judge of character."

He threw his head back. "Then you should be running for the hills."

"Nah, I like what I see, Des Gallagher."

"And I'm grateful you do."

Natalie put her hand on Sam's shoulder as they stood in the doorway and watched Des climb out of his truck. After yesterday's fun with the gingerbread house, she felt as though their relationship had entered a new phase. He waved to them hefting the evergreen from the pickup's bed, then limping up the sidewalk with the tree.

Natalie winced at his motion. She hated that Des was so often in pain from his leg. She had yet to learn what had happened. Several times she'd been tempted to come right out and ask but wasn't quite comfortable enough yet to do so. She didn't want him thinking his limp bothered her by pointing it out. His gait was simply a part of him, like his coal-black hair or brown eyes, and she was attracted to the whole package. Yes, she liked all of him. A whole lot.

Sam hovered excitedly as Des carried the tree into the house.

Des held the evergreen to the side so he could see Sam. "Hey, there, bud. Ready to get this set up?"

Sam clapped and nodded.

Natalie brought out a box of ornaments from the closet. Her mother had given her many of the ornaments they'd used on trees from her childhood after her dad had died. She also had some she and Ryan had collected during their short marriage. Before bringing out the box, she'd removed one that had celebrated their wedding anniversary. But she'd kept the ones Ryan had bought for her celebrating other occasions. Removing reminders of Ryan had not been her intention. His daddy might be gone but his memory needed to be kept alive for Sam, even if it was time for her to move forward. Starting a new relationship didn't erase the past and she'd have to learn how to integrate the two for Sam's sake. She had a few new ones she'd bought at the church's Christmas in July bazaar to signify their fresh start in Loon Lake. So there was a mix of old and new, past and present.

Des got the tree situated in the stand she had put in front of the window. He secured the trunk and she added water.

"We'll string the lights first," Des said as he opened one of the new boxes of lights she'd set on the couch.

"Wait. There's one thing I need to do before that," she said as she set up the folding step stool next to the tree. She got on the top step with her precut pieces of twine.

"What are you doing?" Des put his hands on his hips as he watched her.

"Cat-proofing the tree." She tied the twine around the trunk under the top branches and strung it over the curtain rod. "At least it won't tip over."

"Where is the cat?" Des asked and put his hand under her elbow as she started to climb off the stool; his hand lingered for a few extra seconds after she'd stepped off. Heat flared where his skin had all too briefly touched hers. It made her think of them being together…and alone…

Her heart beat so fast it threatened to jump out of her chest as she continued to gaze at him. She leaned closer and— Sam shifted, reminding her they weren't alone. As much as she might wish it.

"I shut Shadow in Sam's bedroom until I had the tree secured since I didn't know what his reaction would be. You can go let him out now, Sam."

As soon as Sam left to go get the cat, Des pulled her close for a kiss. Their lips met in a heady rush, too rushed and hard to be labeled tender, but whatever tenderness their kiss lacked, it made up for in enthusiasm. A door opened and they pulled apart, both breathing hard.

"Mmm." She licked her lips. "What was that for?"

He shrugged, his gaze on her lips. "Couldn't help myself."

"I'm glad you have no self-control." She gave him a quick peck as footsteps came down the hall. "Me, either."

Before they could do anything else, Sam came back with the cat close behind.

"Here." She handed Sam a piece of paper.

Sam crinkled the paper into a ball and immediately had the cat's attention. He tossed the paper, and the kitten skittered after it, batting it around the room.

"Wow. Do you have a special technique for doing that? Or are you like some cat expert?" Des asked Sam, who rolled his eyes. Des playfully poked his side until Sam was giggling.

Natalie's heart melted as Des interacted with Sam. She couldn't have asked for anything more for her son this Christmas. No matter what the future held, she and Sam would have wonderful memories of their first Christmas in Loon Lake. She knew from experience that difficult memories had a way of bringing the sweetest joy as time mellowed pain.

Still, a ripple of unease coursed through her. What would happen to Sam if Des reverted to his old ways of shutting people out? How would she explain it to Sam? Could she?

She shouldn't let her fears of something that hadn't happened, and might never happen, spoil the here and now, so she shook off the melancholy thoughts as best she could.

By the time Des strung the lights to his satisfaction, Natalie had noticed he was a bit of a perfectionist. They divided up the task of putting the ornaments on the tree.

Des put the ones on the higher branches, Natalie the middle and Sam the lowest.

"Ready to put the star on top, bud?" Des asked after the last ornament was in place.

Des picked up Sam so he could put the star on top of the decorated tree. After setting Sam down, Des plugged the star into a socket on the end of the lights he'd strung.

He stepped back and turned to them. "Are we ready for the tree-lighting ceremony?"

"Ceremony?" Natalie turned to Sam, who lifted his shoulders and held his hands out, palms up in a "me either" gesture.

"Like the town tree. You're not the mayor, but I thought you might like to say a few words," Des said.

She laughed. "I'll pass, but thanks."

"Okay. Why don't we let Sam flip the switch? That okay with you, bud?"

Sam nodded and Des held up the power strip he'd brought with him to plug the lights into. Sam pressed the on switch and the less-than-desirable tree took on a happy glow.

Natalie's heart lit up as brightly as the tree. The three of them—together—made her imagine things beyond this Christmas, things she had no place imagining.

"I saw how fascinated he was with what they did at the town tree-lighting." He shrugged. "I also wasn't sure how many outlets you had since this is an older home."

"Well, I appreciate it and I'm sure Sam does, too." She wasn't just falling in love with Des. Despite her concerns over the future, she was all the way—madly, deeply, hopelessly—in love. A scary prospect, because she didn't know what had caused Des to shut himself away from the world. She suspected whatever scars he had ran deep and many had never been healed.

She glanced at Sam, who was watching Des with what amounted to hero-worship. Yeah, she wasn't the only one who'd fallen under his spell.

"I made lasagna earlier today and I hope you'll join us for supper." She realized how much she wanted him to say yes. Tonight and forever.

He lifted his face and sniffed. "Is that what that delicious smell is?"

Silly, but that simple comment made her stomach flutter. "Yeah, it's one of Sam's favorites."

"Well, after those pancakes, I trust his judgment. Not to mention I haven't had a home-cooked meal in a while."

She frowned, feeling both happy to be feeding him and sad that he had no one to cook for him. To *care* for him. "How long is a while?"

He shrugged but had a strangely impassive expression as if afraid of revealing something he didn't want her to see.

She let it drop. "So no pressure to impress?"

"You've already blown me away with your cookies and other goodies."

"So my cookies appeal to you?"

"That's not all I find appealing," he whispered and waggled his eyebrows.

A delicious tingle ran down her spine and lifted the hairs on her arms at his words. Did this mean he was feeling the same intense feelings that she was? Before she could say anything more, Sam approached Des and tugged on his sleeve.

Des leaned down. "What you need, Sam, my man?"

Sam pressed his tablet. "Love. Tree. Thanks."

"Did you find 'tree' on there?" Des asked and pointed to the tablet.

Sam grinned and nodded.

"Great job. Put her there, bud." Des held out his hand palm up. After Sam gave him a palm slap, Des turned to her. "I'll be happy to help in the kitchen, but first, I have one more thing for the tree."

"Oh?" What more could he have? He'd already done so much for them.

"Yeah, it's in my truck. Let me go get it." He held up his hand as if to halt any questions. "It's a surprise."

She felt like a kid herself as they waited for Des, who came back in with a slim rectangular package. Setting it down, he pulled a small folded knife from his pocket and unsealed the box to reveal a model train and track.

"To go around the tree," Des explained.

"How wonderful," she said, but her voice sounded strangled.

Fearing she might embarrass herself, not to mention Sam and Des, she headed for the kitchen. Bursting into tears would be a bit difficult to explain. How could she explain something she didn't understand? Because as much as she might want to, she didn't have the words to express her gratitude. She couldn't imagine a better father figure for Sam. Des was in the running for World's Best Dad. "Let me go set the table and fix a salad to go with the lasagna."

In the kitchen she wiped her face, listening to Des

talking to Sam as they set up the track for the train. Every so often she heard Sam's iPad talking. Maybe Des had been right that Sam hadn't been ready until now to use it. Or maybe his relationship with Des had prompted him to use it. Whatever the reason, she felt like rejoicing this new milestone—along with celebrating *her* own, newfound bond with Des.

In those dark days following Ryan's death, falling in love again had never occurred to her. Then as she healed, she doubted she might ever find anyone special enough again. Now the possibilities that lay ahead of them were all she thought of.

Chapter Seven

After getting the train set up and working, Des took a few minutes to share in Sam's enjoyment. Although he felt guilty for choosing to put together the train for Sam before going into the kitchen, he suspected Natalie had wanted a few moments alone. After catching her surreptitiously wiping tears away, he let her escape.

Not that he could blame her. He'd been grappling with his feelings because Sam was such a large part of this relationship. At five years older, Patrick had been the only father figure he'd known in his life. Each time he was with Sam, Des channeled his early memories of his big brother helping him, guiding him and having fun.

He stopped in the doorway to the kitchen. Natalie was bending over in tight jeans as she pulled a large pan from the oven, her long hair tied back with a bright tie. He wanted to release her hair and let those silky strands slide through his fingers. When she stood, her face was flushed from the heat of the oven. That flush reminded him of when he'd kissed her, making him want to do it all over again. And again.

He would forevermore consider cookies an aphrodisiac. She looked at home in her kitchen and he knew she tasted sweeter than any cookie she baked. Longing for her sweetness, he yearned to be at home here with her.

"Hey." She set the pan on the counter and pulled off the oven mitts. "Got the train all set up?"

"Come and see it." He held out his hand, hoping she'd take it. She did, and his heart swelled to a size he hadn't known it could occupy in his chest.

They stood in the doorway, the lights from the tree reflected in her eyes. His heart squeezed in his chest. God, she was beautiful.

"You were right," she whispered, turning her face toward him.

"I'm sorry, but could you be more specific?" he whispered back. She narrowed her eyes at him and he touched her chin. "I'm right about so many things."

She rolled her eyes and elbowed him. "I was talking about the tree. It's beautiful…in its own unique way."

He put his arm around her and pulled her closer. "Are you saying you doubted me?"

"I shouldn't have." She pushed out her lower lip. "I'll know better next time."

He gave her a mock scowl. "See that you do."

Sam made a noise and they jumped apart and turned toward him. The cat had caused a train derailment.

"Uh-oh, bud, simulated train disaster?" he asked and Sam giggled.

"Hey, don't go giving him any ideas," she warned, but her lips curved into a smile.

Damn. With only his older brother as an example, he knew his skills as a dad were sorely lacking. Trial and error might work for some things, but not so much when it came to parenting. He sighed. "Maybe the train wasn't such a good idea."

She shook her head. "I'm sure I'll figure something out."

"It doesn't bother you?" His mother would never have stood for any of this. She'd complain he was making a mess that she would have to clean up, despite the fact that he always picked up after himself.

"It's not the end of the world," Natalie was saying. She squared her shoulders and continued, "What will be a disaster—and not the simulated kind—is if my lasagna gets cold. Sam, put Shadow in your bedroom for now."

Sam laughed, picked up the cat and cuddled it as he went down the hall.

Des turned to her and quirked an eyebrow. "Hmm, did you say your father was a drill sergeant in the army?"

She scrunched her face. "Too harsh?"

Des burst out laughing. "Oh, yeah, I could see both of them quaking in their boots."

"What about you? Are you quaking in your boots?"

"You better know it."

"Good. Now march to the table and eat." She turned on her heel and went into the kitchen.

She walked away, her hips swaying in a way that had him groaning, even though he suspected she was exaggerating the movement. Damn, but she was beautiful coming and going. He was getting in deeper and deeper. And loving every minute of it.

Sam came back and Des put his arm around his shoulders. "C'mon, bud, we better get in there before supper gets cold."

After supper he helped her clean up the kitchen. Even mundane chores took on a new meaning when he shared them with her.

"How about we go out front to see how the tree looks from the street," he suggested after they'd loaded the dishwasher and wiped down the counter.

"I love that idea. Maybe we can walk a bit down the street and look at some of the others. A few people have lights strung along their bushes and some of those lit-up deer on their lawns." Her smile turned to a frown. "It won't bother your leg, will it?"

"I'm not an invalid," he snapped, but regretted his churlish tone when distress marred her features. Hurting Natalie was the last thing he wanted, so he made an effort to soften his tone. "I'll be fine."

She opened her mouth to say something, but after glancing at Sam, she nodded.

Des touched her arm and raised his brows in a silent appeal for forgiveness. When she smiled, he released his breath and dropped his hand.

"Ready to go, sport?" he asked, resting his hand on Sam's shoulder.

Sam grinned and gave him a double thumbs up.

He laughed. "I'll take that as a 'heck yeah.'"

They all bundled up and went out into the cold.

"The tree looks so pretty," Natalie said as she stood looking at the house.

"You sound surprised," he grumbled and when she laughed, he flicked the end of her nose.

Sam looked up at Des and pointed down the street.

"I think he wants to check out the competition," Natalie said.

Des nodded. "I think you're right. Shall we?"

Sam went ahead and Des used the opportunity to hold Natalie's hand as they strolled to the end of her cul-de-sac. His leg was sore but the slow pace suited him. Holding Natalie's hand felt too good to worry about the aches and pains he lived with every day.

A car drove past and the driver tooted the horn and waved. As Des returned the friendly greeting, he realized how much his life had changed in the short time he'd known Natalie and Sam. He was doing things he wouldn't have contemplated a month ago, thinking things he wouldn't have even thought of and wanting things he hadn't in a long, long time.

When they got back to the duplex, they admired the tree from the street again. Des clapped Sam on the shoulder. "I declare Sam to be the best Christmas tree picker-outer in Loon Lake."

Back in the house, Natalie told Sam it was time to brush his teeth and get ready for bed.

After Sam went down the hall, she turned to him with an expectant expression. "I hope you'll stay after Sam goes to bed."

Des gave himself a mental high five. Clearing his

throat, he tried to keep the excitement from his voice. "I'd like that."

"Me, too. I'll be right back." She started to walk away but turned back to check on him as if afraid he might make a run for it when her back was turned.

He grinned at the notion and settled on the sofa and put his socked feet on the coffee table.

She frowned and took a step back toward him.

He removed his feet. "Sorry. Is that not allowed?"

"No. No, it's okay to put your feet up. Please." She waved her hand in a helpless gesture. "Is your leg bothering you? I shouldn't have made you walk around the neighborhood in the cold and—"

"As much as I appreciate your concern, I am well acquainted with the word *no*." He forced a laugh. "And I frequently use it when it suits me."

"Of course. I…" Her face red, she gnawed on her bottom lip.

What the hell was wrong with him? He didn't want to fight with her, and not over something so trivial. He got up and went to her, doing his best to disguise his limp. He cupped her cheek. "I'm fine."

When she looked skeptical, he turned her around and gave a gentle shove. "Go. Do what you have to. I'll be right here."

She glanced over her shoulder.

He grinned. "Actually, I'll be over there on the couch."

She started back down the hall and called over her shoulder, "Put your feet up, Lieutenant. That's an order."

"Oh, believe me, I intend to, but tell me something."

She stopped and turned. "Yes?"

"Do you plan on being this bossy later?" He quirked an eyebrow and studied her from across the room.

Her eyes widened and a blush spread across her face. "I guess you'll have to wait and see."

She turned and hurried down the hall before he could respond. Instead of chafing at being bossed around and fussed over, following her commands didn't leave him feeling defensive. Huh, maybe the promise of things to come made a difference.

Chuckling, he went back to the couch and put his feet up. He had to admit it did ease the ache a bit.

She came back a few minutes later with Sam and the cat following close on their heels. "He wants to say good-night."

Sam stuck out his hand and Des shook his hand, then pulled him closer and gave him a hug, which Sam returned.

"C'mon, Sam, I think Shadow wants to go to bed."

Sam giggled and picked up the cat.

His chest tightened as Natalie and Sam walked with the cat back down the hall. What would it be like to be a part of this ritual every night? To belong to something like this, to belong in Natalie's world…forever?

"Did you want to watch a movie?" she asked when she came back into the living room and sat next to him on the sofa. "I promise to stay awake this time."

He had more on his mind than that, but he'd take any excuse to linger. If that meant watching a movie—even one of her dreaded Christmas romances—he'd take it. Putting his arm over the back of the couch, Des toyed with the hair falling over her shoulder. "If that's what you want."

She began to fidget, pulling at the neck of her shirt. "To be honest, I'd rather we uh…uh…" She blushed. "Geez, I'm an enlightened and empowered twenty-first-century woman, so this shouldn't be hard, but it is. And so, so awkward."

Relief rippled through him along with a sexual thrill. Were they on the same page? Looked like his self-imposed period of celibacy was over. He opened his mouth, then realized he didn't have any protection with him. Ha! He didn't have any at his house, either. Damn. "I would love to, but I don't have any—"

"I do," she interrupted in a rush.

"You what?" His heart thudded in his chest. Could she mean what he thought—hoped—she meant…

"I have some." This time her face blossomed scarlet. "When I was in Boston… I…I…well, I figured no one would know me there so…"

"Wait…" He put his thumb under her chin and lifted her head. "Didn't you go to Boston after our third meeting?"

She scowled. "Now you're assuming I bought them because of you."

"Well, I…" *Guilty.* He had made that very assumption.

She poked him. "Of course they're because of you."

He couldn't see his own face, but he was certain he had a silly grin plastered all over it. Pulling her into his arms, he bent to kiss her, but before his lips touched hers he whispered, "We are talking condoms, right?"

"We are. Now kiss me." She sighed and melted against him, their lips meeting.

He cradled her face in his palms and kissed her as

if he'd been waiting for her his entire life. And perhaps he had. Strands of her silky hair caught on the rough skin of his fingers, her lavender scent tickling and inciting his senses.

He'd been with other women and even engaged, but he'd never felt like this before. All his nerve endings were electrified to the point where he expected sparks where their bodies touched.

He left her mouth to kiss his way across her cheek to beneath her ear and then the spot where her neck met her shoulder.

She groaned. "I had a dream about you last night."

"Mmm…tell me more about this dream." He nibbled on her earlobe.

"You'll think it was silly." She ran her fingernails lightly up and down his back.

"Tell me anyway," he urged.

She sighed. "You were wearing dress whites and swept me off my feet."

He groaned. How often had he heard that before? "Are you sure you weren't dreaming about Richard Gere?"

She shook her head. "Who?"

He searched her face but still couldn't be sure if she was serious or not. "*An Officer and a Gentleman.* The movie."

She smiled. "Sorry. That was before my time."

"Mine, too." He found it hard to believe she wasn't referring to that movie. Ashley had talked about that scene, as had other women he'd met.

He wished he could make her dream a reality, but he

also knew his limitations. His days of sweeping women off their feet were over.

That had never bothered him as much as it did now, because he wanted to make Natalie's dreams come true…no matter how hokey or cliché. "If I had Richard Gere's sturdy legs, I'd sweep you off your feet and carry you anywhere you desired. Since I don't, how about I take your hand and lead you to the bedroom instead?"

She placed her palm against his cheek. He leaned into her touch, yearning for that connection with her.

"Sounds like a good plan. I'm capable of walking. Why risk injury before the fun begins?"

He brushed the hair back from her face. There was a vulnerability about this woman that awakened his protective instincts. "If I could make your dreams come true, I would."

She lifted her hand and pressed it to her lips, then pressed her fingers to his lips. The gesture was chaste and at the same time so sensual he experienced her touch all the way to his toes.

What he could or couldn't do didn't seem to bother Natalie. She accepted him the way he was and didn't prattle on about how it was too bad he couldn't fly jets any longer. Was it because she hadn't known him before? Or that she liked living in Loon Lake and wouldn't feel as though she'd been cheated out of something she'd expected from him? Something deep inside shifted around the region of his heart.

Tingling all over, Natalie led Des to her bedroom. Mindful of her son, she locked the door. A lit lamp was casting a warm glow over the bed.

Suddenly shy, her hands shook as she pulled out the

box of condoms from the top drawer. Biting her bottom lip, she set it on the bedside table.

Des choked out a laugh and picked up the box, turning it over in his hands. "Did you get a volume discount?"

"It's been a while and…" She was about to get intimate with this man—at least that was the plan. And yet she didn't want to tell him there'd been no one in the past three years.

He set the box back down and positioned himself in front of her. "Making up for lost time?"

What must he think of her? Why hadn't she taken out a few condoms? "Look, if you—"

He pressed his fingers against her lips. "I'm sorry for teasing. I guess I'm a bit nervous."

Her eyes widened. "Guys get nervous, too?"

He coaxed her into his arms. "This one does when he's with a woman as beautiful as you and when it's been as long as it has."

She blushed. He thought she was beautiful. She rubbed her cheek against the soft cotton of his shirt. He smelled of woodsmoke, pine and fabric softener. "Are you telling me that it's been a while since you…?"

"Don't look so surprised. You've seen where I live and how I treat unexpected visitors." He chuckled.

The vibrations from his deep voice against her cheek raised the hairs on her arm and sent a delicious chill through her. She lifted her face to his. "You were a bit of a grizzly, but in your defense I did barge in. I'm still not sure where I got the courage to do that."

"I tried to scare you off by acting like a jerk, but it didn't work." He shifted, fitting her against him.

She ran her hands up and down his back, her finger-nails scraping him.

"Maybe I'm able to see past that gruff exterior to what's underneath." She placed her palm over his chest. "I see what's in here."

"Ah, X-ray vision. Good thing I put on clean under-wear every day."

"See? I knew there was a sense of humor under there." Any misgivings she may have had vanished. She wanted him and she wanted this. Ached for his touch, his and no one else's.

His eyes darkened as if he'd recognized her desire. "The homemade candy and cookies were a stroke of genius. Did you know I had a sweet tooth? Is that why you brought the candy?" Although it was an innocuous question, his voice was husky.

"When I asked about you, Tavie mentioned that you load way too much sugar in your coffee. She says you're trying to offset all that grumpiness." She had trouble concentrating on the conversation because his hands were under her sweater, roaming over bare skin. His callused hands were causing her breathing to become erratic.

"Ah, but I've been told my grumpiness is one of my virtues," he whispered close to her ear.

She shivered. "You're twisting my words, Des Gallagher."

Working his shirt free of his pants, she slid her hands underneath the fabric and moaned when her exploring hands encountered chest hair.

He groaned. "I love it when you say my name in that sexy little drawl."

"Des Gallagher," she whispered and made sure to drag it out to as many syllables as she could.

"You're killing me, sweetheart. Now it's my turn to make you plead."

He lifted her sweater and pulled it over her head with a crackle of static electricity. "Sorry," he murmured and tried to tame the silky strands.

"It's okay. It gets like this during the winter. I feel like the bride of Frankenstein."

He twined his fingers in her hair, fisted his hand and gave it a gentle tug. "I've wanted to do that for the longest time."

"And I've imagined you doing just that."

He groaned low in his throat and kissed her. She lost herself in his touch as he eased them toward the bed until the mattress hit the back of her knees. She'd told him the truth about wanting his hands in her hair and all over. She wanted this, wanted him. Now.

She laid on the bed and he followed, never breaking contact with her lips. He moved so they were laying face-to-face and cupped her breasts in his palms. The lace of the bra brushed against her nipples, sending fire shooting to the apex of her thighs. She made a sound in her throat and he squeezed with one hand and reached around with the other and unclasped her bra, freeing her breasts.

He kissed and sucked, driving her into a frenzy of sweet, sweet torture.

"Please," she groaned but had no idea what she was pleading for.

He unsnapped her jeans and eased the zipper down as he rained kisses over her stomach. She helped him by shimmying out of the pants, leaving her in nothing but her new pink lace bikini panties.

He groaned and put his hands on her hips and rubbed his thumbs along the lace.

"So beautiful," he whispered and kissed the skin above the waistband, drawing his tongue across the top.

His touch set her on fire and she felt beautiful, sexy and desired, pregnancy stretch marks included.

She pushed at his shoulders. "You have too many clothes on. I want to touch you."

Des pushed himself off the bed and began stripping off his clothes as eager as a teenager being with a woman for the first time. If he wasn't careful he'd lose control with embarrassing results, especially when her eyes darkened as her gaze traveled to his groin.

His pants around his ankles, he froze when she gasped. His scars. Damn. How could he have forgotten about those? Sick to his stomach, he began yanking the pants back up.

"No. Don't." She scrambled off the bed and kneeled in front of him, tugging the jeans back down.

Her fingers traced the angry marks, then her lips followed where those soothing fingers had been. Until that moment, he'd barely acknowledged their existence because they represented all he'd lost, but looking down at Natalie the bitterness he'd carried began slipping away. They were scars, nothing more, nothing less.

Fearing he might embarrass himself, not by loss of sexual control but by bawling, he put his hands under her arms. He urged her up, cupped his hands around her face and gave her a hard, bruising, and yet some-how cleansing, kiss.

When she made a noise, he broke the contact with their lips but continued to cradle her head in his palms. "Did I hurt you?"

"No, I was right there with you," she whispered, and threaded her fingers in his hair, resuming the kiss.

He wasn't sure who moved first, but they were both back on the bed in a tangle of arms and legs.

"Isn't it about time to lose these?" she asked, inserting her fingers under the waistband of his boxer briefs and pulling.

When he sprang free, she reached over. Her touch was gentle, tentative, but his hips bucked under her hands and he couldn't hold back the groan. Growing bolder, she stroked him and he gritted his teeth to hold on to his control. He attempted to calculate lift-to-drag ratios in his head but his brain had ceased to function, leaving him little more than an incoherent fool.

Leaning down, he took the puckered point of her nipple into his mouth and sucked. She squeezed him in response and he grinned against her skin.

He ran his fingers up and down her side. She arched away, giggling.

"Is my Southern gal ticklish?" he asked and touched her again, triggering the same response.

"Yes, but I'm a Muggle, not a Southern gal."

He laughed. "I have no idea what a Muggle is, but I love hearing you say it."

"It's a person with no magical ability. From the Harry Potter books."

He pressed a kiss to that spot. "I'd say you were pretty magical."

"Bless your heart, aren't you a peach," she said and giggled again.

"I have a feeling that's another one of your insults," he said in a voice that was supposed to be stern but he couldn't pull it off.

"Sorry."

"You can insult me all you want as long as you use that voice."

His wandering fingers found a spot that made her moan and his blood began to pound. Teasing forgotten, he used all his skill to work her into a frenzy.

"Oh, please," she begged. "Yes, right there."

He applied a little more pressure and she came apart in his hand.

He scooted up and grabbed one of the condoms and fumbled until he got it opened.

"May I?" she asked as he started to sheath himself.

What sweet torture. Her hands shook as she rolled the condom in place.

"I can't hold out much longer." He moved over her and spread her thighs. "But you said it's been a while and I don't want to hurt you."

"You won't." She shook her head, her blue eyes dark with pleasure and trust.

She trusts me. He groaned again. "Tell me to stop if it hurts and I will."

He took his time until he was satisfied she was ready for him. He pulled out, then thrust into her. Lifting her legs, she crossed her heels around the small of his back and urged him to keep up his pace. When he got too close he slowed down, trying to wring as much out of both of them as he could. Finally, he couldn't hold off any longer and, using his thumb, he brought her to the peak and made sure she tumbled over again.

Closing his eyes he thrust hard and deep one last time before he exploded in a release that bewildered him. He'd never experienced anything this intense and perhaps if he wasn't so numb with pleasure, he'd be able to figure out why or the implications of what had happened.

He stretched out next to her and anchored her against him with his arm. She rested her head on his chest.

"That was amazing." She caressed his chest. "Was it good for you, too?"

"Amazing," he echoed and kissed the top of her head. "I'm glad my behavior didn't scare you away, Natalie."

"Me, too." She cuddled closer, her fingers drawing swirls on his chest. "You seem like such a loner. Do you have any family?"

Did he want to talk about this? He remembered the look of trust in her eyes. She'd trusted him with her heart—and her body—so the least he could do was offer her the same. "I had a brother."

She lifted her head. "Had?"

He puffed up his cheeks and released the trapped air. "His name was Patrick. He was five years older."

"What happened?" She laid her head back down. "Forget I asked. You don't have to spill your guts because...because of this."

"I know." He laced his fingers through hers. "He committed suicide when he was seventeen...went out in the woods and hung himself."

"I'm so sorry. That must've been terrible for your parents."

"It was just my mother. Technically, he was a half brother. Same mother, different fathers. Patrick's father died of a brain tumor when my brother was a baby. Patrick's father was the one great love of my mother's life and when he died, she poured all that love into Patrick."

"But...what about your father?"

"I never knew him. He was married, had another family. His *real* family," he said, blinking back stupid tears pricking his eyes. Looked like shoving feelings you didn't want to deal with down deep just buried them instead of eradicating them.

She gripped his hand tighter. "That's terrible. Your poor mother."

He exhaled a mirthless laugh. "Nah. No other man could hold a candle to the love of her life. She said my father was just some mistake she made."

"So you never knew him?"

"No. I think my mother agreed not to make trouble for his other family as long as he sent support checks. The checks arrived monthly like clockwork until I turned eighteen."

"You never wanted to meet him once you became an adult?"

He rubbed his chest but the constriction wouldn't ease up. "I found him and we spoke, but once my curiosity was satisfied I never felt the need for more."

But that was a lie, because he *had* felt the need. How could he desire a relationship with someone who'd shown no interest in him? "After Patrick died, my mother checked out. She was still physically there, going through the motions, but that was all. As a kid, I was afraid she'd kill herself and I'd be left with no one. As an adult, it made me angry and sad."

She shook her head. "She had you. That's terrible that she couldn't see that."

"My brother was a great guy, no question, but he wasn't perfect, nor was he a saint. But after his death, he'd become the anointed one who could do no wrong. I couldn't compete with a ghost."

"You shouldn't have had to. Is…is that why you don't like Christmas?"

Her voice was thick and when he touched her cheek, his fingers came away wet. The back of his throat burned. She was crying for him and he'd lied to her. "I lied."

"What?" She sniffled. "What did you lie about?"

"I lied when I said I never felt the need for a relationship with my father. I had hoped maybe he'd want a relationship, too. I had convinced myself he regretted his actions." He couldn't keep the bitterness from his tone. "I had this whole fairy-tale scenario built up in my head. Yeah, right."

She sucked in a sharp breath and laid her hand on his thigh. "You had every right to expect more than what you got from him. I'd love to give him a piece of my mind."

Her hand had curled into a fist and he laid his hand over the tight little ball. Such fierceness on his behalf. He uncurled her fingers as the tightness he'd carried in his chest for so long unfurled.

When she sniffed, he put his hands under her arms and dragged her on top of him and kissed her.

"No more tears," he whispered against her lips. "How can we take your mind off all this?"

"Well…" She stretched out on top of him. "I do have all these condoms. Can't let them go to waste."

He chuckled. "They do have expiration dates."

"Natalie?"

Someone was shaking her shoulder, trying to get her to wake up, but she wanted to cuddle up next to… an empty spot. Des wasn't next to her as he had been when she drifted off.

She opened one eye. "Des?"

"It's me." He kissed her forehead.

She opened both eyes and sat up.

Des was leaning over the bed, fully dressed. She glanced around and squinted at the glowing numbers of her alarm clock. It was half past midnight.

"I know you wanted me to leave before Sam got up."

Yeah, she'd said something to that effect before falling asleep. "I didn't mean to make it sound like I was kicking you out, but thank you for honoring my wishes."

"No problem. It's starting to snow so it's best to go now, but if we have an accumulation I'll be back to get you plowed out."

She yawned. "Doesn't the town plow?"

He chuckled. "I meant your driveway, unless you have a snowblower."

She swung her feet over the side of the bed. Standing, she reached for the robe on the bench across the end of the bed. Once she was covered up with pink terry cloth, she switched on the lamp. "No, but I did buy a snow shovel."

"If the forecast is right, we could get over a foot."

She tied the robe's belt. "I bought Sam a child-sized one, too."

"Well, in that case…"

She pushed his shoulder. "I told you, a little snow isn't going to scare me away."

"That's good." He hitched his chin toward the opened box of condoms on the bedside table. "We barely made a dent in your supply."

She patted his chest. "I have no complaints."

Yes, it had been a while—three years—since she'd been intimate with a man, but that didn't explain the incredible night with Des. Adding to their fantastic chemistry was the fact that he'd confided in her, trusted her with a piece of himself he didn't show anyone else. Now she understood him better and had hope for a future together. As trite as it might sound, the world, *her* world, looked bright and inviting.

His arms went around her and hers around him and their lips locked in a kiss that held a promise of more.

There was a noise at the door and he stepped away.

She went to the door, unlocked it and opened it a crack. The cat pranced in and gave her an accusing look and twitched his tail. She bent down and picked him up.

"I usually leave my door open a crack so he can come and go. He divides his time between me and Sam during the night," she explained to Des.

He scratched the cat's ears and tried to give her another kiss, but Shadow stuck his head in the way. "Good thing I'm in such a good mood."

Yeah, she was in a pretty sweet mood, too. A couple rounds of lovemaking would do that.

"If there's some accumulation in the morning, sit tight and I'll come over. You're not used to driving in this."

"But I need to help with the horses. Besides, I will need to learn to drive in the snow because I am here to stay."

"I'll take care of the horses in the morning. And let the plows clear the roads before you get out, promise?"

She scowled at him. "I'll have you know, Mr. Bossy Pants, I've been driving for ten years."

He quirked an eyebrow. "In the snow?"

She stuck her tongue out at him. "Brat."

His gaze zeroed in on her tongue, and his eyes darkened. He seemed to be fighting a battle with himself. Finally, he kissed her again and licked his lips when he ended the kiss. "Remember this. We won't be able to use up your king-size box if you're in traction."

"You do have a point," she conceded, already looking forward to their next encounter.

She followed Des to the door and gave him a kiss. "I want you to know I won't be asking you to make Christmas ornaments again."

He cocked his head to the side as his gaze met hers. "No?"

"It was unfair of me and I want you to know I respect your right not to want to make them. I shouldn't have pursued it once you said you didn't want to do it."

"Thanks, but I am glad you didn't give up easily." He touched the side of her face.

"Me, too, but I wanted you to know I regret pushing you." She leaned into his touch. "But know this. That's the one and only thing I regret."

"I'm glad," he whispered as his lips met hers in a kiss full of promise.

"Me, too."

"Until tomorrow," he said and opened the door.

Hugging the cat, she stood in the front window and watched Des get in his truck and back out of the driveway, missing his warmth already. Her thoughts drifted back to the days leading up to Ryan's death. They'd been arguing over her desire to finish her degree. Ryan had felt it was unnecessary, expensive and time consuming, but she'd disagreed. He'd wanted to talk about it, but she'd been too angry to discuss it rationally so she'd refused. Things had been tense and they'd had no time to apologize and make up before he died.

Anger had prevented her from telling him she loved him before he and Sam had left that day. She'd had every expectation he'd return home and they'd talk about it and come to a mutual decision. She stood for a long time, staring out the window, watching the snowflakes in the streetlight at the end of the road.

She'd fallen in love with Des Gallagher. This was no crush, no sex high. Well, okay, she might still be a little drunk on the passion they'd engaged in, but she was mature enough to separate the two. She'd fallen for him before tonight. How could she not fall for him after seeing how he treated Sam? Des had fit into their lives like a missing puzzle piece.

The cat was kneading its claws on her terry-cloth robe and purring in her ear.

Sighing, she went back down the hall toward her room, glancing into Sam's as she passed. The nightlight cast enough light so she could see he was still fast asleep. Setting the cat down, she went back to her room, put a nightgown on and crawled back into bed. Alone. For now. As she cuddled under the covers with Shadow curled up next to her, she pictured the future. Her and Des sharing a bed every night with no need for him to leave before Sam woke up.

Ryan's death had shown her how random and cruel life could be, but meeting Des had proved that some of life's most wonderful things could also be random.

Chapter Eight

Natalie awoke the next morning to the weight of an eight-pound cat sitting on her chest and a five-year-old boy poking her shoulder.

She lifted Shadow and sat up. "What is it?"

Sam ran to the window and lifted the blind and stuck his head between it and the glass.

"Did it snow?"

She grabbed her robe from the bench and threw it on. At the window she pulled up the blinds, and the cat jumped on the windowsill. Sam kept pointing to the snow. There were a few flurries coming down, but it appeared the major snowfall had stopped. She couldn't be sure.

"Yes, we'll go out, but first, breakfast." And coffee. She needed caffeine. "Go get dressed while I make breakfast."

She threw on a sweatshirt and jeans, stuck her feet into pink fuzzy slippers and went to the kitchen. She had to admit she was excited, too. And it had nothing to do with Des saying he'd come over to help with snow removal. Nothing? How about everything?

She considered the fact that he'd confided his feelings about his father as a big step forward in their relationship. Des wasn't someone who confided in people. That, combined with how he and Sam had bonded, gave her hopes for them as a family. Maybe even more children in the future.

After putting a pod in the coffeemaker, she got out eggs and bread. She'd be lucky if she could get Sam to eat more than a few bites but scrambled eggs and toast would be quick to make.

She was beating the eggs when a horn tooted. Des? She set the bowl down and moved the frying pan off the burner. There was a knock at the front door before she could reach it. Sam came galloping down the hall with one sock on and the other in his hand, the cat nipping at his heels.

"Sam," she cautioned, but he was already opening the door.

Des filled the doorway and she fumbled a bit trying to get the storm door unlocked. She managed to push the little knob and opened the door.

"Hey, guys." Des stepped inside bringing the cold, crisp winter air with him. It seemed to cling to him along with a faint woodsmoke scent.

Sam pointed outside while Des stamped the snow off his boots before stepping into the house and shutting the door.

Des ruffled Sam's hair. "Yeah. Lots of snow out there, bud, but I think you need something more on your feet first."

"And he needs to eat some breakfast," she said. "Maybe Des will join us for some eggs and toast."

"If your mom's cooking, you better believe I'm eating." Des unzipped his jacket and hung it on the coat rack next to the door, then removed his boots. He set them on the plastic tray next to a pair of Natalie's shoes.

"Sam, put your other sock on." She turned her attention to Des. "You're early. Did you take care of the horses already?"

"Sure did." He touched her arm and smiled.

"Have you had breakfast yet?"

He made a face. "Does a Pop-Tart count?"

Both socks on, Sam stood up and gave Des a thumbs-up.

"A Pop-Tart does not count. We're having eggs and toast."

Sam pointed to her and shook his head.

Des laughed. "I think Sam is saying you're…absolutely right. Eggs and toast is a much healthier breakfast."

Sam put his hands on his hips and gave Des a scowl.

"You're gonna get me in trouble with your mom," Des told him and pretended to shadow box.

Sam burst out laughing and pushed Des toward the kitchen.

"Eggs it is," he said, and when Sam's head was turned, he gave her a quick peck on the cheek.

In the kitchen, she broke more eggs into the bowl and switched to a bigger frying pan. Watching Sam and

Des together these past weeks had given her mixed feelings. She was happy they got along so well together, but knew it was already too late to prevent Sam from getting hurt if things didn't work out with her and Des. She glanced at Des. Yeah, Sam wouldn't be the only one getting hurt. She fell in love with Des a little more each time she was with him.

Sam took a seat at the table and began to draw with crayons and a pad that were on the table.

"How can I help?" Des asked.

Fall in love with me, too. "If you want coffee, there are some pods next to the maker. Mugs are in the cabinet above it. Help yourself." She motioned to the coffeemaker.

He picked out a pod and took a mug from the cupboard. "Do you want some?"

"I haven't finished the first yet." She indicated her mug next to the stove. "Although I may need another shot of caffeine to get going."

"Someone tire you out last night?" He gave her a bland expression but his eyes darkened.

Despite the fluttering in her chest, she returned his bland expression. Not an easy feat when she wanted to giggle like a schoolgirl or break into song as if she were Julie Andrews on an Austrian mountain meadow. "Something like that."

Sam got up and handed Des a picture he'd drawn.

Des held up the picture. "I think he wants to build a snowman. Right, bud?"

Sam nodded and Des playfully poked him and made him giggle.

"And so we shall. As soon as we eat our eggs and toast," Des said.

Natalie mouthed "thank you" to Des and dished out the eggs onto a platter and put buttered toast on a plate. She brought them to the table. All they were doing was eating breakfast together but she felt a thrill run through her each time her gaze landed on Des. What would it be like to have this scenario be her future? Waking up to Des every morning, and better yet, going to bed each night with him. Sharing their lives and love. *Don't go getting ahead of yourself, Natalie.*

As soon as Sam had shoveled in the last bite, he jumped up and went to get his jacket and new snow boots. He shoved his feet into the boots and Natalie showed him how the pull-tie laces worked. She gathered her dirty dishes and piled them in the sink.

"Want help with that?" Des gathered the rest of the plates.

She shook her head. "I'll worry about them later. Sam wants to get out there before it all melts."

Des laughed. "No chance of that. It's still coming down."

She shrugged. "Like I said, if we got any snow in Nashville, it disappeared as soon as the sun came out."

"Not much chance of that here."

She grinned and motioned with her head toward the front door. Sam was bouncing up and down, waiting to go out. Des met her gaze and grinned in silent communication.

After getting her parka buttoned up, she put on a knit cap and mittens.

Des glanced at her feet. "Did you get new boots, too?"

"I took your warnings to heart." She put her palm flat on his chest. "I've been taking notes and learning. So be warned, you're not getting rid of me that easily."

He put his hands on each side of her waist. "What makes you think I'm trying to get rid of you?"

"You keep warning me about the snow."

He squeezed his hands around her waist. "I'm looking out for you. Not chasing you away."

She exhaled in relief. "I'm glad because I like it here in Loon Lake and I like you."

"I—"

Sam tugged on Des's sleeve and pointed outside. Des released her and put his hand over Sam's head, adjusting his knit cap. "Okay, bud, let's go build the best snowman Loon Lake has ever seen."

Natalie's heart clenched. What had Des been about to say? Had he been going to return the sentiment? Or could he have been about to warn her not to take this seriously? Tell her not to read too much into what they'd shared last night?

"You guys go out. I want to get some things for the snowman's face." *And to collect myself.* Let feelings that were too close to the surface settle back down. Des had been the first man she'd become sexually intimate with since the death of her husband, so naturally her feelings would be confusing.

She got a carrot and coffee beans from the kitchen and found an old scarf and mittens in a box of things she'd been collecting to donate. Taking a breath and telling herself not to read too much into a comment that Des never even finished, she ventured outside.

"First, we need to make the body parts. Do you know how to do that, Sam?"

Sam shrugged and Des patted his shoulder. "Don't worry, it's easy."

Natalie noticed Des had picked up her habit of asking Sam specific questions, ones that he could answer with a yes or no movement of his head. She often wondered if she should be doing more to encourage Sam to use his tablet for communication. Or was letting him develop at his own pace the answer? Since being with Des, Sam seemed more willing to use his tablet. Maybe Sam's therapist's cautious optimism was warranted.

Des demonstrated how to roll out parts for a snowman with Sam helping him. The two of them pushed the large balls of snow around the yard. Des glanced up at her when they'd gotten the requisite three balls stacked up. She handed him the carrot she'd gotten out of the vegetable bin for a nose, some fresh coffee beans for a smile plus an old scarf and knitted cap to complete his outfit.

"Do you have any old pants or boots Sam maybe had outgrown?"

"As a matter of fact, I have a box of stuff I hadn't gotten around to taking to the charity shop. What did you have in mind?"

"You'll see."

She ran in the house and got the box. Des was whispering something to Sam when she got back. They'd put another small ball on top of the snowman.

Sam ran to the box with a huge grin on his face and pulled out pants and an old pair of boots.

"What have you two cooked up?"

"You'll see," Des said and took the things from Sam. "Thanks, bud. We'll use the leftovers for another face." He glanced at Sam. "Okay?"

Sam retrieved the things from the porch and held out his hand to Des, who shook his head. "I'll hold you up and you do it. Do you want to do that?"

Sam's eyes widened and he nodded. Des held up the smaller ball of snow on top of the snowman's head. He held him in place while Sam placed the items to make another face.

"A two-headed snowman?" Natalie asked.

Des and Sam shook their heads at the same time and Natalie's heart expanded until she thought it would burst. Was she doing the right thing letting Sam get this close to Des when there was no guarantee things would work out between the adults? If they didn't, Sam could be collateral damage. But then, sacrificing her personal life might not be the right answer for her child. If she was unhappy or lonely, she wouldn't be setting a good example for Sam.

Des set Sam back on the ground and headed for his truck. "I think I have some rope. Sam, get some old shirts or something from that box so we can fill out the pants so they look like legs."

Des and Sam stuffed an old pair of pajamas into the pants and Des pushed the rope through and tied the old boots to each end before placing them on the snowman.

Natalie stood back and watched. "Oh, my, look at that. Let me find extra mittens and a knit hat."

In the garage she found some extra mittens and a hat and gave them to Des. He finished arranging the snowman and once they got it finished, it looked like an adult snowman carrying a snow child on his shoulders.

Sam kept grinning and pointing to the snowman. She nodded and gave him a thumbs up. Despite all her optimistic thoughts this morning, her stomach quivered. After one night with Des, she couldn't let her desire go rampaging ahead because Sam needed to be considered in every decision she made.

"Your first snowman and it's a masterpiece." Natalie hugged Sam. "Teddy will be so surprised when he and Miss Addie get back."

"Where's your neighbor?" Des asked.

"They went to visit friends in Massachusetts for the weekend." She studied their snow masterpiece and felt proud. Sam was beside himself with excitement. No matter what the future held, today would be a treasured memory. One they could look back on with joy.

She patted the snowman. "What made you think of this?"

"I'm an artist… I'm supposed to be creative. It's part of the job description." His cheeks had color in them. Whether from the cold air or embarrassment, she couldn't tell.

"You're right. Sorry. I should've realized."

He gave a sharp bark of laughter. "I saw it on Pinterest."

"You use Pinterest?"

He shrugged. "It makes it easier to keep track of some of my designs and inspiration for future works."

"I see," she said. She suspected he wore that gruffness like an outer shell to protect his soft underbelly. She treasured those glimpses beneath his surly exterior.

He grunted. "You see what?"

"You." She smiled. "I see you, Des Gallagher."

"Of course you do." He gave her a quizzical look. "I'm standing right in front of you. Let me get the snowblower from the back of the truck and I'll get your sidewalks cleared."

"Let me get my new shovel and I'll clear off the front steps. The logistics of snow removal are still new to me."

Sam nodded his head and tugged on Natalie's sleeve and pointed to the plow attached to the truck.

"He wants to know if you're going to use the plow."

Des laughed. "It might be a bit of overkill, but if he wants to hop in the back, we can clear your driveway and your neighbor's."

She nodded. "Thanks. As the landlord, I am responsible."

He turned to Sam. "You want to ride in the truck with me while we plow?"

Sam grabbed Des's hand and nodded.

"Okay, but you have to ride in the back, bud."

"I'll have to get his booster seat out of my car."

"I already have one back there."

"You do?" Natalie was surprised and pleased he had gone to the trouble of getting one for Sam. What did the gesture mean? Or did he think it would make things easier when they went around collecting items for the auction?

"Yeah. I remembered what kind you had and picked one up last time I was in town."

She swallowed. "Thanks."

He opened the rear door on the driver's side and gave Sam a boost. "You want to check and make sure I did it right?"

She made sure Sam was buckled in securely, not an easy task considering he was bouncing with excitement. "I hate to ask but could you plow the lady across the street's driveway, too?" She pointed to the Cape Cod–style home across the street. "Mrs. O'Malley's in her eighties and a widow."

While Des worked, she went and got her brand-new snow shovel from the carport and cleared off the front steps on both sides of the duplex.

After plowing, Des got the snowblower from where he had it secured in the back of the truck and did the sidewalks, including Mrs. O'Malley's. Sam used his shovel to clear off the widow's steps while Des did the sidewalk. Natalie stood on her own steps and watched the two of them working. *Her two men.* What? No, she needed to not read too much into this with Des.

The elderly woman came to the door, and Sam and Des stood talking to her. She handed something to Sam and went back inside. "What you got there, Sam?" she asked as the two came back across the street.

Sam held up a toy truck.

"She wanted to pay us but we said no," Des said. "But she insisted Sam needed the truck for his collection."

"She's so sweet. Did you thank her?" When Sam nodded, she continued, "How about we go inside and warm up with some hot chocolate? Sam?"

Natalie couldn't help notice that Sam looked to Des before nodding. Her stomach clenched when she realized all the implications of that simple gesture. Sure, she enjoyed the smile of happiness on Sam's face, but knowing Des put it there was troubling because she didn't know how long he'd be in their lives. Could she count on Des to be here after the auction? How would Sam feel if Des was out of their lives? She definitely needed to look into a Big Brother organization in or near Loon Lake.

They trooped back into the house through the car-port. She helped Sam get out of his boots and jacket in the laundry room. "Go get some dry clothes on and bring me your wet pants."

Des leaned against the door frame as she set the wet socks, hat and mittens on the washing machine to deal with later.

"I think we'll—uh…" He cleared his throat. "I mean you'll need to get him snow pants to go over his jeans and the top of his boots if he's going to do a lot of play-ing in the snow this winter."

"Yeah, I guess I hadn't thought about him being in snow that deep. Shows how totally unprepared I am. The hand-knitted mittens were warm but not water-proof."

He stepped closer, put his arm around her and pressed his lips to her temple. "Like you said, it's your first winter here."

"Then it's a good thing I have someone like you to show me the ropes." She leaned into him, enjoying his solid strength. "Thank you for today."

Having Des to lean on thrilled and scared her. The future held no guarantees. Could she survive another devastating loss? But, by the same token, she couldn't let fear rule her decisions or rob her of a future with a wonderful—if sometimes grumpy—man.

Chapter Nine

Three days had passed since the season's first snowfall and since the temperatures stayed below freezing, the white blanketing her yard, including Sam's snowman, stuck around.

Natalie snuggled against Des as they enjoyed a few stolen hours together in her bed. Brody and Mary had included Sam in a group of kids they'd taken sledding and he'd been excited to go. They'd invited her to go along, but she'd felt it important to release, or at least relax, her grip on Sam's hand. She hoped there'd be many more outings like this in his future, and not just because it gave her and Des alone time they were putting to good use. And making a dent in her jumbo box of condoms.

She caressed her fingers across his chest. "Did you always want to be a pilot?"

"I was always interested in flying." He rubbed his hand up and down her arm.

"After your injuries couldn't you have been an instructor or something? Use your love of flying to teach the new guys." She hated the thought that he had to walk away from something he loved.

He yawned. "I might have been able to do something in the classroom."

"But you chose to walk away."

"I'm not saying I didn't love every minute of it—you have to love it in order to make it through the intense training—but…"

"What? Tell me?" She yearned to know everything she could about the man she'd fallen in love with.

"Flying had been Patrick's dream. After he died I guess I took it on as my own. Not consciously. I don't know… Maybe I thought my mother would transfer all those feelings she had for my brother to me."

"I'm guessing she didn't."

"No. Even in death Patrick always came first." He sighed. "I had always thought being the favorite was a good thing. I was even jealous of Patrick even though he was never anything but generous and protective with me."

"Do you know why he killed himself?"

"I can't be sure but I think having to live up to my mother's expectations added a lot of pressure on him."

"I'm sorry you were exposed to that much dysfunction."

"I survived."

"But it skewed your opinion of families."

He raised an eyebrow. "Has it? Or maybe you're the one with the skewed vision of families."

"I'd hate to think that." She shook her head. Suspecting he was jaded was one thing, but having him verify it another.

He gave her a pitying look. "That's because you're an eternal optimist, ignoring reality."

"Hey, that's not fair." He'd gotten her hackles up with his comments. That expression on his face hadn't helped. She didn't appreciate having to defend something like optimism. "Because I believe in happily-ever-after and happy families doesn't mean I live in a fantasy world."

"It does if they don't exist. Was your marriage to Sam's father perfect?"

Her hands curled into fists. "Of course not. I never said anything about perfection. It's not the same thing. A relationship doesn't have to be perfect to be happy or successful."

His words brought her guilt over the final days of her life with Ryan to the surface.

"Relationships aren't perfect or guaranteed, but we need to try." And she believed that.

"Why put yourself out there to get your heart broken?"

"Because if you don't, how can you say you lived? The people who never get their hearts broken are dead. Frankly, I don't aspire to be dead." The blood pounding in her ears made it difficult to focus on her thoughts. Why had she pursued this conversation when he was going to say things she didn't want to hear? Because burying her head in the sand wasn't the answer, either.

He made an impatient noise. "And you think I do?"

"Not consciously, but not feeling anything isn't living." Her heart broke for him. What an awful way to live.

"Opening your heart to someone, making yourself vulnerable, is asking for trouble. How can you sign up for that? You can't believe all that 'better to have loved and lost than not at all.'" He shook his head and looked at her as if he felt sorry for *her*.

She tried to swallow past the growing lump in her throat. She'd known Des was cynical, but she hadn't realized the extent and that knowledge made her stomach queasy. "I may have lost Ryan but I have Sam and I wouldn't trade any of the pain for not ever having known or loved him."

"Ah, jeez, Natalie, forgive me. I shouldn't have dumped all that on you." He urged her closer. "The last thing I want is to fight with you."

She didn't want to spend precious time with him fighting, either, but she wasn't sure she could accept his view of relationships. She could walk away from what they had, but what would that prove? Would it reinforce his beliefs? But if she stayed, she could show him that loving someone didn't have to lead to heartbreak. She owed it to both of them to try, except she couldn't hold up a relationship on her own. She knew he cared. He might not want to admit it, but his actions had proved that. Even if he denied it, he'd gone out of his way to show them how much he cared. All the things he'd done for and with her and Sam proved that. She might regret it for the rest of her life if she left now.

She relaxed and wrapped her arm around his waist.

Resting her head on his chest, she listened to his beating heart under her ear. "Me, too."

He put his hand under her chin, lifted her face to his and kissed her. "How much time do we have before Sam gets home?"

She smiled. "Enough time enough to make me glad I went with the jumbo box."

Des came back into the barn with the empty wheelbarrow and stood for a moment. Natalie was busy cleaning Augie's stall and he watched her. How had he become so involved with a woman who believed in the sitcom version of happy families? He'd opened up to someone who believed in fairy tales.

He blew out his breath and tried to ignore that uneasy feeling in the pit of his stomach.

"What time are you supposed to get Sam?" he asked as he brought the wheelbarrow to the stall.

She stopped raking shavings and turned toward him. "Addie will bring him home later this evening. Why?"

"I bumped into Brody Wilson the other day and he asked if we'd be interested in a sleigh ride out at his farm. He bought an old one and restored it as a Christmas gift for Mary. She's always wanted to go on a sleigh ride."

She laughed. "Leave it to Brody to buy a sleigh instead of just taking her on a ride."

"Yeah, the guy is a bit smitten. Anyway, he said we were welcome to come out and give the sleigh a try. I guess Riley and Meg Cooper have been out there. So I thought maybe you and I could check it out, just the two of us. Brody said to let him know." He set the wheelbarrow down. "That is, if you're interested."

"I'd love it. Thank you. I've never been on one." She beamed with pleasure. "My first winter in Loon Lake and I'm going on a sleigh ride."

Her reaction made him glad he'd asked her. From the moment he had run into Brody and learned about the sleigh rides, Des had wanted to take Natalie on one. He'd never been romantic, but this was something he wanted to do for her. As much as he enjoyed doing things with Sam along, he wanted to do this with and for Natalie. He was glad she'd felt the same.

He was still trying the ignore the queasiness whenever he remembered how much he'd revealed to this woman.

Had this thing between them moved to the next level too quickly? He knew nothing about maintaining a relationship. Maybe he should stick to the horses. Those he knew about, but the care and feeding of a relationship was beyond his experience.

He might know how to land a jet on a carrier in the middle of the ocean, but keeping a woman like Natalie happy long term…not so much. What did he have to give her?

How about starting with a sleigh ride, his inner voice suggested.

Once at the Wilson's farm, they found one of Brody's horses hitched to a two-person red-and-gold sled in front of the barn.

Des glanced around. "Looks like Brody has everything ready to go for us."

"This is wonderful. It's a one-horse open sleigh like in the song." She turned to him. "I love it."

Her breathless voice tightened his groin and he urged her close for a kiss.

"Ahem."

Caught. Des stepped away but his lips twitched at Natalie's amused grin despite the color staining her cheeks.

"Glad you two could make it," Brody said as he strolled out of the open double doors of the barn.

Natalie threw her arms around Brody in a friendly hug. "Thank you so much for the opportunity. I've never been on a sleigh ride and I've been looking forward to this one ever since Des mentioned it."

"You're most welcome. I hope you feel the same way after the ride." Brody laughed and kissed Natalie's cheek. "I'm glad Scrooge here brought you."

Des scowled at Brody, who had the nerve to laugh.

"In case you get cold." Brody pointed to a plaid wool blanket folded up on the seat.

She nodded. "I make sure to dress in layers wherever I go these days."

Des put his arm around her shoulder. "We'll make a Vermonter out of you yet."

"Says the man who's only been here three years longer than me." She playfully pushed him.

"I hate to break it to you two, but you're both 'flatlanders,' as Tavie would say." Brody laughed.

"So are you," Des told him.

"Yeah, well, we can't all be perfect," Brody said.

Natalie, who was preparing to get in the sleigh, turned around. "Guys, what's a flatlander?"

"It's what the native Vermonters call someone who wasn't born here." Des put his hand under her elbow. "Let me help you up."

After helping her, Des swung up onto the sleigh and settled on the seat beside her. He arranged the blanket around them.

Brody patted the horse. "Ranger knows what to do and he knows his way home. Have fun, you two."

Des clucked to the horse, who took off with a jingle of bells.

"This is perfect." Natalie sighed and cuddled against him.

Des put his arm around her and drew her closer, kissing her temple. This was everything he had imagined. He hadn't done it for any other reason than to be with her and bask in the glow from her smile. He ignored the warning voice that suggested he might be getting in too deep with Natalie. She wasn't looking for anything more than what they had because she had a son to raise, he argued with himself.

He put one arm around her as he held the reins loosely in his other hand. Brody had been right. The horse knew the trail and kept to it at a moderate pace with little guidance from him. Good thing, because his thoughts were with the woman beside him. Maybe he'd come out and ask her what she was expecting from what they were sharing. She snuggled closer and sighed. Maybe now wasn't the best time for that sort of a discussion.

"Des, look," Natalie whispered and touched his arm.

A doe and her fawn were visible through the woods. He halted the horse so they could watch the small family until they wandered back off into the woods.

The deer disappeared from view, but Des kept his gaze on the spot where they'd been nibbling on the bushes. Could he keep Natalie and Sam from disappearing from his life as the deer had so easily moved on?

"It's perfect. Thank you," she said after the deer had wandered back into the woods. "Huh, seems like I'm always thanking you for something. But you've made this Christmas memorable. Not bad for a guy who tries to make everyone think he's Scrooge."

He shook his head. "You've ruined my reputation."

She laughed. "Sorry?"

The horse tugged at the reins, so Des loosened his grip. "I think he's wanting to get back to home."

"I guess I can't blame him. It's getting late but we did have a wonderful ride."

"I'm glad you enjoyed it," he told her and kissed her, putting his worries about what the future might hold on the back burner for now.

The horse sped up as if in a hurry to get back home and Natalie snuggled closer to Des, wringing the last bit of enjoyment out of their adventure.

Back at the barn, Brody came out and took charge of Ranger. Des jumped down and turned to help her. He offered to assist Brody with the horse and sled, but Brody waved him off.

After thanking Brody and asking after Mary and Elliott who, according to Brody, were out Christmas shopping, they shook his hand and got in Des's pickup.

As Des was driving down the long gravel driveway, Natalie got a text from Addie asking if Sam could go with her and Teddy to the movies.

Natalie told Des, adding, "That means we have a couple more hours to ourselves. Will you come to my place?"

"Sure." He arched his eyebrows. "Any suggestions for using those hours?"

"I could make cocoa and we could watch a movie. Or…" She couldn't hide her grin. "I do have that somewhat large supply of condoms…"

"I like the way you think." Des took her hand and intertwined his fingers with hers for the rest of the drive back to her place.

"Did you want anything to drink…or anything?" she asked as they walked up the sidewalk and went inside her house.

Inside, she removed her coat and hung it on a hook attached to the wall in the entryway, suddenly feeling nervous.

They'd joked about using up her condom supply, but having a casual sexual relationship was new territory for her. Were there certain protocols? She—

"Hey, where'd you go?" he asked and placed his hands over hers to still her hand wringing.

She glanced down at their hands. How could she put into words what she was feeling?

He put a finger under her chin and lifted her face to his. His dark gaze searched her face. "If you've changed your mind…"

She swallowed. "I haven't."

He tucked her hair behind her ear and traced the outer edge of her ear with his finger. "You sure?"

"I'm positive." She huffed out a nervous laugh. "I'm

sure you're thinking I'm the silliest woman you've ever met, but I'm just…this is all new to me."

"You're not silly." He rubbed a knuckle down her cheek. "You're the most special woman I've ever known and I'm so glad I met you."

She turned her head and kissed his hand. "I think you mean you're glad I barged into your life and refused to go away."

"No matter how much I growled at you." He caressed her bottom lip. "And I'm thankful you didn't turn tail and run."

"You're saying that because you know you're about to get lucky."

He shook his head. "I've been lucky since you walked into my barn and I'm not referring to what's hopefully about to happen."

She took his hand and they walked to her bedroom.

Afterward she cuddled up next to him and heaved a contented sigh. "This is one of the many reasons why I fell in love with you."

His body tensed and the sudden change in him confused her. A wave of nausea hit her when she realized what she'd said. She hadn't meant to make the big confession now, but the words had slipped out. She might not have meant to say it yet, but she wasn't going to take it back. Her feelings were too big to hold in any longer and she felt giddy with relief at it being out in the open. Trying to hold it in had begun to feel as if she were hiding something, and she hated lying. The truth was she loved him. Plain and simple. She might not be able to pinpoint when it happened or how, but there was no turning back. She was lost.

He pulled away and sat up. "I wish you hadn't said that."

She recoiled as his words pelted her like hail. "Why? Why shouldn't I say it? It's true. It's been true for a while now."

He rubbed his hand over his face. "I thought we were going to keep this casual."

Casual? She might not have had a lot of sexual experience, but even she knew what was between them was special. And yes, she knew sexual chemistry wasn't the same as love, but they'd shared a lot more than what had happened between the sheets. Her throat closed and swallowing became painful. The future that had been so clear hours ago began to dissolve into nothingness. But she only had herself to blame, because all those fantasies of their future together were just that—stories she'd made up in her head. She'd been falling head over heels in love and he'd been doing casual. "When did we say that? Was there a book of rules I should have been following?"

"See? This is what happens when that word is thrown around." His tone and his expression grew hard and resentful.

She flinched at his reply, suggesting he was blaming her for falling in love with *him*. Maybe if he hadn't been so irresistible she wouldn't have fallen in love. So it was his fault. What was wrong with her? You couldn't assign blame when falling in love. It just happened. "That word? You mean *love*?"

"Yeah, that's the one." He jumped out of bed and punctuated the statement by pointing his index finger at her. Anger hardened his features.

"You can't even say it." How could she have gotten this so wrong? Her face grew hot with humiliation. She'd told him she loved him and he was treating her as if she'd done something wrong. As if her *love* was wrong.

"What's happened? What has changed? We're both still the same people we were before I said those words," she said, hating the pleading note in her voice.

But she knew that wasn't true. She had changed it by saying those words. Words he didn't want, wasn't ready to hear because he couldn't even say *love*, let alone mean it. Maybe this was all her fault. No! The only thing she'd done wrong was to fall for a man with so much baggage that he couldn't even say the word. He might never be in a place to be able to process the love she and Sam were offering him. She couldn't think like that. She wasn't going to think like that.

He began pulling on his pants. "I thought we were on the same page but obviously I was wrong."

"Obviously," she repeated drily. She sighed and rolled off the bed and grabbed her robe from the bench at the end of the bed. She needed to cover up, as if pink terry cloth could shield her from all the pain barreling through her system. She pulled the robe tight around her, trying to contain the pain; otherwise her heart would shatter and the pieces would scatter like confetti. She'd never get them all back.

"I'm sorry you find my being in love with you so offensive." Her voice was hoarse and barely recognizable.

He blew his breath out noisily and shoved his arms into his flannel shirt. "I never said anything like that. You're putting words in my mouth. I just—"

Her sorrow turned into frustration and anger. "Maybe you didn't say exactly those things, but as soon as I said I love you, you began searching for your clothes. Now you're halfway out the door. Your about-face has given me whiplash."

"Natalie, I—"

"No. Don't you dare." She spat the words at him. "I'm not going to apologize for loving you, Des Gallagher."

He made a derisive snort and slashed the air with his hand. "You may not apologize, but you'll regret it. Maybe not today. Maybe not even tomorrow. But someday. My own mother couldn't love me… Ashley didn't… How can you?"

"I don't know what your mother's problem was…but the problem was with her. Not you. If she didn't love you or treated you less than you deserved, it's on her. Not you." She hadn't felt this helpless since the day a drunk driver plowed into a crowd of innocent people, changing her life. "As for Ashley… I'm not even going to say what I think of her."

"I never asked you into my life. You barged in and kept coming back despite the things I said. Or have you conveniently forgotten that?"

"No, but it sounds as if you've forgotten what you said an hour ago."

He scowled. "What? What did I say?"

"Nothing of any importance." But it had been important. His words had made her feel as special as he'd said, maybe had even given her the courage to confess how she felt. Those words had changed her life and he couldn't remember them. She swayed and had to lock her knees to remain standing. Putting her hand on the bedside chair for support, she asked, "Let me get this straight so there's no mistake. You're saying you don't want me in your life?"

"Maybe I don't want to be another one of your damned projects! Maybe I liked my life just fine before you came barging in with your endless chatter and fattening cookies."

Natalie closed her eyes as she tried to manage the agony shooting through her body. Ryan's death had hurt and she'd mourned him, but somehow this was much worse. Des was intentionally hurting her, causing the pain on purpose. Inserting the knife and rotating it until all her tender organs bled.

"Natalie, I shouldn't have said any of that. It was mean and nasty, meant to hurt. I'm so sorry. I—"

"No, don't." She held up her hand. Ice spread through her belly. "I'm the one who wanted honesty, remember? Huh, what is that saying? 'Be careful what you wish for.'"

"I shouldn't have said any of that. Please believe me." Now his tone was pleading, as if he was asking her to forgive him.

Unable to take on his pain, too, she didn't know if she had enough strength to handle her own right now. And Sam. Oh, my God, what would this do to him? She should have protected Sam, stepped in when she saw they were bonding.

She shook her head. "If that's how you feel, then you should speak your mind. I'm an adult. I won't lie and say it didn't hurt, but it's better to know how you feel. What I can't forgive you for is Sam. Have you shown any consideration for him?"

He looked flummoxed. "I have been nothing but kind to him."

His expression would've been comical if this whole situation wasn't so damn tragic. "You made him love you. Now you want to back off. He's five... How is he supposed to process that when I, as an adult, can't?"

"What I said... I shouldn't have. I was angry." He reached out his hand, but dropped it when she flinched.

"Does...does my loving you make you angry? Because I never wanted that. And if I could stop loving you, I would. You're not an easy man to love, Des Gallagher. And right now it doesn't feel very good. But that's not how this whole falling-in-love thing works. I couldn't stop it and I can't turn it off so maybe...maybe you should go."

She needed him to leave. Anguish was threatening to overcome her rigid control. If she lost control, she'd be a blubbering mess, saying things she'd regret. Like begging him for things he couldn't or wouldn't give. Des had the upper hand because she'd admitted she loved him, but she still had her pride. Pride might be all she had and it was cold comfort, but it was hers and she was hanging on to it.

"I hate leaving having you think I meant those things." He reached out again, but she backed away. "Natalie, please."

"What you did or did not mean isn't the issue. Clearly my saying I love you freaked you out to the point you lashed out." Her eyes burned but she held back the tears by opening her eyes as wide as she could. She'd cry later when she was alone, because it wasn't going to be pretty.

"I don't see why we couldn't go along the way we were," he muttered.

"Because I have a son and every relationship, every bond, I form with anyone involves and impacts him. He's a little boy and my first duty is to him. I can't have men come and go from his life as if it doesn't matter."

"Christ. I'm not about to abandon him." He rubbed his scalp. "I'm talking about messy emotions between you and I."

"But I can't turn my messy emotions off. I feel what I feel and I'm not sure suppressing them is healthy and now, what I said is hanging out there. I can't take it back…and maybe I don't want to take it back. Maybe ending this is best for all of us. I have an impression-able son to think about. I want him to grow up respect-ing women and—"

He stiffened as if she'd struck him. "Are you saying I don't respect you?"

"No, but I want Sam to grow up understanding that in a healthy relationship both parties share their feel-ings. That—" she swallowed "—one party isn't carry-ing the whole burden."

"What will you tell him about…about us?"

"The truth," she managed through frozen lips. "I'll tell him that sometimes adults can't make relationships work and they end up hurting one another so it's best to go their separate ways."

"Natalie…"

"I think we've said all that needs to be said. I'd like you to go."

When he reached the door, he stopped with his hand

on the knob and turned back, his gaze meeting hers in a silent plea. She closed her eyes.

The door opened, then shut with a soft click that reverberated through her entire body like a sonic boom.

Chapter Ten

Des finished cleaning Augie's stall and moved like a
robot onto the next one. It had been two days since the
scene in Natalie's bedroom. Each hour that passed had
him feeling sicker and sicker. He hadn't been able to
sleep for more than an hour at a time and his stomach
had refused all but coffee and antacid tablets.

The upside was that his bum leg was the least of his
problems and the horse stalls were spotless because the
physical labor suited him. Too bad he wasn't a drinking
man. He might have been able to find some oblivion, but
he was afraid if he did, he wouldn't be able to find his
way back. Another legacy from his mother: addiction.

You made him love you.

Natalie's accusing words echoed and pierced him like
those shards of broken glass he used for his sculptures.

He wore gloves to protect his hands while handling the sharp pieces. Too bad he couldn't have protected his heart just as easily.

How many times had he walked to his truck to go to Natalie's, only to turn around and come back to the barn? What had she told Sam? What was there to say?

Pulling the roll from his pocket, he popped another antacid into his month and chewed. His own father had one up on him, because he'd never formed a relationship with his child. Instead, Des himself was guilty of forming a bond with a little boy, then disappearing.

Natalie was there to soothe Sam's broken heart, but who would be there for *her*? Was she baking cookies? Was the cat still chasing the train? Was Sam using his iPad to communicate more? All questions he had no answers to and might never get. What had he done? He'd blown the best thing that had ever happened to him. He blinked trying to clear his vision, but the blurring remained.

He wiped his eyes on his sleeve before tackling another stall when the sound of a truck pulling up stopped him. Setting aside the rake, he left the barn.

Des saw the horse trailer and his stomach turned to stone. This couldn't be good. *You got that right, Gallagher.* Nothing had been good since that night Natalie ruined what they had going on. A voice shouted that the fault was his and his alone, and as much as he tried he couldn't drown it out. His biggest mistake had been trying to be someone he wasn't. Take that stupid sleigh ride for example. He never should've suggested it. He wasn't a romantic guy.

He shaded his eyes from the sun using his hand. "Brody, what are you doing here?"

"Gallagher?" Brody peered at him. "Hey, man, you look like crap."

"Is that what you came all the way out here to tell me?" He rubbed his forehead, hoping to ease the headache he'd had for two days.

"Nah. I suspect you feel as bad as you look." Brody gave him a pitying look. "Natalie asked me to come and get the horses."

His one link to sanity and she wanted to take that away. Des leaned on the rake. "Does she have a place to board them?"

Brody blew out his breath. "I barely have room but I agreed to take Augie for the time being. The rest are being boarded about thirty miles away until a decision is made about the future of the program."

Thirty miles? Natalie must hate him if she'd let those horses go so far away. "Let me help you get them loaded up."

"Thanks." Brody gave him a calculating glance. "Sounds like you messed up."

Des stiffened at the thought of someone knowing his personal business. What did it matter? Anyone looking at him could tell what a mess he was and pretty much everyone in town would know why. He had been all around town with Natalie and Sam acting as if they were a family. As if he believed in happy families. As if someone like him could be a part of one.

"I'll take that brooding look as a yes." Brody laughed and shook his head. "You remind me of how I was when I nearly blew it with Mary."

"You did?" He didn't know Brody well but he knew from seeing him and Mary together and from town gossip that the Wilsons had a solid relationship.

Brody grimaced as if the memory was painful. "I had to watch her walk out of my life to catch on and smarten up."

"But you're so happy together now."

"Yeah, had to swallow my pride and admit I'd messed up." Brody clapped him on the shoulder. "But it was worth it."

Des shook his head. "You may have worked things out, but I'm not that guy. I'm not like you and Riley."

"What a load of horse manure." Brody laughed again. "Hey, man, we all put our pants on a leg at a time."

Des rolled his eyes. "Let me help you get these horses loaded."

Brody threw up his hands. "So you're giving up? Just like that?"

"You don't understand." Des crossed his arms over his chest.

Brody snorted a laugh. "Yeah, that's what I told Riley Cooper when he tried to talk some sense into me."

It was too late for that. Someone should've talked some sense into him before he'd spoken those awful words. "I'm sure my situation is a lot worse than yours. I said some unforgivable things."

"But see, you don't get to decide that." Brody pulled a toothpick from his shirt pocket, unwrapped it and shoved it into his mouth.

"What do you mean?" He swiped his sweaty palms down his pants.

"Natalie is the only one who can decide if what you

said or did was unforgivable. She's the one that will have to do the forgiving, so it's all up to her." Brody rolled the toothpick around in his mouth before taking it out. "Mary forgave me for being a jackass and from what Riley has told me, Meg did the same for him. Seems women have a great capacity for forgiveness. I'm not saying they won't call us out when we're wrong, 'cause they will, but they also forgive us because they know we can't help messing up."

Was it possible that he hadn't messed up his chances with Natalie? Did he want another chance to be with her and Sam? More than he wanted to fly again, more than he'd wanted anything else in his entire life. He might have suppressed it, but he'd ached to be part of a family, a happy, normal family, all his life. That's why he'd ignored the warning signs in his relationship with Ashley. But instead of learning from his mistakes, he'd made a new one, a colossal one.

Des shook his head. "I'm not sure she'll forgive me."

"Maybe. Maybe not. But I'm gonna give you the same advice Riley gave me when I messed up with Mary."

He didn't want to hear it. Maybe this was all for the best. He could go back to being here all alone. Enjoy the peace and quiet. No endless chatter. No calorie-laden baked goods. What was he thinking? He'd been in hell since he'd messed up with Natalie. "What's that?"

Brody raised his eyebrows. "His advice? He told me to tell her I loved her and that I had messed up."

"And that worked?" Skepticism laced his tone. He had a right to it because he couldn't imagine Brody saying anything near as nasty as he had.

"It did and I thank God for Mary and Elliott. I work every day to deserve the family we've created." He shook his head. "I always thought I wanted to be alone, thought it was better not to take that risk of getting hurt. I'm here to tell you that's a load of hogwash. The best thing I did was to stop worrying about what could happen and make today happen. Embrace all the good stuff I have right now and let the future take care of itself."

Natalie opened the door to the Loon Lake General Store and the bell hanging from the casing tinkled. Something about that old-fashioned sound always made her smile, which was no easy task these past three days. Would she ever be able to smile and mean it? Good thing she'd had a lot of practice grinning at strangers who made comments about Sam.

Tavie glanced up from the magazine she had spread out on the wooden counter. "No Sam today?"

"He went to the library with Addie and Teddy Miller. They were having a Christmas party for the younger kids. He and Teddy are going to help pass out gifts. It's part of my effort to teach Sam about the true meaning of Christmas." Natalie pulled off her gloves and unbuttoned the top two buttons of her red parka. "I decided to use the alone time to run some errands and check to be sure Ogle is still planning to play Santa at the carnival tonight."

Tavie touched her helmet of teased and sprayed hair. "He wouldn't miss it."

"Great." Natalie twisted her gloves between her hands. "I've decided to let Sam line up and sit on Santa's lap by himself. I know I have to start letting him do things on his own, but it's hard."

Tavie nodded in agreement. "Do you think encouraging him to do things by himself will help him adapt to using his tablet?"

"That's the plan." She didn't mention how he'd started to use it but had lost interest when she and Des broke up. Broke up? Had they even had a real relationship? She'd been falling in love and he'd been...what? Having good sex? Bitterness coated her stomach.

As if sensing Natalie's distress, Tavie reached across the counter and patted her arm. "Don't you fret. Ogle knows what to do. Sam will be in good hands."

Natalie didn't correct the other woman's misconception. She loved Tavie, but knew better than to divulge certain things. The older woman would be on an all-out campaign to reunite her and Des. "Thanks. He might not believe in Santa too much longer. I want this to go well since I convinced him Santa knows how much he likes LEGOs."

"Yeah. When my grandkids were that age they couldn't get enough of 'em."

"Sam has been begging for the bigger, more complicated kits. Teddy has some and the two sit for hours, building things."

"Does he know which one he wants so I can tell Ogle?"

"He had wanted the airport but...uh...I think he may have changed his mind." Yeah, she'd done her best to explain why Des didn't come around anymore. Of course that hadn't stopped Sam from running to the window every time he heard a car or pickup go down the street.

It broke her heart each time he came away from the window disappointed and every time it happened, she convinced herself she hated Des. Then her phone would buzz and her heart would jump into her throat in that moment before she picked it up to check the caller ID. That phone made a liar out of her every damn time.

Tavie was giving her a peculiar look so she cleared her head of such thoughts and managed a semblance of a smile. "We ran into Liam McBride in his fire uniform in the parking lot at the Pic-N-Save yesterday. Liam had been at his niece Fiona's school giving a talk about fire safety. He gave Sam a badge and plastic fire helmet he had in his truck. Sam's eyes got as big as saucers and he was looking up LEGO fire stations when we got home."

"That Liam is such a sweet kid. His ma would be proud to see what a wonderful family man he is. I swear, every time he and Ellie bring the twins in, they've grown twice as big as the previous time."

Natalie nodded, grateful Tavie's attention was focused elsewhere. "Ellie brought them a few times to the church luncheon when I was volunteering."

"I'm so glad the younger generation in this town is carrying on with some of our traditions. Not to mention adding to the population." Tavie gave her a speculative look. "I hear tell you and the lieutenant have been seen together. Mitch Makowski says you three were together at the tree-lighting."

Anxious to avoid Tavie seeing how her heart was shattered into a million tiny pieces, Natalie glanced at her watch. "Look at the time. I really need to run. I told Addie I'd watch Teddy for her this afternoon and

I need to check that the auction items are all in place. You'll remind Ogle about Sam?"

"Sure thing, honey. Don't you worry. I'll have Ogle ask leading questions about them LEGOs."

"Thanks so much for understanding," Natalie said.

She left the store confident that Sam's visit with Santa tonight was taken care of, as were the horses. She'd talked with Brody again this morning, and while he'd reassured her everything was fine, he'd put her off again when she'd suggested coming to help with Augie's care. She'd tried to insist but didn't want to argue with Brody after he'd been so nice and understanding with her. Not accompanying Brody when he went to collect the horses from Des's place had been cowardly on her part, but she'd been too raw.

Plus, she'd feared seeing Des again might weaken her resolve and she'd throw pride to the wind to beg Des to resume their relationship—on his terms. Pride and self-respect were cold comfort during the long nights, but she'd make whatever sacrifices were necessary to see Sam had a secure and stable life.

"Yeah, pride's a bitch when you're alone," she muttered as she started her car.

But she wasn't alone, she reminded herself. She had Sam and all the friends she'd made in her short time in Loon Lake. She'd get through this and maybe someday she'd even find a guy who didn't run from love.

Chapter Eleven

That evening Natalie pulled into the church parking lot and found a spot. It was still early and people were just beginning to arrive, but she'd needed to take one last look at the silent auction items. She'd wanted to be sure no one had dropped off anything at the last minute.

Besides, keeping busy was her saving grace. It sure beat sitting alone and sobbing. No, she would save that particular pastime for the long winter nights after Sam went to bed.

She got out of the car and pulled her coat closer around her to protect against the chill as she crossed the parking lot. Addie had insisted on bringing Sam with her and Teddy.

Inside the church she went to the room with her auction items on display. She flipped on the switch for the overhead lighting and froze. Many of the items had been pushed aside to make room…

She shook her head and blinked, but the items didn't disappear. Right there in the middle of the display lay dozens of glass ornaments. Cautiously, as if they might disappear, she stepped closer. On the table was an assortment of the most exquisite ornaments she'd ever seen, each one a miniature stained or blown glass masterpiece.

She glanced around, but she was alone, so she dashed from the room. People were beginning to gather for the indoor activities, but she could see no six-foot-plus lieutenant. Going to the entrance she opened the door and scanned the parking lot. No sign of his truck, either. Her heart squeezed. Des had made the ornaments she'd wanted but hadn't stayed, hadn't wanted to run into her. What did this mean? If not for his absence, she might have gotten her hopes up, but this seemed like a clear sign that he was done with her, with Sam…forever.

Even so, each time a new person entered the building, her heart would stutter. Once word got out about the ornaments Des had made—and she had no doubt he'd made them—people flocked to place auction bids. They hung around to ask about the hippotherapy program and the town's business leaders promised to help get the center back on its feet. Some even encouraged her to consider taking over the administrative side of the business. She promised to consider it.

"Hey, is it true?" Addie came up to her.

Natalie pointed to the table with the ornaments. "See for yourself."

Addie scooted over to get a look. When she turned

back, her eyes were wide and her mouth open. "He did this for you? I take back every bad thing I thought about him."

Dare she allow herself to believe this gesture was for her? "He may have done it for Sam's benefit. He knows how much the horses mean to him."

Addie shook her head. "That's an awful lot of work for a guy who doesn't care. He must've been working day and night to make all these. They're gorgeous."

Natalie brought her fist to her mouth and pressed it there to stifle a sob. Was it true? Or did she want it to be true? "I don't know what to believe."

"Maybe you should talk to him. Find out what it means."

"You're right. He must've dropped these off and left because I've looked all over and haven't seen him."

"Maybe you should look again. I can watch over things in here." Addie gave her a quick hug. "Sam's in line for Santa. Sorry, but we were a little bit late getting here so he's the last one in line, but I kept an eye on him and it was his turn. That's why I came to find you. In case you wanted to go check on him."

"That's fine. Ogle knows what to do." Natalie returned the hug.

Addie's brow furrowed. "What's Ogle got to do with it?"

"He's Santa."

"No, he's not," Addie said. "He helped me unload and carry in the stuff we made for the bake sale."

"What?" Natalie's heart sank, but surely Ogle would have told whoever took his place about Sam.

She hurried to where the children had lined up for

Santa and searched for Sam. He was seated on Santa's lap. She started to rush forward but stopped when she saw that Santa was speaking to Sam, who was grinning and nodding his head. So maybe Ogle did make arrangements.

Santa lifted his head, seemed to zero in on her and caught her gaze. The glued-on bushy eyebrows, moustache and beard obscured his identity, but that gaze made her stomach flutter with recognition. But the memory giving her déjà vu was beyond her reach.

Santa leaned down and spoke into Sam's ear. What was going on? Grinning from ear to ear, Sam nodded, scrambled off Santa's lap and ran toward her.

"Did you tell Santa what you wanted?" She was still confused as to what was going on. And there was something about that Santa…

Sam tugged on her sleeve, pulling her toward one of the empty Sunday schoolrooms.

"Sam? What in the world…?" She glanced down at her son but he giggled and pushed her into the room.

As soon as she stepped into the classroom, Sam scampered off. "Sam, wait! What is—"

She turned and bumped into Santa, who put his hands on her shoulders to steady her and gently push her back into the room. He shut the door and flipped on the overhead lights.

Her gaze met his and recognition flooded into her. "Des?"

He nodded and yanked off the hat and pulled down the white beard. Those dark eyes glittered as he looked at her.

"I…I…" She shook her head but couldn't form a coherent thought. This was all too much for her to process. "I don't understand. What's going on? Why are you dressed as Santa?"

"I convinced Ogle to let me take over for him tonight."

"Why?" She couldn't imagine why Des would dress up as Santa.

"Because I wanted to prove to you how much I've changed since we last spoke."

"You dressed up as Santa for me?"

"Everything I did was for you, Natalie. I made the ornaments for you."

"But I told you I didn't expect you to make any. I understand and respect why you didn't want to make them." She shook her head. "I never should have tried to force you to begin with. I was wrong."

"But don't you see? I'm grateful you did because you've replaced my bad memories of Christmas with good ones."

"You mean that?" She tentatively reached out her hand to touch him, assure herself he was real—and wearing a Santa suit, of all things. He captured her hand in his and curled his fingers around it, his thumb stroking her palm. She leaned toward him, drawn in, despite her caution.

"I still can't believe you made ornaments," she said and her voice sounded breathless even to her own ears. She was beginning to understand the enormity of what was happening.

"Those don't even begin to express how sorry I am."

"They don't?"

"I acted like…" He squeezed her hand. Swallowing

audibly, he started again, "I acted like an ass. Can you ever forgive me for the way I behaved and those things I said? I swear I didn't mean any of it. I was running scared. My—" He swallowed again. "My feelings for you and Sam scared me. Huh, they still do, but that's okay because being without the two of you scares me even more. You and Sam are my whole life, Natalie. I've been so miserable without you. I can't eat. I can't sleep. I want to spend the rest of my life with you." He rubbed the back of his neck. "Heck, I'm not even sure if that's long enough. I want forever and ever. Tell me I'm not too late."

"Oh, Des, I've been miserable, too," she cried and threw herself against him.

He made an impatient noise and reached under the Santa suit and pulled out the pillow he'd had to use as padding. Then he put his arms around her, hugging her close.

"Shh, don't cry. Please. I don't want to make you cry," he whispered. "I love you. Please believe me when I say it. I love you and Sam more than I ever thought possible. What I felt for Ashley is nothing compared to what I feel for you."

"I love you, too." She choked on a sob and clung to him.

He brought his hands up to cup her face and kissed her. He kissed her as if his life depended on what their lips were doing, pouring everything he ever was and ever would be into the kiss.

After long minutes he lifted his mouth and sucked in air. Resting his forehead against hers, he drew in a deep breath and shuddered. "I told Sam I had something for you but I needed his permission to give it to you because he's a part of this, of us."

"What did you need Sam's permission for?" She was afraid to hope but couldn't prevent it from seeping into her.

He pulled a small black box out of the pocket of his pants.

"Santa pants have pockets?" That's what she was getting from all this? By concentrating on the mundane, she hoped to manage her expectations in case that box didn't contain what she prayed it did.

"Fortunately, these do." He opened the box. Nestled inside was a sparkling solitaire diamond. He cleared his throat. "I told Sam I wanted to be his dad and to marry you, but I would need his permission for both."

"You did?"

Des nodded. "I did. And he gave me an enthusiastic thumbs-up. I told him I hoped his mom would be as agreeable."

He dropped to one knee. "Natalie Pierce, will you marry me? I think I fell in love with you the day you came barging into my barn and my life with your baked goods and your big blue eyes. I was lost the moment you smiled and I saw that crooked tooth."

She put her hand over her mouth. "My snaggle tooth."

He reached out and took her hand away from her mouth, bringing it to his own. He kissed her palm, then pressed her hand against his chest. "If not for that tooth, I would have turned away, convinced you were too good for the likes of me. But that tooth told me you were real and drove me crazy thinking that maybe I had a shot at the most beautiful and loving woman I'd ever met."

"That silly tooth did all that?"

"That and the way you clutched your son's hand. I didn't know the particulars at the time, but that act started thawing something that had been frozen in me for a long, long time."

"And here I thought it was my cookies that hooked you."

"Those, too." He grinned and pulled her closer. "Especially those little green ones with the chocolate on them."

"And the sprinkles," she whispered and snuggled against his shoulder. Amazing how she could go from despair to happiness in such a short span.

"Sam put the sprinkles on so I definitely can't forget those."

She pulled away to look at him. "Sam has challenges ahead of him."

His gaze seemed to be asking for her trust. "And we'll give him a solid, loving home life so that he will be able to meet all of those challenges head-on. We'll equip him and his future brothers and sisters with the skills necessary to conquer the world."

"Brothers and sisters?" She hadn't even thought that far ahead. Not tonight, anyway.

"No?"

She smiled and sniffed. "Yes, definitely yes. Gotta fill up that house."

"With kids and animals."

"Oh, no!" Her jaw dropped. "Animals… The horses. I… They—"

"Are safe at my place. I wouldn't let Brody take them. I couldn't let go of that link to you and Sam." Moisture gathered in his eyes as if the thought brought him pain. He blushed. "I may have done some begging. The swine laughed and said it was good to get in some practice before I came to see you."

"No wonder Brody wouldn't let us come and see Augie." She laughed. "I need to apologize to him for all the things I thought each time he made an excuse and put us off. So, was it Brody who suggested you play Santa?"

He shook his head and hugged her closer. "Nope. I came up with that one myself. I knew Ogle always played Santa, so I contacted him this afternoon."

Her eyes widened because she knew you couldn't involve Ogle in anything without involving his wife. "You involved Tavie?"

"I was desperate," he admitted with a sheepish expression. "I'm nothing without you and Sam."

"But you're everything to Sam and me," she vowed and stood on tiptoe to kiss him.

After they came up for air, he rested his forehead against hers. "I'm going to be there for you and Sam for the rest of my life. You have my word on that."

Her heart expanded until it hurt to breathe. "Sounds exactly like my kind of happily-ever-after."

"Mine, too." He took her hand and intertwined his fingers with hers. "Should we go and find Sam and let him know that you've agreed to bless my heart forever?"

* * * * *

MILLS & BOON

Coming next month

SNOWBOUND WITH THE HEIR
Sophie Pembroke

'Tori, sweetheart.' Jasper whispered the words against her hair, kissing her head softly as her cries lessened. 'Wake up, love.'

And she did.

Lifting her head, she blinked up at him, tears still glistening in the half-light. 'I was dreaming…' She shuddered at the memory.

'About Tyler?' he asked gently. She nodded. 'Would it help to talk about it?'

This time, she shook her head, her hair whipping around in defiance. 'I just want to forget.' She looked up at him again, and there were no tears this time. Just a new fierceness to replace the armour she'd lost. Her body shifted, and suddenly every inch of her seemed to be pressed up against him, tempting and hot and everything he'd never even dreamed of.

That was a lie. He'd dreamed about it. Often. Especially since the night they'd spent together.

But he'd never imagined it could actually happen again, not here and now.

She raised her mouth, pressing it firmly to his, her tongue sweeping out across his lower lip, and his whole body shuddered with want and desire as he kissed her back. The kiss was deep and desperate and everything he remembered about their other night together. When she pulled back, just far enough to kiss her way along his jawline, Jasper could barely remember his own name.

'Help me forget?' she murmured against his ear.

And suddenly the heat faded.

Not completely, of course. The lust she'd inspired was still coursing through his blood, and certain parts of his anatomy were absolutely on board with her plan—right now, preferably.

But his brain, that frustrating, overthinking part of him—the part that had come up with a dream of a frozen river and this woman's hand in his—had other ideas.

'Tori...' He pulled away, as far as he could without falling out of the narrow single bed. 'Tori, not like this.'

God, he wanted her. But he wanted her to want him, too. Not just forgetfulness, not just oblivion. He'd had enough of that sort of relationship himself, when he'd first moved away from Flaxstone. The kind of sex that just blocked out the world for a time, that helped him pass out and sleep without dreaming of the life he'd thought he'd had and the lies that had lurked behind it.

He didn't want that with Tori. Not this time.

Continue reading
SNOWBOUND WITH THE HEIR
Sophie Pembroke

Available next month
www.millsandboon.co.uk

Copyright © Sophie Pembroke

COMING SOON!

We really hope you enjoyed reading this book. If you're looking for more romance, be sure to head to the shops when new books are available on

Thursday 28th November

To see which titles are coming soon, please visit

millsandboon.co.uk/nextmonth

MILLS & BOON

MILLS & BOON
MEDICAL
Pulse-Racing Passion

Set your pulse racing with dedicated, delectable doctors in the high-pressure world of medicine, where emotions run high and passion, comfort and love are the best medicine.

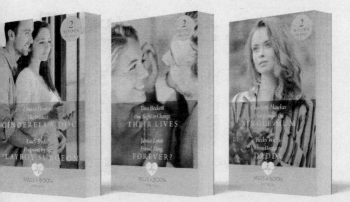

ight Medical stories published every month, find them all at:

millsandboon.co.uk

MILLS & BOON
A ROMANCE FOR EVERY READER

- **FREE** delivery direct to your door

- **EXCLUSIVE** offers every month

- **SAVE** up to 25% on pre-paid subscriptions

SUBSCRIBE AND SAVE

millsandboon.co.uk/Subscribe

WANT EVEN MORE
ROMANCE?
SUBSCRIBE AND SAVE TODAY!

'Mills & Boon books, the perfect way to escape for an hour or so.'

MISS W. DYER

'Excellent service, promptly delivered and very good subscription choices.'

MISS A. PEARSON

'You get fantastic special offers and the chance to get books before they hit the shops.'

MRS V. HALL

Visit millsandboon.co.uk/Subscribe and save on brand new books.

LET'S TALK
Romance

For exclusive extracts, competitions
and special offers, find us online:

f facebook.com/millsandboon

🐦 @MillsandBoon

📷 @MillsandBoonUK

Get in touch on 01413 063232

For all the latest titles coming soon, visit
millsandboon.co.uk/nextmonth

MILLS & BOON

THE HEART OF ROMANCE

A ROMANCE FOR EVERY KIND OF READER

MODERN

Prepare to be swept off your feet by sophisticated, sexy and seductive heroes, in some of the world's most glamourous and romantic locations, where power and passion collide.
8 stories per month.

HISTORICAL

Escape with historical heroes from time gone by. Whether your passion is for wicked Regency Rakes, muscled Vikings or rugged Highlanders, awaken the romance of the past.
6 stories per month.

MEDICAL

Set your pulse racing with dedicated, delectable doctors in the high-pressure world of medicine, where emotions run high and passion, comfort and love are the best medicine.
6 stories per month.

True Love

Celebrate true love with tender stories of heartfelt romance, from the rush of falling in love to the joy a new baby can bring, and a focus on the emotional heart of a relationship.
8 stories per month.

Desire

Indulge in secrets and scandal, intense drama and plenty of sizzling hot action with powerful and passionate heroes who have it all: wealth, status, good looks…everything but the right woman.
6 stories per month.

HEROES

Experience all the excitement of a gripping thriller, with an intense romance at its heart. Resourceful, true-to-life women and strong, fearless men face danger and desire - a killer combination!
8 stories per month.

DARE

Sensual love stories featuring smart, sassy heroines you'd want as a best friend, and compelling intense heroes who are worthy of them.
4 stories per month.

To see which titles are coming soon, please visit

millsandboon.co.uk/nextmonth

GET YOUR ROMANCE FIX!

MILLS & BOON
— *blog* —

Get the latest romance news, exclusive author interviews, story extracts and much more!

blog.millsandboon.co.uk

JOIN THE
MILLS & BOON
BOOKCLUB

* **FREE** delivery direct to your door

* **EXCLUSIVE** offers every month

* **EXCITING** rewards programme

50% OFF
YOUR FIRST
PARCEL

Join today at
Millsandboon.co.uk/Bookclub

JOIN US ON SOCIAL MEDIA!

Stay up to date with our latest releases, author news and gossip, special offers and discounts, and all the behind-the-scenes action from Mills & Boon...

 millsandboon

 millsandboonuk

 millsandboon

It might just be true love...

MILLS & BOON

HISTORICAL

Awaken the romance of the past

Escape with historical heroes from time gone by. Whether your passion is for wicked Regency Rakes, muscled Viking warriors or rugged Highlanders, indulge your fantasies and awaken the romance of the past.

x Historical stories published every month, find them all at:

millsandboon.co.uk/ Historical